Come Home To Erin

Come Home To Erin

Tom Melican

Copyright © 2012 by Tom Melican.

ISBN: Softcover   978-1-4797-4188-5
          Ebook   978-1-4797-4189-2

All rights reserved. No part of this book may be reproduced or transmitted in any form or by any means, electronic or mechanical, including photocopying, recording, or by any information storage and retrieval system, without permission in writing from the copyright owner.

This is a work of fiction. Names, characters, places and incidents either are the product of the author's imagination or are used fictitiously, and any resemblance to any actual persons, living or dead, events, or locales is entirely coincidental.

This book was printed in the United States of America.

To order additional copies of this book, contact:
Xlibris Corporation
0-800-644-6988
www.xlibrispublishing.co.uk
Orders@xlibrispublishing.co.uk
304832

1

PEGGY GILLESPIE JUST wanted to go home. She was a tired and weary woman but she was very happy. Ten days in this maternity ward was enough. Enough of the looking at the ceiling and just waiting. Waiting for the matron to do her rounds at waiting for the consultant when he would come with his flotilla of nurses and junior doctors all fluttering around her bed. Open eyed in admiration as he uttered his fine words. God but she was fed up and had enough

It had been a bit of a drama and a rush getting here but it had all worked out well in the end. Her son was delivered safely and he was a healthy child. She smiled down at him in her arms and thanked the Lord. Thank you Jesus she thought. She was so pleased. The boy did not have a sign of being red-headed. Again thank you God for that. There were enough Jimmy Ruas and Tommy Ruas in the family already. There were ruas all over Gweedore. Up the airy mountain and down the rushey glen. Peggy herself was called Peggy Neddy Rua and she hated the name. There were Gillespies and O Donnells and Coyles in every parish and townland. All ruas. Even poor old Mickey Paddy Joe the postman sometimes did not know where the letters should be delivered. The postmark was often a better indication than the parish address. He knew that a Boston postmark went to one end of the parish and Chicago went the other end. After 35 years on the post he nearly knew from the writing. Partick O Gallagher or Eamonn Coyle could be anyone of a dozen people. But Jimmy Tommy Neddy Paddy always printed the address and Micked Neddy Frankie always wrote with a backward slant. No problem. The letter found its way safely home to the right person

Peggy was christened Peggy Coyle. The old parish priest muttered that he was not sure there ever was a saint Peggy but he was too much of a coward to upset half the women in his parish. So Peggy Coyle went on her baptismal certificate. Saint Peggy or no saint Peggy. Ever since that lady from The Blasket Islands went on Radio Eireann with her book they all liked the name even if the Irish she spoke was as Greek to most of them. That Blasket Island dialect was a different language to the Donegal version

Peggy Coyle never used the name on her baptismal certificate

People asked "Cé leis thú?" 'Whose are you?'

Peggy Coyle could be anyone but Peggy Tommy Rua placed her for two generations. She hated it. Peggy Tommy Rua. Just to say it upset her

What a start in life.

So she had not given birth to another Rua and she was relieved. Peggy was 37 years old and already had a daughter Sinéad. Sinead was twelve. Peggy's husband, Ownie Rua was working in Scotland. Wherever McAlpines had a big job. Construction work on the reservoirs or hydroelectric schemes or motorways, She was never sure where he was. They moved him and his Donegal gang wherever there was a contract.

In his younger days Ownie was a great Gaelic footballer. He had a cushy number driving a delivery van for the Bacon Company. Every morning in to Dungloe and load his van and then deliver all over the county and even down into Sligo and Cavan. Everyone knew Ownie Rua

'Win the county Championship again this year Ownie?'

'Sure thing, sure thing' 'Good on ya, good on ya"

Gweedore won it most years and when Ownie was selected to play for Ulster in The Railway Cup nothing could have been better. Every schoolboy knew his name. He was the best known Donegal player was her Ownie.

They bought a small cottage on the edge of the village and settled down to a quiet family life. As a single man Ownie was one of the wild ones but he changed. Training twice on weeknights and a match most Sundays. He did not stay for the binges after the matches but came home to the tranquility of their cottage. Peggy some times went to the home matches and when Sinead was born she preferred to stay at home and do a bit of needlework. She knew how to do alterations as her mother had worked for a tailor in Derrybeg and she had passed it on to Peggy. Clothes that came from America mostly. Mothers wanted the garments toned down. The children did not mind what shape or colour the garments were but mothers did not like it broadcast that most of their childrens' clothing were hand-me-downs from the States. Pride was all that some of them had left. Peggy did a neat job and was able to earn enough for pocket money for Sinead and the odd treat for Ownie Rua

It was a pleasant and quiet life and they were happy and secure.

But suddenly all changed. The Bacon Company was bought out by a Dublin company and the Dungloe depot was closed. Ownie Rua was out of work. Redundant. Unemployed.

No panic. Sure he would just go and get another job. He was a famous footballer. Everyone knew Ownie Rua, Sure thing. Good contacts. No bother.

But things changed rapidly. Word passed round. No more "Win the Championship Ownie?"

People avoided his eye. He got the odd nod and "Howyah" and then they were gone

Sure the GAA might be able to help. Did they heck.! His playing days were coming to an end. Soon he would be a has been. A nobody on the county scene. Anyhow most of the officials had nothing to give. They were just hanging in there themselves. They were salaried council workers or employed by some government department or were the owners of small companies spread over the county. Any vacancies they had went to their own relations. The Fianna Fail boyos looked after their own and Ownie was not in their circle.Politics, Not for him. All that name calling from the platform and drinking cronies behind the scenes. Not his scene.

He was to turn up at The Garda Barracks and sign on for the dole every Monday. He hated it and did not bother. The big fat gardai were laughing at him

"Lovely to see you Ownie. How is she cuttin?" and he knew they did not give a curse. He drove all over the county looking for work

"Sure times is hard Ownie,God help us. Give us a call agin in a few months"

Some people were not able to say 'not a hope in hell Ownie" to his face and he liked them for softening the despair.

Peggy saw his shoulders drop and gradually he just gave up the ghost. He was feeling so low. Not able to keep his wife and child. Their savings were going fast. She had sympathy for how he felt. Sure what can a man do when he is able and wants to work. He became resentful and angry at the world. It was so unfair. Look at the local TD with his Mercedes and garda driver. Even the Parish Priest has a lovely house and his own housekeeper thank you. Finally he took solace in the bottle. What else on earth could a man do?

Then one night he fell through the door very drunk. Sinead was asleep in bed and Peggy was sitting by the fire with her thoughts. She always waited up for him to come home. He was broken. Full of remorse. "Never again never again "he moaned. But she had heard it many times over the months before. Now even the alcohol had not numbed his feelings of despair

She wet the tea and they sat together on the sofa. A word. No blame. No anger. Just a word. No anger no remorse between them. Till death do us part was what they vowed at the altar. They went through the last few months. Scotland was the only answer. Not over the water to England but to Scotland where most of the Donegal men went to get the start. They talked it through and life looked brighter once again. They would have to live apart but at least they had a way to gain control again. Life looked up

Ownie gave up the drink and painted the front gate. It was good to see him back to his old self again

2

OWNIE SOBERED UP and started going to football matches again
"Nice to see you Ownie" was the usual greeting. They knew he was out of work and had a hard time. But they had nothing to offer. Most of his old teammates had gone. Some had done well and joined the Gardaiand there was an odd pimary school teacher as well. But most had emigrated to Scotland. Gweedore men stayed together and worked as a gang with their own boss man. The ganger. Never promoted to foreman as they moved to follow the work and the bonuses and the overtime. They were not fussy with National Insurance contributions and their tax returns were non existant. Ownie called on the homes of some of his old pals and he got a few names and possible localities wher they might be working. No phone numbers. He would be a lucky man to even get a permanent address.

He called on Tommy Paddy Joe's mother and she gave him the address on the last letter Tommy Paddy Joe sent her but he was warned that Tommy Paddy might have moved on since then

"Sure it depends on what contract they are on" she said. "They can be gone anywhere in a week"

Ownie went to the Parochial House. The housekeeper answered the door but she did not invite him in

"Whaddya want? She asked. Snotty madam was Breege Coyle

"I would like to have a word with Father Friel" he said

"What about?" she asked Snotty. He had\a mind to tell her it was none of her business but he kept his temper

"Well it's a bit private" he said

"I'll see if he is in" and she turned away

Jesus effin Christ he thought. Surely she must know if he is in or out the silly cow. If it were nor for working in the Parochial House she would be footing turf or gathering seaweed with the rest of her family back home on the Foreland

She was soon back at the door and said

"Come in" and she led him in to a bare room with six chairs round the walls and a bare table in the middle of the room. This was where the priest met his parishioners when they called to the HousekeeperShe did not offer him a seat but said the holy father would be with him soon.

He sat on one of the chairs and waited

Fr Friel shuffled in and looked at Ownie

"Well my son what can I do for you?"

Ownie explained that he was unemployed and that he was looking for work,. Fr Friel nodded and said things would ger better.

"God is good" Ownie thought to himself that sometimes the Devil was not bad either but he quietly considered that he might lend God a helping hand and go to Scotland to look for a job

"Well this is my position" he explained. I think the only chance I have of getting employment is if I go to Scotland. I have the last known address of Tommy McGinley, Tommy Paddy Joe, and I wondered if you might be able to contact the local priest in that area or give me an address of the parish priest. Tommy is still a practising Catholic. Well so his mother says.If we could make contact with the priests in that area I might be able to find Tommy Paddy Joe and that would be a great help"

Fr Friel walked over to the window and with his back to Ownie said

"I do not have a Diocesan Directory for Scotland"

Lazy bastard thought Owniebut he bit his tongue. Too much trouble. He could ring up and find an address. Diocesan Directory my eye

"Might the bishop have one?" Ownie asked "he might be able to help"

"Nooo Nooo no" said Fr Friel. "He is too busy a man for us to bother him with small trivial matters. Far too busy"

But Ownie was not finished, "This is not a trivial matter. One of your parishioners, me Ownie Gillespie,needs help in getting employment and you and your church are notready to help me. That is how I see it. Am I right,?" and thenafter a few seconds he added "holy father"

"Don't you get cheeky with me young man. I am Parish Priest of this parish and I deserve respect"

"You will get the respect you earn" said Ownie as he walked to the door

"you are a thundering disgrace to the priesthood, Take that from me and you cannot deny it" and he slammed the door leaving Fr Friel speechless

Then Ownie went to the Garda Barracks

"Jeeze nice to see ya Ownie" said Garda Flanagan, A big fat Connemara man who nevere did a day's work in his life

"What can I do for ya? he smiled

"Any chance you might be able to get me a phone number in Scotland?" Ownie asked

"Well now that could be a trickey one. Where in Scotland?"

Ownie passed Tommy Paddy Joe's letter over and Flanagan read the address

He looked up at Ownie and he smiled again. A great smiler was Flanagan to be sure

"we do not have a telephone directory for Scotland "Flanagan said

"But the superintendent might have one at divisional headquarters" Ownie suggested

Flanagan stopped smiling

"Not on. Not on at all. The Super is a tight fisht from Mayo and it is more than my job is worth to start anything in that line. A real tight git he is. Not a hope. I am very sorry Ownie" and his smile was back on again.

Then Ownie went down the village to the lending Library. It was in a back room of the village hall. There was no reading room but a few shelves. Two for fiction and a one for non fiction. One could borrow three books free of charge but one had to be non fiction

"Ownie, how nice to see you here" a voice greeted him. It was old master Gallagher. "Nice to see you in this place of learning and culture. Not after some books are you?You were not that fond of the books years ago as far as I can remember."

The master was an old adversary of our Ownie. They had crossed swords many times in the classroom but in spite of all that they were very fond of each other

"I have a wee problem" said Ownie

"let me hear it then" said the master

"I need work and I will have to go to Scotland. I have an address of Tommy Paddy Joe and I wonder if he still lives there. If I could contact a priest in that area he could help me find Tommy Paddy Joe and I might be able to get the start

"Leave it with me a mhac" said the old man. Christ he still thinks of me as one of his schoolboys. I wish I had the money and I would take him to Kelly's bar for a wee drop. The master liked a wee dram of the creathure. No better man

A few days later the master dropped in and gave Ownie the address of a parish priest for that region where Tommy Paddy was working. Ownie wrote to the priest and had a reply that there was a Donegal gang working locally and sometimes one or two of them dropped in to attand a Mass. The priest did not know any names but he gave the name of a local public house they frequented

That was enough. Ownie had a contact point and he was on his way

3

OWNIE TOOK THE boat on Friday and found the parish just outside of Perth. Saturday evening he hung about the Catholic Church. Tommy might want to go to Confssion or to Saturday evening Mass. Not a sign.

Ownie was there for the 8.00, 10.00, and finally at the 12 o clock Mass he saw his man

Tommy Paddy Joe himself. The very man. What a relief. He had made contact. Tommy was just his old self. Less of the red and a lot more of the grey in the hair

Ownie walkes over and stood alongside Tommy

"Hello Tommy cunas tá tú?"

"Ownie Ownie. Jesus I can't believe my eyes. What you doin' over here? Tommy asked"

"Its a long story" Ownie said. "fancy a pint and I'll bend your ear"

"bend my ear" Tommy laughed. Now that is a funny You nearly broke my back on the fotball field down in Magheragallen years ago. Rough as a badgers arse you were. Aye indeed. A pint will go down well after listening to that blasted sermon"

"I heard it four times this weekend ' chuckled Ownie

"How come?" Asked Tommy

"I heard you might be coming to Mass here and I did not want to miss you"

"Well four Masses and four sermons. That deserves a pint or two. Let's get them down us" said Tommy

Ownie told him the whole story. The loss of his job, the feeling of despair, the binges, Fr Friel, Garda Flanagan and finally old Master Gallagher his saviour. He wasdown to his last few quid and not a hope of a job at home. They sank a couple of pints and Tommy went silent for a minute. Then he spoke "meet McAlpine's bus outside The Golden Thistle public house at 6.30 sharp on Monday morning and come out to the site and we will see what is going. I will have a word with the foreman and the site agent and we will see what is on the cards. No promises mind you but there is always something somewhere. Now I must be off as the dinner will be ready in my digs for 2o clock. It is always about an hour later on a Sunday to allow for a couple of pints beforehand."

With that he reached over ans stuffed a £20 note into Ownies jacket pocket

"No no none of that" protested Ownie "not another fucking word" said Tommy. "This is from our gang. A quid or so a man and the time may come when some Gweedore man will be grateful for a few bob from your good self. So not a bloody word. See ya Monday" And he was gone

Ownie met the bus and he saw a few from his own parish. He did not join them but sat on his own. Tommy was there on the site to meet him

"First things first" he said and he took Ownie over to a galvanised shed where there was a stove and a pan of frying rashers.

"Give this man a couple of your best" he said to an elderly man who was cooking

"This is our cook Charlie. Charlie will get you anything you need here. He is my right hand man" and he gave Charlie a thump on the back that nearly knocked him over.

Charlie fed Ownie without a word. It was a strange way they honoured each other's dignity. Obviously Ownie was not there for the view. He was out of work. He might be broke or even living on the streets. Charlie had seen it all before. Just look after the man and leave him be. When he was ready he would tell Charlie his story and Charlie was a great listener. As silent as the grave. Not a word and many a time he heard a sad story and he never broke a confidence. The McAlpines agony aunt was Charlie

Tommy Paddy Joe came back in. "I will leave you here and I will be back again in about an hour." Ownie sat by the stove and he helped Charlie do the washing up. Then Charlie haad to go and get some provisions from a shop down the road. Probably another supply of rashers and sausages for his clientele. Tommy returned with the site agent and the foreman. He explained that Ownie was from his own townland and that he would vouch for him. That was enough for the agent and the foreman. Weatherbeaten and crusty old Donegal gangers with their own gangs wre likegold nuggets

'Nothing doing at the moment but come back tomorrow" said the foreman.

Tommy gave Ownie a sly wink. He knew the form. If he wanted a man he eventually got him.

"You can pay me back when you get started" Tommy said as he slipped Ownie a £20 note. Here is the address of a good landlady. I am sending you to her because she looks after my men very well. No drunken carry on or any misbehaviour. I will hear about anything in that line and you will be in trouble. So behave yourself and see ya tomorra" And with that he was gone.

Ownie was lost. Out here in the back of beyond and the Site bus did not go back till the men were ready and had finished for the day

But Charlie came to his rescue. He offered to drive Ownie in one of the site dumpers down to the bus route a few miles away

"What if the police come on us? "Ownie was worried. That would be no way to start his career in the Perth area

"We meet the squad car up here from time to time" said Charlie. "No bother. Nothing like a good bacon sandwich to keep the law on your side

Ownie turned up next morning and he was told to start the following Monday. Not with the Donegal gang but with the sweepers up. Tidying up the site and loading and unloading the lorries. No great rates or bonuses but it was a job and he knew that when there was a vacancy in the Gweedoregang he was next in line. Most of them knew who he was anyway

When he got his first pay packet he sent a telegram home to Peggy his míle stór. Then he wrote a letter. He was not the best with the pen and paper as the master said but he wanted to set her mind at ease after what she had been through the last few months. They now had his address at home and he was looking forward to their letters. Maybe even Sinéad might drop him a line as well. Not to place too much expectation there as she was growing into a fine if awkward young lady. But God knowa she saw him at his lowest and at his worst. But he would make it up to them if it was tha last thing he ever did

Ownie soon found his way. He soon got to know Tommy's gang.

Many's a bacon butty they shared in Charlie's hut. The job was a doddle. He knew that eventually he would join the Gweedore gang. The vacancy usually arose when a man decided he had enough to buy a boat or a lorry and go home to live with his people. But not always. Some fell by the wayside The alcohol and the bookies.

Ownie liked his digs and when he thought he might share an apartment with some of his workmates Tommy Paddy Joe was very much against it.

"Too rough too rough. Too much drinking and the cards. Some of those men are skint by Monday and are looking for a sub. Keep well away."

Ownie stayed in his digs and when he joined the gang and moved with them round Scotland for their work he always stayed with a landlady. He did have the odd bash with the Guinness but that is what Paddies did on sites all over the world. No sweat.

He had his wages paid into a post office account with his expenses paid seperate. Just enough for the odd pint and the fags and the craic. The building industry closed down in July for their annual holidays but not the Gweedore gang. What job they had started they finished. They were the dynamite men who did the rock blasting for the foundations of the hydroelectric dams and the foundations for the motorway bridges. They made the way for the rest. They took their holidays between contracts and Ownie always came home to his loving wife. It was on one of those visits that Peggy became pregnant

4

IT WAS LATE morning when the consultant Mr Lavelle did his rounds. He was a tidy if rotund man with his grey hair Brylcreemed tightly back on his skull. He wore a light blue suitand a waistcoat and a white speckled blue dickey bow over a light blue shirt. Not many dickey bows in That part of the world. Indeed not. Around him gatehered a posse of nurses and junior doctors. Listening to his every utterance as if he were Moses

He picked up peggy's records from the end of her bed and he started speaking to hus assembled followers

"This lady has a daughter aged eten or eleven and as you can see this is a fairly late pregnancy. She had no trouble giving birthbut she is a little anaemic so we have decided to keep her here for a few extra days. She livesalone with her daughter. Her daughter is being cared for by a neighbour so s few days rest will do this woman good."

He looked across at his entourage and they nodded in agreement. Who would dare to question the great nman himself?

"Jesus help me" thought Peggy" Not another few days. I will go out of my mindAll the other mothers have daily visitors. I cannot expect Sinéad to come all this way and Ownie said he would come home when the baby was born and we could all be together. Not much point in coming home for the visiting hours"

She plucked up courage and waited forhis lordship to draw breath

"I feel very well and strong and I would like to thank you all for the wonderful treatment I have received in this hospital"

A good opening that and she saw him swell with pride

"Will you let me go home soon. My daughter and I can manage very well and my husband Ownie Rua Gillespie is coming home from Scotland for a couple weeks holiday"

"Ownie Rua Gillespie" said Mr Lavelle and he rubbed his back with a sigh "I know that name. That name rings a bell"

"He used to play football for County Donegal" said Peggy

"Don't I know it Don't tell me Ownie Rua Gillespie. He nearly killed me once. Never forget him. Never. And he massaged the small of his back again.

"I will see what we can do. We certainly do not want him coming in here. Well I never. And it still hurts. Every day I think of Ownie Rua Gillespie"

And he walked away with this palm on his back and as he was down the ward he looked back and Peggy could have sworn she saw him give her a sly wink Later the matron came and fussed at straightening the bedclothes. Then she said

"We will be letting you go home this afternoon. Change of plan. This Ownie Rua must have been some Gaelic footballer. Pity we cannot get to meet him. I think Mr lavelle is still a little afraid in case you might have a certain visitor."

She geve Peggy the shadow of a smile and then she left. A busy lady the matron as that was the first time Peggy had seen her on the ward

What a relief. The joy of going home and taking her son to meet Sinéad. Then Ownie would be home. We will have a party and a celebration. Invite the whole townland. Nurse Coughlan as wel as she was so kind. AndPaddy Joe the postman who did many a message for her on the quiet. She might even have the young curate as welleven if all he ever did was to call infor a cuppa and a few slices of the boiled brack. They would all be welcome and she had a good few quid in the Post Office savings account

The staff nurse helped her get her few things together

"We do not use the ambulance in cases like yours. We have a hackney driver we use and you will get on well with him. Jimmy Mac we call him. I do not know his real name. Just Jimmy Mac

Peggy did not care who was driving. She was going home

But Jimmy Mac was something else. He was a small wizened man wearing a tweed jacket that had seen better days. It was frayed on the collar and its lapels were bent ove, He had a brown shirt and no tie, But the most outstanding feature of his attire was his cap. It could have been worn by John Wayne in "The Quiet Man' It seemed a few sizes to big for Jimmy Mac and its peak was almost resting on the tip of his nosse How he could see where he was driving she could not guess

"Sit in Mrs Gillespie" he said and he opened the door af an ancisnt Ford Consul

Peggy had her doubts

"Sit in the front seat. It is the best place for the babby and he will not get the draughts from the wondows."

She sat on the front bench seat and placed her son beside her. Jimmy got in behind the drivers wheel and it took three bangs before the driver's door clicked closed. Jimmy gave a wee sigh of satisfaction and adjusted the peak of his cap over his nose.

"All ready to go" he said and he gave the ignition a start but it did not fire. It gave a metallic squeak

"She can be a bit moody at times" he looked over at Peggy and noticing her apprehension he added "but when she gets warmed up she is a great wee motor. Yes she is a fine wee lady"

He pulled out a packet of fags and he lit up

"Like one yourself" he asked and whenshe refused he said "you don't mind if I have one?. It's good for the concentration and I will keep the window open so the smoke does not get to the babby"

Cheeky sod she thought but if I say anything we could have a long sour and dreary trip home

The fine wee lady's engine starte at the third attempt and they headed out of town towards Gweedore.

Jimmy Mac started on his life story from when he left the primary school. I did not worry Peggy as all she had to do was listen. It meant she did not have to say a word. She enjoyed the pasing scenery as She and Ownie did not use this route to the town

Jimmy must have divined her thoughts

"much better this way than over by Dooish and Dunlewy" he said "much safer too and more passing traffic if we have a breakdown. But peggy said nothing. His life story carried on. Two operations and chronoc bronchitis and they had not even reached Creeslough.

When they came to the village of Creeslough he pulled in to a pub carpark. Not a word he switched off the engine and pulled on the handbrake

"It does the old lady good to give the engine a wee rest. Lets it cool down you know.There is a man here I have a message for. You care to come in?" peggy did not know what to say

"I'll sit and wait here. You wont be that long?" she suggested

"Just a few minutes" and off he went

She checked her son and he needed changing so she gathered her things and followed Jimmy Macinto the public house.

There he was sitting at the bar wit a pint of Guinness half consumed and a whiskey chaser.

"Thought I'd have a little freshner for the road. Can I get you anthin?"

"No no I'm fine. I thought I should change him. Where is the Ladies?"

"Frankie, Frankie" he shouted Will ya come out here for a minute. This lady needs you"

Frankie put his head round the door lesading to the kitchen and disappeared. Then Mrs Frankie, she presumed cane outwiping the flour off her hands and apron

"Sorry about this" she said "doing a bit of baking"

"Id like to change the baby if possible" said Peggy

"Sure sure" Mrs Frankie said and she lifted the bar counter shelf Better come out into the back and she took Peggy into the kitchen

Frankie wa seated at the tablein front of a large plate of spuds and bacon and cabbage. He muttered something and carried on eating

"No use going to the Ladies out there" Mrs Frankie said "rather basic to say the least. Come with me up to the bathroom"

They went and changed the baby

"How old is he?. Where are ye from?.Hve you got other children?.Not intrusive. Just inquisitive. Not many little babies drop in to public houses

"A nice cup of tea is what you need. Oh yes yes and not a word. Put yourself and your lovely son down there on the sofa. The men can chat among themselves,Frankie had finished asnd he went back out to the bar.

"I have a nice wee cake here" Mrs Frankie said and she cut Peggey a couple of slices. Maureen was her name and Peggy liked the woman and her kindness. Their life stories wre told and enjoyedThey swapped names and addresses. It was lonely for Maureenout there faraway from her relationsShe said their lad had a job in Dublin and they had a daughter a nurse in Birmingham. It was a bit lonely now almost on her own

Fankie put his head \round the door "Jimmy is ready when you are"

"He never passes without giving us a call" said Maureen

And I thought it was the better roads that had us coming this way. Peggy thought. God I'd better stop this. Getting to be an auld wan hating rhem all. Not good.

Maureen bustled about the kitchen and handed Peggy a parcel

"Sure it's only a bit of cake. I enjoy baking" as she handed Peggythe rest of the cake she had tasted

"It will be something to have with a cuppa when you get home" she smiled

They got hrough Dunfanaghy and Falcarragh without any stops for the poor engine and then Errigal loomed ahead. Soon they would be home. It was a lovely warm feeling. She had read in the Readers Digest that when the Eskimos saw each other approaching they delayed the actual meeting to prolong the joy of anticipation. She could understand that. The world was good. She sat back and enjoyed the last few miles'

Jimmy Mac pulled up outside the front door and Sinéad came rushing out. She wanted to hold her brother

"Not just yet my dear. Wait til we get in to the kitchen. You will have many years to hold him and to play with him. They invited Jimmy Mac in for a cup of tea. But he had to get back to take a few lads to the dogs in Lifford. Maybe a drop of the old malt might have enticed him but sure he might call to see Frankie again on the way home

Mrs Sharkey had seen the car arrive and she dropped in to welcome home the new baby and she just happened to have a pound of sausages and a black pudding and a few rashes

"Sure you will be starving after the journey" Bless her heart. They sat down to a fry and to Maureens lovely cake.

It was good to be home. Peggy and Sinéad just sat and looke at their new babyas he gurgled and bipped.

It was the end of a perfect day.

5

OWNIE ARRIVED ON The Swilly bus the next day. He broke down and cried soft tears when he held his son. He just sat on the sofa and held him and cried. He would dry his eyes and look at him and start all overagain. Soon he did not know if he was crying or laughing. But he was happy

They held a party for the two men in the house. Word was passed round that there was a new son and his father in Gillespies'. All the old gang came again. Even the new curate turned up. He sometime dropped in to have a cup of tea with Peggy and she soon found out he loved ginger snaps. But at the party he could not understand why the tea in the big blue teapot was so popular. Then he had a taste. It took his breath away Potteen with a few of Barry's teabags to give it colour. It was a reserved sin but tonight who cared. Did not Jesus do something similat at the wedding feast at Cana?

The blue teapot was your man and Ownie had to go out to the shed to top it up a few times

"Anyone for another cup of tea?" and a nod was as good as a wink

"What will you call your son?" asked the curate. That was a little problem. Peggy knew very well what she was going to call her son. But not now. Not here. She did not answer the young priest but she asked him if he would bless the child. She nipped off to get some holy water and the curate did the blessing. She had dodged the question

Next day Ownie raised the same subject

"Whaddya think we will call him?" he asked "Ownie runs in the family and there is the odd Frankie and even a Patrick and a Jimmy. Sure any one of them will do. I'll leave it to yerself"

Peggy was very careful "I have been thinking about the name for a long time. If I had given birth to a girl I would have called her Sheila"

This was her softener. Ownie had a sister Sheile who was settled in Boston

"But" she said and she waited for his full attention "there is one name I wold really like to christen him. It is an old Irish name"

Ownie looked at her "What?"

She had his full attention

"I would like to call him Aengus. Aengus"

"Jesus Peggy, that is the name of a boat. The wan we went over to The Aran Islands on"

Peggy sat down beside him and spoke very quietly

"Aengus is not the name of the Galway to Aran Islands ferry. That name is the Dun Aengus, named after a prehistoric fort on Inishmore. The fort is thousands of years old. Even before the Celts themselves. But Aengus was a god of youth and love and poetic inspiration. He was a mwmber of Na Fianna and he was friends with Maeve and Fionn MacCool

Ownie looked over at his young som "Well I never met anyone with that name before. The neighbours will think you are cracked. They will laugh behind our backs"

Peggy took his hands in hers and said "I do not care about the neighbours. It will be a few days wonder. They will get used to it"

"But what is wrong with what the other garsuns are called?" he asked

'She had her answer "All the Paddies, Frankies, Mickies, Jimmies?. They are there in their hundreds. I want my son to be different. I know my son will be different. I was born Peggy Coyle. Was I ever called Peggy Coyle?. Never. It was always Peggy Neddy Rua and now it's Peggy Ownie Rua. On my grave stone they might put P. Gillespie but who will know who is there?Nobody knows Peggy Gillespie. Aengus is a good strong name that can stand on its own. Not another Gweedore anonymity"

"But you can't have him baptised Aengus," said Ownie "Aengus was before religion. He was a pagan you said. There is no Saint Aengus. It is a good job Fr Friel has gone or he would never hear of it' Ownie felt very satisfied that he had put an end to that carry on

"We will just have to wait and see" was all Peggy quietly said.

Afew days later Peggy went to the Parochial House. Fr Friel and the battleaxe Breege had gone and Father Mullarkey and his housekeeper Maureen had taken their place

The housekeeper opened the door and invited her in

"Peggy a stór, come on in. How is the wee man himself? The spittin' image of his father. Good and strong I hear. Have you come to be churched

"What's that?" asked Peggy

"A servive of purification after birth. It's in the Gospel. Our Lady herself had it done" explained the good Maureen

"Well Maureen with all due respect I think I will give that a miss"

They might avail of it to purify the ward in the hospital she thought. But enough of that. Leave that alone

"ActuallyI came to see Fr Mullarkey about the Baptism and Registration of the birth" said Peggy

"I'll get the father for you now" Maureen said

Father Mullarkey came in a few minutes and they settled on a date for thr baptism

"I suppose you are going to christen your son after his father, Owen or Eoin, the Gaelic version. Both Irish versions of the Apostle John. A great name John. Brother of Jesus and he looked after his mother Mary after Jesus was crucified. Great name Owen or Eoin" and he unscrewed the cap of his fountain pen and started writing

"No no father. Hang on father. Wait. I want to call him Aengus"

"What?" was all Fr Mullarkey could say

"Aengus. Aengus" Peggy repeated

It took him aminute to replace the cap on his fountain pen. Then he pursed and moistened his lips.

"That is not a Christian name. I cannot put that on a Baptismal Certificate. Where did you get that one?"

"I got it from a book on Irish Mythology from the library. Old Master Gallagher said it was very interesting" Peggy replied

That Master Gallagher Fr Mullarkey thought. I wish he would keep his mythologies to himself and run the library without all that Pagan and Celtic tomfoolery. But the old master held the upper hand and Father Mullarkey knew that. He said nothing. Fr Mullarkey was not an honours graduate from Maynooth. But he could do funerals and weddings and they all thought he said a lovely Mass. But now he had a Baptism with a little problem. He would try his best

Peggy got in again "I like the name Father and I want him baptised with it"

But the holy father was not finished "Aengus is not a saint" he said "Will you let me call him Owen Aengus or Eugene Aengus and that will cover us both?" he asked hopefully

"No father "she replied. One name only. There are lots of Baptised Patricks and now they say he might never have existed or that there may have been three or four Patricks. Indeed they are not sure which one is the real Patrick' That Old vagabond Master Gallagher again thought the priest. That's where she learned all this. I blame him for all this bother

But Peggy was not finished. She carried on "Then there was Saint Christopher and they threw him out and even St Brigit might be for the bin as well"

Peggy was ready for a fight. If it came to a pinch she would baptise her son herself. God would not mind. But the registration of the birth was necessary and that certificate would be needed later on. It was time to cool down. A bit of the feminine touch

"Father you know all about these things. You have the experience and the wisdom of years in your sacred calling. I am only a poor Irish mother[good line that she thought] and all I want is to have my son baptised in the Catholic Church. Just bear with a tired and weary Irish mother on this one

The Irish Mother bit got to him. He knew he was beaten

"All right Peggy.Come here on Tuesday and we will christen your so Aengus"

The Christening was a quiet affair. Peggy's sister Mary who was married to a Garda in Clifden was one godparent and Eddie Sharkey from the shop was the other. They had a meal and a few drinks at The Castle Hotel and called it a day

Ownie Rua went back to Scotland that Saturday night. Aengus Gillespie was fast asleep under the adoring eyes of his sister Sinéad and his happy mother Peggy

6

HANNAH ROBINSON SAT staring out the window. She was not looking at anything, Nothing at all. It had started raining but it might as well be sunshine for all she knew or cared. The radio was on low and someone was wittering on Woman's Hour. What they were\saying she had no idea.

Then the doorbell pinged and she woke from her vacancy. A Customer. A customer.

"Howya Hannah. Give us four pounds of sixinch nails and four of thim brackets I got last week"

No problem. No problem at all. This was a cash customer. David Robinson, Hannah's father had one rule of trade. No Credit. Repeat No Credit.

Well not exactly. There were six or seven customers who were allowed to sign and run an account. But it can be told there was not a Catholic in that group. Not to be trusted David Robinson said. It was never spoken but they all knew it was cash on the nail except for the chosen few. And only they knew who they were. No hassle. That's how it was.

David Robinson was an Elder in the Presbyterian Church. The Kirk he liked to call it. After all it was the Scottish Army Chaplains who brought David's faith to Ireland in the 17th Century. They got no help from the resident Anglican Church either and since then they had managed seperately. He was very proud of the Burning Bush emblem he had over his door and the Covenant handed down from The Lord Himself.

"Ardens Sed Virens". Burning but flourishing. Not many knew what it was and what it meant, But he saw it every day. It gave him the courage to carry on. Life had been cruel to him. His only son and heir Luke was tragically killed on his motorbike and he had only his two daughters left to help him carry on. Luke on whom he had placed all his own future was gone. His older daughter Ruth had finished in Trinity College Dublin and had a good career teaching in Omagh. So it was down to his other daughter Hannah to carry on the business

Hannah Robinson was his daughter and she looked after the shop. She was on her own. Some days she would not have even one customer and she felt a tired weariness. She could feel her vitality drain away. The local doctor would laugh if she complained. At least her mother Judith Robinson had the housekeeping to keep her busy. But cooking for three was no great burden and Judith filled her time cleaning and polishing and cleaning and polishing. Windows, mirrors, glasses, doors, lampshades. They were done every day. It became an obsession

Hannah had attended the local Catholic Primary school. The National School as it was called. The nearest Presbyterian school was in Strabane and that was too far for a young child to travel so she went to the Catholic school in the village. That did not worry David very much as Orthodox Presbyterianism as practised locally was as far removed from his beliefs as was the Roman Catholic version of Christianity practised in Garton

That meant Hannah had a longer lunch break as the Cathecism class was always the last class before the lunch break and she was excused

But it was a trick they played on every new curate who came to the village. She stayed on in the class when he came to check on their religious knowledge. And if he asked her a question and before the teacher could intervene she would say "not a Catholic Father" and watch his face break into a false smile and all the other children would giggle. It never failed.

After sixth class she was sent to Alexandria School in Dublin. It was heaven on earth. In Earlsford Terrace opposite the UniversityCollege Dublin she could look out and watch the students sitting on the steps outside the Main Hall.There was a school orchestra and she was enciuraged to play the violin, and she reached Gtrade 6 which was quite an accomplishment She passed her Leaving Certificate and then enrolled at the College of Commerce in Rathmines. She shared a bedsit in Upper Rathmines Road and the freedom ws stimulating. There was the Abbey, The Gate, The Peacock and even the Gaelic Damer Hall. All the famous playwrights and then there was the National Gallery and Library and The National Museum to broaden her mind. Irish music in the pubs and basement clubs with their hint of nascent republicanism and Sinn Féin. David Robinson wouls have taken her home if he had any idea of what she was experiencing. Confined to Garton she would be

Then she discovered the Rathmines and Rathgar Musical Society. They used her local The Loft. Not that she drank anything alcoholic but they did lovely open sandwiches. The R&R asked her to come along to rehearsals. She was in heaven. She loved helping out. Making the tea and washing up. Then it was suggested that she try for a place in the chorus. They said she might have a voice. Go to Mr Gleeson in Phibsboro. She did and her voice got stronger and he advised her to modify her pronounced Donegal accent. Her wild Donegal accent he calles it. No Place for Barney McCool in the R&R. She improved and she was given her place in the chorus. The thrill of the first night in the Gaiety. The excitement. The adrenaline rush and the endorphin release after. She could swear everyone in the audience was looking at herself. What a change from the gloom of Garton. But to be part of the whole performance. They told her she could sing and left it at that. No great pretensions. After performances the cast went back to The Loft in Rathmines. Even the ladies knew that half a pint when added to another half pint made the world a better place. The craic was mighty. Hannah stuck to her Ginger beer. Non alcoholic but looked like the hard stuff.

She was with two of her pals when this man walked over

"Can I get you girls a drink?"

He bought a round and told them he was Des Shanley

Hannah had noticed him beore but they had not been introduced. Her eyes seemed to stray in his direction and he caught her looking at him. She quickly looked away and hoped she had not gone the usual beetroot. Later on she had another peep and there he was, peeping at her. She reddened again.

But tonight she had her friends beside her and she felt at ease. Soon she and Des were deep in conversation and the other girls drifted off. Subconsciously they must have felt they were outsiders. When the barman called closing Hannah and Des Shanley knew a lot about each other and they seemed to enjoy each others company.

They made a date to go to the pictures at The Savoy and afterwards they dropped in to Slatterys for the music and the craic. They were soon regarded as an item by the rest of the company. Hannah even went to Parnell Park on Sundays to watch Des Shnaley's team play. He was captain of Na Fianna and when theyheld their annual dinner dance in the Gresham Hannah was there with her friend Des at the top table

What her father would have said and done had he known?. Football matches on a Sunday, on the Day of the Lord, the Lord's Holy Day, and a boyfriend, a city boy at that. Not to mention that he was a Catholic. And a Catholic teacher to boot. Des was a science teacher at one of the Jesuit Colleges in the city and his hobby apart from Na Fianna Football team was collecting rare maps and old books. He was 26 years of age but as a Dub. he was much more experienced than his younger Donegal country lassie.

"Imagine" he once said "me a Dublin RomanCatholic and you a Donegal Scottish Presbyterian. Chalk and cheese or what?"

She did not reply and he did not expect an answer. They both knew she would have to go home to Garton when her commerce course was complete and she would have to help her father. Ruth was settled in a good career in Omagh and ws engaged to be married. Hannah knew she would have to return to her parents, No secrets there. Tht's how her life ws happening. Soon it was time to go home.

To Garton in East Donegal. Few people would haqve heard of Garton. Her friends held a farewell party in the loft. She held back her tears and hugged them all goodbye

Des whispered through her tears that this might not be a fnal goodbye and that the fates might have something in store. He did not hang about and was gone. Hannah stayed awake all night and got the early train from Amiens St.,. Her father was there to meet her on the platform in Strabane. She was so delighted to see him that she hugged him and kissed his face and ears. He shrank with embarrassment and looked round the station to see if anyone had noticed her behaviour

They had not much to say to each other. He had never been to Dublin. Belfast was his city. Dublin and John Charles McQuaid was something he did not care for. He hoped she had not learned any other funny antics strs as well as the hugs and kisses

Hannahs mother Judith was happy that her daughter was home again. Hale and hearty. But beneath the surface there was a sadness. They knew that their young daughter had come home and home to stay. For a young woman there were many more exciting places to live than the village of Garton

7

HANNAH WAS HOME and back in the shop. Her sister Ruth was now engaged to be married to Daniel Crossan, She was supposed to be sharing a flat with a girlfriend but she was sharung the flat with Daniel. In reality they were living together. What her father would have made of her living in sin was beyond anyone's imagination. Sometimes she took Daniel home for Sunday lunch and on other Sundays she took another teacher namedTeresa her supposed flatmate to the Garton homestead just to have her parents believe that Teresa shared the flat. Daniel worked in The Northern Bank and he would get very favourable mortgage terms and they were saving for a deposit. David Robinson would no doubt help them in this but as Hannah was slowly discovering there was no great fortune from Garton. to share out. She was able to read the accounts now. They made depressing reading.

Some times Hannah would go over and spend the weekend wit Ruth and Daniel

She almost asked the question

"Do ye . . . . ?" bur Ruth's raised eyebrow was enough. Nothing more was said. Nothing needed. Even when Daniel was promoted they would keep the house in Omagh and he could come home come home at weekends. The Six Counties were not that big and the bank would surely give consideration to their domestic arrangements. But the bank did not approve of marriage under a certain age and Daniel had some time to go. Ruth was sure they vetted prospective partners as well and she hoped her CV would pass muster. If they looked at her father's CV they would make her Chairlady of the group she thought. David Robinson was the bedrock of society. Poor Ruth she had no idea how perilous was her father's financial position.

It was no surprise that Daniel was amember of the Orange Order and every year they went to Rossnowlagh for the 12th of July. Not much ito do in Rossnowlagh but have a picnic and walk the strand and listen to the bands and the speeches. William of Orange won the Battle of The Boyne on the 12th of July 1690 and saw off James and his Catholic followers. But Hannah learned when she was in Dublin that the Pope was on William's side and that the Te Deum was sung in Rome to celebrate William's great victory. Not that she cared very much either way

She once went over to Raphoe to watch the 12th parade there and she found it quite amusing. Some of her customers who did not have a penny to ther names were out there on the street in sashes and top hats with walking sticks and rolled umbrellas. Toomuch like Charlie Chaplin at his best

She pitied the Gardai walking alongside the paraders keeping an eye on the village troublemakers. The big fat sergeant of the Gardai had warned "No trouble now me boyos or it will be a night in the cell. You might get away with it today but be sure I will make you sorry sometime later." He might as well have printed it on a leaflet.They knew what he meant and there was no trouble.

But sure the other crowd were just as bad with their Hibernian regalia and their march as well. What were they celebratinganyway?. Where do they come from?.She knew the Drumboe Commeration was for men killed in the Civil War but surely all that was past and gone. In a war the edges get a bit blurred. Let bygones be bygones. We are all in this together and let us make the best of it

What she enjoyed most was when Daniel took them on trips to Innishowen and Buncrana and around Bloody Foreland., Errigal, Gweedore, Carrick and Sliabh League. They took a trip to Arranmore and went even to Tory Island and visited the Tory School of Painting. Primitive, and she thought she could do as well herself but then she always thought Picasso was a bit of a fraud. All this sightseeing was a delightful change from the Sundays her father would have her at the Kirk reading the Bible and singing those mournful hymns. But she needed the breakShe thought the change from her life in Dublin would take some time. And it did.She took driving lessons. Patsy the driving instructor was a man of great patience and the lesson was held in silence. Not even so much as a tut. But at the end he would ask "now where did we make a mistake?". She could tell him every mistake she made as that was when he ticked on his pad with his pencil. It always worked. On her official driving test she never met another mechanised vehicle,. She could have been the only motor on the Donegal roads that day. She passed the test

8

LIFE WAS SLOW in Garton village. Hannah was bored. The quietness was eerie. Sometimes even the birds were silent. There were days when she thought not a motor car passed through. The main arterial road to Lifford was over the hill and the passing traffic did not disturb the silence. She got her old violin out. At Alexandria she had been in the orchestra and had made it to grade 6. She took the violin down to the shop and set up her music stand there. Often when the doorbell did not cling loud enough the customers stood and listened before banging on the counter. She often thought back to Slatterys and the Irisnh music and the craic and Des Shanley. When her father was away she tried a reel or two. No great shakes. Not too clever. She would never be a Maguire or a Coleman but she managed. The slow airs were better a la Tony MacMahon. But they were all so sad. Caoineachs. Weepers. That is what they were. She needed a bit of Mozart or Chopin to get to her heart and make her feel better. With her new driving licence she set out further afield and she started taking violin lessons with Herr Kreid in Londonderry. She was not allowed to call it Derry. Only the Fenians called it Derry and that was not allowed in David Robinsons home

Herr Kreid suggested she take further examinations and she could qualify as a music teacher. But Hannah had enough with the shop. All she wanted was to hone her skills for her own satisfaction. He suggested that she join the local musical society. After all was not Londonderry famous for its famous Londonderry Air, Danny Boy and who had not heard if its recent composer Phil Coulter. Hannah attended a few times but she did not find it to her liking. It was too concentrated and dark. There was none of the mad spontaneity or the R&Rin Dublin. She even found the city threatening as she drove by the Brandywell. So she dropped out and only came to Herr Kreid for his tuition and his hilarious accent and his good company. But things were still too quiet. She asked the lady in the library in town if anyone was interested in playing in a group. No not one. So she placed an advertisement in The Donegal Democrat

"Young lady wishe to form group for light musical and classic favourites"

She got 20 replies. She made a mistake in not giving a location and there was a reply from as far west as Dungloe. She got replies from 6 violins 3 piano players. An accordeon player a clarinet and a keyboard player. Flute and whiste players galore.

The piano wa the problem. No one could haul a piano round. There was a piano in the village hall but it needed tuning and anyway the place was too cold for what she had in mind. She had to do without a piano player. They arranged a rota to play in each other's houses and in a few months they were up and running. They did not have a definite number of players. Just whoever was free turned up. They offered to play at the Kirk bur David would have none of it, He had been to a service in Strabane and there was a quartet there playing "Blowing in the Wind" and that ws enough for him. Dear Lord what was the world coming to.? One might ask

Should they give themselves a name?Tee hee. Why not?Just for.Why not? Just. And so the Garton Players was formed

Herr Kreig could not control his curiosity when he heard and he called in on one of their sessions. He was not over impressed by their music but he praised their diligence and he invited them to come to Londonderry to his house. They faithfully promised. But he could not wait and in a few days they had a letterwith a list of suggestions and a promise that he would like to hear them again when they had practised as he had suggested. They looked atv each other and there was a heavy silence. No comment

Mrs Bell was a boss lady in the local I.C.A. The Irish Countrywoman's Association. Her husband was a builder and he did business with the Robinsons. He had a building gang of four and as an Orangeman he was kept busy with the members of his own Lodge and by the wealthier Catholics. He was very reliable if a little expensive but he always completed and that is what you had to pay for a job well done. Mrs Bell got to know Hannah and she invited her to come to a meeting. She would enjoy it. Yes she would.So off she went to an I.C.A. Meeting. Most there were older than her but they were\a jolly lot. It was as if they had escaped from their husbands and were intent on enjoying themselves. They had visiting speakers but their main fun was in their own competitions and the exchange of recipes. Hannah thought their coffee was extra special as welland she found out the recipe A cup of Cognac in the pot helped the flavour. No kidding.

Judith Robinson was a little peeved when Hannah replaced the old candlewick bedspread in her room with a patchwork one she herself made with I.C.A. instigation. It lifted the whole bedroom

And so life went on. Day after day. Some of Hannahs serenity returned. It was always implied that she would marry and carry on the business. A nice solid Presbyteriam lad. But they did not live around Garton. There was Ivan Ashe who dropped I for the odd purchase but he never came to the Kirk. He was probably Church Of Ireland and they were mostly the old Anglo Irish landowners. The only men she met was the odd travelling rep or an odd Garda who might drop in for a cup of tea. Killing time. Up here in Donegal on border duty and very lonely away from their families. But the overtime was most acceptable

She tried fishing on the Finn but the local angling club did not welcome newcomers and had little time for women. Then there as s dispute over fishing rights. It had always been free since time began and the "No Fishing" signs were a cause of animosity to the absent landowners. And a Presbyterain might be considered a spy in the camp. She found the fishermen a close and envious lot. Jimmy Quinn was the most successful local fisherman and there was a whisper that he did not always use the rod and line. Nod nod.

So it was back to the Garton Players. They offered to play at Mrs Bell's birthday party. It was her 60th and she was not shy about being 60. Boasted about how well she was for 60. There were\a few of her friends who rembered that Mrs Bell was never much at the sums in school and that maybe she had not improved in the meantime.

Still it was the Garton Players' first public appearance. They had cards with their name printed and they gave them to all the guests. If Mrs Bell thought they were good enough then many of the others might think so as well. Their big break came when the local Master of the Orange Lodge held a party for his daughters coming of age. The girl had been an intern in the Republican Party in Boston for a year. It was ironic that ifshe had similar party affiliations at home her father would have disowned her. Anything was better than the Kennedys as far as he was concerned

Soon the Garton Players had a select clientele and they disreetly started charging fees. The did not charge fees as such but left it open to the person who invited them to play to make a donation to their expenses fund. Money was never mentioned. "Leave it to yourselves.whatever" But Hannah knew them all and she had no doubts that their details were passed round and their remuneration was discussed in many a kitchen. Who wanted to be thought of as a cheapskate?

9

AENGUS GILLESPIE JUST hated school. He hated it. Every minute. Bean Ui Ceallaigh[Mary Paddy Frankie] his teacher had never met anyone like him before. Carysford Teacher Training College had in no way trained or prepared her for this. On his first day at school Aengus did not seem to mind. It was a taster, and he decided he did not like the taste. Sitting at a desk all day and no running around. No thank you this was not for Aengus. Then there was that awful cocoa that Bean Ui Ceallaigh[Mrs Kelly] made him drink at lunchtime. "To make him grow into a big strong man like his father." He did not want to grow into a big strong man. He wanted to be at home with his mother and hs best pal Toby the dog and to play with Sinéad. Sinéad said she loved school. He did not care. She was a girl. Let her. All the girls loved school

Mrs Kelly asked the master to have a look at this young man. Just have a look at him. On the quiet. He did.

"Son of Ownie Rua. I might have guessed. Don't worry too much. He will settle in time. Ownie Rua's son. Well I never" and master Kennedy rubbed the small of his back where Ownie Rua had placed a knee some years ago.

"My God" he thought "someone is going to get a bad back in years to come"

He spoke quietly to Mrs Kelly "just keep him busy. Keep him occupied" was the only advice he could offer

"I would like to live to get my pension and die of old age" said Mrs Kelly, hoping for some sympathy. But the master only smiled weakly and hurried back to his own classroom. Much safer there.

Poor Mrs Kelly. She did her best. Plasticine, crayons, slates, coloured pencils; all day long until Aengus was so tired he almost fell asleep at his desk. Peggy told her it was the best week of her life, as when he got home and had his tea and had a play with Toby he was ready for bed even before it was dark

Slowly he settled in. The game of football in the school yard at lunchtimewas his sole reason for going to school at all. But again here he was different. He played by his own rules and he was banned from playing for a week. He found that he could not do what he liked. No use complaining. There was no room for a mammy's pet in Dunmore School. It was a hard world but soon he was able to go to school on his ownand join the other pupils as they pased by his home. He was becoming more independent

Funny how people change. Soon he loved going to the school Then it was his First Communion. All that fuss. Auntie Sheila and her husband Andrew were coming over from Boston for the big day. Ownie was taking a few days off to be there. But nothing was that simple. First there was the questions in the Cathecism to learn and all the long prayers. Fr Kelly dropped in once as the day grew closer. All the questions and answers. He praised the communion class for their knowledge and that meant they were ready. "Word perfect" was what he said. Aengus himself asked Peggy at home to answer some of the questions and she definitely would never pass. She got cross with him when he told her so and she said that she knew what she meant even if the words were not the same as in the Cathecism. Bur she had failed and he told her and that was that. Move along there !!

Mrs Kelly would never pass his mother Peggy. He had to call her "Miss" now instead of Bean Ui Ceallaigh or Mrs Kelly. It was easier as well.

She said his own words were no good and it had to be what was written in the Cathecism or not at all. He was able to answer every question "word perfect" as Fr Kelly had said and he was able to recall what page number the question was in as well. Miss said that was not necessary as Fr Kelly could look it up in the Cathecism himself if he wanted.

He got a new suit and shirt and a tie. Auntie Sheila gave him a dotted one like they use in the movies but Paggy said he looked bad enough as he was. He wore it for the photographs Auntie Sheila took for her own album. They all wear them in America she said

"Don't chew. Don't chew" they kept repeating. Swallow the Host "Swallow Swallow"

There was a big Mass with singing and incense. Then he had to go up to the alter rails and open his mouth wide and the Host was placed on his tongue and the priest said Latin words. No problem, he remembered the "swallow, swallow" instructions and he closed his mouth. But it stuck to the roof of his mouth. He stopped on the way down from the rails and someone gave him a push from behind. But it was still stuck. He stopped again and again he got a push as he was holding the line up. He put his finger in his mouth snd dislodged the Host with his thumbnail. There was a bit of a titter from the front benches in the church but he made it safely back to the First Communion bench and the rest of the class.

Peggy was mortified. Everyone would have seen what he did. And all the timeds he had been told the correct thing to do.She was cross with him. Silly little monkey.

But she soon forgot about it and they had a great day. Lots of sweets ans cake and ice-cream at the village hall. Fr Kelly came as well and when he asked Aengus how he felt on his big day he got the reply that "it was not worth all the bother". Sheila and Andrew booked two caravans by the sea at Portnoo and they all went there on holidays. Sheila and Andrew and Peggy and Ownie went to the Hotel there every night for a few drinks and Sinéad stayed with Aengus and Toby to stop them from tearing the caravan apart. Ownie had to leave after a few days. A very proud and happy parent.

Ownie was thinking it was time for him to come home again. He was a ganger now with his own Gweedore group of men. He and Tommy Paddy Joe[MacGinley] worked close together with their gangs. They had a good reputation and they were never without work. There were always jobs waiting for them. But this First Communion made him realise what he was missing. But what could he do at home?. Buy a lorry? Run a hackney car?. They might have to move elsewhere and buy a shop or a business. Something somewhere will turn up. But when and where.

Sheila and Andrew were so sad to go home to Boston. They had no children themselves and they really enjoyed the disorderly and almost chaotic life of the Gillespies.

The years moved on and Aengus moved in to the Master Kennedy's classroom. Things changed overnight. No fooling about any more. Some days the master would be absent and his wife came in to take his classes. They all loved her. She sat at her table and read them stories. There were rumours that Master Kennedy was fond of wee drop now and then. Sure did not the man deserve every drop. It made no difference to his pupils or to Aengus. He loved that man. He would not have a bad word said against him. The man could not do enough for his class. Sinéad got a scholarship to secondry school. It was all down to the master Kennedy. He had her sitting t on her own at one side of the room and gave her extra tuition and work to do. She worked away on her own and she won a scholarship. Fees all paid. Thank you Master Kennedy

Peggy and Aengus and Toby had the house to themselves. Aengus could turn on any radio station he liked. No arguments. He could read the Sunday Independent witout having to give the centrepiece out. But they wre so delighted to see her again when she came home on holidays and they gave her a free run of the house.

10

THE GARDA SQUAD car pulled up at Peggy's house. No sirens and no flashing lights. The squad car is never a good sign. A policewoman knocked on the front door and was admitted. Policewomen were new to Ireland but in this case she was best suited to her task.

For she had bad news. There had been an accident in Scotland and Ownie was involved. Ownie was injured. That was all they had at present but the Superintendent was on the phone to Scotland trying to find out the complete story. It was not good. There had been an underground explosion and two Gweedore men were dead.

The Garda Superintendent himself came out to the house and to confirm the bad news. He read from a prepared statement

"It has been confirmed that there was an explosion underground at the construction site of Auchtermore Hydro scheme outside of Perth in the county of Perth and Kinross. There have been fatalities. A Mr Owen Gillespie of Gweedore\ and a Mr Thomas MacGinley of Gweedore. If I might add they are better known locally as Ownie Rua and Tommy Paddy Joe. I am grateful to the local postman Mickey Paddy Tommy for giving me their local identities. Thank you all and may God give us strength on this awful day"

Everyone was stunned. There was no point in wondering why. Was there a kind and caring God up there somewhere? Did God really care? Fr Kelly came to the house and he prayed for the repose of Ownie's soul. It did not mean a thing to the family. His soul they did notknow. But his body they did. And they would never see him again. Never again. When his body did arrive it would be ain a sealed coffin the coffin would not be opened and there was the unspoken thought that some of Ownie's body would not be in the same coffin. The Lord be with us this day.

Old master Gallagher from the library came and sat with the Gillespies, He had seen similar tragedy when a herring fishing boat capsised some years ago. The poor priest was lost. He had been in the parish only a few years. Nothing that in a lifetime. He was not one of them. Only one of their own could feel and share in the grief they carried. The wise old master went to the doctor's and came back with some pills that he advised Peggy to take

"Only for the first couple of days. Otherwise you will be just a zombie" Peggy did as he advised and she spent her time sitting and looking at the bare wall. And instead of having every visitor cry and weep with Peggy the master opened a Condolence Book and and had the visitors sign their sorrows and best wishes. At least Peggy was not exhausted by the whole population of Gweedore. Peggy knew very well that Tommy Paddy Joe's relations were suffering as well ad she new that when the funerals were over they would get together and there was still life to be lived and the bereaved had to soldier on

Sinead came home and was not able toaccept what had happened. Where was God.? Why did it have ro happen to my father?. He was a good man. Rough on the football field but he was a good man. Her exams were coming up but she let them pass. She was in no state to sit an examination

Aengus seemed the least damaged. He had only known his father when he came home on his short holidays. He knew of Ownie's great reputation.But then he was too young to appreciate what he would miss for the rest of his life.

MacAlpines did not fail in their duties. Next morning their Dublin agent was at the door

"Any money problems we can help with?" But they had enough for the present time at least

"The company will fly both coffins to Ballykelly Airport ans we will have hearses taake the coffins to the church or to their respective homesteads. No cost to the families. Peggy had\the coffin taken to the house. She wanted to spend this last night with her Ownie. She told the children she did not want Ownie to spend the night alone in the cold chapel. It was hard for her to accept that her Ownie was dead and that he could not feel the cold any more. She sent the children to bed and she sat beside the coffin. They found her the next morning in an exhausted sleep on her chair and her head on a pillow she had placed by the coffin.

The local G.A.A. Did him proud. They had a piper and a guard of honour of his old teammates in the club colours by the graveside. The County Board sent most of thir senior officials and the radio and the local press covered the funeral. The national Irish Press had an article on "One of Donegal's Greatest". Flowers and Mass cards aplenty and the odd most welcome cheque. There was a large wreath "From the Gweedore Gang". No names no addresses. Sheila came over from Boston and stayed for a few days. Poor Sinéad was inveigled to go back to school. It might be best for her as hanging about the house was not doing her any good

As for Aengus it was hard to know. He lay on the sofa with his pal Toby and he barely spoke. It was hard. There was no way round it. Ownie was dead and gone. All this stuff in the Cathecism about going to Heaven and the eternal life did not register with him. Neither did the "looking down and watching over us" bit help him I any way either

The cold reality was that they would have to come to terms with the death and get over their loss. Fr Kelly dropped in from time to time for the chat and the cuppa and the brack. Bless his heart. He took Aengus to MacCools park in Ballybofey to a football match and he made enquiries about Sinead's progress at her school. Sadly she was not doing very well and it was suggested that she mightbe better off at home with her mother

Master Kennedy gave Aengus a busy time at the school

"Get it right. Do it again. Keep up. Listen. Listen to what I tell you Well done my son. Now let's do it again. Not bad. Give it another try One more time Well done. I could not do it better myself"

Things quietened down. A substantial money order came from The Gweedore Gang. Even Peggy knew this meant there was a site collection and every man had to fork out. You never know when it might be your family. The old master wrote to MacAlpines asking if there was any monies coming to the family, Accident compensation or the like. He got a big cheque from the company. They explained it was from their Benevolent Fund. There was no accident insurance compensation as The Gweedore Gang worked The Lump. The master explained that Ownie and his gang did not pay any Income Tax r any National Insurance payments. They wrere paid by the amount of work they completed. Almost by the cubic yard one might say. Thy agreed with MacAlpines on a price for a particular piece of work and when it was done MacAlpines paid up. Usually to the head man, the ganger, and the ganger didvded the monies to the men, That is one of the reasons the Gang was so close. It was none of MacAlpines business what the Gweedore Gang did apart from the tasks they were paid to do. The Gang was a unit responsible to themselves only.

It was well known that the quickest way to clearDonegal men off a site was to shout "Tax Inspector"

So what she had now saved in the Post Office was what Peggy and her family would have to manage on. Her old sewing machine was back in full time employment. Any alterations, tucks in. lets our. Waistbands. All come to Peggy's' Well and good. But there was still a problem with the unsettled Sinead. Nothing they could do to help her. She was a very unhappy person. Almost ill. Sheila heard of the problem and offered that Sinead come and stay with them in Boston to recover. The change of scenery and new people night help herand her Irish heritage might be to her advantage. Peggy mentioned this to Sinead and she was happy to go to Boston

There was no American wake the night before she left. People dropped in to say goodbye and to slip her a few pounds and for her to remember them when she made her first million. Peggy was easy about her leaving as she knew Sheila and Andrew would look after the lass. The child deserved a chance to live her life. And live her life did she again. Within weeks she\was working in the office of Patrick Horan Attorney At Law. Patrick was second generation Irish from Claremorris. Within months she was promoted and Patrick himself suggessted she attand law school

She could attend lectures by day when necessary and make up the time in the evenings or on Saturday mornings.

He muttered something about jewellery and diamonds and polishing

11

AENGUS WAS NOW in the 5th class. He was one of the senior boys now, Big chief Aengus. But Master Kennedy might have other ideas. He took Aengus and three other boy to one side

"Here's how it is. No talking, no cod acting and heads own all the time. If you have any problem just raise a finger and I will come and help you. It will mean you four men coming to school half an hour earlier and staying on half an hour in the evening. Have a word with your parents and come back to me. If you do not want this there is no problem. You can sit back like the rest of the class and carry on as before. But if you do come in then be ready, No whimgers no crybabies. It is all or nothing and you willwork as you have never done before."

All four accepted the master's challenge. The I.N.T.O.made a complaint about the abuse of the primary school system and how it gave some pupils an advantage, Of course it did. But any other teacher was free to do the same. Not to mention those who could afford private tuition. Were they not buying an advantage?. The department of Education sent an officer to see what it was all about but he was a Gweedore man himself and knew the Master personally and the whole fuss died of inertia. And so Aengus and his three companions started on their course. Whenever they showed signs of slacking the master mentioned some past pupil's name and said "Look at him now, He sat in those benches and look at him now. You can be the same.". The Primary Certificate was a doddle. But they wre entered in three Scholarship entrance examinations. They were stiffer and wider examiations. Aengus was not sure but the master confided in Peggy that Aengua was a sure cert to win any of the scholarships. The last day before the Summer holidays and the last school day for the senior class the master did not teach at all. He sat at his table filling on forms. Th class was very subdued. It was as if theywere wary of the outside world.Not hope for some of them. The master knew this very well and he was not able to face his beloved children. Some he knew t would proceed to further educat ion ;even to the local technical school.But there were no prospects for a large number of the class. There were no apprenticeships or factory jobs for them. Too young to join the army. There was talk of a fish processing factory in Bunbeg. But the Fishery Board was in no hurry and the politicians had no need to nurture the electorate. The men in the Dail, the Irish Parliement, fotr that region had comfortable majorities. No need to get excited. It was marginal seats that would get the goodies in the pre election run up

Aengus was ready for anything. Sinead was doing well in Boston and was on her way to becoming a fully fledged attorney. She was earning enough to send home the odd dollar. From his father's genes Aengus was interested in playing football. He and his pals went to the nearest football field nearly every evening on the way home from school. It was the local Soccer team's pitch. Strangely in Gweedore there was agreat tradition of playing soccer. Possibly from the emigration to Scotland. Many of the Glasgow Celtic team had relations in Gwedore and came on their Summer holidays, No one bothered about the Ban. The Ban meant that if you played Soccer or Rugby or any of the non Gaelic games or even if you attended any of those games then you could not be affiliated to any of the Gaelic playing clubs. But no one in Gweedore paid any attention and there were Donegal County players playing Soccer for professional teams all over Ireland, But because the local team's playing field was so far away Aengus and his friends lacked any supervision or organisation and they stopped playing their football

With his father Ownie not being there Aengus saw more of his grandfather Eugene Coyle. Eugene had an old tin whistle and an old flute and he often played for Aengus. He gave Aengus the tin whistle and they tried to play together. Aengus was interested and the old man began to teach him some of the tunes in his repertoire. What he sould not play he di diddled I died them. The old mouth music. Aengus learned the airs ut he was not able to play them. But he kept on trying and Peggy banned him from playing in thehouse. Out to the shed he had to go as it was driving her mad. If she heard him trying to play Carolan's Concerto once more she might finish up in the asylum

But then came a break that lit his enthusiasm. Ciaran MacMathuna had a programme or two on Radio Eireann. It was traditional Irish music. Ciaran came to Donegal to tape Maire O Cathasaigh for his programme. He was also very keen to tape John Doherty but the problem was that John was a wandering minstrel and he did not stay very long in any one place. Aengus knew where he lived when he was at home. John did not carry a fiddle. He was fond of the drop and a fiddle would not last long on his travels. Wherever he stopped the word was spread and a session was soon organised

So Aengus took Ciaran half way up the side of The Blue Stacks and they found John Doherty "at home" in his small one roomed thatched sottage

After a few naggins or six the session was in full swing and it lasted until the wee hours of the morning. It was daylight when they came down from the mountain with their lungs full of turf smoke and their clothing smelling of sheepdogs. It was a great experience for a young garsun.

Sinead must have heard of this expedition for weeks later there came a parcel from Walton's of North Fredrick Street. The people who have "the music you know and love" and he opened the package and just looked. A Concert Flute. This was too much. But the old master [he from the library] saw the flute on one of his visits and he dropped in with a record of Mozart's Flute Concertos

"That should keep him going for a couple of years" was all he said.

Just a lifetime thought Peggy and she offered the master a wee drop

"against that cold North wind"

Then that letter came. He had won a scholarship. Yippee yippee. Dancing and screaming he raced round the house and then cycled over to Master Kennedy's house

"I could have told you that months ago" was all the master could say as Aengus grabbed and smothered him

"Now come in and meet my wife. I believe you two know each other". Aengus shook hands with Mrs Kennedy and then they all had nothing to say. But the master went and got his fountain pen and started writing.

"Here is a little motto that I want you to follow for the rest of your life"

"IT MATTERS NOT HOW STRAIT THE GATE
HOW MANY PUNISHMENTS THE SCROLL
I AN CAPTAIN OF MY SHIP
I AM MASTER OF MY SOUL"

He shook Aengus by the hand and clapped him on the back and said

"Now young man off you go"

12

THE SUMMER WA soon over and it was time to go College. Aengus was ready. He had been ready for weeks. His suitcase was full of what the college suggested. They named a shop that carried suitable clothing. But Peggy when she saw their prices knew better, She found an Indian who travelled round in his van and when she offered to pay cash he could not believe it.Most of his customers paid on the "never never" instalments. The clothes might be slightly different from what the expensive shop was selling but knowing Aengus after a week or so they would be in tatters anyhow. No one would be able to tell

There were two other boys from the parish attending the same college and they agreed to have Aengus share their hackney car. So it was a full boot and three cases on the roof rack. Jimmy Mac the Garage was the driver and he asked for Jasus sake could they leave some of the rubbish at the college if he was to collect them for their Christmas return home. He did not want his effin springs broken or the effin Garda stopping him for a dangerous load. And if they wanted to eat their sandwiches then they should tell him and he would stop and they could eat them on the roadside thank you

"What if it is raining?" theyasked

"Tough" was all he said. A man of great personal charm was Jimmy Mac the Garage.

Later on in years Aengus was able to go by bus when he knew where to change buses and when he was strong enough to carry his cases. By then he did not have to carry so much as he was able to leave some of his gear in a locker at the college.

Boy was he impressed when he saw it for the first time.!!! It was massive!!. Bigger than any building he had ever seen before. They drove up a sweeping drive to an arched elevated entrance to the collegeThis might be the only time he went through this door the other boys told him. It would be the tradesmans entrance for him from now on. He could see rows and rows of windows looking out on the playing fields.

All the new boys were collected in the refectory. The" mice" as they were called by the older students. They were told they would spend that night together in St Enda's dormitory which was the first stairs just outside the ref. There they would stay for a night or two there and then they would be allocated a permanent bed in other dormitories for he rest of the year. Supper was at 6pm and a glass of milk at 9 and then prayers and bed. When all the mice went to St Enda's dormitory to go to bed there was a priest there walking about silently to see that everyone got a bed. God but he looked tough. He did not say much but just looked and pointed. Bet he was a full forward when he played fotball Aengus thought. Then the priest bellowed "Settle down" and it was lights out. Soon the whispering began, the lights were switched on and a loud voice commanded" Not another word. Li.sten to me. Not another word from anyone. Understand"

God but he had a fearsome growl

It was hard work, Aengus did not know his way about the college and he was late for Mass on the second morning. He saw the Dean give him the eye as if to say he might be one to watch out for. But he soon settled in. There were lads from Cavan Sligo Leitrim Mayo Monaghan and some from further afield as their fathers were Old Boys. Life was easier as the weeks passed and Aengus made one very good friend. Brendan. Brendan was from Monaghan. God how Brendan would have loved to have been born in Kerry or Cork or Cavan or any of those great footballing counties. Brendan was football mad. And poor Monaghan did not have a good team. But Brendan was a true Gael. He supported his home county.

Monaghan, give us a break. God bless his heart!

And Brendan knew what very few people knew:Monaghan did win one title. Years ago it was. In the mists of time

"What year was that again Brendan?"

"What are you on about now?" asked Brendan

"You know. The year Monaghan won the All Ireland"

Brendan always rose to the bait" Naw naw.I told ya that they did not win the All Ireland"

"What did they win then?"

"They won the Ulster Championship. I told ya many times before so stop takin' the piss"

"Sorry Brendan. I forgot. But the Ulster Championship is something to be proud of, Innit?

"Bollix" whispered Brendan. Brendan knew that he was being baited and that Monaghan won the Ulster Championship when it was only a clib championship and that was back in the time before the County Championship was started. Aengus was on Brendan's side and went easy on him. Donegal were a poor team as well and had won very little. They blamed the emigration to Scotland. No doubt Monaghan had a reason as well only no one had found it yet.

But Brendan hiself was a tidy footballer and he was always picked early on when teams were selected. Nippy player would fit his description. Sometimes Aengus thought that Brendan did not run about on the playing field but stayed fixed to the same spot and the other players knew where to put the ball for him to receive it. That was a sure score for Brendan had a deadly left foot

They were good friends and spend many hours walking round the playing fields. The priests did not like students hanging about the corridors or the window ledges. Brendan had been to the Summer School in Rannafast and he was a fluent Gaelic speaker. Even if he spoke Irish with a Monaghan accent. And he knew about Gweedore Especially Asteoiri Gaoith Dobhair. The Gweedore Dramatic Society. His father back in Monaghan ran a drama club and Brendan was familiar with the Gweedore lot as they were well thought of all over Ulster.

But that was not all. Brendan had another hidden talent. He coulsd play the guitar and there was a small music room in the college wher he retired to practise. On his own in his own quiet way It was a room hidden away from the general college hubub.

Aengus did not mention his flute until he had spent some time with Brendan and his strumming. Aengus was embarrassed by his own lack of talent but Brendan insisted they play togetherand Brendan was Aengus tutor.Then one of the lay teachers heard of their playing. He crept up on them and was listening outside the door of the music room when they found him. He was so enthusiastic and nothing would stop him from joining them. He was an accomplished musician. Piano, violin. He took them under his wing. A free tutor. Master Jordan decided he liked the two boyos and he came to teach them and to develop their musical skills. He was from somewhere outside Sligo. Music was in his mother's milk he told them. Coleman and all that lot. He had no respect for the wild Donegal fiddlers. They sounded like the bagpipes going into battle.Mr Jordan organised some of the older bys and they formed a group. They were relieved of Sunday morning study and he came in every Sunday to the college to train and to conduct "his orchestra"

Aengus soon found out that having had a famous footballer as a father was of no use to him on the college football field. He was not big for his age and many a time he finished fsce down in the mud. But he grew and filled out physicslly and he eventually made the college senior team. But there was no pleasure in playing for the team. The Reverend Dean, Fr Duffy was always on the sideline shouting at and criticising his players. The referee at one match, and they swear he could not have been a practising Catholic, blew his whistle and stopped the game, Then in front of everyone he came over to Fr Duffy and asked hin to shut up or else to leave the sideline as he the referee was sick and tired of listening to the abuse being thrown at the boys. Did r Duffy shut up? Did he hell. But the referee went down in history and down to Hell if Fr Duffy had any influnce in that quarter. As Summer aooroached the football season ended and the preperations for the coming examinations began. Exams took precedence over everything from now on. The Leavin Certificate and the Ciil Service examinations. Junior Executive officer in the Civil Service was a post coveted by most school leavers and the college had a good record there to defend.

It was not easy for the students. Irish was obligatory and Latin was added to the curriculum by the Church in case any decided to follow in the priesthood. The focus was on answering examination questions. Knowledge for its own sake and broadening of the mind was for those who could afford it. Here at the college you needed only to answer examination questions. Memorise vast pieces of poetry and and quote them in your answers, Everyone knew that poetry indicated a learned mind. Some of the masters both lay and clerical were tired and cynical men. Sarcastic and sour. They had their time and they were ebvious of the possibilities open to the students. The young priests did not want to be in the college at all. Teaching Latin to boys who hated the subject instead of being out there in a parish saving souls. Nigeria or Tanzania would be preferable than supervising boisterous boys in the Ref or in the study.

The college headmaster or the President as he was called felt it was all beneath him. He was a Monsignor and one day hope for the Mitre and the big ring. All he wanted was no trouble. Just keep the place ticking over and all would be well. None of this modern approach to education. If it was good enough for his forefathers then it was good enough for the boys under his headship.

Aengus passed his Leaving Certificate with honours and got a call to St Patrick's Teacher Training College in Dublin

13

AENGUS HAD TO wait until Seotember to go the the Teachers' Training College. Sinead invited him over to stay in Boston but he knew she had contributed to his college expenses so he would stay at home and get a job He did not like to cause any more expense and he needed some cash. He was lucky this time, He got a job as a bus conductor with the GNR. The Great Northern Railway. Strange name for a bus company but the buses were only a recent addition to the old railway company. He was the bus conductor between Ballybofey and Derry. There and back twice every day during the week and once on Sarturdays and once on Sundays. The pay was not great but it was better than loungeing at home. There was a suggestion that he might consider Scotland but the thought caused him some unease

He took digs in a private house in Ballybofey and he shared a room with another young man who worked for Bord na Mona. A firm that had started using the local peat bogs for turf and compressed briquettes But there was a very good football field in Ballybofey. McCools Park, named after a local Republican Patriot. Every evening there was a group of men kicking a ball in the park. Not really a match or training but one lot in the goalmouth and the others outfield and they kicked the ball in and out of the goalmouth.

This did not suit Aengus and he started running and training in the adjoining football pitch. Soon he was joined by two others who were interested in keeping a high standard of fitness. One was a Garda from Mayo and the other a Customs Officer from Kerry. The trio concentrated on stamina and general fitness. Aengus went home to play for Gweedore and he was selected to play for the Donegal Minor Team. It was not a great minor team but they had one outstanding player

49

in a John Campbell from Dungloe. It was the team policy to let Campbell have the ball when they wete in the opposition half of the field and let him use his superior skill to score for the team. It was a bit much to expect Campbell to carry the other fourteen members of the team and they were knocked out in the second match of the championship. Aengus was disappointed with the way the county team was run. They got no refreshments at the Clones march and when he was injured and had to leave the field he had to find his own way to the nearest Casualty. They did send an official to collect him but the coach didd not go to Ballybofey to drop him home. They left him at Lifford and it was lucky for him that his friend the Customs officer was on duty and he got Aengus a lift vto Ballybofey

Aengus enjoyed being a bus conductor. It was never boring and he met so many different people. There was the big rush during the Glasgow Fortnight when all the Donegal relations in Glasgow came home for their annual holidays and Aengus had to collect them all in Derry for mid Donegal. They would come home to the mountains and the hidden valleys for two weeks and every night they invaded the town and drank the pubs dry. No hassle.

They were a hungover lot when it was their time to go back to Glasgow

One of Aengus' important tasks was to get the Sunday News Of The World. It was banned in the Republic and that made it more in demand and he had regular customers waiting for his return from Derry every Sunday afternoon. They also did a midweek trip out to Glenties and to Portnoo. Through Brockagh and thr Gealic speaking Fintown area. He hoped that John Doherty might get on his bus but buses were not John's mode of transport.

Then his time was up and Aengus went to St Pat's in Drumcondra Dublin to train as Primary School Teacher

14

AENGUS ARRIVED AT St Patrick's Training College. It was set back from Upper Drumcondra Road. This was on the North side of the city. North of the Liffey by the Tolka river. History has it that it was the incoming tide and the overflowing Tolka river that caused the Danes to panic and Brian Boru won the Battle of Clontarf. There is no monument on the site or a commeration of the Battle but there is a Lemon's Sweet factory thet gives off very appetising smells.

The College itself was almost hidden from the road and was not an outstanding piece of architecture. But for Aengus it had some outstanding features. It was only a few hundred yards from Tolka Park Football Ground and Croke Park, the headquarters of the G.A.A, was just down the road. So he could watch the Soccer on Saturday and the Gaelic on Sunday. He had saved from his holiday job and he bought a racing bicycle with drop handlebars and about thirty gears. The student's equivalent of a Ferrari

The College had a good football team. Erins Hope it was called. They had some intercounty players in the college and three of the students there had won All Ireland Medals with their own county teams. Aengus was out of his depth but he scraped by in this company and he just made the team. They did not win anything in his time there but to play with and against top class players was very very educational. He soo realised that this was all that was educational about St Patrick's Training College. The lecturers came in and read their notes and the students copied them down. Word for word and that was the last they saw of those men. Off they had gone. No discussion. No debate. They might as well have posted the lectures. Yet the bonus was that the same lecturers set and marked the examinations and there were very few failures. No problem.

Aengus got involved with a Dublin City Charity, Catholic Help. A Friendly Society that visited the down and outs in the inner city, Aengus and some of his fellow students would go down the back streets to the hovels and the doss houses to meet the poor men. They doled out cigarettes and Catholic newspapers. Fags he could understand but what use was The Catholic Herald to Alcoholics and the needy. Four or five men in a room with a slop bucket in the middle of the room. He ran a raffle and a whist drive to get some mney but it had to be sent to the Central Fund and could not be given to his needy men He went round the local shopkeepers begging for food, clothing, anything; but they could not identify with those in the inner city and he was not overwhelmed by their generosity. But he worked at it and he was noticed. The Dean had seen what he was doing. He did not know it bit he was in the Dean's good books.

Aengus had to learn how to teach so he spent two weeks in a classroom at the Model School attached to the Training College. This ws a primary school with children from the locality but the teachers were picked for their teaching ability. He was expected to sit in the class and watch the class teacher and then to stand before the class and teach them. He just had to see how it was done and then do it himself. He was never told what to do. You just had to pick it up. Listen and learn.

Then there came his first trial lesson. His examination. With an assessor sitting at the back of the class. The assessor was a fussy little man with halitosis and nicotine stained teeth

"No no no" and he shook his head "You will have to do better than that" and he stormed off

The class teacher heard all of this. He himself was a robust Kerryman who had come to Dublin for his family's education and he had little time for "those little Hitlers" He was just tagging along to retirement with the help of a flask of coffee laced by a few naggins of vodka and afew slices of sponge cake. For the ulcer you know

They sat down andorganised a plan of action. He would teach the lesson that would be Aengus test piece. They practised until the class was word perfect. The children loved it too. Better than hide and seek or snap any old day. And it worked. "Remarkable" was all old smelly said. Aengus had passed with honours

15

NEIL O NEILL is head of the family. Mary is his wife and they have three children. Two sons, Eugene and Shane, and a daughter Maureen. Neil always had trouble with his forename. Some pronounced it Nile as of the river where Anthony and Cleopatra cavorted and others pronounced it "neel" as an "eel" wth an 'n'. The man himself preferred the 'eel' version. Many years ago in the time of the War of Independence and The Civil War not many would recognise the name. But they knew of 'Badger' O Neill or even "The Badger". Those who watch David Attenborough on TV will understand. Badgers are nocturnal. So was Neil O Neill in those days. Nowhere to be seen by day but when darkness fell he was in his element

Neil is a small farmer. He has a small farm in the parish of Garton. The farm is called 'Lochbeg'. No one ever asigned the name. It was always called 'Lochbeg. 'There is a small lake above the house and that is the reason for the Gaelic name. It means "little lake"

Neil himself is not of farming stock.His people were sheep men from the mountainside above the Drumkeen area. It was a remote and isolated community. You never passed through the place as it was not on the road to anywhere. Many a visitor there found the road ended in a stack of turf or a boghole. There was a church and a school and the Post Office was down on the main road. Just in case the Post vans got stuck. But do not belittle the people who live there. They are a close community with old Republican feelings. It was never openly declared but there was an undercurrent of belief that the First Dail[a Republican one] was never rescinded and that all subsequent governments of Ireland did not have any legal authority. The Drumboe Martyrs would always be remembered. Those martyrs fought the enemy by the side of their own and then when they were prisoners of war they were murdered by thir own kind. Never forgotten but buried forever in the folk memory

Neil met Mary at a dance in Letterkenny and they liked each other. He thinks they fell in love but he was not sure what love really is. Erroll Flynn and Rita hayworth fall in love but he was not sure love was for sheep farmers. But he liked Mary and she said she liked him and that was good enough. They got married and Neil moved down to Lochbeg. Mary's parents wery very old and she was caring for them. She had a brother Liam and sister Josie who had emigrated to America many years before and she had lost contact with them. There was a hope hat they might make it home before the old parents died. But Mary dared not hope. Not all who went to America were a great success in spite of what those left behind might care to believe. So Neil settled in at Lochbeg. They had three children and buried the old couple between the Chapel and the river Finn. Indeed Neil was no great hand at the farming. A field of spuds, a bit of meadow and a few animals. He cut and saved the hay and fattened the bullocks for the Fair Day. Then the Cattle Mart opened and he bought calves for fattening. That got him into turnips and swedes for their feed. But he was a mountainy man and his real love was sheep. Not the sheep he was reared sheepwith., the mountain sheep. How he loved them. Now he bred the bigger sheep for their meat. Marinos, Suffolk. Leicester and of that type. But he did not trust the Mart, Those dealers with their big Mercedes cars. They had it all sewn up. He went round the local butchers and dealt directly with them and soon he had a ready market. Then the electricity came and they had an electric pump and water on tap from the well

Life was getting better. Transport would be a blessing. Mary liked to go in to the town on Saturday evenings. To Confession and to meet old friends and a bit of shopping. And a bit of gossip. It would be nice to be driven there and collected instead of having to walk home with the shopping hanging from the bicycle's handlebars and the carrier overspilling. Such luxuries. But a tractor would be more practical and a tractor it was.

Neil was quite happy with his farming.The neighbour who bordered his farm was Ivan Ashe. Ivan had about 400 acres of good fertile land. He was a very respected member of the Church Of Ireland. It could be said that he was of Anglo descent. But Ivan's family had been in Ireland for more than 600 years and that is long enough to be considered an Irishman. Ivan was one of nature's gentlemen and he and Neil got on well. Ivan knew Mary's parents and her siblings before they went to America. All he ever said was that there were few oppertunities of employment in those days and there was only emigration for the many. Sometimes his stock might break in to Neil's land but it was no great isue between them and even if one of his dogs worried the sheep Neil let it pass.

After buying the tractor Neil called on Ivan and offered his services. If he ever needed any ploughing done

"I have the old tractor and I am getting the hang of it. If you ever need a man I am there. No prizes for my ploughing but I am there if I can be of assistance"

Ivan was delighted. "there is many a time I could do with and extra man. It's a deal. You're on"

And so an easy partnership began. An odd day here and there and Neil was paid. Sometimes he might do a few hours and he would not accept any money. He liked being good friends with Ivan

One day Ivan said something strange

'You might stock the loch" Stock the lake? Sure there might be a few perch in the lake. Neil walked around it that Sunday. The lake was about two acres in size, whatever that was in square metres, and there was a wood on one side. Trees that grew there there naturally. Nothing planted. He heard the odd cock pheasant over the years but the Strabane Gun Club were not interested and the locals would say they had the shooting rights for centuries. Surely he could not charge them for shootin the odd effin pheasant? Getting high and mighty. A long way from Drumkeen he had come.

But stock the lake with with fish?. There was free fishing on the Finn. Salmon and trout. The local Angling Club had signs for reserved fishing but they did not have a bailiff and he doubted if they had any rights. Further up the river at Cloghan there was a bit of trouble over that. Maybe he should get a boat for the children. But Mary would worry in case they fell in and drowned. They had enough to occupy them. As his own mother would say "It is far from a boat they were born". He thought he had better stick to the sheep and the cattle and keep on to the end of the road. "Was that a song? "He asked himself. Getting funny as I grow older he thought.

With his tractor Neil was able to go back to the mountain. Back to the bog above Drumkeen. You can take the man out of the bog but you can never take the bog out of the man. He loved looking at the fresh scraws. He did not cut the growth from the top of the turf bank but cut through it and every sod of turf had a wig rough grass or heather on one end. The banks were only one sod deep so each sod was all the depth he could cut. It made for easier spreading of the sods as he could throw them back from the bank himself as he cut them. With his tractor and trailer he could sell sa few loads and make a few pounds. But what he really liked was the splendid isolation and the feeling of freedom he had up there. Get the fire going and the kettle on and a couple of wodges or Mary's French Toast and he could stay there all day. In a good Summer the turf would dry and save themselves but if the weather was poor the children were conscripted to help with the footing. To stand the turf sods against each other so the wind and the sun could dry them. The children thought the ride to the mountain in the trailer was a great treat but after an hour or so on the bog they had enough and he had to save the turf on his own.

And so the years passed He got on with his work. Eugene his eldest lad showed no signs of doing any farming. The master said he "had great hopes for the boy" and certainlyhe had his head in a book most of the time. In Neil's eyes he was a bit of a mammy's boy, a bit of a pet. But he did not interfere.

Maureen and her mother he left to get on with it. 'Wimmin' he never understood.

Shane, his younger son. was different. He was growing up fast and was a handful. Thying to do Roy Rogers on a pig's back or wheeling his motorbike tyre down the stairs. Shane took his motorbike tyre everywhere. He rolled it along with the leg of an old chair he found in the shed It was his horse "Trigger".

He tied "Trigger" by the school gate and Mrs Reilly said that anyone who interfered with Trigger "would have her to deal with"

Eugene was an altar boy and that was the one thing Shane envied. To swing the thurable and to bang the bell at the Consecration, and sitting facing the congregation during the sermon and holding the paten at the rails for Communion

He took his First Communion. No bother. The new curate sometimes called in to check that the class was getting on well with their Christian Knowledge. The master would ask the questions and the curate sat at the back listening, Shane asked to go to he toilet and when he returned he stood by the curate and saw he was doing the Irish Times Crossword. The curate looked up and gave him an elbow and a wink. They met weeks later after Mass on Sunday and the curate said

"Shane O Neillit is? I remember you from the last visit to the school. Good man. You must soon be ready for helping me on the altar. Let me know". That priest was not slow. He knew the price of silence, Shane was away. That was all he needed. With Eugene dressed in a sheet they practised "Mass" in the front room and he was ready in weeks, and he was an altar boy.

Then one day he was rummaging upstairs in the loft when he saw this old battered case. It was an accordeon. A Hohner button accordeon. Mary said her brother Liam used to play a bit before he left for America. Liam was not spoken of very often by his sister. But Mary was glad the Shane found "the box" as she called it. Shane went to the front room and started to try and play. By the time he had enough he was able toplay "Theree Blind Mice" and he felt like Joe Burke. Then he started on "The Rose of Aranmore" and was doing well he thought until Neil "For Christ's sake" told him "to give his ears a rest". So now he had to retire to the shed. He did not mind. He had found a new plaything. A new Pal

16

THE END OF the term and the course was approaching. Aengus would be a qualifued National Teacher. An N.T

The Dean approached him

"Gillespie" he said "Have you any idea where you want to work?" Aengus muttered that he did not mind that much where he was employed

"How would you like to teach in the City?" the Dean enquired

"I would like that very much" said Aengus, thinking of all the football matches he could attend and all the cinemas and the Phoenix Park

"Well I can get you a job in the city on one condition" said the Dean

"What's that?" asked Aengus

Well its a bit complicated "said the Dean. "I have a great pal who is a priest in Finglas and he runs the local Gaelic football team. A real nutter he is about his team There is no great tradition of football in that area and he has trouble getting local players. He has contacts. And I am one of his contacts and I send him suitable players. You and I know that you are not the best player that ever played for Erins Hope but you are a good sound man. The type of man Fr Crowe is after and I have mentioned to him that I might be able to get you to play for his team. Here is the bargain. He has a relation in the Christian Brothers, Brother Kevin, and Fr Crowe can get you a position in the city if you agree to play for his team"

He stopped for breath "How about that?" he asked.

"thatis fine by me said Aengus" what is the name of the team?

"Na Fianna" said the Dean. "not a bad team at all considering the club is not that old. It was originally founded for the shop assistants in the city and was named C.J. Kickhams and then moved out to the North Side of the city. So that is that.

Will you go down to William St Christian Brothers school on Saturday and say Fr Crowe sent you. Ask for Brother Kevin there"

Aengus did as he was told and met Brother Kevin who was the headmaster. He gave him a warm welcome and a ghastly cup of tea from a teabag and the kettle he boiled in his office. He was most apologetic but would Aengus mind if he had one of the otherbrothers show him round the school and show him the room that Aengus would be teachin in

"Holy mother of Jesus" was all Aengus could say when he was shown his classroom Under his breath of course with the holy brother beside him. John Wayne had better cell for his outlaws in Didge City he thought. The brother was rabbiting on" how he would like it when he settled in and that "we have a very dedicated team here". Aengus felt sorry for the poor man. He was doing his best. Brother Kevin was probably in hiding somewhere. Keeping out of the way. And rightly so thought Aengus.

Aengus could not believe what he saw.It was a dark and dim and dreary room. Paint was peeling off the walls and some of the desks were broken and they were held together by lengths of electric cable. The floorboards were uneven where the knots in the timber stood out and the windows were dirty and badly in need of a clean. At least there was none broken. A big blackboard on an easel stand was in one corner and there were two naked bulbs hanging from the ceiling.

But he had agreed with the Dean he would stay in the City and this was reality

. He did not expect to go to Terenure or Rathgar but this was stretching things to the limit. But he would not back down. No Surrender. With his Northern accent he had better not say that out loud. Too much like the Twelfth and the Battle of the Boyne.

He had to get fresh air. He managed to open a window and he peered out. A broken concrete yard was what he saw. It was given the grandiose title of Assembly Area. It most definitely was not a playground. Might suit the army. No use picking on this Brother. "Very nice" he lied

"What is the name of the teacher who is retiring? Aengus asked

"He is a Kerryman from Listowel, A Mr O Shea. Come in on Monday morning an meet him. He teaches first Class. That is the class you will be teaching. They come here from the Sisters of Mercy at the Convent and you will be their first male teacher"

The school was a couple of streets back gfrom th opulent glitter of O Connell St. Even though it was only two streets back it was part of poor Dublin. It might be the Fair City of Molly Malone and her wheelbarrow but wher she laid he head to sleep was another story and no one dared to sing about that. The school children were the ones who called out "Evening Herald" or "Sudday Indo'on the streets selling the newspapers or they were the ones who stacked the fruit stalls in Moore St. on Saturday mornings. Dublin Corporation had tried to rehouse them in Drimnagh and in Ballyfermot but they drifted back. They missed the humanity of their old squalid living quarters. Having your own indoor lavatorydid not compensate for the feeeling of loneliness. They had to get the bus to work and the last bus home again was 11.30 and sure that gave no time to drink up and then head for home. So theyreturned to their old haunts and Summerhill and Ballybough bustled with life again

So these were the children he would teach.Where to start and where will it end? They had not given him any idea in The Model School in Drumcondra. The children there were from middle class homes. Well mannered and well behaved and more importantly they were well fed. And the teachers there were very experienced. But his ganng of children were different. Would they be like from Chisty Brown's "My Left Foot" or would the Sisters of Mercy have them tamed. They might be Irish copies of Denice The Menace or the urchins from Dickens

Aengus went back to St Patrick's and spoke with the Dean

"Now do not worry" the Dean advised "You will cope. You will not be expected to turn them into little angels with academically gifted holy halos". Not that funny Aengus thought and he wished it was that easy

"Come on come on" the Dean went on. "Any man who could hold Jock Haughey to a single point in a Championship match will find these children easy to manage. Look at me here. I was thrown in to this job as Dean here and given 200 sex starved young men to handle. So off you go on your holidays and come back fighting fit. Na Fianna have an early start and Fr Crowe is rarin' to go"

Aengus stayed on at the college and on Monday he knocked on Master O Shea's classroom door

The master opened the door "Dia is Muire dhuit" was his greeting. Help thought Aengus. Not another Gaeilgeoir.

"Ta me go maith and how is your good self Master O Shea?"

No need to ask where O Shea came from. A Kerry accent that would have done John B. Keane proud

"Nice to meet you boyo. Brother Kevin said you might be coming aboard"

Master O Shea was a cartoonist delight. Women have handbags and toffs have bowler hats and umbrellas. But teachers have jackets. Not your ordinary man in the street jackets. Jackets with pockets where a couple of newspapers and a paperback would fit. There was always a double split in the the tail of the jacket to allow for an expansive rear end. An egg or a gravy stain on the front lapels and a pipe sticking from the breast pocket. He had a dark green shirt and a brown tie and a shabby corduroy trousers and a pair of desert boots

"Come on in" he said

There was a general hubub in the clasroom and he stood and said one word "Cuineas"

And there ws quiet. Jesus could not have done better

O Shea gave a good smoker's rattled cough and spoke to his class

"Now men listen. This is the new teacher who will be coming here after the holidays. His name is Aengus Gillespie and he is a good football player and he comes from Donegal. He is a lucky man. He will not be teaching you ruffians but he will be taking the new boys from the Convent."

30 pairs of eyes peered at Aengus. A new master. From Donegal. A footballer

"YouRovers or Shelbourne?" a wee voice from the back asked

"Don't be daft" sid O Shea. Real football. Real football. Gaelic football. Not the one you fall over if anyone comes near. Croke Park football. The real stuff"

There was a class groan. GAA, Bloody GAA. All the inner city went to Dalymount Park. All the Dubs. Croke Park was for the bogmen. The Culchies. Nuttin' surer. The Dubs only went to Croke park when the Dublin team was playing in the All Ireland Final and then they commandeered Hill 16. That was The Dubs own territory

Then from the back again "Can you play proper football sir? Like Soccer sir?"

Yes I can" said Aengus. I had a trial with Swilly Rovers"

"Somewhere in Siberia" was a loud whisper

"Never heard of Dilly Rovers sir" said the young boy. Titters all round

"Now that is enough" said O Shea. Open your books at page 36 and he had them mark the word they had to learn to spell

"Dilly Rovers Dilly Rovers. I'll get to you later Mulligan. Smart Alex" and he smiled at the young boy. Then he took Aengus over to the window

"You will be all right here. I came up here for the children's sake and now I am going down to a caravan I have by the Corrib. A bit of the golf and the fishing. Heaven on earth down there it is.Herself was a teacher and she is now going to The College of Art. Fancies herself as a bit of an artist. I told her that sh could come with me down to Galway and do her Paul Henry bit. No chance.That is beneath her. Abstract art and all that baloney. But you will like it here. They grow on you the little blighters. And the Christian Brothers are doing great work. One or two of these lads might make it to further education. That is if the parentas are ready for it. Some might make a success of retailing or in the motor business but most will end up as shop assistants, road cleaners street traders or even bus conductors. But we can help them. We can train them to have a happy life if not a prosperous one"

He stopped and looked at Aengus

"I'll bet you think I am a sanctimonious old fart" he laughed

"No no I do not "said Aengus" but I have learned more in the last half hour than I did in 2 years in Drumcondra. A new insight into teaching. I like it. I like it and I want to play my part. Jesus what am I saying?. If the lads at home could hear me now?.Skint and here I am going to save the world. Get a life. Get a life Aengus"

But he felt good. Better than he ever felt about the life that was before him. Come on ye Dubs. Come on ye Dubs He was ready for them

17

GOD BUT SHANE loved trying to play on the box, When Neil was out he played in the front room ; otherwise known as The Parlour when important visitors were expected. But most of the time he played in the shed

His partner in their secret was transferred and another curate arrived. Shane served Mass for him on Sundays, The young Curate thought he should visit all the families in the parish as the old Parish Priest, Father Carr, was almost bedridden and to cross over from the Parochial House to the Church was as far as he travelled.

Father Morris was the new curate's name and he called up to Lochbeg to visit the O Neills at their home. He was in the kitchen having a cuppa when Shane arrived and threw his schoolbag on the table

"Hello Father Morris" Shane greeted him

"Fr Morris replied" Hello Shane "Then he continued" Between you and I could you leave off on the Morris. If I answer to Fr Morris soon they might start calling me Mini, or Minor or God forbid, Morris Thousand. Just call me Fr Barry and I will come running. Theis is the first time we have had a shat, The other curate told me about you and that you were a man to be trusted"

Mary was puzzled. What was she missing?

"I see an acordeon in the corner" Fr Barry continued. "Who plays?"

Mary spoke up "my brother Liam played before he went to America and now Shane is trying"

"Mammy" Shane said." I cannot play that much. I only know a couple of tunes"

"Never mind that" said Fr Barry" Give us a belt on the box." Shane went all shy and stuck his hands in his pockets.

"Will you go on outa that and play the father a tune" said Mary

Shane rumbled through "Kelly the Boy grom Killane and he got their applause. He felt more confident now and he gave them "Drowsy Maggie". Nice and easy as he was still not that confident

"Great show Great show' said Fr Barry" would you be interested in learning more?" he asked looking at Shane. But Mary was in there fast. The word 'learning' was mentioned and Shane was highly allergic to that word. 'Learning was anathemato her younger son. Learning. Yes. School was enough

"Of course he would" she answered

Fr Barry sensed he might be in a sensitive area. "I might be able to help you there" and he did not know whether to look at the mother or Shane

"Tommy Martin, Tommy the postman. Tommy is your man.I will have a word" and he was so glad he did not say'about you" adfrighten the young man

"No need father" said Mary. He pases te road every day. The O neills had and arrangemeny with Tommy Martin. A brick was placed by tree at the bottom of their lane and that was an invite for Tommy to call up. The O neills did not getmany letters but the brick meant a nice cuppa or maybe a wee dram. Tommy often posted the odd letter for them or carried a message to a neighbour. Tommy was a member of Cumann Ceoltas Eireann. C.C.E. The traditional Irish music gang. They met once every two weeks in Doherty's lounge in Lifford. The craic was goo. A car load from Garton went to most sessions. Soon Shane was a regulatr.Just be at the bottom of the lane by 8pm and he would be picked up

At fist Shane went along and listened. He did not take his box.But he listened carefully and the melodies became embedded in his brain. But Toomy insisted that he take his box to the sessions. At first he vamped with whoever was playing solo and he gradually improved

Then one night Tommy stood up and called for silence. He said there was a yong man in the room who had never played in public before and he thought there was no better place for him to start than here and tonight So he told young Shane O Neill that the floor was all his

Before Shane had time to refuse Tommy had him on his feet in front of the ready listeners. Shane played a simple reel without any left hand accompaniment. He managed it and he sat down to a generous applause. Bloody hell he thought. Glad that's over

One of the older box players came over

"Where are you from son?" he asked

"Garton" Shane said

"I know it well. I have a cousin there. Paddy Murphy in Shipston"

"I do not know that end. We live in Lochbeg" Shane explained

"Hang on for a few minutes after. My name is McCloskey and I am from Omagh. I have something that might interest you."

Later on that night he showed Shane how to use the left hand on the accordeon. He explained all about chords and their corresponding right hand notes. He went to his car and gave Shane a print out that showed how to play the bass. He gave Shane an instruction manual as well and told him to keep it until he had mastered what it contained. It was like magic. Practise practise and again and again. Omagh advised him to come to every session. As he improved he made sure he was always at the bottom of the lane on time. And if Shane was getting better at the box so was Eugene improving at school. Master Byrne called up to tthe house one day, When Neil saw him coming his first thought was what had Shane done now.Never a minutes bloody peace, But Master wanted permision to enter Eugene for a scholarship examination.He was sure Eugene would win a scholarship and he himself would glow in the honour that would bring to himself and to his backwoods school. Neil and Mary were delighted, Eugene woulsd be the first on either side of the family to get to boarding college. He would never make a farmer but he was fond of "the learning" and so much the better, The master gave him extra homework and Mary put an electric bar in the bedroom where he ciold study in peace.

But how could a man study with that squeeze box on the go all the time?. Chugging away most evenings. It might be acceptable if there were tunes being played but having to listen to the same notes being mangled was too much. Shane was not trying to play Eugene maintained but was just acting the maggot. But Shane was trying in earnest to master the chords as he was told.

Fr Barry heard ot the trouble between the two boys. He had been calling rgularly to help Eugene with his Algebra. Algebra was on the examination curriculum and it was not taught in the Primary schools. So Fr Barry helped him out whenever he got into difficulties.Shane was trying out a tune for Fr Barry and Eugene came down the stairs and asked "Can you keep the noise down a bit?"

"Noise, what noise?" snorted Shane." That is not noise. It is Irish music. The music of out forefathers"

"Well our forefathers did not have to listen to you making such a bad fist of it" said Eugene and he smirked at hisown repartee

"Now easy lads, easy" said fr Barry "this needs sorting." The problem was discussed and Fr Barry asked "Can Shane play outside in the sheds?"

I have been playing out in the sheds all Summer, But it is co cold, It is icy out there now, One could die of the cold" said Shane "Whata pity" quipped Eugene "do us all a favour"

There was asmall shed outside that was used for the pony trap years ago and was not being used for anything now. "I have the answer" said Fr Barry

"The Confessional"

"The what?" both boys asked

"Well as you know "continued Fr Barry" we got new confessional boxes in the Church. The old ones were all right for the parishioners but for the priest to sit there for a few hours was torture. The old confession box is still at the Parish House and it could be converted into a suitable playing area for Shane. And we could set it up in the shed"

They went quiet. It took time for what he said to register

So the old confessional was loaded on the tractor trailer under the cover of darkness and taken to O Neills shed. They fitted glass where the curtains were and opened up the divisions inside and fitted an electric light and an electric fire.

So in th very box where he made his First Confession Shane began practising his accordeon, Fr Barry was a happy man and as he drove home he hummed a happy tune and he smiled to himself. He drove to the Parochial House like a man who had something on his mind and was enjoying the thought.

18

AFTER HIS TALK wit Master O Shea abnd the Dean Aengus sold his bicycle and took the bus home to Gweedore and he spent a few days with his mother. He was now on the Government payroll as a teacher in Wulliam St Christian Brothers' School. He could have rested at home and kept his mother company as he was being paid anyhow. But he decided to go to England and take a job and save more money and that would set him up well financially. Most of his pals who had obtained teaching positions were doing the same. I was a good way to get some cash and he knew he would like to buy his own transport.

The usual tedious trip fron Dun Laoire with some drunken men and tired mothers trying to keep their children in tow. It was a wearyAengus who arrived at Euston Station and he made his way to digs he had booked in advance through the Irish Centre in Camden Town. His digs were on the Edgeware Rd. on the north side of the city and a tired Aengus rested for all of the next day.

Then he went to MacAlpine's Central Office and asked for a job. He had often heard the best place to get a job on the building sites was to go to an "Irish" pub wher he would meet many a site ganger. But Aengus did not know any "Irish" pubs and the Cental Office seemed the best bet to him. He was right and he was told to go to a site in Fulham. He went there and was told to start work the following Monday.

Back to the digs and to his room. There were two beds in the room and a small table. The other occupant had a suit hanging an the back of the door and he had a suitcase under his bed. That was all. Another Irishman on a building site.

Aengus was entitled to a breakfast but any other meals had to be paid for at the table, Cash on the spot. Many of the residents were not regular in their habits and sometimes an evening meal might not suit their agenda. There was always fish and chips anyhow. His roommate was a Mayo man whom he never saw by daylight as he was gone by dawn and did not come to bed till very late, Usually well tanked. He smoked in bed and threw the cigarette ends on the floor. To Aengus' dismay. He used all of Aengus aftershave when Aengus forgot to put it back in his suitcase.

On the Fulham site Aengus was put in the concrete gang. Ready mix taken by crane to be spread by the gang into the ready prestressed steel concrete bays. A gang of 8 and he was soon one of the lads. He told them he was a small farmer's son and that he had left the farm to come over to earn enough to clear some of the old man's debts.

He was not happy sharing with the Mayo man and he went looking for a bedsitter. He got an address in Islington and he took a bedsitter there. It was an attic at the top of a four storey tenement house. Aengus was the only white person in the building and it was a rough living quarters. The big rent collector came every Friday night kicking at the doors and shouting "rent" and if there was no reply he swore again and said" he would not put up with any of this fucking carry on"

Aengus shared a kitchen down on the third floor with an Asian family. They came to watch him cook and he was honoured until he was told that they were afraid he would use the utensils for pork, or was it beef, and that would make them unclean for themselves to use after him.

Then he found an Irish eating house, Not a restaurant but an ordinary terraced house where the Irish navvies went to eat, You took what was the menu for the day. Boiled bacon and cabbage and mountains of potatoes. The house speciality was a huge black pudding and a mound of mushy peas on a plate of mashed potatoes, All with your own jug of gravy. There was no alcohol allowed but the tea was strong enough to trot a mouse on

Aengus settled in his bedsit with a skylight open to the stars and a shared kitchen on the floor below. As the last man in the concrete gang he was given the job the rest did not like, He was in charge of the vibrator. It meant he had to put a vibrating machine into the poured concrete and especially in the corners to guarantee that the wet concrete filled in and did not leave any air bubbles in the prestressed steel,. The work was not heavy and the chat and the stories and lies were passed over and back among the men. There was a small canteen that did baps and strong tea but it was the Jamacian 'Orlando' who drove them crazy when he opened his thermos and had his chicken and rice while thay pulled on their butties.There was a Donegal man on the site. A steel fixer from Fanad. He and Aengus met but they were not chatting buddies. Then one day Fanad came over to where Aengus was reading the paper

"No page 3 then" Fanad said

Aengus smiled and let it pass. But Fanad was not finished

"Reading the poxy Telegraph then? Whats wrong with the Mirror or The Sun?"

"Nothing at all" said Aengus "I just like this paper and it give the news about the old country'

"You should get the Irish Post if yo want to read about Ireland. You can get The Irish Press or the Irish Independent if you want to. In any paper shop"

Fanad went on

"Maybe in Camden but not in Islington" said Aengus

"Islington" said Fanad "Jesus is that where you live?. Just order them in Islington. OK?"

"I must do that" said Aengus cooly and walked away

Fanad sneered "Fucking egghead. Fucking brains. Hi Brains give my love to all the shites in Islington. Fucking brains is what you are and all that lot in Islington"

The rest of tha gang heard it all and the name stuck. Poor Aengus was known from then on as "Brains". It was "Brains come down here" and "Brains willyou do this?" and soon no one knew his Christian name. 'Brains' it was from now on.

An agent from the Transport and General Workers called on the site and advised that they be unionised. He explained the benefits and they all agreed it was a good idea. He asked for a volunteer to act as shop steward and he got no one. But Fanad stood up and said 'Brains' was the man for the job. They all cheered and so 'Brains' was shop steward. He had to collect a shilling a week fronm the men. The concrete gang, the steel fixers and the scaffolders' mates all joined.There was a crew of Shuttering carpenters who would not join. They were a Pakistani gang and very close. They had no need of the union as they looked after each other. A carpenter's mate on one job would appear as a fully qualified carpenter on the next site and his fellow men would carry him until he learned his trade. Nothing like that for the Paddies. If you wanted a safe and steady job then go to Luton or Ellesmere Port and work in the motor assembly line.

If Aengus thought that being site steward made him important then he was mistaken. He was still on the hated vibrator. No one gave a damn. But he started thinking. Most of these men did not know how their wages were made up. They took the packet and the sooner they got to the pub the better.In his gang, Aengus knew, there were times when they were slack, waiting on the steel fixers and the carpenters to finish so they could then pour the concrete. Other weeks they were run off their feet. But it made no difference tio their wage packet. He knew the brickies were paid on what they dd and maybe there might be a system for the concrete gang

He went to the site agent's office

"Whaddya want Pat?" asked the agent not looking up from his desk

Aengus did not reply

"What is it Pat?" the agent asked again with his head still looking at some very important business on his desk and he flicked his cicarette ash into a tray

"Are you speaking to me?" said Aengus

"Well there ain't no one else in the fucking room is there Pat?"

"Let me tell you one thing" said Aengus. "My name is not Pat. My name is Aengus and you will address my by that name when you speak to me in future"

"Ok Ok I am a busy man Pa- sorry, Irish name is it" said the agent

"Yes it is. A E, N G U S. I cannot spell it any clearer. You got that? Aked Aengus.

"Yea yea. Angus like in the Aberdeen Angus but with an E, Good name that haha"

What is your name sir?" asked Aengus

"Owens David Owens" he replied

"Well "said Aengus "David Owens, I will call you Mr Owens and you may call me Aengus, Aengus Gillespie"

"Ok Pa . . . Aengus. Ok Aengus what can I do for you?"

Aengus replied very slowly and carefully "I have been elected Shop steward for the site. Transport and General Workers Union. I work in the concrete gang. We are interested in how many cubic yards or metres we pour every week" he asked

"How the hell do you expect me to know what concrete you lot do every week?. You think I have nothing else to do" said Mr Owens "Now stop annoying my head and give me a bit of peace." Mr Owens was getting annoyed. These bloody Paddies. Getting a bit too smart by far.

Aengus did not get rattled but turned to leave and said

"I will not bother you any more. You are a very busy man. But would you like me to find out for you?

Then Aengus stopped at the door and looked back and said "I can get our Union guys at head office to contact your head office and they might be able to help us"

"Hold on. Hold on" Mr Owens came out from behind his desk" what's this all about then?" he asked

"Its like this" said Aengus. "we pour a lot of cement. We do a good job and we think we should get extra money when we earn it. A bonus for doing very well. Others on site have a bonus system. The steel fixers have"

"How do you know thar? "Mr Owens asked

"I can call one in if you like" said Aengus Mr Owends ignored that suggestion. Aengus carried on

"You can tell from your invoices and delivery documents what concrete we do every week. You can deal with me and we can discuss it here or I can get one of our top men and one of your bosses to come down to have a chat with me here and we can trash it all out"

Again Mr Owens was agitated. "No need No need "was all he said. What the hell was the job coming to with Paddies talking about invoices and cubic metres. Then he spoke again "It will mean a lot of work for me and I am a very busy man as it is" Mr Owens went back behind his desk and stood by a cabinet with his back to Aengus and remained silent.

There was a lull. Then Aengus spoke again. "Just listen to me Mr Owens. The paperwork is already there. If you like I can drop in and do it for you.Anytime you like. My gang will not mind and the union will not have any objection. We need not go any further. No one need ever know" Then he waited, This was the moment of truth. That was the sweetner. It is now or never.

Mr Owens needed time to think. He stayed at the far end of the Office. As far from Aengus as possible. Finally he said "All right then. Leave it with me. I will sort it out. That OK?"

"Sure thing" said Aengus" but in the mentime when you are doing the sums we will be happy with £2 a week bonus. That will be £16 a week in bonuses you will have to pay the concrete gang"

Aengus knew that £16 was chicken feed to Mr Owens. He could hide that in the office petty cash. Mr Owens was on the fiddle. God only knew what he was pocketing

The deall ws done and there was no need for friendship any more so Aengus turned as he reached the door and he said

"Two pounds to eack member of the concrete gang. That will cost you £16 pounds every week. If we are due more than that I trust you will see to it. I would hate us to fall out over this. Thank you from all the concrete gang. Thank you Mr Owens" With that he was gone

"Ok Pa. Aengus" said Mr Owens but he was alone in the office. He went to a drawer in his desk and he necked a bottle of Vodka until his hands stopped shaking. Better keep clear of that one he thought, Fucking Paddies who can read and write and understand invoices

Aengus was the star man among his mates. He pleaded with them to tell no one else on thr site. In his mind it was a dodgy deal between himsolf and Mr Owens and if it got out the whole deal might come undone Was there honour among Thieves? Sure man sure. Sure there was.When their own skins were in danger. His own gang were very appreciative and they offered to relieve him of the hated vibrator, He refused their offer, He was just one of the gang he said. But the next week his rate of pay was increased by six pence and hour and he felt a bit guilty. Judas and all that. But his biggest surprise was when the site foreman gave him the keys and said he was then responsible for opening the site in the morning and locking up at night. At least two hours overtime every day. He had to admire Mr Owens. That meant the foreman was tied into whatever little scheme he had going and it made sure that no one squealed. Every man has his price.

19

FATHER BARRY MORRIS did not like his own name. It was too machanical for Holy Orders, Fr Riley might be better. At least it was a better cl ass of motor. Fr Temple. That would be a nice naoe he thought. But he had to accept the name he was given.

Fr Morris was born in Buncrana, His father Michael Morris emigtated to America in his late teens and he did very well in the building trade. He left his girlfriend Siobhan behind in Ireland but unlike "Many Young Men of Twenty", as soon as he had the fare he sent for her and they were married in America, She got a job as a housemaid and trained to do some cooking and she soon was a cook in Poloski's Diner in Boston. They worked all hours and saved their money and when Siobhan fell pregnant they came home to Buncrana. Michael put a deposit on a small pub in the town. Another returning Yank ready to lose his money the locals thought, But Michael was different. He was younger. Not like the retired policemen and firemen who came home to slowly lose their retirement monies. Michael built on to the old building and he kept a clean and neat public house. No drunkeness or dieorderly conduct. "Respectable" is what Garda Sergeant O Toole would call it and he often took his misus there for her sweet sherry and a couple of pints for himself

Siobhan was cooking the evening meal when a customer remarked "God that smells great. You got any to spare?" and so the idea was born. Early every night she would start cooking and as the smell of frying bacon and sausage wafted into the bar Michael would ask "Anyone for a bacon sandwich?" They soon went on to baps and burgers. It was soon a regular trade and they put a menu and a price list in the window and Buncrana had its own "Innishowen Diner". Nothing fancy but sit at the bar or with the bottle of Tomato ketchup do your best. Michael had been a keen Gaelic footballer and he took an interest in the local football team. He used his American contacts for a few dollars to get the team going again. Money was scarce around Buncrana but there was a nucleus of strong Donegal men in Boston and Micheal was not proud and was not shy in asking for help.

So Barry Morris knew about pubs and cooking and eespecially about washing dishes. He went to Secondary School in Derry and passed his exams. He was no great student and University was never considered. He had no idea of what he wanted to do and Michael was not happy having a young man staying in bed all morning

Barry felt there should be more to life than this. Then The Redemptorist Fathers came on their parish mission week, thundering from the altar and threatening damnation on them all. Poor Mrs MacShane would go down to hell after calling Minnie Kelly a silly auld bitch and Jimmy Quinn was sure he was damned as he liked more than a skinful most Saturday nights. When ever he had the money that is. Barry thought he would like to work among the opeople. He asked the parish Priest and he got sponsorship from the Diocese of Westminster in London. He went to All Hallows in Drumcondra, It was back to the olden days again. The Irish would be saving the souls of the British as it was many centuries ago in the time of St Columbanus.

Barry Morris had a lovely time in All Hallows. The regime was pretty lax and the studies did not overtax his brain. He took life easy and did not bother that much No great student was our Barry. Just keep under the radar and cause no trouble. He found Church St. traditional Musician's club and went there regularly and he bought himself a banjo mandolin to pass the eevenings in his room,He attended Philosophy lectures in University College Dublin but he was no Aristitle and he enjoyed the antics of the lay students who took Philosophy.

He was odained in The Procathedral in Dublin and after a weeks holiday in Buncrana with his parents he sst off for London.

Canden Town was his base. The Irish abroad were his parishioners with some of the West Indians and the Chinese coming under his chaplaincy. One of his duties was to meet the boat train at Euston and see to the young Irish arriving with a suitcase and a few quid. He had a listof safe lodgings and the rest he took to The Irish Centre where he was Chaplain.

He made contacts in the building trade and cultivated the foremen. He was known to British Rail, London Transport. MacAlpines, Murphys,and numerous small companies around his district,

He went to the Irish Club in Eaton Sq. wheree he met the graduate Irish and he often dropped in to the Galtymore to hear the visiting Royal or The Clipper Carlton Showbands. When ever there was a function at the Irish Centre in Camden town and especia;lly if there might be a dignitary there Fr Barry made sure that many of his contacts got a place of honour. He patrolled the streets at night helping the druggies, the alcoholics, the homeless and the people of the night. The poor addicts and alcoholics. He could not cure them but his heart went out to them. His whole soul cried out to Heaven for help. The help did not come and the bishop decided that FR Barry had given his all. A broken priest is like a wounded soldier and is best that he be helped back to recovery. So Fr Barry went on retreat to Hawkstone Hall in Shropshire to reinforce his vocation and to strengthen his resolve and his bishop decided he had given enough to the diocese and that was to be rewarded by his being allowed to return to Ireland. There was always a place in Donegal for another priest and Fr Barry was sent to Garton.

He would be Curate in Garton with the very old Fr Carr as his parish priest. Fr Carr was in his eighties but he had served his bishop well and the bishop was allowing him to stay as a parish priest with an active curate. He was content with his meditation and his Sunday Mass. The congregation at his 12oclock Mass had dwindled to those who had grown old with him and sometimes when he was deep in prayer one would have thought he was asleep were it not for the clattering of his loose dentures. His quiet and sacred offering every Sunday was half way to Heaven for most of his congregation

So Fr morris was in charge of the running of the parish. There was the Parochial House, The National School. The Village Hall, the St Vincent De Paul Society, The legion of Mary. These were all his responsibility. Then there was the Catenians and the AOH hovering out there but he left them to their own devices and he let them get on with their own business.

But he had a dream. He had a great secret dream. There was a spark back there somewhere.Many years ago there was a great Garton football team. The Garton Gaels. It was his dream to revive the old club and the old pride of the parishioners. Yes he would like to see the young men play for their parish again. It was a dream, a personal and silent dream. Dream on. Dream on. But it would have to wait its turn.

It was hectic. First things first. The parochial house and the church were in need of urgent repair. There had been nothing done for years and the bishop could not understand this sudden need for all this money. But builders had to be paid and there was no money in the parish coffers. The Sunday collections were small, So Fr Barry did what his father Michael Morris would have done. Have a concert. He spoke from the Altar. If there was anyone out there who could act or sing or dance or play an instrument then would they please come forward. Of if they knew of anyone who could, then please come and give their names. There was a hum of agreement from the congregation. Sure there is not an Irishman who does not think he could do better at 'the acting' than Peter O Toole or Barry Fitzgerald. Even better with a few pints.

The I.C.A. Ladies came to the rescue and the Strabane Operatic Society only needed the nod.Soon it built up. The concert was a great success. He organised

Whist Drives and Bring and Buy Sales and the Parochial house got a facelift and the Church roof was repaired

This is what he had dreamed of in his dark moments in London. Having a people waken to their possibilities and their hidden talents. He was getting to know these people. They came to confide in him in the Confession box. There was the confident and there was the frail and he hoped he might have an influence in their lives. Some think the Cartholic Priests have a lonely life without a family. He Fr. Barry Morris had the biggest and most lovable family in the world and he asked his God to give him the health to stay with these wonderful people

20

AENGUS WAS GETTING fitter and leaner as te weeks wenton and he felt he could go and enjoy some of Londons night life. In the Dirty Duck with the gang he drank Ginger beer and non alcoholic beverages. This causeed some merriment.

"Cor blimey. An Irishman what dont drink". He had heard of a dance hall in Victoria that was used mostly by students. He went there one Saturday night. He liked the easy way the men and women mixed in the hall. He was nursing a coffee when this young lady sat at the table

"I hope you don't mind but my feet are killing me" she smiled

"No. Not at all" Aengus said. They both sat watching the dancing and he asked her "Where are you from?"

"Boston" she replied

"I have a sister in Boston. An attorney. WithPatrick Horan" he said

"I have heard of the firm but I do not know anyone there" she said

"I suppose you have met the Kennedys "said Aengus.

"Not a chance. All our lot are Republicans. Wasps" she said with a shrug.

Thety started talking politics. Her name was Fiona, Fiona Bruce. Aengus was away. His favouritr topic. History. How Fiona was an Irish name and Bruce was a Celtic King of Scotland and of part of Ireland. She probably knew that already but she listened.

She said she "was not really in to history" but she\was over on a Fulbright scholarship and she was doing some research intoCharles Dickens. She was supposed to stay in Oxford or in Cambridge but she found London more alive and more exciting. She could go to any of the colleges when ever she bneeded.

Then they danced and fell into easy compnionship. She had her head on his shoulder and her cheeknext to his. Cloes dancing is what the Redemptorist Fathers on the mission back home would call it. He was in trouble. Not withhis conscience or feeling of sinning. It was with himself. Holy Jesus I am getting a hard on he thought. What the hell could he do?. He\couldfeel her stomach pressing against him and he was sure she could feel his erection.

Fiona looked in his face and said "this is nice" and she wiggled her hips aand pulled him closer. He forgot his embarrassment. Soon it was time for him to leave. The last bus was at 12 and he was not familiar with the tube to Islington late at night. He said he would have to leave but suggested that they make a date to meet again. She asked where he lived and she said "I know that area. I have a Mini and I will drive you home. They danced on and as they wetre leaving the dancehall she sid she had to go to The Ladies to freshen up as she must look a sight after all that dancing

She stopped outside his front door

"I have only an attic bedsit" he said

"Yes but an attic bedsit with a window to the stars" she said. I would love to see the stars from a Dicken's attic window. Much better than anything the Spires at Oxford or Cambridge can offer"

In the bedsitter she was so keen to look out the attic window and see the rooftops that she grabbed a rickety chair and climbed halfwaty out the window. Al Aengus could see was abare backside She was not wearing ant panties, as she herself might say. As he helped her down she toppled sand he grabbed her and they fell over on his bed. She soon had her hands on him and it was not long before he ejaculated. He was so upset and he said would clear upthe mess

But she shyly said "here" and she handed him her silk scarf that she had used to collect his sperm.

"We can wash it out in the morning" she said. She pulled him close and said "lets getto bed' and she reached for her handbag and pulled a box of Durex.

"Come on big boy" she said. "The night is young. Let us have some fun"

It was daylight when they were both replete and she left to go home. They were lovers. Sometimes she came over to savour the Dickens atmosphere but they met most times at her place. He often went there straight from the site. He bought some better gear to wear as he did not like going there in concrete smelling clothes. But Fiona loved taking him to the shower and washing down the concrete and his sweat and their own emissions from their bodies

He knew she had other lovers. The empty aftershave bottle and the cigarsmell. But he did not care. She knew much more than he did but he was a willing pupil and she was a wonderful teacher. He was not in love but they both loved the sex and the romance. Fiona knew he would be going home to Ireland in the Fall but she knew she would give him memories to take home with him. How right she was. Aengus handed in his notice and left the site.on Friday. He went o say with

Fiona that night and they had a Chinese take away. He intended taking the boat train on Saturday evening. However, he just made the Monday evening train and he slept all the way to Holyhead. He bought a Heinkel scooter with his holiday savings and he set off home to Gweedore. He was back in Dublin the following Saturday for school on Monday.

He was ready to take them all on.

21

HANNAH ROBINSON WAS bored. There had not been one customer all morning.She longed for the bell over the door to tinkle. At least it would be somebody to talk to. Her father David spent all his time out in the yard or on the road looking for business. He was not successful and business was slack. They wre off the main passing road for casual passing trade and the local business was slack. A bag of nails, a few screws or a light bulb.

Life at home was getting tense. David withdrew to himself even more. He read the Bible and his religious tracts and said very little. He would not discuss business affairs with Hannah. It had gotten to the stage where the reps phoned ahead. She was delighted to hear from them at first and then she realised they wre not interested in her well being but were assessing if it was worth their while calling at alland if she had any orders for them. There were letters from the bank which she opened and she was dismayed. The Robinsons wrere eating into their capital and they were slowly going broke

"Father is it true that we are in financial trouble /" she asked

"Who told you that? Do not bother your head. I will take care of it. Now off you go young lady" and then he called after her "and not a word of this to your mother"

Again she brought it up "Dad are we inin trouble?. Tell the truth"

He could not lie "Well things are a bit slow at the moment but they will improve, Now you are not to worry your little head"

"her little head. Her little head?" Now was the time to say her piece and she did

"Father let me say something. You and I are in this together. It is only you and me. I want to play a full part. I am not a little child. I want o play my part. Will you let me help?" she asked

"What can you do little one?" he aked plaintively

"Forget the 'litle one'" she said sharply. The days of the" little one" are over.let me play my full part in the business" she said.

"But what can you do" her father sighed "Luke and I had it all planned but The Lord took him from me and his death on that motorbike finished that dream. It broke my heart, never got over it. But if it was The Lord's Will who am I to question that?"

Time for The Lord to pull his finger out she thought. Instead she put her hands on his shoulders, looked into his face and said "let me take Luke's place" David Robinson was not convinced. "Sure a womsn would be lost in Luke's place"

Hannah sat him down. "Now father listen to me. I am not trying to show off. The whole world is changing, We have women TDs, women doctors and surgeons, women police, women running large international companies and here in Donegal we have women engineers on the Council payroll. When Peter Sweeney in Lifford died of his heart attack his daughter Angela took over and she has made a great success of the business, She has six shops now. She did it. I can do it. We can do it. You and I. I have the education and I know the business. Let me out from behind the shop counter and we can get going again. You cannot be expected to do it all at your age. Let me help"

By the time she had finished sghe was standing over hi with her fists clenched, full of determination. He looked up at her and he stood up and he touched her cheek and he nodded.

She had won him over

Nothing more was said and Hannah set about saving Robinsons from insolvency. But where to start?. She had a good history of saving in the Credit Union. But they dealt in small and medium amounts. The bank manager knew of their problems. It was he who sent those threatening letters and he was a nervous and fussy little man and he would be no help

As they said in Rathmines College of Commerce it was "back to basics"

What do people always need?

Food, clothing, shelter warmth. And entertainment. The food and the cloyhing and the shelter were well supplied by the shops in town and by the Counci. But the warmth and the entertainment?. She knew she could never manage without her little gas heater, Superser. On its own little wheels and you could move it from room to room.

Then there was the TV. She saw how people in the rural areas loved their television programmes. No licence was needed as the channels were from Northern Ireland. Not many could afford to buy a television set but for the price of a couple of packets of fags or a few pints one could hire one.

Gas. Now that might be the answer. She drove to Dublin to the Calor Gas Company and she was promised an agency. When she was cleared by the bank he was in business and she put their sign over her shop door. Then she moved all the spades and shovels out of the shop window and replaced then with her gas fires and gas heaters. But what sold best were the gas pokers. Word soon passed round. No more problems starting the fire. The poker was all you needed

Then she approached the Television Rental Companies. No good.

"Not enough demand in your area madam". Some bloody pen pusher. What did they know?

This time The Credit Union came to her rescue. She showed them her detailed plan[thank you College of Commerce Rathmines for that] and they agreed to finance her. She bought 12 television sets. (9 to go out on rental and 3 as back up in case of breakdowns.] Money always in advance as sometimes the pint might make more sense than payment to the lady. The Credit Union were happy with her success and when she had hired out her supply they let her buy another dozen sets. Her plan was working. Televisions and gas pokers and gas heaters

She noticed a young boy peering in the window. He was there again the next day. Eventually he came in tio the shop

"What's them things in the window?" he asked

"Gas pokers';' Hannah said

"What are they for?" he asked

"You stick them under the turf or the coal and they light the fire." she explained

"God that's handy" he said" no need for matches ot rolled papers then?" he remarked

"Not at all. You need a match to light the gas poker and it helps if you have kindling sticks to catch and set the fire" she told him

"How much are the kindling sticks?" he asked

She told him and he gave a soft whistle and "Nice little earner" was all he said

He thanked her very much and said goodbye. Cheeky little monkey she thought. But she had not seen tha last of the cheeky little monkey. He was back again an a couple of days. No hanging about this time

"Miss Robinson I am here to do business"

What's your name?" she asked

"Shane O Neill" he said and he carried on "I can do cipini or kindlings as you call them for much cheaper"

I am sure you can "said Hannah "but you need a shop to sell them. How old are you?"

Shane O Neill did not answer the question

"If you sell my cipini you need only pay me half he price you charge for them. I can delivervevery day. Is that a deal?"

"Deliver every day?.How?" she asked

"On the carrier of my bike. That's how. Let me drop in a few bundles and see how they go" he cheekily replied

Hannah could only but agree

"Drop me in a bundle or two and we will see how they go" she said

"It's a deal then" and he put his hand out to nbe shaken." Settle every Saturday evening. OK?"

He gave her a big smile and he let himself out

The cipini were at her door the next morning and every morning after that until she had apile of bundles at the back, She stacked a few at the front and they soon began selling. People liked the scent fronm the burning cipini, She told Shane and he said it must be the old apple tree branches he was using. Then he went home and collected all the apple windfalls and mashed them in a barrell and topped it upwith water and he soaked every bundle in this mix,. If they liked the apple scent then he would supply it. The Cipini Trade might be flourishing but there were hitches in the Television Rental business. She had over 20 sets out and 5 on standby. Repairs were the problem. Breakdowns were her headache. She could not leave the shop to do a course herself. There was a group in Strabane who were raising money for a young RAF man who was injured in an accident. She went to one of the charuty fashion shows and she met Chris Williams.

He had been a technician in theforces and he was discharged as he was confined to a wheelchair and was unable to climb into the awkward spaces of plane engines. The RAF were prepared to finance some retraining for him. It was not enough to keep a married man and his family and Hannah suggested he join her enterptise. She would pay him a salary during his retraining and when he was trained he would come and work with her. This was between themselves and she paid into a seperate account in the Republic of Ireland. On her side of the border. He qualified as a TV technician and he came to work for Hannah. He came to Garton every day and soon the business was running smoothly. But he found the daily travelling rather cumbersome and he set up a repair shop in his garage and Hannah delivered her sets there to be repaired. His reputation grew and soon he had plenty of work. But he did not forget how Hannah had helped him and her televisions got priority. Hannah's help was not forgotten

22

AENGUS WAS FIRST down to breakfast in his new digs in Ranelagh. He was sharing with Tipperary Pat. Pat was a Civil Servant or something. He would find out. Pat was in no hurry to get out of bed whatever he did for a living. But Aengus wanted to be at the school as soon as the caretaker opened. He made sure all the desks were in line and all was neat and tidy. He opened the windows to let in the Dublin smog. No Atlantic breezes like in Dunmore National school.

He walked out into the yard to familiarise himself with the morning proceedings. Boys arrived in dribs and drabs and formed loose lines towards the main building.

There was no sign of his class

Then it all happened

Two sisters of The St Vincent De Paul Order with thir huge white wimpled headdress were herding abiu 50 people in to the school yard. The sisters stood out like two large yachts surrounded by busy tugboats. Women with children in tow. Sisters, aunties, grannies and any other woman from the street. This was one of their big days. The Holy Sisters herded the whole gang straight in to his classroom without as much as a glance at anyone else. Like two sheepdogs wit an unruly flock. The room was packed and Aengus had to push his way to the front, From the looks he was given he might have been intruding on their scene himself.

Then Brother Kevin the Headmaster came through the packed room with a sheaf of papers against his chest. The women must have known who he was as they let him through. As the waters did for Moses. Otherwise he might have to crawl over a few babies

"Your attention please" he called and he might as well be whispering into a gale.

"Quiet" he shouted and he banged the table with the blackboard cleaner.

"Thank you, thank you" and he looked around

"Welcome to you all. I see some faces here again. Nice to see you regulars again"

And you will see us many more times some of the women thought. It is not our fault. It's the men. Only one thing on their mind.

"As some of you know" and He smiled at the ladies "I am the headmaster. I am Brother Kevin the head master" Aengus cuold see some boredom on their faces. So what?The headmaster. Heard it all before. And maybe a few times more if himself at home keeps at it every bloody night.

"I woukd like to thank The Holy Sisters for bringing the boys down here and for looking after them the last two years. This is Master Gillespie who will be looking after your lovely boys from now on" Got that in nicely" Br.Kevin thought

"Now I am going to call out the name s of the boys and I want each boy to sit on the seat where I point"

Half an hour later all the boys were seated with all the women lining the walls of the classroom

"I am a busy man and I will leave you now" said Br. Kevin/. "I will leave you in the hands of Master Gillespie. God bless you all" He stopped and waited. As if he expected a round of applause. Not a sound. Not a clap. They all looked at Aengus. All he could see were eyes. Questioning eyes

"Will the mothers come forward and stand by their boys?" he asked. "and write down their full names and addresses

The nuns stepped forward." We will help out there." They knew that some of the mothers could not read or write and they would be embarrassed before the New Master. Things were sorted out and then there was a feeling of a job well done.

Aengus thought he might say a few words

"Thank you all for coming and our thanks especially to the Holy Sisters. My name is Master Gillespie and I come from Donegal and I am looking forward to teaching your wonderful children." Aw my God over the top again he thought. The mammy will know her little Jimmy is not wonderful and she will be delighted to get him off her hands now the holidays are over. Thanks be to Jesus. And the mammy has turned up today to see what the new master looks like and to have a chat and a wee nip in Mulligan's bar and lounge on the way home.

But Aengus was new to Dublin ladies. He went on

"Now the paperwork ids done we can get to know each other." He looked around. He need not have bothered. They were chatting among themselves before he had said a word. This Culchie of a master had no idea ' Some of them had done this day three or four times before and they had heard it all and they might hear it again. The Catholic church and its Vatican Roulette. They gathered in bunches and ignored Aengus. One dear lady came over to explain that Fintan might be absent on the odd day as she herself had a "poorly chest" and was 'given to the coughin.'" and that she could not leave the house. It took months for Aengus to realise that the "poorly chest" was Mulligans Bar and Lounge

Lunchtime and they wre still there. Aengus went to the teachers' staffroom. A central table and a few chairs and a single hanging lampshade lighting the smoke filled room,. There was very little conversation but plenty of fags and some were reading the newspaper. He was given a nod of acceptance and that was all. Few of the teachers bothered with lunch but there was the odd one who nipped out to the pub to "ease the vocals",

Back in the classroom he shunted the ladies home and reminded them to come back at 2 pm and collectthe children. He nearly said "little darlings" but enough was enough.

The class settled down and he said he would read them a story, He suggested "Cinderella "but the groans and the looks of disgust stopped him there. He had a copy of "Riders to the Sea" in his briefcase and he read it. They loved every word.

As the children were being collected he heard one little boy say

"The Master done a play for us, All about the sea and Culchies getting drownded"

Aengus went to Easons and bought sellotape and safety pins and lengths of plastic and he made name tags for all his boys.

23

HANNAH HAD OFTEN seen the sign on their way to Bundoran. But her parents were anxious to get to the sea and she did not stop. But today she was on her own and the sign "Furniture Bought and Sold" half way through The Barnesmore Gap had her intrigued. She followed the sign up a twisted lane into the mountainside. As long as there was room to turn the car she was not worried. Buying and selling was her livelihood now, and she was a business woman. Even the lecturers in Rathmines recommended that you be aware of what was happening around you. Good busines they said. And Hannah wanted to be good business, and if you don't mind, a good business woman

After what seemed miles she came to a broken down barn. What a barn was doing on a mountainside she could not guess,, But when she looked inside she could not believe her eyes. It was an Aladdin's Cave up here in the Donegal mountains. Furniture of every kind. Some was fit for burning but she could see some good quality chairs and tables.

An elderly unshaven man in a dirty Duffle coat came from the back

"Lovely day thank God" he said

"Yes a lovely day thank God "she replied. She hated herself for her fatuity. Just to please the old man

"I just saw your sign on the main road and I thought I would give you a call. Never noticed it before" she lied. God I am getting worse she thought

"Been at it for 30 or more years now. At least 10 years up this mountain." he said

You have some lovely stuff here "she said as she picked her way through the stacked furniture. "I cannot believe my eyes. Out here miles away from anywhere. You have enough here to furnish the Finn and the Lagan Valleys

"Yes" he said "I do get customers from Ballybofey and as far over as Lifford and even from Omagh and beyond. On their way to Bundoran: the Sunday trippers. But they only buy what they can fit in the car so I carry a lot of knick knacks. Years ago I shipped a full lorry load to Glasgow every week and we sold in the Gorbals. No trouble then. But I am too old for all that now and the wife and I have retired up here where there is space and the quiet freedom for the dogs

How wrong can one get?. It is a philosopher I have before me. And she thought he was a silly old unwashed man. "a quiet freedom". I wish I could utter gems like that.

"Do you buy?" Hannah asked

"Not any more" he said "I used to do all the old country house clearances but now I only buy what people bring in. They know that if it is worth anything I will offer them a fair price. But no. I do not buy much any more. Its the old ticker you know" and he put his hand on his chest

Hannah bought a fireside scuttle and tongs and went on her way.

But she was excited. She had an idea. Her father was not happy with the bundles of Cipini outside the shop and TV sets all over the floor inside. But he had agreed to let her manage things in her own way and he ha to admit she was making money again. But he did not mind being poor as long as he had his pride. Hannah understood how much his standing in the community meant to him and it was important the local people though well of David Robinson. What she had in mind would need considerable management and careful diplomacy and it would take some time.

There was groundwork to be done. David disliked the cipini and the gas cylinders around the front door. He would not even mention the cipini. It was a gaelic word after all. Selling sticks that a schoolboy gathered. Beyond contempt. But he was a silent man when she showed him her profits from the very same sticks. She compromised to save his feelings and she moved the firelighters to an outside shed and she put a notice in the window that they were on sale at reduced prices. David suggested they might do without the gas cylinders now the TV business was doing well but she reminded him that he promised to let her run the business her way.She knew that his standing in others eyes was important to him. He would not mind being poor if the neighbours did not know. If Hannah had not come home he would have had to close down the business and live in isolated penury. She jollied him along

"Marks and Spencers started from a wheelbarrow and the Kennedys in America from the illicit sale of whisky" she said

"Who wants to be like the Kennedys?" he snapped

Oops, a bad example there, she thought but she spoke up

"Look at Anton Rogers" she said "a few years ago he was on his knees literally, with his trowel doing kitchen floors and now he is a wealthy man. A big giver to Charity and his photo in every paper. Not to mention what he gives to the political party. No one tells Anton that they can remember when he did not have two pennies to rub together. Everyone tells Anton how much they admire him and his money. They do not care where he got it" David looked away and said nothing. He knew Anton well and he knew how generous he was with his money. Then he spoke

"Yes. Anton has done well for himself"

Now she decided was her time

"I was thinking of starting as an auctioneer" she said and she very deliberately used the word 'auctioneer'

There was an auctioneer in the Masons and David knew him. If she said she was going to open an auction room he might have dismissed it as a knacker's yard

But he was listening to her.

"Do you hav to pay any entrance examinations or do any courses?" he asked

"Not that I know of' 'she replied. You pay a registration fee and I suppose they check if you have a criminal record and you possssibly need a banker's reference. I can sort that out".

She took his silence asagreeing with her suggestion. She started getting the place in order.The large store room was cleared out and a smooth concrete floor laid and then covered with a light wood laminate. She had three full length windows put in a side wall and had filament lighting along the wall and in the ceiling.

She now had an empty store room and David was very proud. She went to Derry and came home with a large sign which she placed over the front door "Robinsons Auctions" it told the world

Then she applied formembership of the Association of Auctioneers.She rang the local papers and invited their editorial staff to a gala opening function of Robinsins Auctioneers. She had to pull rank for alcohol to be available at the function. Plenty of alcohol. She got her publicity and in return for her promise to advertise with them she got front page photographs.' New Business in Garton' was one headline and another was "Hannah is Happy".

But when they had all gone she sat and thought. What is all this? Not a storeroom any more. And after all the money she spent. A gallery? No. Too posh. Not a Hall. There was a hall in the village already. It had to be 'Auction Rooms' So "Auction Rooms" it was.

She placed her first advertisement in the local papers

"YOU SELL – WE BUY. WE SELL – YOU BUY. Robinsons Auction Rooms. Auction the first Saturday of every month,. Come and see us"

Now there was three weeks before the next first Saturday. And she had nothing to sell. But people dropped in. Out of curiosity. Hannah remembered the old man in Barnesmore Gap and she followed his example. She herself went to ountry auction sales and she came home with car loads of brick-a-brack.

She placed chairs around the new auction room and practised her selling chatter. None of the "what am I bid what am I bid? But just a quiet "anyone care to make an offer?"

The first Saturday twelve people turned up so it was low key. But word passed round and gradually their trade increased. There was no fee. Leave your item and get a docket. If it was sold the auction room kept 10% of the selling price and if it did not sell after three auctions the owner had to take the item home

There was no valuation service and this caused problems. Most people overvalued their property and if they did not take Hannah's advice on a selling price and when the property did not sell after three auctions then they had topay 1% of the price to cover administration costs. It stopped people from being silly and it was fair to all. No favourites. She got a well earned reputation as a fair trader and her trade volume increased and her auction rooms were on their way to being successful. She was a busy lady.

Sothebys and Bonhams here I come. Dream on.

24

IF AENGUS HAD difficulty in remembering their name s so did the children have trouble recalling Aengus' own name. "The Master" was usually good enough. But hey thought his proper name was something like the statue in the G.P.O. They knew it was not Cuchulainn so they did the next best thing and they christened him Finn MacCool "like them fellas long ago"

He handed out the name tags and he warned that they were not be taken fronm the schoolroom. Were they heck?Those tags were more highly regarded than any bravery medal. Some mothers put them up there beside The Sacred Heart Picture and the little red Eternity lamp. Many years later in Boston the Mayor came up to Aengus and took his hand from across his jacket lapel to reveal "Declan Molloy 'on one of Aengus most cherished name tags.

"Well I never" was all Aengus could say and when Declan's wife addressesd Aengus as 'Mr Finn" he knew it was the real thing. But he did not have the heart to tell her that her beloved husband was never known as Declan. His real name was "Sniffer" among his pals

Back at the school Aengus set about his classroom. He went to World Choice in Grafton St. and explained he was a teacher in William St primart school and asked if they had any old posters to brighten his classroom walls

"That crowd will not need the Bahamas posters" a little nobody from the back tittered. But Aengus spied a good looker with the name tag "Yvonne" so he spoke to Yvonne as if the others did not exist. He left with an armful of posters and a feeling that he would like to call in there again. A little sweetheart was that Yvonne and a nice name as well. Not too many Yvonnes in Gweedore

Because the boys were so young the day was dinvided Ten minutes break every hour and half an hour at 12.00 for a lunch break and home again at 2.00 pm.They stayed at the school for the half hour break and ate in the classroom. Aengus saw what they had and some could do better. So he wrote in capital letters on the blackboard and he had the class copy it all down on the sheet of paper he had given each boy

"Well done my men" he said. "That is your very first letter. Now keep it safe and take it home to your father and mother." It was a request for any old cups or mugs so they could have a drink at the school. He got a collection of cups and mugs and two electric kettles. Then he went to Brother Kevin and said he was thinking of making a cup of tea for his class. Br. Kevin went pale "This is not Bewleys, you know" and he thoufght Fr Crowe had sent him a right one here

"It is only a cup of tea" said Aengus. Even the building site workers have a tea break"

"It will bring the rats in" protested Br Kevin

You mean more rats thought Aengus but he shut it

"I promise you the rats will get nothing. We will sweep up every day. The cleaners will never believe it and think of the good habits the boys will learn." answered Aengus

"This is not Cathal Brugha Domestic Science Academy you know. The Three Rs is enough for us here" remonstrated Br Kevin

Aengus carried on "Let me have a go on the quiet and see how I manage. Some of those little tykes come in on an empty stomach and a cup of tea or cocoa will lift them."

"Ok then" said Br Kevin" but do not get the idea thst we are allRobert Carrier"

Thank you "said Aengus with a smile and he felt that Br Kevin would have said 'Robert fucking Carrier" but for the fact he was tha headmmaster and a Christian Brother

But Aengus was getting there. He had the permission and all he needed now was the provisions. He went to Liptons and he was given a chest of tea and Barry's of Cork sent him a consignment. Bewleys came up with the goods and Lyons gave him vouchers to use in any of the major grocers. Then he went after the cash. The Sick and Indigent Innkeepers gave him a good donation. It was not their area but if he was stuck he was to call again. The St Vincen De Paul were doubtful. It might set a precedent. Precedent my arse he almost told them Come down to my classroom on a frosty morning and you will see a precedent. Eventually they gave him some money and Thanks be to Jasus they finally agreed to a monthly donation.

Milk was the problem. Bottled milk. He was not able to get a delivery to the school and the local shop stopped doing milk years ago. If they were paid all they were owed for milk they could goto Costa Del Sol for the restvof their lives. He asked help from every Government depatrtment and he did not get any replies

Poor innocent Aengus. He called at the Pro Cathedral and met one of the priests. He just laughed. Help the poor and needy. Sure they had the upkeep of the bishop's Mansion in Drumcondra and that was enough. Ha ha, help the poor and needychildren. Stop pulling me leg. Poor old Noel Browne got short shift when he tried tio help the poor and needy mothers and children. Get off with ya!. Then he heard of a Fr. Mulrine who was working in the area. He had been a member of a religious order but had come out and was now working with the poor and needy. He ran an underground support for the people of the streets. Aengus met him and they had much in common. Fr Mulrine and Aengus formed a breakfast Club and the oparents took to it. It relieved them of their feelings of inadequacy. By helping there they were doing their part. Paying their debt to society. The odd dishevelled parent might arrive with the child late for class and he would slip Aengus a note for "the tea fund" or the odd box of biscuits that had "fallen off a stall" and was not suitable for resale. ButAengusdid not accept fruit of any kind. He knew that fruit was what the Moore St traders sold but he promised to keep the room tidy and fruit could be messy. He organised a rota for the clearing up and awarded stars to the best team at the end of the maoth.

Br Kevin called in and said everything was fine but to remember they were not running a drop in centre. That was not true. They did not drop in. They were already inside. It was trying to get out was the problem.

Then there was the problem of "the Irish" "an Gaeilge'. DeValera kept on about the Revival if the Irish Langusge. And him not an Irishman at all. Born in America and with an American citizenship. It saved his life in 1916. The doddering old man rambled about "comely colleens dancing at the Crossroads" Bet he had never heard of The Crystal ballroom or the National and the Royal showband. And he wanted the children taught through the madium of Irish. That would be verybuseful in Moore St or down the docks. Fluent Irish speakers would do well there

Aengus asked Br Kevin for advice. All he needed was for an inspector to come and give him a hard time. Br Kevin was as patriotic as the next man and he advised that the teaching of Irish was not a priority. He saidthatveven the Department of Education did not press De Valera's wishes

So get in there Aengus. Tell them what you are going to teach them Yjhen teach them then tell them what they have been taught. Aengus did just that. Twenty minutes a session. That was their concentration span. Then theyb had a bit of a sing song and would start af=agin The other teachers wondered.How were they training the youg teachers in St Patricks nowadays, Singing at 10.30 in the morning?

He encourage his boys. It was never "no good" but always "Good. Now try and do better". And his star system. A star for spelling, a star for writing, a star for attendance, and most important of all a star for the boy who tried the hardest. To award this star to a backward child was truly divine. The swagger as he wore it home and around the streets and possibly in bed. One proud mother had her son's photograph taken with his star and she was disgusted when The Evening Press would not publish it, Some stories are hard to believe but you never know!

There was still more work to do on the classroom

"Mind if I do a bit if painting?" Aengus asked.

"National College of Art?" asked Br Kevin. Jeeze he has a sense of humour that man, thought Aengus

"No, just the walls of my classroom" he replied

"See what you can come up with" Br Kevin wearily replied. He knew Aengus was a great scrounger and beggar. Let him have his head

Aengus was away, Round the shops again. Any old brushes or tins of paint of any kind? Any colour except black or brown or any very dark colour. He colleccted a few gallons of paint and a satchel of brushes. That was fine. But where to start? He asked his boys for advice. "Now men what colour for this wall? What colour for the ceiling? Will we do the door Will we wait until the holidays or will we do a bit every weekend?". They did not know

On Monday morning there was a heavy rattle on the door. Aengus opened it to a dishevelled man reeking of fags and stale porter

"I want to speak to Finn MacCool"

"I am he, and my name is Master Gillespie. What can I do for you?"

I am Paddy Gorman and my nipper Eamonn is in your class. I have 5 children and Eamonn is the only one who fu--- who likes coming to school. Bloody fu--- bloody marvellous. Sorry master about thelanguage but it is fu--- sirry master it is bloody marvellous"

Eamonn is a good wee boy" said Aengus

"Good? Bloody fu--- bloody good that's what he is.If he keeps this up he will finish up in Earlsford Terrace with all them Culchie fu--- sorry with akl them Culchie University Perfessors. He might be tha first Dub up there with all the Culchies and all the foreigners up ther in the University as well. He tells me you want to paint the classroom. Now let me axe you a question. What the fu--- sorry what do you know about paintin'?"

"You have me there" said Aengus

Paddy Gorman carried on. "Well we was chattin' in Moloney's Bar the other night. You ever bin there? Well we was chattin' and the wimmin think you need a hand as you is makin' a great fist of teachin' the weans. I am a paintin. Contractor meself and I have a few men who work for me. The salt of God's earth they are. The salt of the fu--- sorry the salt of the earth they are. And we thought we might be able to help you out. We are slack now and there is a bank hioliday coming up and we thought we might strip the room on Friday night and do the undercoat on Saturday, the finish on Sunday, and clear up on Monday mornin'. Whaddya think?"

"I could not afford it "Aengus said

Give us a fu--- Sorrry Give us abreak. We will not charge you. You look after my son Eamonn and that goes for the other men too. I will be in contact nearer the date. OK? Might we see you in Moloneys some time?

Br Kevin was not too keen. He knew there were parents' groups in Dun Laoire and Rathgar and at Terenure and posh places like that. But William St?

"Thety will burn the place down or tear it apart "he said. But Aengus was not having any of this

"No they will not. Give them a chance. It will mean a lot to them that they have helped out. I find they are good people and it is our fault we do not understand them. I am sure there is more alcohol taken in some homes in Terenure and the likes than there is in Moloney's Bar and Lounge"

Aengus gave Br Kevin the lecture that would do him good

"All right, All right. Leave you in charge" he agreed

The room was painted. Not according to the colour scheme Aengus had in mind

"Leave it with me" said Paddy Gorman. "the professionals know best"

Even with a pint or four taken our Paddy was boss man

"Rule number one" he called out. "No smokin' on the premises.

Rule number two.Do not interfere with my decisions. Do not tell me how to decorate a room, Thank you"

He had sheets put over all the desks and over the floor. A break every two hours and two bottles of stout. Afterthree breaks he said they had enough bevvy and they carried on until it was time for Moloneys and there they stayed until the Garda squad car arrived and told them it was time they went home to bed. Not many argued with Lugs Branigan and his squad of heavies

The children loved the new cclassroom.

"Me old fella did that. Naw it was mine"

The room looked three times bigger and even the hated Inspector said it looked "ana mhaith" in his best Drimnagh gaelic accent. Very good it meant to those who could understand his strangulation of the ancient language

Not a word from the Church and there was a feeling of unspoken disapproval coming from the staff room. Where would it all end? Would they all be expected to do something similar?The INTO were approached but after the John MacGahern case they did not want any more trouble,

So life went back to normal again. Aengus read a story or a part of every evening for the last 15 minutes of the day. Long John Silver, Treasure Island, Swiss Family Robinson, and and then on to Maurice Walsh and Walter Macken. He told them of Na Fianna and the Tain Bo Cualinge and Maeve and Finn MacCool. Cuchulainn was their favourite

"Me mammy kisses his toes every time she posts a letter in the G.P.O". Donie Ryan said and then he asked" why are the crows sitting on his shoulder? Cheeky monkey. He had heard the story often enough.

25

SHANE WS IMPROVING very fast on the accordeon. Out in the shed in his Confessional box he was not deafening anyone's ears. Fr Barry dropped in from time to time to see how things were coming on and to help Eugene with the Algebra. Timmy Martin was the man for the lifts to Doherty's and his man from Omagh looked after him and encouraged his progress. At home he listened to Ciaran MacMathuna on the radio and he was so frustrated that he could not remember and learn to play all the tunes. Omagh heard his moaning and suggested a tape recorder might help

Oh Yeah?. But a tape recorder costs a fortune and where could he find one?

Order one from the music shop in Strabane he was told.

He went to the music shop and he asked the man behind the counter and he took a tape recorder out and he taped Shane's own voice. Jeeze he was mortified. That squeaky voice, was that him?Did he really sound that funny?. If he sounded like that he would never say another word

"Dont be silly" the man said "we all think our own voices sound funny and different. You sound like any young man from Donegal. You will never be asked to read The News at Ten but there is nothing wrong with your voice or your accent"

"Makes no difference" Shane said "I can't afford it"

"You could pay a deposit and then something every week" suggested the man

Shane was aghast. The dreaded "never never" Molly Flanagan bought a new radio on instalments and she was branded for life in the parish. They were all talking about her.We will all be like the person in the Bible who finished up in the hands of the moneylenders?.

But Shane went past the shop every time he was in the town. Just to look at his hearts desire in the window. The shopkeeper recognised him and soon they were on nodding terms. But the price kept them apart. Shane called in and aked if there might be a cheaper one or an old one. The man said he only dealt with new equipment but there was a man in Derry who might have a cheaper one. It was a Pawn Shop run by a Mr Isaac Woolf. He found the shop in Derry but there was no tape recorder in the shop window. He asked inside and Mr Woolf went out the back and came in with a battered looking tape recorder.

They tried it out together and Mr Woolf said it was in good working order and it had only been handed in as the owner needed the money for the fare to America. He, Mr Woolf himself, would vouch for its working order.

"Would you take a deposit from me and keep the tape recorder here for me until I have paid the full amount?" Shane asked

"I have never done anything in that line before" Mr Woolf said "would you mind me asking what you need it for?"

Shane told him "I play the accordeon and I want to tape from the radio to learn more tunes"

Isaac Woolf smiled. Isaac was a cantor in the Synagogue. A fellow musician. He would help this young man. But first things first.

"What if someone else wants to buy it?" he asked

"Thats my tough luck. If you get your asking price then you sell it" Shane sadly replied. "Take it off the market for two weeks and let me get some money and if I cannot raise a good deposit then you can put it back on the market and sell it"

"How much can you put as a deposit?" Mt Woolf asked

Shane made his offer. All he had at home from his dealings with Hannah. Mr Woolf shook his head "Ill need more than that" he said

"Would a few bags of spuds and a few dozen of eggs be any good?" Shane asked

"What kind of potatoes;? Asked Mr Woolf

"Arran Banners, fluffiest potato there is in the world. Melt in your mouth. You will never again eat any other kind when you have tasted these. And the eggs. From my own Rhode Island Reds. Every hen a personal friend of mine. Big firm yolks. Food from the Gods. Change your whole life" Shane told him

Isaac looked at this young man. Shane O Neill. He, Isaac Woolf, had been in the hock business for over 40 years; and at the sharp end as well. He had met crooks and thieves and he had survived. He lookeed at Shane again and the thought that a seasoned old cynic like himself had a heart somewhere. He examined the unlined face of the boy again and he felt a fellowship with this manchild. He would do him a deal

"All right then, potatoes and eggs and I will take the recorder off the market"

They shook hands on the deal and Isaac knew that no other person than this Donegal boy would ever have that recorder. He would wait for his money.

The poor hens must have thought Shane was gone crazy. He sat watching them and if one of them gave as much as a cackle he was out to the henhouse to collect the egg. He told his mother of the deal he had done with Mr Woolf and she told Neil and she asked for his help

"Two bags of spuds? What for?" Neil asked

"For a tape recorder for his music" she told him

"Whats wrong with his music? He never stops playing. Always at it"

"He needs more tunes and a tape recorder will help. That is all he wants. You give Eugene everything he asks for" she said

That was below the belt. They knew Eugene was thinking of the priesthood. Neil wa not a great man for the religion but a priest in the family was the wish of every Irish mother and he liked the thought himself,

But he would never admit it.

"All right then" he grumbled. Secretly he was pleased. He hoped Shane would stay on with him on the farm and he wanted to have a happy and contented son beside him

Problem solved? No not yet. How was Shane going to get the spuds to Derry. Fr Barry heard of the predicament and he had the answer

They loaded two sacks of Arran Banners and three dozen eggs on to the back seat of his car

"Some spuds for the Convent" he told the Customs Officer

"Carry on Father" was all he was told

They stopped in Carrigans for a ginger beer and Fr Barry said

"I have an idea that might help us"

Shane liked the way he said "us"

"I think we should go to The Credit Union in town" Fr Barry continued "They area non profit making organisation that lends money. Not huge amounts but enough for the needs. Write your plan of action down and call in and see them. They will ask how you intend to repay their loan and ifyou have a plan written down they will know you are a businessman"

Shane glowed with pride. A businessman?. Me a businessman?. Yea man Yea.

So Shane went to the Credit Union.One of the girls in the Office came out and said she had heard him play at one of the Garton School Concerts. They seemed to know a lot about him and where he was from. It never occurred to him that Fr Barry might have passed on the word. When his application was passed the girls thenmselves had a little celebration and one made a secret phone call." Someone special "she told the others and it was "not what they think." It ended with "thank you Father"

So Shane paid Mr Woolf in total and he took home the tape recorder. But Mr Isaac asked if he could drop in a bag or two of the spuds any time he was passing as some of his friends liked the taste of Donegal Arran Banners. Good idea.

26

AENGUS HAD PROMISED the Dean in St Pat's that he would play for Na Fianna. They used to be C.J. Kickhams fom the drapery trade but now they were reformed as Na Fianna. They were a strong club. Mostly of men from the country but now with the end of the ban there were men from the city joining them. The Dubs were coming in. For many years the G.A.A. scene in the city was dominated by the same clubs. Vincents, Clann Na Gael, Na Garda the Civil Service but with the removal of the ban new clubs were coming forward.

Aengus enjoyed playing for Na Fianna. Especially when he played against former well known players who were past their prime but who continued playing at a lower level as they were not yet ready to retire.

All at the veteran stage but a joy to watch with their dodges and tricks to compensate for approaching middle age and declining fitness

Aengus loved playing against Vincent's. They were a team of Dublin born only players and they had a condescending attitude to the country men they played against. They were the Dubs and they had no respect for the Culchies

Aengus was picked to play against Vincent's and he was delighted that Ollie Freaney would be one of his opponents. Ollie was a God among the Dub followers. He had been a county superstar for years and he had won every medal there was. But the years were catching up on Ollie and he did not care to accept it. He still played, as he loved the game and the banter and the clash of personalities on the field. He was famous for his insuling remarks to the Culchies. But it was only part of his game. Just as boxers stare each other before the big fight and then are friends for ever after.

They were playing in Parnell Park which was Ollie's Home ground. He spent most of his adult life in Parnell Park

He swaggered over to Aengus and asked "Which part of the bog are you from, Culchie?" and he did not wait for an answer. Let the Culchie stew and lose his temper was Ollie's technique. Aengus had been warned that this chat might happen and he took no notice. He waited. He waited until the next high ball came their way. Ollie rose majestically with his hands ready to catch the dropping ball. Aengus did not bother with the ball but he caught Ollie as he landed and he flattened him. Ollie was turned over a few time before he knew what had hit him

He was delirious. "Ref ref" he shouted "Blow your whistle. Ref blow the bloody whistle. A foul. a foul. a bloody foul" Aengus stood over him and reached down to help him on his feet and he said

"Now now Ollie. No shouting like that little Ollie. And which little girls' school did you come from?"

Ollie swore an oath and he said Aengus would be sorry but Aengus reminded him "Now Ollie you know the nuns in thse convent do not like language like that. Go and wash your mouth out'

War was declared and they had a right battle for the rest of the game.

Afterwards they sat in the clubroom together and when he heard Aengus name Ollie just looked

"From Gweedore?" "Yes" said Aengus." I am a primary teacher in the Brothers in William St."

Ollie looked at Aengus again and said "The only time we played Gweedore I was nearly crippled by a chap called Ownie Rua, a bloody head case. He nearly broke my back with his knee"

"Was that in Clones in the Gael Linn Club championship?" asked Aengus

"Yea, how did you know? Asked Ollie

Ownie Rua was my father" said Aengus.

"Holy Mother of God" said Ollie. I might have guessed. How is the ruffian?"

"He was killed in an accident years ago" said Aengus

"Oh God Aengus I am so sorry to hear that and all the things I said about him. Didn't mean them"

"He would have been best pleased to hear you speak of him as you did "said Aengus

Ollie and Aengus looked out for each other every time the teams met and they remined life long friendly enemies.

The social side of Na Fianna was not great. Most of the lads were country men and they were in digs or flats all over the city and they went back to friends or pals or their girlfriends in their part of the city. It ws a drink in the clubhouse and "I must be off" as they checked the wristwatch

Aengus and Tipperery Pat decided to move from the digs to a flat. Anywhere not too far from Redmond's Bar and Lounge and Marios Fish 'n Chips, The new flat was a bit of a tip but they managed. What Pat did in the Civil Service was never clearly defined except thet it was not very much. He worked for the Department Of Posts and Telegraphs and he had something to do with the locating and financing of Public Telephone Kiosks. The great perk was when he had to check on the proposed site and that meant a trip down the country and a hotel. It was a change from sausages or Marios fish and chips. Their social life was the cinema or Redmond's Bar or the odd trip to the dance halls inTown. They tried some of the tennis club dances but they were made to feel complete outsiders there. Cliques with their posh Dublin accents, frightfully posh, actually,frightfully, actually.

Soon it would be the Summer holidays and he was offered a job teaching in one of the Summer Colleges in Donegal but a lazy holiday at home with his mother appealed to him more. There was a suggestion that he might like to help in Sunshine House in Skerries but he wanted to go home. He made arrangements for some of his boys to holiday in Sunshine House and he went bhome to Gweedore. His mother was at the door. Waiting. Sinead was getting married and she was having the wedding in Boston.

Holy mother of God!!!. Never a dull moment.

27

WITH HIS EGGS and potatoes Shane soon paid off his debt. He dropped down with Fr Barry and a back seat load to Isaac Woolf from time to time. But his trade with Hannah went into decline. There is no way she could have the cipini outside her showroom doors and with the gas pokers the demand had dwindled. Indeed she was thinking of giving up the hardware and the TV business completely and concentrating on her auctioneering. Shane was not too upset as he had nearly shorn Lochbeg farm of all its foliage. But he was getting on very well with his music. He taped all of Ciaran's programmes and he added to his collection of tunes. Tommy Martin was so proud of his prodigy and he insisted they go to Rathmullan to hear a piper that was supposed to be a s good as Paddy Moloney of The Chieftains and to take his tape recorder with him as well. When they got there who was sitting in the front row but the brave Fr Barry Morris himself.

He said he was only passing through but all the others there knew him and spoke to him as a regular and finally he opened his bag and he gave them a few tunes on his banjo mandolin

Tommy Martin chastised him "You never told us you could play. Never" he said in disgust

"Aw come on," said Fr Barry "I am no great shakes. My father has this old banjo and sometimes I have the odd belt on it. I am too embarrassed to let any one hear me play. Honest Honest"

Priests do not say "honest to God" thought Shane. Especially when they are telling lies. But it began to make sense. His interest in Shane's playing and things musically Irish in general. He was a different priest. Old Fr Carr would not know the difference between Val Doonican and Elvis Presley never mind Irish music. And the banjo mandolin was a difficult instrument to play. Well done Barry Morris. And a Holy Father as well. Good on Ya.

All Shane said was "Take the banjo mandolin up to the house and we can go to Confession together"

Tommy Martin could not believe what he heard. Was this a new type of Confession?. One never knows. With the new Pope and the nuns wearing ordinary dresses now. What next? But he kept his mouth shut.The sessions in Doherty's carried on as before and Fr Barry came along but he would not play. Omagh was there and he thought Shane was good enough now for him to have his instruction book back. Then he invited Shane over to play in a concert in Omagh town and Shane stayed overnight. Omagh introduced Shane to one of his neices who was going to go to England to study nursing when she was older and to stay with her aunties over there. They shyly said hello but Shane was struck. He thought she was just lovely. An Angel. She said her name was Rita and then she was gone. Rita Coyle. Rita Coyle and she was going to be a nurse in England when she was older

Master Byrne called up to the house. He said that Eugene had done very well and that Shane might follow in his path. But Neil was not happy "One scholar in the house is enough and I have a daughter to provide for as well as another son" said Neil

"He has the brains and I can aim him in the right direction before I retire" the old master said

"Thank you Master" Neil said "but I have always hoped that Shane would stay on the farm with me and take over sometime"

"He could always come back later and take over" the master replied

"It never works "said Neil." I see bent old farmers dying on their feet and their sons driving a lorry or fitting tyres in some garage and they will never come home to settle. They will sell the old home. "Come home to that slavery?" they say and they do not want it. Farming is not work. It is a lifestyle. There is no beginning to the day nor is there an end to the day at evening time. Some days nothing needs doing and other days there is not enough time. No nine to five hours as the farmer walks his fields through his animals. No great wealth but who is to say his lifestyle is inferior"

The master said nothing. He nodded. Sometimes the quality of life was not apparent to the casual observer. His own teaching career was coming to an end and all he had ever wanted was a quiet life. But Eugene did him proud. He had won a scholarship and he was set on an academic caereer and the master could not have hoped for a better end to his teaching. His "back country school" had won a scholarship. The master was unperturbed. He had spent 40years in a back country school and what had he to show for it? Not much he thought. But there were many others who thought different

Eugene came home on his holidays,. Some of the holiday. He and Shane did not get on well. Because a man did not know the capital city of Bolivia or the name of a chap who crossed the Alps on an elephant did not mean he was a "thickie" as Eugene tended to imply. He was getting more and more studious and introverted and he did not help on the farm at all. Mary was worried in case he was not eating the right food and that he was not sickening for something. Neil just said "Let him get on with it" and did not bother.

Soon Eugene was spending his holidays with his college friends and he only stayed at home for the Christmas break. Neil some times lost his temper and barked at his older son and this led to days of sulking

Shane thought Eugene should help out a bit more. He could cut the hedge around the house and clean out the cowshed. But no way. He avoided work. He read The Messenger, Blessed Martin, The Far East and any religious book he could find in the public lending Library.He tried to have them say the Rosary in the kitchen but the dog kept licking their noses and the prayers were abandoned.

Maureen was attending the Convent in Strabane. She caught the CDR diesel train every morning. The rail track was not far from the house and though it was not an official stop Brendan the driver always let her hop on if she was there. The boss in Stranorlar knew about this arrangement and as long as they were careful he did not mind

Maureen's books and her course was different from what Eugene had studied as her examinations were in the North and she had a different prospectus. But Maureen was a good student. She got on with her work and hail rain or snow she was there for the train. She never complained.

Then one day a big car drove in to the front yard and a stockily built grey haired man got out. He stood looking round and leaning against the side of the car

Shane saw him and went forward. He might be from the Ministry of Agriculture

"Mornin'" said Shane "Can I help you?"

The man was crying'

"Can you take me to Mary O Neill?"

"Mammy mammy, come out here, a man wants to meet you" Shane shouted towards the house

Mary came out drying her hands on an old towel and she ran to the stranger and silently they embraced and hugged. Then she turned to Shane and said" This is your uncle Liam. He has come back home. Thanks be to to the Lord and His Blessed Mother"

They went in to the kitchen and Mary got the whiskey bottle but Liam said that he would prefer a cup of tea. They sat and chatted for a while and then Mary sent Shane out to fetch his father

"A wee drop in your tea?" Mary asked

"No this is fine. Just fine" Liam said

"Then I'd better put the bottle away "she said "no use getting himslf started so early in the day. There will be time later"

"Lots of time" was all Liam said

Neil came running. He stopped in the doorway. He did not know how to approach this man. He had heard stories and more stories so he stuck his hand out and Liam grasped it and held him by the arm as well. They looked at each other.

"Welcome home" said Neil

"Thank you and it's nice to be back. Thank you very much, very much" said an emotional Liam

"Like a wee drop?" asked Neil

"No thank you. The tea is just the job" Liam said and Mary smiled at him in gratitude

"How about a fry" she asked

"Oh God yes. It is years since I had the full MacCoy" he said

"Right then" and she got the frying pan "you must be starving" she said

"I landed at Shannon yesterday morning" he told them" and I had a few hours in Limerick and then I headed North. I had a meal in Athlone and a coffee in Sligo and now I am ravenous"

"Good" said Mary and she got to work with the pan. Liam said he had come home for a week or two and then he would go home again to Brocton

"Where is that?" he was asked

"Just outside of Boston" he said

Liam's story was a long and tortured one and he had come home to find peace of mind. When he went to America he hung about in New York and about Moran's pub. It was a rough pub and he got casual work labouring. As a recent immigrant he was soon conscripted. He did not like the army and the army did not like him and he went absent without leave . . . He was caught and was retrained in the roughest corps and he was sent to the front line in Korea as a member of a parachute regiment. He loved it. The fear, The adrenaline, the amphetamines and of course the bottle he always carried in his rucksack. Wild and out of his mind on the drugs and the booze he attacked and cleaned out a Communist dug out. He was promoted to Sergeant in the field. He was awarded the Silver Star for his bravery and he came home to New York as a war hero. He was given a cushy job as an agent for a brewery. A cushy job?. What job?. All he had to do was entertain the company guests. Meet up with the owners of the bars and entertain them. That lasted a time but Liam did not. The alcohol took over. There was no Liam. There was the booze and an empty bottle. He drifted and lost many years. Sleeping rough on the streets and in back alleys and trying to avoid the cops. They loved to pull in the drunken Paddy. He was lying in the gutter when a man sat beside him and said "I can help you if you let me"

This was a new one to Liam. He agreed to meet this man the next day when he might be able to understand what it was all about. He thought of his mother and father and he decided they were having a word with the Almighty on his behalf. His new friend was named Jumbo. He was an alcoholic had been in the gutter and now he was doing social work for The Lost Souls. A Charity

He got Liam in to Rehab. Liam listened and he recovered his life. He started work again and now he was the owner of a small firm doing building renovations and extensions. He told them in Lochbeg his story.

Bit by bit, as when he felt they were ready to hear all the gory and sad details. They were sad for him and they were proud of him. He had made his way back and now he was safe with them. He told them they were going to have a week's holidays with him

"But we cannot leave the farm" they protested

"No need to leave the farm at all" he said "we will use the farm as our holiday base"

He took them all over the county and they feasted in the best hotels and restaurants. He bought presents for them all and food for the home and they had a wonderful time. Shane took him to a session in Doherty's but he was not that enthusiastic. Best left alone. He said he had tried to contact his sister Josie in America but she had passed away ten years earlier. Again he did not go in to details. But she had two daughters and he still had hopes of finding them and they might like to meet their Irish cousins,It was sad.

Murrays came to Lochbeg and installed a large colour Television.Liam could not understand how they ever managed without one. The night before he was due to leave he held his Americen Wake. He said there was no American wake went he left the years ago as no one knew he was going away. He just stole off in the night. But this was different. It was a party for all. He had a catering company do all the food and the clearing up afterwards. Then they sat down and he said a few things

"I have been a scoundrel in the past. The night I crept away and went to America I stole £500 from my mother's room. From under the carpet where she kept her savings. That money would have been for Mary's wedding and Mary's dowry. I must make compensation for my own peace of mind. Tomorrow morning I have a hackney car come to collect me. I am leaving my car here. All the documents are up to date and I have transferred the ownership to Neil. I am leaving an envelope on the dressing table in my room. No complaints. No comeback. This is more for myself than it is for anyone else. Now goodnight and sleep well." He began to weep and he went to his room.

The hackney man woke them with the blasts from his horn. No polite knocking on the door for him.

Liam was packed and ready to go. They all felt there should be a priest to bless his departure. Words? No words. Just the silence and the pain and the tears and the wonderful happiness that he had come home and that he was well again

The sealed envelope. It was a banker's order for £2000. Holy Mother of God!
Next day a Post Office delivery van pulled in to the yard
"An item for Mr Shane O Neill" the man said "Sign here"
It wa abig box with a huge lable
"Waltons" for the music we know ans love'
There was a card attached "From your Uncle Liam"
It was a chromatic button accordeon.
Hohner's finest and latest model.

28

AENGUS WENT HOME to Gweedore on his Summer holidays. Six whole weeks to hang about and to relax in whatever sun there came. But not on the beach. Swimming in the Atlantic and lying on the beach was for visitors or the pupils at the Summer Irish School. He would bet that 80% of the Gweedore people could not swim a single stroke. Swimming was for swimming pools and heated at that.

He was not very long at home when he knew his mother was worried.Sinead was engeged to be married. Most mothers are delighted when their daughters are betrothed. Aengus had read Sinead's letters to his mother. She had explained that her fiancee was an attorney like herself and they both worked in the same legal company

But Peggy was not happy. His name sounded funny. Yehudi Levi. Was he a darkie?. He might have more than one wife. Aengus knew that with a name like that Yehudi was Jewish. He had no trouble with that. But Peggy?. He would have to take things very gently

Peggy went on and on. This Hudi, what did he look like? When she was told he was Jewish she wondered if he had a big long beard and those funny long ringlets. And did he wear a funny hat like Moses?. There was no way she could ask Sinead on the phone, That wan Mary Paddy Jimmy in the post office would hear it all and then everyone would know. Even the sergeant in The Gardai had to ask herto stop listening in and to get off the line. So for privacy the letters flew over and back across the Atlantic. Yes mammy Yehudi is Jewish, Reform Jewish. Not as strict as the Hasidic with the long hair or the Orthodox with their long coats and their beards and big hats. His grandfather came from Russia and started a bakery and then a restaurant and his mother worked in the fashion trade until she started her family. Yehudi has 4 brothers and 3 sisters, Honestly you will like him. You will ger on well together

But Peggy ws still worried. Boston was far away and Sinead was marrying a stranger. Aengus expleined that if she married a Kerrymen she might be further away in Tralee. It is easier and quicker sometimes to get to Bostom than to Tralee. He explained that Boston had been Sinead's home for many years now and all her friends were there and Hudi had a big family there as well Peggy knew all this. But secretly and she would never admit that she wanted to show Gweedore and all the world how well her daughter had done. Some of the glory would reflect on herself and she liked the thought. Hudi might want to get married in a Synagogue and she did not know if there was one in Donegal at all. Certainly there was not one in Gweedore.

Aengus stayed close and helped her. Nothing had happened yet. They might fall out and not marry at all. Let things settle a bit. All he really wanted was for his mother to take her time to accept what was going to happen.

"That Sinead was always strong willed" Peggy complained "Always wanting her own way"

"She is a grown woman and a qualified Attorney" Aengus reminded his mother "wait for her answers to all yourquestions. Write to Auntie Sheila and see what she says"

Auntie Sheila's letter was very reassuring. Hudi is from a very nice and very respectable family and he treats Sinead like a queen. His family are of the Jewish faith but not of the radical or extreme type Then she wrote what Peggywas waiting for. He does not look at all foreign. If you met him in the street he could be an Irishman. There are Connemara men who are more foreign looking. God but that set her mind at rest. Gradually the panic eased and Sinead marrying Hudi did not seem so disastrous. But Aengus had to leave home and return to Dublin. He had to play fotball for Na Fianna. He stayed with the past captain of the team. Another teacher called Des Shanley. Des was a teacher in one of the Secondary Schools. But teaching was a distraction as far as Des was concerned. His main interest was in ancient maps and manuscripts, First editions were wghat he lived for and if they had the author's signature then he would certainly offer is life. His flat was like a museum with books and maps and manuscripts all over the place. He did not have a cleaner as his maps and scripts were too valuable and precious to move. It was a brave man who would go to the toilet at night in the dark for fear of doing very expensive damage on his away. Aengus never knew Donegal had so many writers. Starting with the Four Masters and MacGill and The O Griannas,Sheamus MacManus and not to mention O Searchaigh and Friel of recent years. He spent a few weekends immersed in Culture with Des. Then he went back home and he was so glad he had been there to help his mother with Sinead's news. He himself was looking forward to going to Boston to the wedding and to meet his inlaws.

29

THE ONEILLS HAD a very pleasant problem. They had too much money. Well not too much but more than they ever had seen before never mind having it all to themselves. And a big car as well.

One thing was certain. The money was mother's. No question. She would have a washing machine and a dish washer and a big fridge and an immersion heater and shower. What to do with the big motor car?. It was like the one Keane's had for their funeral service. Neil traded it in for a Morris Minor Estate and he came home with hundreds of pounds as well. Shane suggested a multi plough for the tractor and a power saw that would work off the tractor was purchased as well. Neil was doubtful about the saw but when he saw it in action and the way it cut the logs he was convinced. Shane still had the idea that the Robinsons might sell logs. After all he was a businesman now. Well he soon would be.

Shane loved the Morris Estate. He called it Fr Barry Minor but his mother soon put a stop to that

"Show some respect and don't be so cheeky"

He did say it once to the Reverend Father but Fr Barry was deaf in that ear and did nor hear him. They took Maureen to Strabane and had her have her hair done and then to the ladies' outfitters and she picked and pleased herself. They gave her a Parker Pen and a new leather briefcase.Shane washed and polished the Minor every week. He had been driving the tractor since his legs were able to reach the pedals and the car was no bother. He often sneaked down to the shop in the car.

It had to happen. The squad car pulled him over and Sergeant Thornton beckoned him to come

"Sit in Sonny. We need to have a chat"

"Driving licence? No"

"Insurance? No"

"I thought so. Under the Road traffic Act 1932 you are committing a road traffic offence." He was not sure about the 1932 but it sounded good

"You should not be on the road at all. It is a criminal offence. How far have you driven?" The sergeant knew very well how far Shane had driven but this was very enjoyable

"Only from the house" said Shane

"And where may I ask is the house? said the Sergeant

"Loc, Lochbeg" stammered Shane

God but he was enjoying this was Sergeant Thornton

"Now Mister Shane O Neill from Lochbeg in the parish of Garton, listen to me and listen very carefully. I should give you a summons and take you to court "and he reached for a folder. He paused and he could see the fear in the boy's eyes. H looked at Shane and waited and pursed his lips as if he was considering taking out a summons

"But Mister O Neill" the sergeant went on "I am a nice man. Yes I am. I will not summons you this time. I will give you a warning instead. If I ever catch you as much as dropping a sweet paper I will have you up in Court.Count your lucky stars that it was me Sergeant Thornton who caught you committing this serious crime. You are one lucky man"

"Yes Sergeant Thornton Yes I am. One lucky man I mean. And Thank you"

The Sergeant spoke again "Now drive very closely behind me and I will lead you home"

Shane saw the trouble this would cause. If either of his parents saw the police car coming they would think "What has Shane done now?" and he did not want that.

So he asked in a small timid voice "Sergeant Thornton Sir, could you stop at the bottom of the lane and let me go on up on my own?"

"Ok Son.Ok" and the sergeant gave him a friendly punch on the shoulder "but remember I will be keeping an eye on you"

Good old Sergeant Thornton. A Connemara man who had settled quietly in the town and had lately moved out to a house in the village. His children were growing up nicely and the job was by then a cushy number. It was to his own credit that the town was so quiet and respectable

When he came there years ago, were blackguards fighting and shouting in the night and upsetting everyone. The Sergeant dressed up in a dirty old overcoat and with a scarf pulled over his face he hung about the streets and the alleys fot a few nights. When he knew what was happening he flashed his torch into the eyes of the biggest of the hobos

"What the fuck you at?" was the response he got

"Come here you" the sergeant said and he opened the dirty coat to reveal his garda uniform

"Fuck off" said Jimmy Quinn

Not me" said the sergeant and he grabbed Jimmy" coming to the station with me you are me laddo"

He threw Jimmy into "the cell". It was a windowless all concrete room with no toilet facilities. It was seldom washed out and it was ripe. After an hour Jimmy had enough and he shouted he wanted his attorney

"Watching too many movies Jimmy. No attorneys in this town. Shut up and be quiet" Jimmy did not listen but he kept on shouting for his rights and he thought he was winning whem "the cell" door was opened. But all he got was abucket of rancid piss and water in the face. He was doused all over. He thought he would die. This was no way to treat a human being. In Catholic fucking Ireland. That bollix Thornton. He would pay for this. Let him just wait. He would make him pay. But then his bravado lessened as he shivered

"Can I have a word with the sergeant?" he quietly asked in what he thought was a humble tone

"No hope" said a garda." He has gone home and will be back about ten I the morning. But if you behave and do not tell the Sergeant on me I can get you a cup of tea" said the Garda.

"Thanks Guard. Any chance of a can of Lager?"

"Not a hope".

The sergeant came in at about ten and released the shivering Jimmy. Jimmy swore at the sergeant and said he woud be a sorry man for what he ha done. The sergeant laughed

"All I did was take you in for your own safety. You were a danger to yourself. Might have fallen in front of a car, Drunk and disorderly Breach of the peace. Right Guard?"

"Sure thing Sarge" said the Guard

"What about the bucket of dirty water? Jimmy asked

"What? What bucket of water?" asked the sergeant, "Well I never. Come on Mr Quinn.?

"Stop telling the porkies. It's the mind playing tricks. You had a few too many. Your imagination me boyo. Badly treated me eye. How many places will give you a cup of tea at 5 in the morning?. Sorry we had no bicuits" and he laughed

Then his whole tone changed "Mr James Quinn listen to me. Every time there is any shouting or any trouble in this town after dark I will hold you responsible and I will find a way of having you in here in "the cell" for a nice cup of our tea. No more shouting or acting the blackguard. I will blame you every time. Got it?"

Again Jimmy's vocabulary was limited

"Fuck you" and he left the room

But the town became a quieter place and people could sleep in their beds when to pubs closed and the dances were over.

Weeks later Mr Finneran the local solicitor phoned. When the sergeant heard who was calling he took the phone from the young guard.

"Is that yourself Mr Finneran? "He asked" Sergeant Thornton here. Mr James Quinn?When? Did we?. I must look it up. Send me your files and I might be able to find ours. Must be in the Superintendent's office. Me too.Lovely to hear from you" He put the phone down and gave the young guard a sly wink

Amonth later Mr Finnegan was on the phone again and the Sergeant took the call

"Lovely to hear from you again. No. We have not fotgotten.In the Supers Office. Yes I will tell hin you are not pleased. So busy. Its the Border duty you know. I hear you are Captain of the Golf Club. Great honour. The boys here say it is time we gave you all a visit up there, neglecting you we are. Ha ha indeed.When I was in Clontarf we had The Royal Dublin Golf Club on out patch. Yea, Great player he was.No one better than Our Christy O Connor. But do you know? Some high court judge objected and he complained to the Garda Commissioner and we were told to leave them alone. They could find their own way home and there was no need for the squad car to hang about. And all we were doing was our duty. Looking after them. Yes I know.I know, Might give you a wee visit. Good golf. Byee"

The Sergeant put the phone down and said

"That should keep him quiet for his year as captain" and he hummed a tune.

Sergeant Thornton was a very busy man. The trouble in The North and the border patrols had not started when he came to Donegal. Instead of spending time in his garden and with his wife and young children he was spending it in a squad car. Hours with young Gardai who who thought it was great fun to pass wind in the car and whose trousers smelt of stale piss. But his meeting with young Shane was what he enjoyed. Crime Prevention was the fancy name they had for it. Common sense was what he preferred. On Saturday nights he collected the car keys from certain people as they arrived in the town and told them to get a lift home ot to find a sober driver to drive their car and they could have the keys back. He never had a complaint and he was sure his name was often silently added to the Rosary Trimmings in many a kitchen

Shane stayed off the road. Back in Lochbeg he was getting restless. Eugene was annoying him

"Go on. Go on. Ask me any battle., Ask me the capital of any country" Mary had to intervene

"Shane does not care who won any battle. He is going to be a farmer and what he does is more important than the dates of battles. He can drive the tractor and milk the cow. So off you go and leave him alone and stop annoying him"

Shane came home with the news that dear old Master Byrne was about to retire. He was going back to Carrick to be with his relations

Fr Barry announced from the altar that the dear Master would soon be leaving to his well earned retirement and that the parish would like to make him a presentation. Fr Barry would set up a committee to organise a retirement party and anyone who wished to help would be most welcome.

They all knew Master Byrne was no great shining star. But he had served the people for as long as anyone could remember and they were fond of him. He opened his school every day for over 40 years. It was never openly said but they all accepted hat they were in his debt. He was always there. Even if it was only to help them fill in Government forms. He was part of their parish and now they would give him a good and well deserved farewell.

30

PEGGY'S MIND SETTLED down and she accepted that her daughter wa getting married to the man of her choice. And it was time for Aengus to go back to Dublin. He dreaded going back to the flat in Ranelagh as when he left it was very untidy but now things there would be chaotic. But he was surprised. The flat was neat and clean and tidy. Tipperary Pat said that was the way he liked things and with Aengus not there he was able to tidy the place as he liked and wanted. No offence meant. What really happened was that Pat's sisters asked to spend some of their holidays in the city and stay in Aengus' room

They were so digusted with the state of the whole flat that theyemployed a commercial cleaning agency to come and clean and fumigate the place and they hired a cleaner to come every week from then on. Aengus was so embarrassed and he thanked them.

But he was looking forward to meeting his ruffians again and from the way they greeted him it was clear they did not mind coming back to school He thought they would have grown bigger. They were the same size as six weeks ago!. But they had grown in other ways as he soon found out. Up to all the tricks. One evening his Heinkel would not start. He tried a running start. No good. He tried again and by now there was a good few looking on. He stopped. Exhausted. Then one of his boys came over and removed a carrot from the exhaust pipe to the applause from the watching gallery. Sure the poor Master was a Culchie from the back of nowhere

They were given back their old room as it was suitable for their Breakfast Club. Things were running smoothly now.The class was well trained and they followed the leader, The Master. They were well ahead of their class learning schedule but he wanted more. Manners and Consideration. Think about the people around you. He took them to Dalymount Park and to Croke Park on guided tours. Theywent to the Dublin Zoo, The National Museum, The National Library and the Narional Gallery. He led them round the paintings in the Gallery and then half the class was missing and he found them tittering at a Rubens.The Three Graces

"They was wearing no clothes sir" Aengus was a popular teacher in a depressed area only a few hundred yards fom the glitter of O Connell St

When he went back to Ranelagh he went to a different city.The residents of the flats and the bedsits and the boarding houses were not city people and they had no affiliation to the locality. They could be years in the street and never know their neighbour. Their relative affluence made them immune to comradeship.

His boys and their parents might be vagabonds and devil may cares but they had a humanity and a feeling for living and a feeling for each other. No Angels. But human beings who fought with each other and made peace. Interwoven and intermixed to form a close fabric ; in and out of each others apartments and rooms; No need ever to knock;borrow a cup of sugar or a jug of milk or in a crisis a few quid. They had nothing the pawnshops would value so they coped among themselves. A win In The Hospital Sweepstake was their dream and a couple of pints or six in Moloney's bar and Lounge at the weekend kept them going from week to week

Mass on Sunday from the back seats in the ProCathedral and a crafty fag out the back during the sermon was all that they needed to avoid The Mortal Sin. Nicknames, jeering, drunkenness. Laughing crying and always gabbing. Always talking. This was where O Casey and Behan learned their dialogue.

Aengus was in his element

Then he made a big mistake. He took them to the Christmas Pantomime in The Abbey Theatre. The parents wrere doubtful but the Master knows best. The Panto was in the Irish Language and the Dubs in the tenements had no great love of the Gaeilge. It was never mentioned but the poor of the city mocked and jeered at the IRA prisoners as they were marched down the docks on their way to English Jails after the 1916 Rising

It was not that they disliked the IRA or the Republicans but for Jasus' sake it had nothing to do with them. It was for that crowd out in Terenure and Rathmines. Republic me arse. It never helped to sell the apples in Moore St or buy the clothes for the childer. DeValera never called in to visit. Never. Big Jim Larkin was the only one who ever cared about them and he would have them all Communists. And in Holy Ireland!!!.

The Panto visit did not go well. At first the children were quiet but the Gaelic was beyond them and soon they were talking among themselves. There was a lot of shushing from the other theatre goers and the the children started giving the cast on the stage a shush as well. Poor old Joe Lynch had to come forward and do what William Butler Yeats did years before and ask them to be quiet. He did not say "You have disgraced yourselves again" as William Butler said but that was the end of the show, Cheers and shouting and they all went out on the street and then back home or to Moloneys

They held a meeting to discuss what went wrong. To their minds it was the Culchies in Cork or Kerry or in The West Of Ireland who got all that was going by way of Government grants and the like. Grants for speakin ' Irish. All this carry on about the Irish Language. It was left to the Dubs to look after themselves. No grants for speaking Dublinese

Aengus tried to explain that inner cities always suffered and had the poor. He mentioned London and the Cockneys and he was told it served the bastards right, Roight Roight.Mistake there thought Aengus. He should have said Paris

They went to Moloneys and had a few. They were into culture now. Maybe Brendan Behan himself might call in but he was going to McDaids up by the Green now. Posher crowd. Ever since "the Quare Fella" took off and he went on Television with his cousin Eamonn Andrews. Known to them all as Blessed Eamonn Android.

Tipperary Pat knew a place to go. St Mary's Irish Club. If you wanted the real Irish music. It was behind the Four Courts and the Bridewell. Aengus took himself there and he found his spiritual home. He dared not take his flute there as this was of a different quality. But as well as the beautiful music there was a strange undertow in the club. "Sean South of Garyowen" got a rousing reception and "My Name is O Hanlon" brought the roof down. There was a collection hat by the door but there ws no one attending to it. It may heve been on trust or just that no one paid anything in. It became one of his regular haunts and he was soon able to say that he sat next to Barney and Ronnie and other famous singers and players

Then he went to Connradh Na Gaeilge club in Harcourt St. Down the steps to the basement. They were all native Irish speakers but it was a different dialect to his own. They all seemed to come from Connemara and they spoke so softly in whispers. Not like the harsh and hard edge there was in his own Donegal dialect. He was told a poet from the Aran Islands was a regular there and a Professor from Trinity College but Aengus missed the lucky nights. He heard Dominic Behan sing a solo in the pub and he heard Patrick Kavanagh give a solo recital to the wall in Leesom St. late one night.Not for those of sensitive disposition.

Home again for the Easter holidays and Peggy was at ease. There was talk of Sinead coming home for a holiday. They were not sure if Yehudi was coming with her. Hudi they called him now and sure there were Hudies galore in Gweedore. Sinead sent photographs and Peggy was very relieved. No long black beard. He looked more Connemara than Jewish. He could have come from Rosmuc. Not that she was sure what a Jew should really look like.

Then it ws back to school for Aengus

Br Kevin called for him

"Well done Aengus. The best I have seen in my years of teaching. You have the rare gift of being an excellent teacher. But I have bad news. You must part with your class. Your class as it moves up will be taken by Brother Lynch. No fault of yours. It is The Brothers' policy. It makes for equality of teaching. Boys will meet excellent teachers like yourself and with luck they will meet very few poor teachers. But over the years it evens out and has they meet a variety of personalities it helps with their development"

Aengus sat down.

Br Kevin carried on "I can let you have any class you wish. 4th class? Good for the football'

Aengus was numb. To think of all the plans he had for his Jackeens, the little villians, the ruffians, the little devils, the vagabonds. And what would the children and the parents think? That he had abandoned them?. "Christian Brothers' policy" be damned.He felt betrayed. He knew he would always be looking to see how his old gang was getting on. OK, he was only theitr teacher for a few hours every day but they were part of his life now. He knew their strengths and their little weaknesses and he wanted to help and advise them as they grew older. Which boys to steer towards higher education and which to send to Paddy Gorman and his paint brushes.

Tipperary Pat picked out his mood and thought he was starting the flu'. After a few pints in Redmond's he started talking. He would have to leave. If he stayed it would happen again in another two years. It was too much to ask

Tipperary did not agree. He knew about these things. He had dated almost every student nurse in the Mater Hospital and he knew how these things happened

"Doctors and nurses do not get upset when a patient recovers and goes home. So snap out of it" he advised.

"Tipp you do not understand" Aengus said. "Doctors and nurses work as a team and there are others in the team. Almoners, physiotherapists and all that support. But I work on my own. Me and the class. No one else involved. I know the boys and I know their parents and I want more than teaching them the three Rs. I might be a fool with an idiot's dream. If I am, then I will have to find another occupation. But I cannot carry on in William St, and with the Christian Brothers. I will need to try my dream in another place

Aengus asked to meet again with Br Kevin. Br Kevin nodded and smiled weakly. He knew,

That horrible tea and powdered milk. Aengus asked for black coffee, Not a man for luxuries was Br Kevin

Br Kevin spoke first "Well Aengus let it all spill out. Just you and I. No one will ever know what passes between us"

Aengus repeated what he hadsaid to Tippereary Pat in Redmonds. His dreams and how he hoped to realise them.

"I am so sorry" said Br Kevin" but they are not my rules. For all I know I might be a cook next year in a Reform School in Letterfrack in the back of beyond. I am but a small cog in this organisation and my considerations carry no weight. That is how it is. You are one of the best teachers I have ever met and I would love to see how your class would develop with you as their master over the next four years"

"Is there any way around it?" asked Aengus

"No way. Life can be a bitch, which is the only word I am allowed to use"

Aengus thanked him and said "I would like to try a country school where I can be of use to the children and to the community. My own primary teacher was a man like that." Br Kevin spoke again

"A beautiful concept. A vocation. I was like that once but I signed away my destiny with a vow of Obedience. Now I do as I am told and to the best of my ability"

"Will you help me find a suitable post?" Aengus asked

"Indeed I will" Br Kevin said "I will write you a glowing reference and I will pass the word among our communities all over the country and let them tell me of anything available, even before it is advertised." Aengus applied for every job interview and he sent a SAE withhis applications. He got very few replies. When there was a vacancy the choice was limited by blood or by marriage.

At some interviews Aengus had to control his temper. Some doddery old priest would ask why he was unemployed. A young and fitman like him should find it easy to get employment. Why was he unemployed?. Had he dome something wrong?. All he could do was give them Br Kevin's personal phone number and ask that they have a chat with his former headmaster

One morning Br Kevin came running "Come come and see me. See me now. Now." He was bouncing with excitement

"perfect perfect, the very job the very job"

He is going to have a heart attack thought Aengus

"Sit down sit down" Br Kevin carried on "I was never so excited. This job is made for you. In your own county as well What could be better?" Aengus was of the opinion that certain places in Donegal were best avoided but Br Kevin was not having it.

He raised his hand and commanded silence

"Aengus not another word until I am finished. A three teacher school in East Donegal. A wee village called Garton not far from the border. Lifford and Strabane the nearest towns. The old teacher is retiring and going home to be with his relations. They have not advertised the vacancy. I know the parish Curate. He was the Chaplain in the Irish Centre in Camden Town and then I was with the Reform School in Dublin and he helped many of our boys get employment in London. Some who fell by the wayside owe him a lot for his help in getting their lives back together. We were friends back then and we have kept in contact ever since. Fr Barry Morris is his name and he knows where I am now and he has asked my help in finding him a teacher. Although he is only the Curate he is in effect the parish Priest as the old Priest nominally in charge is feeble and aged. We have had a chat on the phone and I have told him all about you and he would love to meet you and show you round and that you stay the weekend with him"

"Sounds good to me said Aengus "I will go up and meet him"

31

IT WAS MID morning when Aengus arrived at The Parochial House in Garton. He pulled a lever on thr door and he couuld hear bells clanging inside. A grey haired lady came to the door. The Priests' housekeer

"Yes?"

"I have come to meet Fr Morris"

"Who s shall I say it is?" the housekeeper asked

This was a housekeeper he could not tell as she would not be told any unnecessary information

"I have and appointment to meet him this morning. He is expecting me and he will know who I am'" Aengus told her

"Fr Morris, a gentleman to see you" she called up the stairs

"Coming, coming" a voice called and Fr Morris came bounding down the stairs. A fine big strong man just showing a few grey hairs

"Thank You Bridie" he said and he waited until Bridie had gone and closed the door behind her

"Aengus Gillespie" said Aengus

"Barry Morris" and they shook hands. "Welcome Aengus. You are very welcome and thank you for coming all this way. Come on up to my study"

Aengus looked around him. Brown linoleum, brown leather chairs, brown curtains and brown wallpaper. The stairs was brown as well. There was a stained glass window of an Irish Saint with his crozier and shamrocks sprouting behind him. It had got to be your man St. Patrick.

Then they entered Fr Morris' room. It was another world. It was a big and cheerful room with some Paul Henry prints on the walls and a Keating of an Aran

Islander over the fireplace. There was a framed picture of Paraic Pearse and a glass framed copy of the 1916 Proclamation in position on another wall. He had two well filled bookstands and in the corner a radiogram and a television. There was a divan bed by the back wall away from the big bay window and a portable gas heater. There was a firegusrd with a picture of the General Poat Office in Dublin and it looked as if the fire was never a regular fire in the grate

"Tea or coffee? Asked Fr Morris

"Tea please"

Fr Morris went over to a side table and plugged in the kettle and they settled down with the teapot and a packet of chocolate buiscuits.

"I do not bother Bridie too much "Fr Morris said." She cooks a main meal at lunchtime every day and if we are out we let her know. She comes in every Saturday to do a bit of baking for the Canon. Soda bread for him and shortcake for me. I cook the breakfast for myself and the Canon. Not much. Before I start I prefer to be called Fr Barry. The Morris bit is open to all sorts of remarks

Br Martin has told me all about you and what you have achieved in Wiliam St. A light in the Darkness. And much more. Let me tell you what we have to offer here in Garton"

And for the next hour or more he went into details of what he had in mind for the patrish

"Br Kevin has told me how you like to play an active part in the community. In the parish in this case" Fr Barry said

"Yes" said Aengus "In my own case it was a teacher called Master Kennedy in Gweedore. He changed the lives of so many people over the years and I would like to think I can do the same"

"We are on the same wavelength" the priest replied and he let Aengus carry on and reveal his soul. He told the priest what he had in mind and how disillusioned he was when he was not allowed to follow his dream in Dublin

They went over to see the school and Aengus was impressed, Three classrooms and a toilet at either end, and spare room for storage, a good sized yard to play in and a corrugated shelter at the far end of the yard. There was a good concrete wall round the whole site and a gated entrance at the front on to the road. Compact and complete

"I would like you to meet the other two teachers" said Fr Barry. "Mrs Collins is married to a local farmer and Mrs Brady's huasband works in the Council Offices in Lifford. Both are settled and there will be no resentment at your coming.

What do you think? Would you like to be Principal Teacher at Garton National School?" he asked

"Yes I would" said Aengus

"Done" said Fr Barry and they shook hands

They went back to the Parochial house and signed the bnecessary papers and Fr. Barry said they should call on the two lady teachers who were to be his assistant teachers.

"I would like to meet Mr Byrne as well" Aengus said and that was arranged.

Fr Barry had a word with Bridie and they called on Mrs Collinss and on Mrs Brady. After the obligatory cups of tea they were on their way again.

They collected Master Byrne and they went to the Hotel. It was a long and leisurely dinner. They all had stories to share and tell. Fr Barry told of his attendance at the Irish music sessions in Church St and at The Maples Hotel in Glasnevin. Aengus regaled them with his time on the buses and on the building site in London. Fr Barry came back with his time doing Philosophy in U.C.D. and his time in Camden Town

Master Byrne was a slow started but after a couple of glasses of wine and a wee drop of the craythur he was in full flow. He told of 40 years teaching in the parish. It was local history coming alive. They saw the master safely home after a great night out.

"You stay the night. I told Bridie to make up a bed for you and your breakfast will be at 8am

Aengus did not sleep much. He was down at 8 for his breakfast to find Fr Barry with the frying pan

"I always do the breakfast when I am here and I take the Canon something to eat as well. Bridie does it when I am away and that is how we manage. The Canon stays in his room most of the time and the Bishop told me that was what the elderly and frail man wanted and that I was my own boss here as long as he was informed of any major changes. Suits me fine. I love it here."

Aengus went back to Ranelegh on Sunday a happy man. Fr Barry sounded all right. He knew of teachers whose managers did not speak to them, never mind helping to run the school. But not here in Garton. He and the priest would get on fine

On Monday he called in to see Br Kevin. He said thet he knew everything already

"I might have guessed" said Aengus a littje piqued, But then it was Br Kevin who got him the job and that was how the system works. So get on with it.

Br Kevin wished him well "I am delighted for you. I know you will have a great life in Garton. Fr Barry is a good man. I am sorry to lose you. My best wishes go with you"

Aengus did not wish his class to know until nearer the time and he got the usual

"Any Indians? John Wayne know you are coming? Smoke signals?"

But the real question was "Will you ever come back and see us again?"

"Don't be silly." Aengus told them. "Donegal is only a three hours by motorcar and there is a bus up and down from there twice every day" he said but he had to turn about and face the window. No point in letting them know ho much he was going to miss the little rascals

He told the members at Na Fianna that he would be leaving. They took it in their stride, That was the way things happened when country men played in Dublin. They come and they go, No great deal.

But word soon got out that he was leaving and some of the committee decided to have a farewell do. They ordered a cargo of Kentucky Fried Chicken to be delivered to the Clubhouse and washed it down with the beer, There was a general feeling that Aengus would be missed and they all wished him well

Des Shanley came over and asked

"When did you decide to go to Donegal? All a bit sudden this, isn't it?"

Aengus was a bit embarrassed that he had not kept Des in the picture but they had not met recently

"It really only came up in the last few weeks" he lied

"I had a girlfriend from Donegal once "Des said." Hannah Robinson. We send each other Christmas Cards but I supposew she has another boyfriend now. Nice lass she was, Very nice. Well you know where I live and never come to Dublin without giving me a call. Remember that"

They shook hands and Des went on his way

Aengus got a letter from Fr Barry saying that he had arranged digs for him in the same house as Master Byrne until he was settled in and then he could make his own arrangements

Then who came to the classroom door but Paddy Gorman. Sober as a judge and he informed Aengus that they were having a farewell hooley in Moloneys Bar and Lounge and that "his presence was expected". Paddy was very proud of those words as he had been practising them all day in front of the mirror. His wife Mary told him not to be such "a silly old goose"

Aengus turned up to his farewell party. It was a long night. The beer and the whiskey flowed and the craic was "odious" as they say in Monaghan.

It was a noisy night

Then Paddy Gorman stood up and banged his glass on the table ans called

"Ordther Ordther. Quiet if yez please, Ordther" and he banged the table again

They were ready to listen

"No if yez doint moind I would loike to say a few words" Paddy began

"Thank you Paddy, thems enough words now" someone said

He ignored the remark

"As yez know Oi am not much good at the speechin'

Not much good at the fuckin' paintin' either" a voice from the back said

This called for a reply and Paddy said

"Its all right Jimbo. You are in Moloney's and it is Friday night"

Paddy looked over at Aengus and said

"Poor old Jimbo. Not the full shilling" and he gave Jimbo a wink

"Well as oi was sayin' and Oi tank yez all for not buttin' in, "Paddy went on "this man Finn, sorry Master Aengus Gillespie is the best master in the world A remarkable master"

"Speak English Paddy. We dont do remarkable. Where was you reared?"

But Paddy carried on

"One of the best,. One of the very best. One of the best"

"needle stuck in the record" someone shouted. "Not an LP we hope"

Paddy carried on "one of the best. One of the best" He looked down at Mary

"Mary Mary, I said that twice. Have you got the speech in your handbag?

Then he appealed to them

"Will yez listen?" he wailed. "A man is doing his best. I aint no orator"

"An orator. An orator. Where do they sell dem tings?Not on the stalls. Get him. A fuckin' orator". General laughter and merriment

They had their fun. And that was enough. Paddy was one of their own and they wold never want to humiliate him. Good heart has our Paddy. They listened as he rambled on

"Finally" he said to a murmur of assent "I would loike to present him with a Dublin County G.A.A. Jersey" and he waited for the cheering "and a Shamrock Rovers one as well. That was a signal for wa few verses of "Molly Malone" from his listeners. "And she wheeled her wheelbarrow"

Aengus knew what was expected. He thanked them all for the wonderful leaving party. He told them of the great honout he had in teaching their wonderful children and how much he enjoyed teaching the little rascals. He thanked the parents for their support in everything he tried to do and for painting and decorating his classroom. He was leaving because of events that were beyond his control and as for the two lovely jerseys they had presented to him he had his doubts. After what the Dublin team had done to the Donegal team and the thrashing the Shamrock Rovers had given Finn Harps he would only feel safe to wear the jerseys in bed

"Finally" he concluded "I would like to say one thing. Paddy Gorman is an orator. An Orator, and Orators are hard to find. So treat him well" and he started on "For he's a jolly Good fellow"

Aengus teaching career in Dublin had come to a pleasant end.

32

FR BARRY TOLD them all from the Altar that he was giving Maaster Byrne a farewell party and that anyone who wished to help was welcome. Everyone and anyone joined in a frenzy of baking, pie making and sherry trifles. Fr Barry invited Aengus to come but he declined. This was Master Byrne's big night and all the attention was his. The big surprise of the night was Macra na Feirme. The Young Farmers. Posh title but they were only sons of local smallholders who sometimes met for a pint in Cooney's bar. But on Master Byrne's night they turned up early with a tar barrel sawn in half and they lit a fire in it and roasted a piglet over the red hot coals. Roast Hog they said it was. Very popular in New Zealand they said. Fr Barry had intended that there be no alcohol but looking after Hog Roast was thirsty work and there was a crate of stout in the car boot. Who would deny them?

The hall was full and alive. Past pupils who seemed as old as the master himself. With the donations he collected Fr Barry presented The Master with a music centre. A radio, a tape recorder and a record and a tape player all in one. Modern science in action, and with the quiet monies that he had been given there was a nice cheque as well.

Fr Barry read out all the telegrams of congratulation and good wishes to Master Byrne. From all over the world. New Zealand, Australia, Boston Tanzania and the list went on. There was a telegram from Shikoku

"That is in Japan" Fr Barry told them "It is from little Sammy Kelly who is now Mr Samuel Francis J. Kelly and who is President of Sumoko Corporate Finance"

That made them listen.

And now they would soon have a new Master. Would he change things? Would he stay? From Dublin. Would he miss the City lights?

"He is from Gweedore" someone said. That raised an eyebrow or two. Know anyone from Gweedore?. Some of therse Gweedore men can be a handful. Remember the time Garton Gaels player Gweedore and that redheaded madman almost crippled Francie Cooney with his knee. Rough and tough they were. When the Cooney brothers stopped playing no one else bothered and Garton Gaels just died a slow death. The old field and the ball alley was still there but it was only used for pitch and toss after Sunday Mass and the odd kick about around the broken goalposts.

But this new master might be a footballer. That woulsd be great. But they would have to wait and see

33

SHANE WAS ALMOST afraid to play on the new Accordeon. He christened it Liam so he would think of his uncle every time. He played in front of the mirror delighting in how well he looked. He was shy to take it to Doherty's but Fr Barry insisted. Omagh was very interested and he asked if he could have a go on it.He made magic. The fairies themselves could dance to him. Shane was in awe but Omagh told him not to be so silly but to go home and practise. Practise, practise. They taped Omagh playing a few reels and hornpipes and Shane was told to learn the runs and little additions to the melodies. Slow down. Slow down. Some musicians go hammer and tongs. As if they were in a race.Donegal musicians are too fast and too hectic. Too wild. Let the melodies have time to sink in. Give the brain time to register, Not mad and wild like the Atlantic storms over the mountainsides but soft and leisurely like the gentler Summer breezes so one can appreciate the perfume of the flowers

Technique can be learned but feeling needed sympathy and soul. From the inner soul. Maguire was a great fiddler but his playing lacked soul was Omagh's opinion. He might have a point there.

Fr Barry encouraged Shane and they practised together and they taped their duets. By now Shane was a regulat altar boy and Fr Barry was surprised how quickly he mastered the Latin responses. Eugene was sworn to silence when he came home on holidays. It would not do if the prieat heard of a vestment bed sheet around the shoulders and a jam jar as a chalice and Shane saying the Latin responses.

All was fine until politics reared its head.

Neil said the Holy father was talking rubbish

"You mean to say that there was no need at all for the 1916 Rising?" asked a puzzled Fr Barry "But you fought in it"

Yes I did" answered Neil. "We in The Irish Volunteers had no option. When the British murdered the 1916 men we were made IRA men overnight. And we fought the British Army, We attacked an army barracks and shot the odd soldier or policeman"

"That's what won us our freedom" said Fr Barry "the bravery of the Republicans against superior forces and that forced the British out"

"Hold on there a minute" said Neil "Just think back. Redmond and Dillon had been promised Home Rule. It was passed by the Commons and not by the Lords. But the rules were changed and Home Rule for Ireland was in the pipeline. There was going to be Home Rule for the awhole of the island. The Orangemen objected and they formed the Ulster Volunteers to oppose their being part of Home Rule for the whole Island. They did not wish to be part if it. Now the Orangemen then would have to fight the British if they wished to get their own way. There could have been an Ireland in the Commonwealth. A state of Ireland. There might have been a seperate State or dominion in the North of Ireland but still part of the Commonwealth State of Ireland. The Border question might have never arisen as it has now. There might have been no War of Indrepedence and no horrendous Civil War"

But" said Fr barry "If there had been no Rising we would not have got a Reopublic"

Neil was sharp "We did not get a Republic. At that time the British Empire was past its best and we would have been given what Canada and Australia were given. It was 1947 before we declared we were a Republic and it was not announced from the Dail but from somewhere in Canada. To be truthful no one cared a damn by then"

Fr Barry was not finished "When Carson and Bonar Law started their campaign DeValera and Collins knew that armed forces and a Rebellion was the only thing that would work"

Neil replied "You know DeValera never wanted a Rising"

"Don't believe you" said Fr Barry

Neil carried on' "DeValera was a young teacher out in Blackrock College. He was born in America and was sent home to Limerick to live with his uncle. He only joined the Gaelic league because he fancied Sinead Flanagan who taught Irish at their place in Parnell Sq. He later married her"

"Yes but DeValera fought in the Rising and was in command of and defended Boland's Mill" said Fr Barry

"You are right there" said Neil "but the IRB took over the Gaelic league and the Irish Volunteers and used them. DeValere joined the IRB but he soon resigned. He really was a pacifist and a pragmatic politician. He had a great desire for Irish freedom and he wanted to help achieve it. He was a true IRA man. A patriot. And during the Civil War he kept his head below the parapet"

Fr Barry asked "You mean De Valera was never a man for the gun?"

"Yes Indeed I do. DeValera had to carry the extreme Republican faction with him and he talked Republican but he was a pacifist, Later on when he was in power he had some of the gunmen interned at The Curragh and he had one or two executed"

"He would never have signed the North away like Collins did" said Fr Barry

"What else could any of them do?" asked Neil" force the Unionists into a Republic. The Ulster Volunteers had about 120.000 men, all armed. The IRA and the IRB was a rag and bone outfit. Not a hope in hell. Not a hope

Even Collins, the Big Fella knew that partition was inevitablle and he wanted to use it as a step on the way to complete unity of Ireland"

"Neil" said Fr Barry "you do surprise me. I respect your viewsand we might agree to differ"

"Yes and there is a lot more you should know and they will not tell you the truth. Sometimes it is better not to know. All this trouble on the Border. It breaks my heart to see Irishmen shoot and kill each other" Neil said

Fr Barry did not concede "It will all be worth it if we get a 32county Republic. A United Ireland" he said

Neil shrugged "Yes I would like a United Ireland. If only to end all the bitterness and the murdering. But I can tell you it will make no difference to anyone living here in Garton. The same crowd will take over and we will not see any difference. But we must accept Orangemen as true Irishmen now.They are as much Irish as the Kerrymen. They insist they are British. Of course they do. But if you ask a German or a Spaniard what Nationality the Orangeman is, they will say 'Irish'. They cannot change that they are Orangeman and we cannot change that they are Irishmen. The Orangemen have been here over 400 years and there is not a person in America who can claim that length of American heritage"

But Fr Barry protested" do you not think the Catholics in the North deserve our help.? They are the underprivilged"

"Underprivileged?" snorted Neil "they get free education up to university level, free medicine and a fine old age pension. And what have we got here? Nothing. Nothing. Only the fat cats and the poor. In this country the only people we know who are privileged are the people who are related to the political party men. Even the judges here are political appointments"

Fr Barry thought it was time to quit.He was very surprised with what he had just heard from a man who knew what had happened and who had his own ideas and who would not easily alter them. The War of Independence and the Civil War had left a deep mark on Neil's soul. He wondered how many old IRA men had their idealism beaten out of them and were now embittered over the whole system

"Does not know what he is talking about" was what Neil said to his wife Mary after Fr Barry had gone

But they remained friends and had many a good chat. No politics. They were both interested in Ancient Irish history and folklore. There was the old Beltony Stone Circle near Raphoe and that was just over the hill from Lochbeg. The old Celts might have lived by the lake. And so life went on

Eugene came home sometimes on his holidays and Shane was slowly paying back the Credit Union his debts. Mary offered to settle his account with The Credit Union but Fr Barry said it was bertter that Shane do it himself in his own time. Accordingto his business plan. It gave him a good whatever. Profile they called it.

With his new power saw Shane tried to sell logs. Hannah Robinson did not want them but she told him how to have leaflets printed and to pussh them through letterboxes in the town and soon he ahad enough clients, He did not want to ruffle Sergeant Thornton's feathers again and he had Neil as delivery man and drive the tractor and trailer.

Then Master Byrne retired. Poor old Master Byrne. Shane liked him. The Master knew that Shane had no great love of the learning and he let him go on his own way. There was none of "your brother would have" or "your brother did". All Master Byrne said was "carry on". It was Shane's last year at school when the new master came. Master Aengus Gillespie. Funny name that Aengus Was it foreign? Japanese or Indian?. And he spoke wit a funny accent as well. Half Donegal with a touch of Dublin. Barney McCool of Coolaghey and Ronnie Drew of the Dubliners,. And he spoke Irish so fast that they duid not know what he was saying. Then he would slow down when he saw the look on their faces. Shane did not mind as he would be leving school before Christmas

Master Gillespie and Fr Barry seemed very pally and Fr Barry was always dropping in for a chat, Master Gillespie was a good footballer and there was talk he might start a team in the village. Shane hoped Fr Barry would put in a good word for him. Shane would give anything to play for a proper football team. A proper team with jerseys and numbers and on a proper football field. He had been to McCool Park and he was bored. But a Garton team would be something else.

When Master Aengus asked who would like to come and train and form a football team Shane's was the first hand to shoot into the air. There wa a giggle round the room

"Whats so funny?" Aengus asked

"He is no good sir. He is too rough and he gives free kicks away when there is a referee"

Aengus looked again at this young tyke. Not bad for a start. Rough I can smoothe and fashion. I can mould and shape the rough. Plenty of that will suit. He went over to the lad and put his hand on his shoulder

"Good man Shane. I will put you down for training"

The new Master had made a friend for life

34

AENGUS CAME BACK to Garton a week early. He ad been appointed to the post on the last week of term before the Sunmmer holidays but he did not need to attend the school as Master Byrne was still in charge. This arrangement was made so that Aengus would be paid during the Summer holidays. So Aengus was back to an empty school on his first visit as principal teacher. He spent the time tidying up the playground\and his own classroom. He swept the floor and washed to windows. He did not go near the other rooms. Mrs Collins and Mrs Brady were rulers of their own domain and were to be treated with respect and kindness. He had his note book and he jotted down his thoughts and ideas, He cut up a white shoe box and made his name tags as he did in William St. and waited for the first Monday of his new teaching career

Mrs Collins said it was the first time in all her years teaching that no one was late for school on that Monday. The children were sitting on the school wall when Aengus arrived and they went straight to their desks

"How did they know where to sit?.Thay are all in a higher class this year" Aengus asked

"Master Byrne had us all arranged in our new places the last week before he retired "he was told

Now they were ready and watching. There was only one class that was new to Aengus room. They were the class that had moved up from Mrs Collins room. Mrs Brady's room was the biggest room in the school. She took the infant classes who roamed about freely as they got used to being at school. Then Mrs Collins took over from Mrs Brady and the children were in to formal learning. First Communion and reading and writing and the dreaded tables were recited in a sing song by the whole class in unison. One gets used to the noise.

Aengus assembled all the children in Mrs Brady's room. Three to a desk, sitting on the floor between desks and around the walls. He stood by the teacher's table and looked around the room. All those innocent and wide eyed little faces. This is what he was born for. He had come home. He felt weepy and he had to wait. He saw Mrs Collins look over at Mrs Brady and smile. She knew how he was feeling. He cleared his throat and started

"My name is Aengus Gillespie. Aengus may be a strange name to you. Aengus was an old Irish warrior and he awas a friend of Finn McCools. You call me Mr Gillespie or just Master and I will call you by your first names. Your Christian name. Mrs Brady and Mrs Collins and myself will be looking after you all every day here in this school. We will all be great friends. But we will all work hard and we will enjoy our work. If there is anything worrying you please come and tell me. If there is anything we teach you and you do not understand it then please ask us to explain it again. You are very lucky children to have Mrs Brady and Mrs Collins to look after you. And Fr Barry as well. Now you all know where your seats are and go there quietly. No pushing or shoving. Quietly."

They went to their seats and he held a roll call. There were missing names but they were pupils who had left. He handed out his tags and he had them write their names and soon all was done

"Do not take your name tags home" he said. He remembered Dublin.

It was all new to him. Three classes in the same room. He never had that before and he had never read a textbook on how to manage. They were at different levels, He set one class to transcribe from theit Reader, anothr to do sums from their arithmetic book and he started reaching the third class in the room

He drew a map of Donegal on a blackboard and he put a big X where Garton was. Then he put another X where Gweedore was and he said

"This is where we are now in Garton and this is where I am from Gweedore"

There was agroan fro the back of the class and they all tittered

"Who likes Gweedore so much?" Aengus asked. A boy at the back raised his hand and lowered his head but Aengus was able to read his name tag

"Shane" he asked "Why do you not like Gweedore?"

"Because they always win at the football sir" Shane said

"Well Shane, you and I might be able to change that" Angus said and he left it at that

He saw how the three classes in on room worked. Those doing the arithmetic and the transcription were listning to what he was teaching the other class. They were learning by osmosis as it were.

Lunchtime came and they spilled out into the playground. They had their sandwiches and soon they were running all over the yard;

The day was soon over. He was exhausted. He had been a bit emotional he supposed. Even if he lasted as long as Master Byrne he doubted if he ever would have a better day. But it was not over yet. Fr Barry called in.

"I was going to give you a couple of weeks to settle in, But I could not wait. How are things?"

Aengus scratched hisbhead "Do not get me wrong. I am not going to say all is perfect. No offence but do not expect me to keep my mouth shut"

"Gotcha" said the priest. "I can see this is going to be a wonderful combination. Holy Mother of God you are here only four hours and you have me all nervous. What is on your mind? Hit me now"

Arngus quietly said

"I want radiators in the classrooms"

"You must be joking" was all Fr Barry could say

"No joking Father. No frozen children in my school" Aengus said

"But we do not have radiators in the Parochial House" said Fr Barry

"More fool you. Beg your pardon Father. That was out of order. Uncalled for. Sorry Father" Aengus apologised

"No no not at all. But radiators? That is far and beyond my remit" Fr barry protested

"Well then" said Aengus "some heat in every room. Gas is not suitable for children and as you inply radiators are too expensive but I thought electric wall heaters might be the answer"

"Funds might stretch to that" were the actual words that Fr Barry said and they were words that he might hear repeated to his face many times in the years to follow.

Then he made one of the greatest mistakes in his life whan he asked

"Anything else?"

Aengus was away" A water heater for hand washing, a cooker for the spare room,. Tarmac for the playground and an outside shelter, an electric kettle or two, a good sized dining table, the Public Library bus to call once a month and if you have any money left an extension by the front door"

Angus then took out his note book

"Enough Enough" cried Fr Barry "I have gone dizzy"

"You did ask" said Aengus "but I do not need them all today. I might be here for a long time". They smiled at each other. They both understood.

Aweek later there was aknock on the door. An elderly man stood there. He said nothing. He looked at Aengus

"Good morning" Aengus ventured. Might as well see if it speaks

"You the principal teacher?" the man asked

"Yes I am. What can I do for you?

"Priest said you needed heaters"

"Yes we do"

"What kind?"

"Radiant heaters"

"Where?"

Life and soul of the party this man. Laugh a minute

Aengus spoke "Where ever you think is the best place. I will take your advice on that"

David Robinson, for it was he, grunted into his overcoat and took a jotter from his pocket. He looked up and around the room and Aengus saw his face clearly. It could have been carved from a bar of soap. A block of Sunlight. Not a muscle moved and those big dead eyes. Had he not blinked you would never know there was anyone at home. Tall and stooped and a strange yellowish skin. Foreign? Might have Indian blood.British troops served in India. But the few words he spoke were definite Donegal and Lagan Valley

Mr Robinson went round all the rooms with his tape measure and his jotter. He was in no hurry and he double checked every measurement. The children were quiet and silent as thay watched

Then he spoke

"Thats all. Send a man to fit next week" and he was gone.

Aengus was no wiser. But the children knew who he was and they told Aengus about the Robinsons and their shop. A man arrived the following week and fitted the wall heaters and Aengus stayed on after school to help him complete the job

Aengus called in on Fr Barry to be told that was his lot for the year and he would have to raise any other money himself. The parish kitty was empty. Cupboard bare. But Aengus had been there before. No rush. No hurry, And so the year went on. Two senior boys left school. One was the cheeky chappie, Shane who wanted to be a footballer and whose brother was Master Byrne's claim to fame.Shane might be going to the Technical College. The other boy would hang about the house at home. He might as well have stayed on at school. Pity. Again money was the problem. He had no hope of getting a job until he had grown bigger and stronger and then it would be London or Birmingham

Aengus set about looking after his school. Money was again the problem. He might cadge a few pounds off some of the locals but they would remember and avoid him thereafter. It was back to the old reliable raffle. He had the tickets printed and the boys set about selling them all over the parish. Na Fianna returned his ticket stubs with a nice cheque and their best wishes. He sent a few books to Ollie Freaney and he got a cheque for £100 and a nice letter hoping he was enjoying the bog and not to bother coming back to the City. Ollie wished him well and that he stay as faraway from him as possible

Even with the wall heaters he decided they needed a fire in the fireplaces. The electricity bill was causing Fr Barry some ache. He bought some turf and who should arrive at the door but young Shane O Neill and asked if Aengus would buy a trailer load of logs. Good price. Special price for the Master. Change the accent and he could have been in Moore St. A few months ago he was in the back seat of the class doing his spellings and here he was doing his dealer act. The bold boyo. Aengus bought a trailer load and he promised he would buy more when he had the funds

"We do never never" the cheeky monkey said as he walked away with his hands in his pockets. Tony O Reilly had better look out and Charlie Clore might mind his back as well.

One of the parents dropped in a load of turf and Aengus had enough for the year and Fr Barry was happy

Poor Fr Barry. Aengus had other things on his mind and the priest did not know it yet, No hurry Aengus thought. God but he was enjoying this. Living on the limit. Today was fine and tomorrow was not bad but in the distance and in the long run he would have to survive and survival was success in the game Aengus played.

35

H E WAS GOING to train for a team A real team. a Garton team. Shane was delighted. He was always told he was never any good, Eugene kept on saying it. Now he would show them. He might never score great goals like Kevin Heffernan or Sean Purcell but not many will get past him on the field. Bill Shankly would describe him as an outstanding stopper. Yes he would. He looked up at the master in devout gratitude and he saw the master was smiling to himself

Then his school career ended very quietly. No fuss or cermony. It was just that one Monday morninghe did not have to go to school. So he lay on in bed. Then he rose and wandered about the yard, Then he wandered up to the loch and had a look around. Then he came back to the house and he had a cup of tea. Then he sat by the unlit fire and he switched on the radio. Gay Byrne was wittering on about how wonderful he himself was. Shane was bored. He got on his bike and cycled in to the town. He was going to be a farmer. But he knew very little about farming. Suppose he had better learn something. He went to the lending library.

"Good morning, May I be of assistance" asked a white haired lady with her hair tied back in a bun

"I have left school and I want to be a farmer" he said

"Now that is a wonderful ambition" the lady said and she smiled

"Where can I learn farming?" he asked

"Well I really am not sure. There are Agricultural colleges and there is The Albert College attached to University College Dublin" she said

"Dont want any college" Shane was nervous. All he wanted was to be a farmer. Not to learn at a college. The nice lady called out

"Mr Mullarkey" and a man came from behind. He had an important air about him. Thick horn rimmed glasses and his hairwas brylcreemed flat on his head with a mid forehead parting

"This young man wants to be a farmer and he wants to know where he can learn farming" the lady said

"Thank you Matilda, I will look after him now" Mr Mullarkey said and he looked at Shane

"Come over here and we can sit down and have a chat"

Mr Mullarkey was a kind man and he listend to Shane. Then he suggested that Shane go to the Department of Agriculture office. It was where the Agricultural advisors worked from. The Ags, as they were known locally

"You cannot miss it" Mr Mullarkey said" It has all the Volkswagons parked outside"

Shane had no trouble finding it he went through to an inner door and knocked

"Yes come in "he heard and there were four men very busy studying their desks. There was a steaming coffee cup on each desk and fags still smoking in the ashtrays. They listened to his story and they told him they had no idea how they could help him. Their job was the artificial insemination, land drainage, stock numbers. They knew nothing at all about farming. Again they repeated the names he heard in the library.

"No good "Shane said" where can I learn farming here in the Finn valley?.

Here. Not in Dublin. Here at home" Shane pleaded

Jesus he is just a child they thought. Just out of the Primary school What can we do to help him?.

"Give us your name and address and come back next week and we will have some information that might be of use to you. We will have a discussion among the staff and we will see what we can come up with.Leave it with us and we will see you next week"

Next week they were more prepared

"We know where you live and we know who you are and your family situation, Fr Morris is one of out rural contacts. We think that the first thing you will need is some bookkeeping. No need to look alarmed. Nothing fancy. Just to know what money is coming in and what money is being paid out"

Another man chipped in "You will need to know how the tractor works. A bit of motor mechanics will come in useful. Self repairs on the spot are important so welding is in the plan. General farming around the farm you can pick up from your father Neil"

They know my fathers name thought Shane and he felt a bit uneasy

They carried on "If you ever need any help please come in here. We might not know much but we know how to find what we are looking for. We have been in contact with the local Technical School and we think you should give them a visit"

That word School again. But one of them said

"No need to worry. Juat call over and have a chat with Mr Monaghan the headmaster. He is a pleasant man and we have told him about you and he is anxious to meet you. You will make him a happy man if you go over to meet him."

Shane went to the Technical School and there ws a message that Mr Shane O Neill was to go to Mr Monaghan's home residence

Mrs Monaghan met Shane at the door and treated him like a long lost friend. She had tea and biscuits readty for them as they sat in the lounge. Then Mrs Monaghan left Shane and her husband together to have "their little chat"

Mr Monaghan took out a biro and a notepad

"I am ataking notes." he said "Not of anything you say but to remind me in case I forget anything important"

He went through Shane's case in great detail. Not for his own curiosity he said but to decide what was best for Shane's future. Then he said

"Shane I have all the information here in my notebook. It is confidential I will not divulge anything personal you have told me. But I would like to discuss with my staff as to how we can help you best. We need to arrange a timetable so that your sessions do not clash. Come and see me next week and I will have something definite for you. But before you go let me remind you that we are not pressing you to do anything we say. It is entirely your decision and whateever you decide to do we will help you"

Shane went home and he told his father what had happened and what he had done. Neil agreed that he was on the right track and that he should continue with his" plan." He nearly said the dreaded word "education" but it was gradually appearing to Shane that the Tech was another form of School and he had enough of school. It was true that he knew some of the other lads at the Tech and they did not think of themselves as scholars. Fr Barry was having difficulty with a hornpipe and he called to see Shane for advice. He tried the melody over and over again but still it was not right

"Suppose you are a busy man now Shane, a full time farmer" he said and he still did not get the melody right

"Not that busy. My father was able to manage when I wa still at school and he can manage just as well now. I just hang about mostly. Not doing that much"

Fr Barry was really concentrating on his playing

"maybe you should go to the Tech for a few sessions". He was careful not to use the word lessons as had been Mr Monaghan.Shane looked at him hard and long. But the music was really difficult and Fr Barry was bent over his banjo mandolin.

Was this all organised?. Was Fr Barry up to his tricks again. Maybe Omagh was in on it as well and even Liam that time when he was at home. To get him back to the Tech. Back to school. Were the seeds planted over the years and the idea was not his own at all?.

Next day he mantioned to Neil hoew helpful thhey all were in town. Helping him to get the right sessions in the Tech.

"Aye son Right there" was all Neil said and when he mentioned it to his mother she just said "right there son" as well

One night at the table he said he was going to give the Tech a try and they saidin unison "whatever you want son". They might have been practising.

But now his mind was made up and he was ready for his destiny. It was his own decision and he would no longer be the dummy in the house. Maureen was doing well in the Convent and so was Eugene. He would show them. Maureen was definite she would be a nurse and Shane often took her on the tractor to catch the train. Surely Sergeant Thornton would not be up and about that early in the morning. Maureen was a great student and she helped with the housework as well. But in the last few months she was having trouble. In this her final year at the Convent her train had her late on the same day for the same lesson every week. It was not her fault as that was when the train arrived. But the nun could not see that and Maureen was being told off and she was getting upset. Fr Barry heard them discussing the problem and they shut up as he came nearer. Things changed and Maureen was allowed to sneak in to the back of the class without any word of reprimand. Some might put it down to the candles Mary lit in front of Blessed Martin De Porres or even to the power of prayer in general. But sometimed God Himself needs a wee nudge and bit of a push and Fr Barry was yer man. Aye indeed.

36

AENGUS HAD FINISHED his sandwiches and he was looking out on the schoolyard. The boys were playing football. He remembered his own schooldays and a lad who was magic with a tennis ball at his feet. Last week he read that the same lad had scored the winning goal for Glasgow Celtic.

There did not appear to be any future stars playing in Garton School playground but there were some very muddy boys who came in for lessons after the break. The state of their clothing and their shoes. He tried to clean them up and dry them off and when he suggested that they not play at lunchtime and that he would take them to the football field they were delighted

They played twice a week on the field. In the evening after school. No football jerseys or shorts but at least they could change when they went home. Some tried to play in their bare feet. "Can run faster sir" but the pigskin ball was too heavy and Aengus got a lighter ball. They were having such a great time that some of the older girls asked if they might be allowed to play as well. "Even as Goalkeeper sir?". No.

Fr Barry heard about this new development and he often came along to watch. When the boys saw him o the sideline they raised their game. A clap fron The Father invited a swagger and the chest expended. It was the Garton version of The Papal Blessing

"You think we might get it going again?" Fr Barry asked

"Dunno" said Aengus and he waited. It was his dream. "they had a great team here years ago" said Fr Barry "when the Cooney brothers were playing. It would be mighty to get it going again"

"Why not?" said Aengus "whatdya think?""

"If you are, then so am I" said the priest "the genes must still be there. We could start with the juveniles. It will not be easy. Finn Harps are just up the road and Soccer is easier to start with than the Gaelic football. You ready to give it a try?" he asked and he looked at Aengus. Aengus put his hand on Fr Barry's shoulder and softly said

"let us dream our dream. Let it begin"

And so they started their journey. Where it would end was part of the magic. A Juvenile team and maybe a Minor team but a Senior Team was not feasible. Emigration would have taken its toll by that age and there were no incomers as there was in the bigger towns and cities,. But dream on dream on. The word was passed round. That the Garton team was being reborn. Out of the attics and the garden sheds and back rooms came a motley collection of jerseys and togs and socks. A patch added here and a bit of darning there and a team took to the field. Football boots were the problem. They were expensive to buy. And boots had to fit. Some of the boyslooked and walked like ducks as they came on the field wearing boots a few sizes too big

Aengus did what he was best at. He went on the scrounge. He went to Finn Harps, McCools. Derry City and as far as Sligo Rovers asking for cast offs and worn boots.He and Fr Barry got very handy on the cobbler's last and they repaired and mended everything they could use

The first group from the school soon grew. Boys from outer ends of the parish came to join in the fun. In the beginning it was all kick and rush as they all followed the ball. As they improved Aengus divided the boys by size and then by ability. Soon they were playing 7a side. They arranged a game againstMcCools. McCools had a full team and Garton were a man or two short so they chopped and changed, Everyone got a game and there might have been 17 or 18 playing on the Garton side at one time. No one can remember the final score. If one was kept.

"One of the best days of my life" said Fr Barry"

"Me too" said Aengus. Wouldn't it be wonderful if we had a little clubhouse where we could entertain after the game, Tea and buns."

"We could win the Sweep as well" said Fr Barry "but good thinking"

But their immediate problem was a set of jerseys. It was all right playing among themselves in whatever their mothers fashioned for them but a proper set of jerseys had to be obtained. It was of yet a dream. Aengus got a price list from Clery's in Dublin. Too much even to think of it.

And the raffles monies were for the school heating

"Dont bother me" was all Fr Barry would say

Then he arrived at the school all smiles. A happy man. He had a cheque made out to Michael Morris

"That is my fathers name and the cheque is from The Shamrock Club in Boston. He was a member of the club when he worked over there. They heard about our team and the cheque is for us to buy the jerseys"

"God bless The Shamrock Club" said Aengus. Then there was what colour jerseys they should buy. Red was always associated with Ulster and the Red Hand of the O Neills. They should get a plain red jersey. The mothers could dye a shirt red and that would do for playing in the field among themselves in the meantime, but the Club jerseys would be red with a prominent Red Hand

Now a name for the club. It had to be Garton Gaels. G.G. GG a watermark for excellence. Now they had the club colours and the club name but they were short of players. Lots of youngsters and in a few years they might have a Minor team.

Fr Barry got more involved and so did the whole parish There was serious training. Even the teenagers came along to watch the juveniles and soon they wre training andand playing. A team was taking place. A seven a side team at the very least. A good seven. The fittest in the county and with the loose marking in the seven a side games they were a match for any side. Their fitness was their secret weapon. The old past members remembered the old glories and they came along to help. They cut the grass and tidied the field and replaced worn goalmouth patches. They looked after the nets and they gave ribald encouragement. They did not modify their language in the presence of the Holy Father,Sure he had heard it all before. And Fr Barry was delighted. He could see and feel that there was a soul in Garton and that it was beginning to stir again

37

SHANE DID NOT have to go to the Tech every day as Mr Monaghan organised a suitable rota for him. He was doing bookkeeping, machine maintenance, welding and carpentry. He always came straight home after lessons. Neil was always about and the two of them sat with the teapot. Shane got to know his father better

Neil also gave Fr Barry a few history lessons when he called. Not what was in the textbooks. Neil had been there and he knew the inside story. What he did not witness he learned from the lawyers, professors,teachers and the hard men he shared prison cells with. There was even a history don who joined them in Drunmkken and he would have them all as followers of Larkin and Connolly. What was good for Russia and places like that might not suit Drumkeen or Garton. Neil knew all about Johnsons Motor car of the song but he got very tetchy when Drumboe was mentioned

"we did not need to murder our own" was all he would say

Fr Barry brought up the troubles in the North. Neil admired Hume and Fitt but he wanted to know what marching ever achieved

"We have to get close to the centre. The centre of power. The big money men. The police and the army are chick feed. Plenty more where they come from. Shoot and kill a soldier or a policeman and Stormont or London does not give a damn. The poor bastards in the RUC are only doing what they are told so they can feed their families. And what good does a bomb do in a restaurant full of women and children?. But a bomb in the financial centres of London or Zurich will make them jump to attention"

"But the Yanks are on our side" said Fr Barry hopefully

"Our side. Our side? Whose side are we?. The Yanks only care for themselves. If Hitler had won in Europe they woud have settled with him. It took Pearl Harbour for them to enter the war and it took the sinking of their ships in the first World War. On our side? Don't make me laugh. Even the Kennedys are only after the Irish vote" then he stopped.

"How is the music coming on father. You getting the hang of that banjo thinga majig?" Neil changed the subject

"Getting on fine" said a chastened Fr Barry who had been given the sharpest lecture on politics he could remember

Fr Barry knew that it was not right to have Neil lose his serenity and his temper over Irish History and how it differed from what really happened. He wanted to know the inside story. They say that history is written by the victors and Irish History was not taught beyond the end of the War of Independence. It was all right to fight the Brits but fighting your old fellow comrades of war was a different and a sad story. So that story was not told. In Garton and at Lochbeg they lived in a quiet backwater even though they were close to the Border,The odd few shillings was saved by smuggling but if there was smuggling on a large and commercial scale it was well above their heads. The greatest irritation was the military patrols on the back roads. On the unapproved roads. The roads used by the people as they crossed over the border and back in their everyday living. Some of the bridges were blown up by the military and that caused detours and inconvenience to the locals. There were squad cars and military patrols meandering the roads at night and once on their way back from a session in Omagh they took a shortcut and they were stopped buy an armoured car and 4 soldiers with machine guns. They were searched and the car was stripped and the corporal was on the phone in his Scottish accent. Finally they wre allowed to to proceed on their way. Not much fun on a night out. But there you go.

Shane liked the Tech. He learned about big ends and points and carburettors and he learned how to weld a gate and he made a wardrobe for his room. The bookkeeping was different but he managed. Profit and loss he could understand and double entry made sense. Money in and money out. No big deal. But as he grew older and as he took more part in the farm the money in was giving him a worry. He was uneasy. There wa not much coming in. He sold the odd tractor load of logs and he had other dribs and drabs and apart from the odd beast they sold at the Mart there was no income he could see. He was grown up and he wanted to do more but he was limited in what he could do

38

IT WAS NOT a loud bang. More a ruffled sound or a thud. As if someone had kicked the wall of the house. People went back to sleep to be woken by the siren of an ambulance. You could see when the bang had come from as there were flames lighting up the night sky. The Gardai cordoned off the area and closed the road. It was two cars that collided and then caught fire they said.

Then the true story broke. Young Eamonn Slevin was dead. He was in the car that caught fire. Some say there was a bomb in the car. No one was sure. There would have to be an inquest and they would have to wait for the State Pathologist to come from Dublin

All the classes were quiet that morning in Garton School. Some of the older boys knew Eamonn. He was in 5th class when they started school. He went to England as a young man and when he came home he got a job with the Electricity Supply Board as a linesman

His body was kept in the morgue in the town and when the authorities were finished it was released. It would be a big funeral as Eamonn was a good athlete and a footballer. Fr Carr left it to Fr Barry to make all the funeral arrangements. It would be long drawn out affair with the large expected attendance. Fr Barry asked Aengus if the school children would form a guard of honour at the church and Aengus took them down and they had a practice session. The Athletic Club asked to carry the coffin and their offer was accepted. Fr Barry asked Shane to play at the funeral Mass. He would play after the Communion when the congregation was settled and before the panegyric that Fr Barry would give. Something very Irish and simple. There was a big crowd who went to the rails to receive Communion. Then Shane played. Softly and slowly he let the the sad notes float over the congregation. Then he gave them the strength of the music and then he faded away and let it die as he finished. There was silence

Then someone blew in their handkerchief and the sound released in the body of the church was like the Atlantic waves on the sands at Bundoran.

The coffin was crarried to the grave by his fellow athletes and lowered into the grave. Fr Barry moved forward with the altar boy and the holy water. There was a commotion and three men in dark berets and sunglasses came out of the crowd and fired three volleys over the grave. In a flash they were gone again. No one moved. Fr Barry continued with the blessing of the coffin. There was no need to ask anything. They all knew. "Our Day Will Come" was written on many a Telegraph pole.

There was a Garda on duty outside the graveyard directing traffic and all he said was "what shots?"

There was a silent collection in the church and at the graveside, notes only. The Slevin family were given a large donation to cover their funeral expenses. The result of the inquest and the post mortem was never made public. Weeks later there was an Obituary in An Poblacht announcing the death of our brave comrade in arms Eamonn O Slevin who gave his life for Ireland.

For years there had been trouble sll around them. But this was the first time it was that close to Garton. It might be right in amongst them for all they knew. A young life was lost. Were there others to follow? Who was anyone or anybody any more?

The people of Garton were saddened at the death of one so young but life had to carry on. They knew there were patriotic Irishmen who wanted a United Ireland and who were prepare to die for their beliefs. There were the gatherings at Drumboe and the Orange Marches on July the 12th for the battle of The Boyne but that was all in the air. All above their heads and it was for those who lived in the past. Who really cares that much about the Battle if the Boyne or indeed the 1916 Rising?. Far more important to them was the price of a loaf of bread or a packet of cigarettes. Give them a decent wage and you can have Stormont, Westminster or Kildare St. ruling the country. All the same to them. Give them a quiet life and the money to rear their families in peace and comfort

But the funeral brought excitement to the village. The national newspapers gave it wide coverage and the TV did as well. Did you see your man Gerry Adams at the funeral?. Well he was. Of course ghe was. Everyone knows that.

Then there were the overweight men in suits hanging about. Asking questions. Special Branch written all over them. Who could be bothered telling them anything?

"Who played that tune at the Mass?" Aengus enquired

"Shane O Neill. From your school. But he might have left before you came" replied Fr Barry

"I remember him" said Aengus" he stayed on for a few weeks after I arrived and he turns up for the football. Never be much of a footballer but he can play on the accordeon"

"That he can do" said Fr Barry." he is a bgood wee lad. Well not wee any more. He is nearly a grown man now. I know the family and he is an up and coming accordeon player. A bit of an entrepreneur with his spuds and his blocks and his eggs"

"I know him" said Aengus "he offered to sell me logs on the never never for the school"

"Yea, thats him. He plays some nights in Doherty's in Strabane. You must come. If you enjoyed the music in Church St. in Dublin you will like Doherty's"

Fr Barry collected Aengus and took him to Doherty's. Shane was surprised to see his old Master there but he played a few tunes when he was called. At the bar Aengus bought him a Coke

"Good playing you did there" Aengus said

"It was all right" Shane said "that chap over there in the Aran Gansey is coaching me. Omagh I call him as he come s from there"

"Not much more he can teach you" said Aengus

Shane looked at Fr Barry "Where is your banjo mandolin Father?" he asked.

Aengus stared at the priest "banjo mandolin, what banjo mandolin?"

"Fr Barry is a whizz on the banjo mandiolin, nearly as good as Barney McKenna" said Shane

"I see" said Aengus looking at Fr Barry "we have a little secret have we?"

Fr Barry stammered "I have an old banjo mandolin of my father's. But I am useless"

"Ger off yer liar" said Shane. Then he apologised. No way to speak to the holy father

"I have only a few tunes to keep up with Shane" said Fr Barry

"Now I get it" said Aengus "you two play together?"

"Yes. Sometimes we have a pactise in Shane's house" said Fr Barry "and that reminds me, Br Kevin told me you have a flute in your bag and you played it in William St. for the children. No?"

"Yes, I have an old flute and I did play the odd tune for the children.Just to keep them quiet. But Dickty Rock and Brendan Bowyer were more to their taste." Aengus saw four eyes looking at him and he knew what was coming

"I will pick you up and you can come with us" said Fr Barry

"No no. Not Doherty's please. Lochbeg farm please" pleaded Aengus

There was no escape. It was Lochbeg. He felt safe enough there.

Then one night Fr Barry saw a light in the school. The electricity bill was bad enough without that kind of wastage so he stopped at the gate. He heard the music and he looked n the window and there was Aengus playing his flute. He stole away. Things were looking up. Aengus was not as far advanced as the other two and at first he just tagged along. He could manage the slow airs but the reels and the hornpipes had him floundering. Soon Neil was threatening to leave home from all the playing and the music around the house and the trio went and practised at the school. Tommy Martin found out about this and he wanted to have a session at the school and have the Doherty's gang come over but Fr Barry said the insurance would not cover them. A little lie is no sin Aengus thought.

The trio sounded sweet but there was something lacking. They needed a drummer or a bones man or a bodhran to give them an earthy contact. Omagh came to the rescue. He taped them playing their tunes and he had a drummer play wearing his headphones to the silent recorded tunes and he taped the drummer. All they had to do was play the recorded drummer as they played the melody. Some might say it was cheating but there you go.

It was backing music. No one died and it hurt no one.

Shane was growing very fast. He had his driving licence and he would like more freedom. Neil was very reluctant to let him have the car. He himself had only ever had a bicycle as a young man and that was good enough for Shane he thought. They did not see eye to eye on this. Shane wanted more freedom. The Credit Union came to his rescue again. He had a good financial record with them and they financed his Honda motorbike. The release. The feeling of freedom. He could take off to Derry or to Omagh or over to Bundoran on Sundays like most of Northern Ireland did. He had a carrier box welded on and he and his accordeon were free to travel. But now they were a trio and he he did not want to be disloyal and go off on his own. Fr Barry was the driver and the other two were happy passengers. The warmth and the luxury of the motorcar. Even Aengus was getting tired of his Heinkel. It was handy in the city for nipping about and parking was no problem. But Donegal was much bigger and much wetter and there was parking space galore. He bought a Morris Estate car and it was a bonus that he could take the childrens' exercise books home to mark and correct instead of having to stay on and do it in the school.

Life in Garton was placid. Aengus had a fuel shed built with the football team as labourers. With his raffle monies he bought a gas cylinder and he set up a tea room and the children had a morning cuppa and ate their lunches there in comfort. Some of the footballeres came and painted the classrooms. Not in the Paddy Gorman style but it brightened the whole school

The children were flourishing. He did not have any corporal punishment but he used his old star bonus system he found so very successful in Dublin. He used what had worked so well in William St.

Friday afternoon was story time. The infant classes had gone home and he moved all the children in to Mrs Brady's large room. He was well into "The Swiss Family Robinson'; when the door burst openand a big florid man entered without knocking. Aengus was facing the door and he continued reading as if nothing had happened

"What's going on here?" the intruder asked

"I beg your pardon?" Aengus said

"No need to beg my pardon. What the hell is going on here?. I am Feardorcha O Cathain the school inspector" the man said

"Aengus Gillespie" was all Aengus replied

"I know who you are" O Cathain said

"Would you please leave the room and knock on the door and wait to be admitted?" said Aengus "I am teaching a class here and I cannot have people come in as they like"

O Cathain almost shouted" Let me tell you I am not 'people'. I am the schools' inspector and I have the authority to come in as I like"

"I am a teacher in this school" Aengus calmly replied "and we teach the children good manners. It is bad manners what you have just done and it is giving these children a bad example. Just bad manners"

"I will give you manners Gillespie" O Cathain was getting more excited "And what are these children doing sitting all over the place and round the fire?. They are at school and they should be taught in a correct manner. Get them back to their desks and I will give them a few tests to see what they are being taught. Knock knock my eye. I will give them knock knock"

O Cathin set about the class. Question after question and when they answered correctly he moved quickly on. He spoke in Irish and when Aengus told him they were taught through the medium of English he did not listen. He was a true Gael and the children should know The National Language. Little Gerry Dooley was not the brightest wee lad in the school. But he did his best and with his poor health he missed many days. But God Bless him he did try. He stumbled on a question and O Cathain was on top of him. Like a Rottweiler. He kept on and on and called him a stupid boy. Gerry started weeping and Aengus moved to console the child. O Cathain would not have it

Three o clock came and Aengus said it was time to let the children go home. O Cathain hammered on" you can go home when I say you can go home"

Aengus went and held him firmly by the elbow "That is enough for today. We are going home and so are you"

"Take yourhands off me. Dont you dare touch me. I am the inspector and I have the right to inspect the class at any time" he said

"Another time Mr O Cathain" Aengus said as he smeltthe alcohol "and when you are sober"

Gerry Dooley did not come to school the following Monday but Mrs Dooley did

"I am not one to cause trouble but what happened to our Gerry on Friday?. He will not talk about it. He just sits there crying. It breaks my heart. He will not come to school and he has his heart on a star for attendance this term as he has been well all the good weather. He is at home now staring into the fire and I cannot get a word out of him. Maybe I should take him to the doctors'" Aengus explained that the Inspector had been on Friday and he was short with the children and especially with wee Gerry

Later thatmorning Tommy Martin came with the post and Aengus was informed thsat there would be a Grade Plus Inspector's examination of the school at a date to be arranged. This type of inspection was for failing schools and it wouldgo on Aengus' teaching profile. Who would know in future years that it was that clown of a man O Cathain who was the instigator?. But it woukld be on Aengus' record. O Cathain should have been sacked years ago but the Department of Education did not want all the trouble and they thought he could do no harm up there in Donegal.

Now Aengus was in his sights and in his firing line

Mrs Dooley must have gone to the Parochial House. Next day Fr Barry arrived at the school with Mrs Dooley in his car. He had his serious face on

"What is this all about" he asked "young Gerry Dooley?"

Aengus told them how the inspector insisted in speaking in Irish and how he picked on Gerry. As he was leaving Aengus called Fr Barry back and he told him in detail all that had happened

"Leave it with me" he said "When O Cathain comes againjust send himto me. No bother, Fine just fine. I will handle him"

Then he turned to Mrs Dooley "Come back with me to the parochial House". He went inside and came out with an old Beano Annual

"For Gerry" he said "tell him Fr Barry sent it"

Two weeks later O Cathain came. Fr Barry was waiting at the school gate. He invited the inspector to the Parochial House for a coffee and then he asked

"What is this I hear about you?. I have a mother complaining of your treatment of her young son"

"I do not know what you are talking about. I was only doing what I am paid to do" O Cathain replied

"You behaved disgracefully. And confidentially you were under the influence of alcohol" said the priest

"I deny both allegations. I was acting in a professional capacity"

"No you wre not" said Fr barry "you rushed in to the classroom without the courtesy of a knock on the door. You showed no respect to a fellow professional"

"Well maybe I did walk in" said O Cathain "but they were sitting on the floor and some even had cups of tea"

Fr Barry continued "You broke in to the classroom and you were rude and threatening to the teacher and to his class"

"Come on Father. I do not need permision to enter a classroom"

But Fr Barry was not having that. "You do in Garton. Yes you do in Garton and do not forget that. You spoke to the children in Irish and you asked questions in Irish"

Yes I did "said O Cathain. Irish is on the curriculum"

"Only as a subject" said Fr Barry

O Cathain was away on his favourite hobby horse "It is our national language and it should be spoken as often as possible" and he continued along those lines

But Fr barry had enough

"National language? Stop trying to fool me. Aengus is one of the few in this parish who can converse truly in Irish. Take your own name You are not O Cathain. That is an affectation. I know that your birth and marriage certificates and your passport say Fred Keane and as a child you wrere Freddie. Now Freddie you go and get your act together"

I will not be apoken to like that" said Freddie and he rose to leave

"Sit down" Fr Barry ordered him" You behaved like a drunken lout. You treated a young child badly. So badly that he will not come back to school. Then you threatened the teacher. Now you are going to write a report on this same teacher. I want you to listen very carefully" and he srtpopped

"Listen very carefully. Listen to what I have to say. If Aengus Gillespie does not receive a very favourable reportI will personally see to it that you will regret that report until your dying day"

"You cannot threaten me like that" said O Cathain "Dont make me laugh" he said

"Now take my advice and go home to your family. You can write your report in the peace of your home. I do not wish to have to call on the help of what is politely known as The Donegal Mafia. Best not have them involved or you will be a sorry man"

"Father Don Corleone Morris? Ha ha. Thats a good one ha ha" Freddie Keane laughed

"Laugh away said Fr Barry." Ha ha and ha ha again.Every Donegal policeman, every Donegal priest, every Donegal Civil Servant and every Donegal politician will have your name in their books and they will know who you are and how you behaved"

"Bollicks father" said Freddie Keane and he walked out

Feardorcha O Cathain spent the morning at the school and he made a great show of filling out his official forms. He had his lunch in Cooney's and headed for home. He loved living in the North side of Dublin and going to Croke park and to Dalymount at weekends. He stopped in Omagh and had a pint.Just over the border and near to Monaghan Town he was stopped by a Garda car

"Just a routine check sir. Your driving licence and insurance please"

Where were the bloody diocuments?. He opened the glove compartment and half a bottle of Paddy Power fell out

"Oh dear," said the guard "You been drinking sir?"

"No No gusard. I just had a pint wiyth my lunch that's all"

"Fraid I must ak you to come to the station sir. The Super is a demon on drinking and driving. Just lock your car and we can go to the station."

"But I am not drunk. I can walk a straight line" protested O Cathain

"Not my decision sir. Superintendent MacGinley is the boss and he has laid down the law"

So O Cathain was taken to the Garda Station. Two hours later the Sergeant said he was free to go. Sergeant MacFadden said he was sorry for the inconvenience. O Cathain expected a lift back to where he ahad left his own car.

"Sorry sir but the squad car ha been called out to an accident. We can phone a hackney car for you if you wish" said the kindly Sergeant Mac Fadden in his Donegal accent.

He got to his car and the half bottle of Paddy Power was on the passenger seat. He had a nip to help his nerves and he drove oon

Holy mother of God here they were again when the Garda car stopped himm outside the village of Slane

"Been drinking sir?" the garda asked as he saw th Paddy Power bottle on the pasenger seat. Sergeant MacFadden had passed the word alng that they were to look out for a red Cortina with a Dublin registration and here he was. Back as before to the Garda Station. They held him there as Sergeant O Donnell had just gone out on patrol and he would not be back fot a couple of hours. When Sergeant O Donnell arrived he was "very sorry. This was a terrible way to treat a man" and he let him drive on and he hoped the early morning traffic in to the city "would not hold him up"

Feardorcha did not write his report for some days. He had time to think things over. When he did sit down to write it all he wrote was "Highly Satisfactory"

Not a word of the Irish in his report. Feardorcha O Cathain was becoming Anglicised. Bless Him.

39

MAUREEN O NEILL never complained that her brothers were getting all the attention. Eugene awas treated like a God and Shane was always up to some tomfoolery. She went about her way quietly. She passed all her exams and the Convent suggested that she take higher ones. But all she wanted was to be a nurse and she went to Altnagelvin in Derry and then she went to Cardiff to do her midwifery. She wrote home fom time to time to tell them all how she was enjoying life in Wales and how hectic it was in Cardiff

Back at Lochbeg Shane was finishing up at the Tech. He was not in line for any diplomas or qualifications as his course was specifically designed by Mr Monaghan to suit his situation. He got The Farmers Journal and The Young Farmer and he studied them for ideas. Great ideas if you had the money. Sometimes when he had what he thought was a bright idea his father would not listen. Often he saw Neil looking at him and watching him and when he caught him looking he would give a grunt or a hmph as much a to say "just get on with it and leave me alone"

He knew he loved his father and he hoped his father loved him but sometimes there was a coolness that he found hard to understand. He knew his father had seen things during the Troubles but he was never told the full story. Neil was a hero in the IRA and he had done wonderful things but there might have been another side too. Did he do things that were haunting him now? Was that the reason he was sometimes so tetchy now?. Might be old age?.

Ivan Ashe was a great help to young Shane. Shane went to him for advice and if he said "Ivan told me" or "I was talking to Ivan and." it was agood way of having the old man stop and listen to what he had to say

Shane went round the hotel and collected the leftovers and any unused food and he boiled that with the potatoes for his pigs. Labour intensive is what The Young Farmer would call it and he soon reverted to tillage. There would always be a demand for wheat and corn and spuds and turnips. So he set about the ploughing and the harrowing and the sowing. As he grew older he was less gung ho with his father and they began working as a team and they treated each other with respect

Maureen was happy in Cardiff. She has a boyfriend. They would all like him. Geriant Jones. A junior Registrar. She would like for him to come home with her on her next holiday. He could stay in the hotel in Lifford and he would be no trouble

Of course he could come. They would all love to meet him. And they would meet her and Geriant at Strabane Station

The train pulled in to the station platform. Doors were flung open and there was Maureen. She looked lovely and Neil took her suitcase

"Careful daddy" she said "it is very heavy. Geriant will carry it for you" and she looked back at Geriant

Holy Mother of God. Neil was shocked. He hoped he was dreaming. Geriant was a black man. What was he going to do? He was told Geriant was a Welshman. He stuck out his hand and Geriant shook it "Pleased to meet you Mr O Neill" he said

Neil said he was pleased to meet Geriant as he shook the man's hand. It did not feel any different. He took another peek at Geriant. He was not black at all. Not like the black babies they collected for at the school. He had another look. Geriant was a good looking felllow. Well his skin might be a bit darker or even dark yellow brown but he looked fine. No fuzzy black hair or big thick lips. Maureen kept a non stop prattle and Geriant kept saying "Yes Maureen Yes Maureen" and they sat together in the back of the car. Neil now had a good look at Gerient in his rear view mirror. Nice collar and tie as well and a tidy haircut

Mary really took to Geriant. She gave him a great big hug and asked if there was anything he did not like to eat

"Everything. He eats everything" Maureen told her "and plenty". Mary soon had the lamb chops and the roast potatoes on the table

Neil was disappointed in himself. He would have to stop this silly thinking. Here was a well educated Welshman and he should be treated accordingly. The meal was a success. Geriant was good company and he amused them with stories of his student days and the Welsh Rugby scenario. He had a soft Welsh accent and beautiful manners. He and Shane carried on as if they had known each other all thir lives. When it was time for Geriant to leave for his hotel Neil was a bit embarrassed when Maureen kissed her boyfriend goodnight and said "see you in the morning darling"

And what about Mass in the morning. Maureen said he was a Baptist. A Welsh Baptist. That sounded all right to Neil. At it again Neil he thought to himself. Come on now. Give it a rest. Just stop it.

Geriant phoned early the nexrt mornuing. He had hired a car and he would be over later. He arrived with a bottle of Jameson's Redbreast and a bottle of Tio Pepe. Tio for the ladies" he said

Mary head never tasted Tio Pepe but after a single glass she saidd she could feel it was doing the old rheumatism good and she would have another. God is good.

Maureen said that Geriant should see some of the Itish countryside and that they would go touring for a few days. Neil was happy with that.

Shane approached the delicate subject "Dad you do not seem happy with Geriant"

"He is the first black man I have ever met" said Neil

"He is not black Dad" said Shane. Nor is he coloured. He is dark skinned. His name is Jones. Jones in Wales is like McFadden or O Donnell in Donegal. His father is a GP in Swansea. His mother is from India. He is half Welsh and half Indian"

"Not from Africa at all then? Said Neil

"Ah, come on Dad. You must be having me on? I cannot believe this. He has never set foot in Africa "said Shane"

"Well I'll be damned" said Neil. He was playing the old soldier now. Letting on he was so far behind the times that it was not his fault. Cute old fox. It had worked for him before.

But Neil was now a different man as far as Geriant was concerned. They chatted all the time. Man United, The Triple Crown. Plaid Cymru, The Esteddford. They were good pals now. Geriant did not leave without leaving something behind. He mentioned how he would love to spend a day up by the loch fishing. The solitude and the singing of the birds and he might even catch a fish. Little did he know but he had touched a latent chord in Shane's mind. Shane did not know it either but it would rise to the surface in its own good time.

40

SINEAD WAS COMING home on her holidays and Hudi was coming with her. He would be no trouble and Sinead would see to everything. Peggy thought that Sinead might be able to handle everything in Boston but in Gweedore there were the neighbours and theeir backbiting and jealous whispering. Sinead did not care what they said or thought but then Sinead did not have to live in Gweedore. They had booked a car and they took their time motoring up from Shannon Airport. They called at Galway and saw the Claddagh where Columbus called as he was on his way to discover America. Sinead explained that Columbus was a bit late as there was an Irishman called Kevin who had found the place many centuries before him. He asked if that was even before the Kennedys. Ha ha, very funny is Hudi. They called in on Yeat's grave in Drumcliffe and looked up at Ben Bulbin. Hudi was too kind to say they have bigger molehills in America. He had heard of boastful Yanks

Peggy had roast chicken and they opened a bottle of wine. Sinead got straight to the point and said that she and Hudi had been living together for two years. As long as The Canon or Fr Kelly did not know that was fine with Peggy. Aengus stayed at home for a few days. There was not much in Gweedore for a visitor. Hudi loved the Ulster Fry and all that rubbish about not eating bacon did not apply to him anyway. Just bring it on.

Peggy's sister Mary who was married to a guard from Connemara was now living in Blanchardstown outside Dublin. They booked in to the nearby Holiday Inn and Peggy stayed with her sister. Aengus took them on a tour of the city with his old pal Tipperary Pat. They called at Slatterys and O Donoghues and dropped in to McDaids in the hope od meeting some of the literary clientele there. They did the haunts of Beckett, Swift, Wilsde, and Shaw. They called in at McDaids in the hope that Behan or Kavanagh might be there. But thos two wre playing truant. They saw the Book of Kells and did some shopping in Grafton St. Then it was homewards. They were stopped and searched in Ballygawley by a Scottish soldier who avoided their eyes. It was arelief to rest at home and it was time to discuss the wedding. Hudi and Sinead were definite that their wedding would take place in Boston. Hudi's large family lived there as did all their friends. Boston it was. Then they would come home to Gweedore and ahave another wedding.

"Two weddings?"

"Why not? Anyone can have two weddings as long as it is to the same person. You only break the law if you marry again while stiil married to the first person" Sinead said

They had their doubts but Hudi and Sinead were lawyers and they knew that the religious cermony was secondary. It was the State Registration of the marriage that was important

"But should a marriage be registered twice?" They did not know and cared less. Who in the Courthouse in Lifford would call up Boston to ask about a wedding in Gweedore?

Aengus and Peggy were coming to Boston with all expenses paid. No arguements. Job done.Hudi asked to be married in a Synagogue. All his friends and family wrere Jewish

"But Sinead you are a Catholic" Peggy said

"Mum, yes I am" said Sinead "but not a very good one.I cannot remember when I last went to Confession or to Mass"

Peggy went on" but the Jews were the ones who crucified . . . ."

Aengus cut in" Mammy the followers of Jesus were Jews and Jews only to begin with. Then St Paul got them to allow outsiders, Gentiles, in. Then the Romans under Constantine accepted Christianity. To keep in the good books of the Romans the Christian altered the story of the Crucifixion. History was altered. It was the Romans who ruled Palestine when Jesus was alive and it was the Romans who crucified Jesus. But history was changed to suit the Roman Empire. Anyway if the Jewish method of killing was by stoning.

We are not all angels but neither are we all evil was what they agreed on in Gweedore that night

They fixed a date for the wedding in Boston and they thought they might have the Irish one when they came home again.

"Leave it with you to arrange the Irish one" said Hudi

"Sure thing" said Aengus. "I am friends with an Irish priest and I will have a word with him". Aengus was happy how things were coming on. He knew there were things that Peggy need not know. They never told her that Sinead was having tuition in the Jewish faith with a view to conversion. She was very keen to be accepted in the faith before they had children. The Jews had almost a Divine

Command to have many children and the children were of Jewish descent through the mother. If the mother was not Jewish the children were not Jewish. The father did not matter. Even if he were a Rabbi. But Hudi and Sinead were independently minded people and they were able to decide what they wanted together. They would live their own lives within the laws and with respect for each other and let the world outside squabble.

This might have been too much for Peggy Tommy Rua but as Mrs Gillespie and the mother of Mrs Sinead Levi she would have to adapt to the world that had changed since she learned her Catechism at Primary School. Her sister in Boston was happy with Sinead's new husband and that mollified her fears

There were no tears when the young couple left to go back to Boston. Peggy was going to be so busy and there was so much to be done.

41

SHANE WAS BECOMING an accomplished accordeon player. But that was easy for him

What he really wanted was to be a footballer. He tried his hardest. He turned up at every training session and he was one of the fittest in the squad. But on the field there was something missing. He never seemed to be in the right place. Something about spacial awareness the master said. Lack of it.

Training was getting intense now and Aengus made changes in the format. He divided the playing field into squares and you had to stay in your square but you could move into one other square when it was necessary. There were days of practice whe Shane never touched the ball. He was always in the other square.

But he practised at home. He got an old leather football and he filled it with rags and a chopped up bicycle tyre and he kicked this round the field at Lochbeg. He would kick the ball with all his strength and then run and catch it. Neil looked on in disbelief. This cannot be his son

Then the Master approached Shane and said "I think you would make a good goalkeeper" In truth he was one of the few tall enough to reach the crossbar

"Would youlike to give it a try?" Aengus asked

Would he like to give it atry? He would give his right arm to be picked for the team. He was in Heaven. He was suited to the position. He was tall and from his practising in the field at home he had a very strong kick. This was noticed when he took his own kick outs and soon he was taking the free kicks out the field as well. This often meant he had to race back to defend his goalmouth and sometimes it was not funny. But he had found his niche. A Garton jersey of his own. He hung it on the back of his bedroom door and he washed and ironed it after every game

To be truthful they were not good footballers. They were not strong enough to play against regular club teams. But Brother Kevin again came to their rescue. He arranged fotball matches against Christian Brothers' Schools. Omagh. Ballyshannon, Derry, Limevady.

Transport was now the problem. They could squeeze a few into Aengus' estate car and Fr Barry could manage a few more but there ws 15 in a team and then there was their football gear as well. Then they always took a few substitutes as they liked to give everyone a game.

Fr Barry had an idea. He took a photograph of the team in their Garton jerseys and sent it to The Shamrock Club in Boston. Thy thanked him for the photograph which now had pride of place in the club and they wre including a donation that might solve Garton's transport problem

A minibus was too expensive so they bought a Bedford van and they fitted benches in the back and a roof rack for the footbal gear. Some of the gang had notions of days out by the sea in Bundoran or Rossnowlagh but Fr Barry was very definite. They would share the van with the ICA, Macra na Feirme, the Young Farmers. They would all have the use of the van. There were trips to Clones for the football and to balance things out Knock Shrine got a few visits as well. They had a day at the CCE Fleadh Ceoil and Shane was thrilled and he mentioned it to Omagh. Omagh smiled and said "Soon it will be your time but not yet"

Aengus decided they might enter a team at one of the Parish Sports Days. It was Seven A Side with not too much physical contact. Very few of the teams that entered had any training. Usually it was seven lads who joined together for the days fun and for the lark.

But the Garton 7 was different. They trained for Seven A Side matches specifically. Aengus drilled them session after session. Possession, possession. Possession was the vital factor. To kick the ball aimlessly was a major crime in the Master's code. Keep the ball until you can pass it to one of your team mates and when your team has the ball keep away from the opposition so you can be ready and free to receive a pass. He drummed it in to their heads. Listen listen. Thick bloody shulls. And they started winning and as the games went on their fitness counted. And they had substitutes to replace weary players. Garton Gaels wre a winning team at that level.

But they had a long way to go before they could even think of playing the better and bigger clubs.

But the dream was still alive

But Shane had a dream ogf his own. They had a lovely letter from Geriant thanking them all fot the lovely holiday an he sent a gift for the family. It was a box with fishing rod. The rod was only three feet in the box but it extended to 12feet whe it was drawn out. Mary said it was not much use to her and Neil was not bothered at all. But Shane remembered Geriant's remark about the loch and he decided to go up there fishing. He set night lines as well and he caught some funny fish. He took the fish to the AGS and they said they were Chubb or Roach. Not the usual trout or perch that was normal for Donegal. They got on the phone and contacrted one of their fishery men in Dublin

The Dublin fishery expert arrived at Lochbeg. Sheamus Ignatius Dowling. Known as Sid. Sid knew what he was talking about and he said that some tribe, even a prehistoric one, must have imported these fish to Lochbeg lake. He had never come across this kind before in Donegal

"There is an ancient stone at Beltony by Raphoe. Beltony Stone Circle. Thousands of years old" said Shane

Sid was very interested. "You might have your own national monument here" he said. "have you found any funny shaped stones or bits?"

"No not really" said Shane "We do not come up here all that often. My mothers name is Carolan and that might give us something in the history books. But I was thinlking of using the lake"

"Like what?" asked Sid

"We might stock it and let the fishing" said Shane

"Naw. Not much hope. There is free fishing on the Finn River" said Sid

"Any chance of a development grant?" asked Shane

"New one on me" said Sid "let me see what I can come up with. There is a strange type of fish over in Loch Eske near Donegal Town but this one here is a new one to me"

Sid was as good as his word. He called in to Lochbeg many times and had the cuppa and the snifter. He got a result. The Department of Agriculture and Fisheries would stock the Loch. They have a hatchery in Dundalk. They will stock the loch and they will retain the right to research on the fishery developments. This is to be a quiet project and no information is to be released to the press. Some fish were caught and taken to Dundalk and the loch was stocked

Shane had the job of feeding the fish. A bucket of pellets twice daily. He swore the fish were able to tell the time and were waiting on the dot every day and there was one fish who winked at him when he fed them.

Neil ws disgusted. One born every minute he thought.And a son of my own as well.

42

AENGUS STAYED ON in Garton when the Summer holidays started. He had work to do. There was plenty of time to go home later and stay with his mother. He started painting the school. Fr Barry was deaf to his complaints. But his painting was progressing very slowly and he would not have the job finished before the holidays were over. So he placed a notice on the school gate

"Can you use a paintbrush?

No experience needed

Good cup of tea"

Help arrived and the job was done. He kept on about the state of the shool yard. The Department of Education did not want to know and the Diocese was not bothered. O Cathain only stayed a minute ir two when he clled and he said it was not his concern. He could not get away fast enough. Garton was not his cup of tea.

Aengus got quotes for tarmacadam but Fr Barry would not even look. But he had a contact

"My father was friendly with a man in Boston.Sheamus Cleary. Sheamus was amember of the Shamrock Club with my dad. He is now manager of Rowanstown Co. in Dublin. They are a Tarmac firm and they are doing a job at Omagh General Hospital. The man there to ask for is Sean Hegarty"

They set off for Omagh and they asked for your man Sean. He was a big genial redhead with a Fainne. If you had the Irish he was prepared to speak to you in Irish

Fr Barry managed a few words of greeting in Irish and then Aengus gave him the full Gweedore works. Fluent Gaelic. Sean was impressed.

Here in the middle of the Six Counties and they were conversing in the old native language

Fr Barry told him what they were after. No hope. They might have a few bits and pieces over after a day's tarmacading but never enough to bother with. Then Fr Barry began to hum a tune and went over to the window. Aengus had heard the tune somewhere before but he could not remember when or where. Sean Hegarty went over to Fr Barry and they had a quiet word

"Thank you Mr Hegarty for listening to our begging" said Fr Barry as they prepared to depart.

"I cannot promise you anything" said Sean "One never knows how Head Office will react. Public relations and all that you know. Slan abhaile" And the Irish speakers parted and Sean Hegarty polished his Fainne for good luck

"What do you think?" asked Aengus on the way home

"We are in there. Just take my word for it" replied Fr Barry as he concentrated on his driving. Eyes on the road.

A week later they had a letter from Mr Sean Hegarty. He explained the situation. They usually had some tarmac left over at the end of the day's work and the site had to be clean for the following morning's arrival. He would phone them any day there was a surplus. It was too far for a tractor so Ivan Ashe lent them his pickup and trailer. They went to Omagh evey time they got the call and soon the school yard was tarmaced. Another job completed

Then there was a headline in The Donegal Democrat

"School Inspector Drunk in Charge"

The defendant Feardorcha O Cathain denied that he was over the limit. He had only taken two drinks at most

Sergeant Thornton gave evidence that there was a phone call to the Garda Station that a member of the public was driving erratically "on the public highway"

Mr O Cathain said he only had two drinks in Cooney's Bar and Lounge and that the drinks must have been spiked

Cooney's solicitor took grave exception to this insinuation and he called on Cooney's barman to give evidence. Mr Gerard Dooley, the barman. said he was very busy on that night and as far as he was aware Mr O Cathain was just a customer and he did not pay particular attantion to the amount he drank

Mr O Cathain was found guilty and his licence was suspended and he was fined

Mrs Dooley was a very happy lady with the way her husband gave his evidence and she gave him a great big hug when he came down from the witness box.

Fr Barry took the paper to the school and read it to Aengus

"I know Gerry Dooley is from Donegal and he is eligible. But Sergeant Thornton is a Galway man. But do you think we might make him an honourable member of the Donegal Mafia?" he asked. Aengus let on he did not hear that remark

The school was freshly painted and the yard tarmaced. Aengus felt he had done his bit and he went home. Peggie was worried. It was the old problem. What was she going to wear?And at her only daughter's wedding.And not in a church but in a Synagogue. And in America with posh people. Lawyers and DAs and judges. She did not know. But Sinead did.She was to go to Magee's and ask fot Miss Garvey. Miss Garvey would see to Paggy's needs. Aengus was to go there as well and get a new suit and all was charged to Sinead's account. Not to worry about the flight. A car would collect them and take them to the airport and there would be someone there to look after them. They would be met at Boston and taken to Sinead's home safe and sound.

She asked how the arrangements for the Irish Wedding were coming on. She would like to have about 40 of her friends and neighbours at the Irish wedding but she would leave it all to Aengus and his friend the priest.

She had no worries but that Aengus would arrange everything. Sinead does not do worries. But Aengus had a wee problem. Well not a problem really but a great opportunity

Jimmy Beirne had died.Jimmy was a Civil Servant who had come back to Garton to be near the dog track in Lifford. Greyhounds were\his life. His family were all married and settled in different parts of the country. Jimmy's wife decided to sell the house and go and live with one of her sons in Swords outside Dublin

Fr Barry was very excited "here's your chance. Made for you.Lovely house. Go and buy it. Make an offer"

Aengus went to Kings and was given the asking price and he had a look at the house. He liked it and the big garden at the back where Jimmy kept his greyhounds. Kings asked who his solicitor was and in a panic he gave Sineads name.Mrs Beirne was very anxious to move andKings said the price was very reasonable as Mrs Beirne wanted a quick sale.

And was Mr Gillespie himself interested in buying the property?

His giving an American DA as his agent had thrown them. They thought it might be a returning Emigrant who was the client. Aengus told them that he was interested and they politely suggested that they could arrange a mortgage for him. A loan to buy the property and he paid it back over the years and finally the house would be totally his

Then there arrived a package from Sonead Gillespie DA. Patrick Horan Ltd.,Attorneys at Law. Sinead wrote that Kings had sent her all the details and she though it was the ideal house for Aengus.She had chacked the deeds and had a valuation done and everything was in order. She had been in contact with her company's agents in Ireland and she had arranged finances for him. She suggested a mortgage and a man from the Educational Building Society, the EBS, would call on him

The EBS man came and Aengus bought the house. Mrs Beirne said Aengus could have what furniture she did not take to Swords as Jimmy, God rest his soul, was always picking up stuff at auctions and there was no room in Swords for all his rubbish

Because of Mrs Beirne's kind gesture the house did not feel empty. Aengus put what he needed in one room;A bed, a sofa,and a TV set.

But the other vacant rooms haunted him.He called in on Miss Robinson and hired one of her TV sets and he bought a gas heater. A nice young lady was this Hannah Robinson he thought, and she helped him with the furnishings and she told him when anything suitable came in to her auction rooms. Soon Shane O Neill was at his front door with logs "at a special price for the Master"

Then Fr Barry and Shane and Aengus used the front room for thir music practice and the house was living again.

43

THE GRTON GAELS Seven A Side team was winning regularly at the different Parochial Sports days. Shane had a few statuettes in the window at Lochbeg. Dust gatherers, his father called them

The Fisheries Department man, Sid, called every month and he did his measurements or whatever. Things were coming along well and he was very pleased. There were some nice fish in the loch was his opinion

"Would it be all right to fish for them" Shane asked him. Sid gave a positive answer" If we are to treat the loch in a natural way then it should be fished. The fish were here before us and no doubt you have the fishing rights. The local angling club might be interested"

The local angling club was not on Shane's agenda.He thought of fishermen on the loch at least a thousand years ago and them offering their sacrifice to the Gods at Beltony Stone Circle. He saw a programme on TV where the fishermen fished all night and threw the fish back in again. That would suit fine. Catch the fish, weigh it and have your photograph taken with the fish and then return the fish to the loch. You might catch it again next week. The AGS told him of fishing clubs who fished lakes and ponds and they never killed a fish. They even banned barbed hooks so as not to damage the fish. There were lakes in Fermanagh and Cavan where the same fishermen came every year to fish.

He got a copy of Coarse Fishing and he placed an advertisement

"Secluded Loch. First fished thousands of years ago. Listen to the birds and the foxes. No motor cars within 600 yards"

He got replies to the advert and he forwarded photographs of the loch and the wood. Four miners from Nuneaton were his first clients who booked two weeks on the loch. Shane did not know what to do next. On TV one of the fishermen slept in his tent with his Jack Russell.

He went to McGills and he hired a 4berth caravan. But the miners wanted the sound of nature and they preferred to sleep in their tents. Shane returned the van and got a refund. Those four suited him very well. But some of the other bookings he hoped to receive might expect accommodation. It was back to the Credit Union. They had a thick file on him now. He had his business plan ready for their inspection and he was told to carry on. He bought a six berth caravan and parked it in the wood by the loch. He got an Elsan toilet and he went to Hannah Robinson for a gas cylinder and rings and he was ready

The Nuneaton four passed the word and Shane got many more bookings and he was able to buy another caravan for the wood beyond the loch

Mickey Traynor asked if the visitors ever tasted Poteen. It was a dangerous game the poteen. He mixed some with yellow lemonade and he sold it as Garton Glory. It went down a treat. They were all sworn to secrecy and Shane never said a word to Fr Barry or to Aengus. But Neil often wondered why the visitors were so fond of the lemonade

In spite of all his dealings and schemes Shane was restless. The farming was all right but he was not settling down. Some of his old friends had finished their schooling and were going out into the world. One or two were at University and they talked of the dances and the girls and the great life they were having. Those who went to England came home with the Periwinkle shoes and drainpipes and the Teddyboy walk and swagger

Earning big money man. Big money. Yea man Big dough.

And here he was at Lochbeg with a few pounds and it was not his own money. It went into the farm accounts. He knew it was needed there. Profit and loss and all that. And his father was close and tight about money. Neil never had money to throw about. And it never seemed to bother him. He just did not seem to care

Shane mentiomned that he might like to go to America. Just as a passing remark. No one seemed to hear what he said. They were too busy at their tasks

Next day Mary asked "Are you not happy here son?"

"I am happy here mammy" he replied "but if I go to America I can earn money for the farm"

She sighed and said" But we will miss you so much" and she carried on with her work. Neil said nothing. But Shane was aware thet he was constantly watching him and the old man was very quiet. His hurt was painful

One night when they went to Cooneys for a pint and at th pub door Neil stopped and stood. He came close to Shane and he put his hand on his shoulder and said "You wont leave me, will you son?"

It was too much. His voice was gone. Shane had to turn away and he said

"No not leave you. No not for ever. Just to see the world and earn some money for the farm"

"Think it over son" was all the old man said. He had aged in a few minutes and his hand shook as he lit his cigarette and nothing more was said. But someone must have leaked. The Master, Aengus, called in for a chat. What the hell was happening he wanted to know?. It was only a short time ago Shane was sitting in the school in his short trousers. And now he was a young farmer. Many an Irishman in Birmingham and London would gladly change places.

. He had loving parents and a farm that would be his. Aengus told him of his own father Ownie Rua and his tragic death. Now that was a hard way to live

Then came Fr Barry. The whole world knew his business thought Shane. But Fr Barry assured him it was between the three friends. No one else had any idea. He would blame the Celtic genes. Some say we are the lost tribe of the Wandering Jews. And things are never what they may seem. He had worked in England and the fancy shoes and the swagger does not tell the truth. Some are in their forties before they settle and their youth never existed. Hard grind and few of the human graces. No football in the evenings and no Irish music. Irish music abroad was not for the Paddies. It wa for the second generation who had used the education and moved to the middle or the professional classes. Even in America all the Irish do not finish as millionaires. I know of one family who saved for 30 years to come home and flash the dollars. I know as I have met those sad people. If you do well in America you will not come home and if you fail over there you will be too proud to come home and admit the failure

Then Eugene got a word in

"Garton not good enough then?Whats wrong with him? Going to make a million in the States?"

Shane told him to fuck off and to stick to his Hail Marys. That had Eugene sulk in his room for a days. Maureen came home on her holidays. She wa finished in Cardiff and was now working in Leeds Maternity Hospital

"Where is Geriant?

"Geriant?. Well now Geriant is a Consultant in Edinburgh Royal. He got his Fellowship and he is hoping for a vacancy in South Wales. Got a card from him at Christmas"

Later she had a word with Shane

"Whats all this about America. Are you unhappybhere in Lochbeg?"

"Maureen" Shane spoke to her "We grew up here in this house together. You left to qualify as a nurse and now you are a Sister with your own ward in the hospital. I have not been anywhere or done anything. I do not have control over my own life. SometimesI do not have the price of a Mars Bar from the travelling shop"

Maureen understood. She had found her space and her freedon in her profession. Now Shane needed his own space. He was almost a grown man There would have to be a family meeting

She asked Neil if he would agree to a chat about Shane and his new idea. He grunted and said "OK"

Mary was delighted that something was happening as the O Neill family was dying around the kitchen fire. Maureen said that Fr Barry was a family friend and that it might be best if he came. Indeed she had an idea that her mother was confiding in him all the time. Eugene had gone back to Maynooth thank God. Peace in his absence.

The Meeting was held with Fr Barry in the chair. Literally.He sat in the big armchair by the fire. TV off. He did not have them sit around the table or have them facing each other. They sat wher they were comfortable and where there was a seat.

Fr Barry threw a few thoughts in the air. "There might be a wee worry in the house. A small worry that we might like to have a chat about. As I see it Shane is a little unsettled. Young men get unsettled. They want their own space. Look at the birds in the air and the animals in the field or in the wild. And see how they demand and fight for their on territory. We might not recognise this in ourselves but we are animals too and we have some of the same inclinations. But there is one big difference. We have reason and common sense and tonight we are going to use our reason and our common sense on this wee problem we think Shane has. I will act as referee and I will not allow any name calling or raised voices. Nice and easy. Nice and calm. I will allow everyon to have their say but they must ask my permission first. No butting in. Maureen you asked for this little chat. Let us hear what is on your mind Maureen"

Thre were interuptions fron Shane and his mother when they thought Maureen was in error but Fr Barry bade them silent with a dismissive wave of his hand. Whe she was finished he allowed correction of the facts only. Points of information he called it

Mureen said she was upset with what was happening at home in Lochbeg. She said she did not take sides and there was no one to blame. Surely God and His Holy Mother would have father and son stay together. Then Mary spoke and she said it would break her heart if Shane left, She had seen sons go and promise to return and they never did and she did not want that to happen here. Please God we can work it out

The men were more cautious. Say a bit and watch how it was received. Shane spoke of his thoughts and that he never realised they would cause so much trouble. But he would like them to answer some of his thoughts. He was to inherit the farm. Someday?. When was someday?. When he was 60 years of age?. And who was going to make the decisions about the farm?. Especially where money was concerned. How was the farm going to carry on in future years. Would it progress. Was progress nacessaary?Should they buy more land?. Or sell some land?. Down by the road or up by the loch. Shane kept an eye on Neil as he spoke as it was between them the problem had arisen. He expected the old man to get very angry. Instead Neil seemed very settled and at ease.

Fr Barry took notes of what was said and what was suggested, He read this over and adjusted what they were prepared to agree on. Then he read it again and they agreed it was a fair account of what was said. He told them it was not a legal document but just an account of what was said

Neil rose from his chair as if he had just woken up and he said

"let us get this whole thing legally documented and sealed. I want Shane to inherit the farm and I want him to have it as soon as is possible. This has been on my mind for some time but I was not able to put it into words or into action.This talking has cleared my mind and I would like the issue finalised and closed. I have no doubts. I trust Shaneto run this farm. This farm is Shane's farm. I will work alonside him but he will make all the decisions. His word will be final"

Shane thanked his father and said he would not be a know all, but that he would refer to his father every time there was a decision to be made and if his father did not agree then he would not go ahead.

Neil walked over and embraced his son and in a broken voice asked

"Will ye all kneel down with me and say a decade of the Rosary?"

The teapot was filled and the cake tin emptied. Mary suggested a wee drop for Neil but he saisd he did not fancy one. Long may it last she thought and then she herself had a Tio Pepe. For the rheumatics you know

The matter was not raised again until a letter came fron Callaghans the solicitors

Would Mr N O Neill and Mr S O Neill call in at the office at their convenience. Neil and Shane signed all the documents and the farm was Shane's and his parents had the right to live in the farmhouse as long as they lived

Shane pulled in at Cooney's on the way home.

"This calls for a celebration". Neil demurred but Shane insisted. Two pints and a Redbreast chaser and they were on their way home. Neil did no drop off to sleep as he ususlly did but he sat upright in the car. Shane looked over and he say the old man was weeping

"Whats up?" Shane asked

"Nothing nothing" the old man said and he reached over and touched Shane s cheek and said

"This is the happiest day of my life"

44

HANNAH ROBINSON WAS a very busy lady. A busy executivve business lady. Her father David died as he had lived. Quietly and without fuss. They held a service in the Kirk and they buried him out the back. Judith did not last long after her husband and she joined him and her son Luke behind thr Kirk

Hannah was left to manage on her own. She had inherited no debts but there were some British Steel shares. She cashed the shares and had an upstairs bathroom installed and she divided the house into two apartments. She lived in the upstairs one and rented out the other

Gradually her business changed. Life in Ireland was changing rapidly. There was a Garden Centre in Lifford and only a few years ago that would be unthinkable. Percy Thrower on TV with his Fuschias and Gardenias had a lot to answer for. There were Fine Arts programmes on Television showing stately homes and fine old pictures. Hannah was aware if The Hidden Ireland and she enrolled in Fine Art Appreciation Course at Queens, Belfast. It was exciting as all the students were going out to look for the hidden treasures. She felt like some of the old gold diggers in California did with their tents and spades.

Her territory was the North West. From Innishowen in Donegal to Rosses Point in Sligo. From her days in Dublin and her visits to The Abbey Theatre she knew of Yeats and the Gore Booths and Countess Markievitz. The Gore Booths had a Mansion in Lisadell beside Drumcliffe in Sligo. Yeats and Lady Gregory would have been visitors there and she knew that Augustus John was often in the area. He travelled in his trailer with his lover Dorelia McNeill. Augustus was a lover of the Romani whom he called his Gypsise. Not the common gypsies but his own kind. The Gypsise

And Hannah believed that he might have paid for hospitality by the odd portrait or sketch

So she concentrated on that area and she saw what she thought was of interest. In a country house sale. She asked the vendor to withdraw it and she told him of her hunch. It might be worth more than what he might get at the auction and she would share with him

The family was a genuine and likely one. Of true Anglo Saxon descent. Landowners, but cash poor.

She was backing her instincts. There was no proof of provenence but she did not tell the outside world. If the word got out the countryside would be flooded with dealers. She took it to Dublin and had it looked at. It was a John sketch. When it was cleaned there was a faint signature and date. It was accepted as a John. Hannah sold it to a collector from Trieste who thought it migh be a portrait of James Joyce. She got press coverage as The Donegal Treasure Finder and there was a mention on Ulster Television of her great find. No one would ever claim that Augustus John was up there with The Masters but there were not many Irish artists of note and it was to her credit that she recognised and saved his sketch

Hannah was getting a reputation now among the art world. She travelled all over the North West and she was accepted as an honest and fair and most importantly a discreet dealer. Her discretion was a great advantage as many an old Anglo family was short of cash and her name was passed among them as a quiet person to help them.

Peprestenatives from the Dublin art dealers called in to see what she might have. She had a letter from Des Shanley wishing her well and that he knew all along she would be a great success. Good old Des. When Sotherbys asked her to represent them in the area she knew she had arrived

But it was not easy to leave the past behind. Shane O Neill kept calling. They had finished with the cipini and the logs. But he called in for the chat. Cheeky young man. She enjoyed his company

Then there was the new teacher who had bought Jimmy Beirnes house and who called in for bits and pieces, He was very pleased when she told him that old Master Byrne was her teacher in the past. Curiosity got the better of her and she invited herself over to see his new house. It needed so much. Curtains and chairs and tabled and bookcases. Her suggestions were never ending and he reminded her that he was living on a teacher's salary. But they exchanged stories of their times in Dublin and they found they had similar taste in music

She was telling him about a boyfriend she had in Dublin when the doorbell tingled and Fr Barry came in. She changed the conversation. Of course\she knew who Fr Morris was and she knew all about the football team and the village hall

"And what is that music I hear from Jimmy Beirnes house?" she asked

"Just a few of us playin tunes" they said

Aengus tells me he plays the flute and what do you play Fr Morris?"

"Call me Fr Barry please "he said" like the rest do. I have an old banjo mandolin"

"Well for a banjo and a flute you make a strong and beautiful sound" she said

"Well we have another player. An accordeon player. From the farm up at Lochbeg" said Fr Barry. "I do not suppose you have met him. Shane O Neill"

"Met him?. met him? And she slapped the shop counter." Do I know him? Do I know him?" and she looked at them both "I do not believe this. He has been in and out of here for years selling me cipini, logs, potatoes chickens and a turkey and now you tell me he can play music as well. This I do not believe"

"He is an accomplished accordeon player" said Fr Barry. "Shane O Neill on the accordeon, this I have got to hear" Hannah told them

"Come on Friday to my new house" Aengus said

"I must check my diary she lied. There was nothing in the world that would keep her away

As they were leaving she called aftervthem

"Aengus you ever met Des Shanley?" and before he could reply she had gone out the back

They all met on Friday. Shane was not in the least nonplussed. He asked Hannah if she was all right for logs and that he was doing great value in chickens now as well. The men played and they stopped for a wee drop of the Creathur. Hannah went to her car and returned with a bottle of Chianti and they had an enjoyable time

Then Shane spoke up. It had got to be Shane she thought

"Miss Robinson I know you play the fiddle, sorry, the violin"

"Who told you that?" she asked

"I often heard you when we were in business" he sid with a look at the other two. In business.That should impress

She had been found out

"Yes I do play a bit" she confessed "on the quiet. No great shakes"

Fr Barry spoke "Now Hannah tell the truth. No fibs to a clergyman. We can check on your education and on your music history"

She had better come clean

"Yes I play the violin. I can read music and I have passed some examinations and I have played in a quartet"

"Can you play the drums?" Shane asked

"Quiet you!" said Aengus" thats enough from you" They were happy with the news. A violin player

Aengus whispered to her "If you knew Des Shanley I'll bet you can sing as well R&R and that crowd" and he did no wait for an answer

"Next week bring your violin" said Fr Barry

"But I will be hopeless at the jigs and the reels" sne said
"Not to worry" said Aengus. "Just join us and we will make music"
The thought delighted her. What would her father think of her?. Playing this Irish and Pagan music. All those Kathleens and Rosaleensand Roisins and O Houlihans. And she the daughter of Scottish Presbyterian Settler descent.

45

IT WAS TIME to get ready for Boston. Peggy took her daughter's advice and went to see Miss Garvey. Miss Garvey was of the older genertion and she had little tinme for the modern styles. Couture was the word she used. Peggy did not know much about Couture either and so she did not feel deprived

They mixed and matched and they finished with a Donegal Tweed outfit. Peggy came over to stay with Aengus in his new house and she met Hannah Robinson. Hannah was a great comfort to her. Peggy was unsure and Hannah gave her advice and confidence

Aengus had to make his own choices with the help of a nod from Fr Barry.

The hackney car collected them and they were met at the airport by a courier who booked them into The Airport Hotel. Aengus would have liked togo to the cabaret in the Bunratty Catle but Paggy was exhausted and they had an early night. Sinead met them at Logan Airport Boston and they went to her apartment.

From then on it was a crazy succession of meeting future inlaws and dinners and strange food and drinks. The wedding at Martha Rd. Synagogue passed in a haze. It was too much to retain ;with the Chatan and the Kallah and the Canopy. Then a reception at the Boston Harbour Hotel and more dancing and speeches

Aengus was asked to speak. As far as he knew he had given his sister away in the marriage cermony but it was all so sudden and so unfamiliar that he was not sure.

He praised his sister and his mother and he said he had listened to an unfamiliar language and that he would speak to them in another ancient language and he said a few words in Donegal Irish. He mentioned that their forefathers might have had much in common as some say that the Celts are one of the lost tribes of Israel

After the wedding the pace slowed and they enjoyed the hospitality. Strange customs and rituals. Shane felt at ease with the religion that entered every aspect of their lives. It was different from the bent knee at the chapel door in Gweedore. This was a living breathing force and he could feel its comforting embrace

They were very tired and they flew straight back home to Ireland and Gweedore and prepared for the Irish wedding ceremony.

Fr Barry came over to Gweedore and officiated at the second wedding. He had made arrangements with the local Parish Priest and all went well. The local curate dropped in at the reception and gratefully received a sealed envelope. After a week at home with Peggy, Sinead and Hudi came over to Garton to stay with Aengus and to see his new house. They admired his home, made a few suggestions and presented him with a colour television set. Nice one Sinead. Luxury and style. Then they went home to Boston and everyone collapsed for a lazy week's rest

Sinead was not finished. She wrote to say that the house was too big for a single person and that he should let some of the rooms. The estate agent thought it was agood idea and EBS had no objection He fitted a shower in the bathroom and acquired two tenants. Each had their own private room and they shared the kitchen and the bathroom. He converted the garage into a common room and he put his new television set in there. He had a cleaning lady come every Monday morning. Sinead insisted on this as otherwise the place would end up a tip. One of his tenants was a clerk in the Council Offices and the other was an AG in town. They bumbled along with the odd discussion over whose socks had been hanging in the bathroom for weeks. The mortgage payments were no longer a problem

Aengus thought the Friday night sessions might suffer. But the house was always vacant for the music on a Friday night. The Ags man went home to Monaghan and his girlfriend and the Council man had a best friend in the pint of Guinness and was never home until the small hours of Saturday morning. When the electricity bill soared Aengus had coin meters installed and it worked well

As he looked out on the big garden at the back where the greyhounds were kept Aengus thought he might make better use of the space but there was plenty of time.

46

SHANE WAS NOW the owner of Lochbeg farm. In the documents and in the deeds. But he felt no different. He had known for many years that he would inherit the lot. Eugene never showed the slightest interest in the farm and he barely visited during his holidays. Maureen had her own life and was living in Sheffield. She liked it there and maybe it was more than the scenery. They all remembered Geriant with affection. But Maureen and Geriant went their seperate ways and they parted on good termsMaureen had hinted that she might like to come and nurse nearer home in the future

At home on the farm Shane and the old man carried on as before. But something had changed in their relationship and they could not put their finger on it. It was never their way to go about hugging each other, They argued and disagreed as much as ever. But this time with a certain respect. They listened and heard what the other had to say. Shane drove them to Cooney's regularly. Not to get blotto but to sit and have a chat

Shane had a secret motive. It was well known that Neil was an officer in the IRA and that he had a big part in The War of Independence. Neil refused to be drawn. He kept his secrets. Hidden away in the townland of Lochbeg in the parish of Garton in the back of beyond where time and the world seemed to pass them by. There were marches and shootings and bombings. Some as near as Claudy and there was the death of young Slevin but yet the village seemed to sleep through it all.

"What was it like in the old days?'" Shane wanted to ask. But he knew he wouls have to wait until his father was ready and in his own good time. He thought that a few pints might loosen his tongue. But it was not Neil's tongue that was the trouble. It was his mind. And it remained closed. Finally Shane asked the question

"I know, and we all know, that you were Commanding Officer of the Drumkeen Flying Column. Everyone knows more than I do"

"Son, somethings are best left" Neil replied

"but I could have a Republican hero as my father and I do not know anything" said Shane

"Some day I will tell you the whole story" said Neil

"Just tell me a bit to be going on with" pleaded Shane.

"put the kettle on and we will sit and have a chat" Neil said and he went on

"Yes I was in command of the Drumkeen Flying squad. We trained and practised in the bogs between Stranorlar and Letterkenny. We only had a few rifles and very little ammunition and some of the men never even got the chance to fire a shot. We were ready for the big day when we would rise up and declare our freedom. It never occurred to us that we were a ragbag collection with no arms and no ammunition. We were Oglaigh Na hEireann and that was all that mattered. All of Ireland would rise up with us on the big day. Then there was a mix up in Dublin and we did not know what we were to do. The RIC nabbed me and I spent a year in Mountjoy Jail. It was not all that bad as the warders were Irish and they did not treat us badly

But I benifited from the imprisonment. With me in Jail were Professors and lawyers and some very well educated men. It was like being at University with all the classes and debates

I was released and came home to take command again. This time we had no orders from High Command. The Ard Comhairle. Then Barry and Tracy did a bit of a job at Solohead Beg and the war started again

Thats enough to be going on with" and he stopped the story

"Thanks Dad. I will be back for more" said Shane and he thought of what he had just heard.

It was beginning to make sense. Here was a man who did not boast about his exploits. But Shane knew that his father considered 1916 a failure and that it achieved very little. He knew that the street urchins and the Dublin poor jeered the IRA men as they were marched to the docks on the way to English prisons. It was the murdering of the insurgents by the British that claimed world's sympathy and specially the interest of the Irish in America. The story was very interesting and Shane knew that some day he might hear what really happened from his father who had been part of it all.

He asked his mother if she could tell him anything

"I only know bits of the story. We never talk about it much. All I know was when the Free State was formed every man was a hero and claimed a pension" she told him

"Dad never got a pension?" Shane said

"No, and he never mentions it. You must have got him on a good day for him to say anything at all"

But Shane saw his father in a new light. He had a story that was worth telling if only he could get him going. But he would have to wait until the old man was ready and in the meantime there was a farm to run and a living to make

Eugene's ordination was coming soon. The big day would be in Maynooth. They thought he might be ordained in Letterkenny but he was the only ordinand and it was cheaper for the church in Maynooth. Fr Barry suggested a welcoming home party but Fr Carr said it would cost too much. Aengus and Hannah came to the rescue. They organised some supporters and they hired a minibus. Shane would drive the family car, and Aengus the minibus and Fr Barry would squeeze the rest into the football van. All three loaded vehicles headed for Maynooth. Hannah stayed at home as she thought the elders in the Kirk might be upset if she went.

The whole gang booked in to The Holiday Inn in Blanchardstown, only a short drive from Maynooth

Close family members were given places near the front of the church but behind the College Staff. What a pompous lot. They never spoke to the parents,. Not a word or a gesture. They live in their own wonderful presence. As if the ceremony was just to get rid of the hicks they had been training for the past years. Sinead's wedding in Boston had more to offer and the wedding in Gweedore had more soul. The Ordination was for the College of Maynooth. Parents and guests did not matter. It was a relief when it was all over

Then it was time to go home Over the Border and past the Customs Hut at Lifford there was a cavalcade of cars with headlights on awaiting and they were escorted in to the village by The Raphoe Pipe and Drum Band. Fr Barry had organised the whole show and Hannah who had stayed behind made sure that everything went to plan.

Fr Barry welcomed the new young Holy father and apologised for the Fr Carr's absence due to his ill health. They had a meal in the parochial hall followed by dancing. Eugene thanked them all ans he got a great cheer when he mentioned Master Byrne who had started his education. Fr Eugene was safely back home in Garton

47

EUGENES HOMECOMING WAS a great success but he was very disappointed at the small congregation that turned up for his first Mass in the church, Sure they could go to Mass at any time. No bother.

A nun from the convent came with two medals for Neil and Mary. The inscription was "My son is a priest". Neil hid his behind The Sacred Heart picture but Mary wore hers to Mass on Sunday. It looked very nice the neighbours smiled

But the Ordination cost the family money and Shane did not have a lot to spare. People at the homecoming reception gave Eugene envelopes. For the young priest. But who paid all the expenses? Eugene gratefully pocketed the money and Shane did the farm books and there was a gap where the money was used on the ordination.

Shane talked it through with Neil and mentioned it to Fr Barry. The priest agreed but what could one do? There was no way the diocese would help. The bishop ran a tight purse. But Shane did not see it like that. Tight purse my eye. Could he not drive himself about in a Volkswagon Beetle instead of that big limo and a chauffeur

Neil wanted the quiet way

"Let him have the few pounds"

"A few pounds" snorted Shane "let someone give me a few pounds. How hard we have to sweat for a few quid. He does not even put petrol in the car. He should stay at home and stop his gallivanting. All this visiting and his First Blessing with the hand out. But no petrol for the car. Says he is saving up in case he is sent to a poor and backward patish"

Neil tried to defend his son Eugene "He will need a car to visit the sick. He could not really go on a push bike. Could he now? Tell me"

"Did Jesus have a car or a bicycle?" asked Shane but he knew he was losing the argument and he finished with "Let his parishioners help him out then or the bloody bishop"

Eugene was posted to Glenmore. It could not have been a more remote parish. Deep in the Bluestack Mountains. The Parish Priest, Monsignor Brennan, was a retired Professor of Philosophy from Maynooth and he was more interested in Socrates and in Thomas Aquinas than he was in his parishioners. Monsignor Brennan was a feebie for the diocese as he had been on the staff of Maynooth and Maynooth was a College of the National University of Ireland and the good Monsignor was on a very nice pension. He was however the author of some very learned tomes on Thomas Aquinas and he knew more about Aristotle than he did about running the parish of Glenbeg. Summa Contra Gentiles was more to him than the times of the Sunday Mass. It was not his fault that he was isolated out in the mountains

But that was of no consolation either to Father Eugene O Neill. Monsignor Brennan let Eugene have his car but when he was away doing further research Eugene had to make do and he once did an Extreme Unction visit on O Reilly's tractor.

Neil was not happywith how things were with Eugene. The young man was not independent. He was proud of his son and he suggested to Shane that they give Eugene the deposit on a car and leave him to pay the instalments himself to the Credit Union

Fr Barry had a word with Shane and they got a Ford Anglia for Eugene. Nothing was said but Shane felt that his mother made some of the repayments to the Credit Union

Out there in the far beyond and no friends close. Shane said Eugene was welcome to call at Lochbeg any time and the priest dropped in for a good fry up on the pan and a few bits to take back to his remote parochial house

Gradually he became more isolated and withdrawn. He did not have any official holidays but he could have a day off when Monsignor Brennan was in residence. He needed the breaks. The parochial house was cold and dark and empty. His own room was dismal and damp. Some days his only contact with the outside world was to see the GNR bus pass on the main road far away up on the main road. There was no daily Mass as no one came to attend. Monsignor Brennen advised him not to bother about Mass for the people every day. No one cared. Fr Brennen did not wish to make a collar for his own neck. Eugene was sure Aristotle would have phrased it much more eloquently

48

FR BARRY ENJOYED the Friday sessions. The highlight of his week. Better then Doherty's in Strabane or the one in Omagh. The friendship and the camaraderie and of course the food. Aengus and he were like brothers. Young Shane was another thing. He admired his cheekiness and his self confidence. He was a different person completely to his brother Eugene. The old man Neil was a difficult one to handle and Fr Barry avoided politics with him. But that lad Shane?. Where would he finish?. It was a pity he missed out on Higher education. He would have lapped it up and he and Aengus would have guided himalong the right lines. Pity, just a pity.

But the young man seemed happy as he was. Much happier now that he and his old man had settled their little difficulty. Maybe it helped that Eugene was off their hands at last.

Hannah was making a big difference to the music sessions. She brought a softness and a gentleness that made it all the more pleasing. Looking at them now playing and their faces aglow with the music Fr Barry felt a great love for them all

They practised every Friday and soon it was time for them to perform in public. To sit on a stage and bash out the reels and the hornpipes would soon have an audience bored. Playing as a Ceili band was different as the dancing and the sexual attracrtion kept the listeners' minds occupied. But unless one was a connoisseur of techniques and of regional music variations then the continuous playing was boring

Hannah asked if she might make a suggestion

"I had a teacher in Derry who does music arrangements. It might be a good idea for him to hear us play. A German. Herr Kreid"

They went to Herr Kreid. He was delighted to meet his old pupil and he listened to their music.They explained what they had in mind and he agreed

"What you need is not a ceili band. Too many ceili bands. All over the place. What you need is the soft and the gentle kind of the music. Hornpipes and reels with the easy melodies. No rush and tumble. You play for the angels. You play for the sads and you play for the joys and then you finish with a gusto. You might have a love tune and then a weepy sad Irish tune but you finish to leave everyone happy and smiling. Leave it with me. I will arrange for you. I am a happy man"

But there was one problem.They did not have a vocalist. Herr Kreid said they needed a vocalisst

Aengus looked at Fr Barry

"Father you do a good job at the Benediction on Sunday evenings"

"No no, not at all" said Fr Barry "I cannot carry a tune. I just shout as loud as I can. But did I hear someone mention the R&R?. Did someone say they spent some time with The Rathmines and Rathgar musivcal Soociety?"

Vacant and feigned looks all around "The R&R?"

"Aw come on come on. Not that. Give me a break" wailed Hannah "that was in confidence. Totally in confidence"

"Hannah" said Fr Barry "confidence is psrt of my calling and keeping secrets is an everyday thing with me. We are not breaking any confidence. I will bet there are hundreds in the R&R who remember you"

"Ok Ok so I was a member of the R&R but I was no great singer" she said "But" said Fr Barry "you do not have to be a Bernadette Greevy to sing with us. It helps if you are a bit adenoidal with a catch in your throat. A teardrop in your voice. Ruby Murray. A bit of the rain and the mist"

The argument went round and round. They tried to get her sing Not a peep.

Shane said he would sing, He would be a singer if no one else would. He would show them. Nothing better in his mind than the mike in his hands and an adoring audience. Not Maio Lanza but he could be a Barry Manilow. Yea man yea.

They let him sing. He tried. And again. It was too much. Sniggering and coughing they listened as he gave "Mary of Dungloe" a very cruel death

Hannah went to make the rtea

"Milk is gone sour" she said but hey missed her joke

"Thank you Shane for that wonderful demonstration" she said

"Of how not to sing" added Fr Barry "Come on Hannah. Give us a few bars"

She sang "Down By The Sally Gardens" and they applauded

"She has the wrong shape of a mouth for Irish songs" Shane remarked and he hung his fhead

"We will have no more silly remarks" said Fr Barry. "Hannah has a grand voice. No more remarks. Hear that now and I mean it.We can have her learn to sing like the best of the traditional singers. As good as Dolly herself and even Dolores Keane.

"Well that's it for tonight said Aengus "I cooked a chicken this afternoon and Shane has brought some sausages"

There was some serious eating to be done

The next Friday was going to be a very crucial meeting. Fr Barry warned the two other men. Hannah had to be converted and he did not want any mistakes, . . ." So softly softly and no silly remarks" he said and he looked at Shane

They decided not to do any playing. Tonight was a night for talk

"I sing this way" said Hannah "It is the way I was taught"

"Yes Hannah we know that the way you sing is the correct way" Said Fr Barry, "It is the correct way for Gilbert and Sullivan and for formal singing. But there are other ways of singing. In the church we have Gregorian Chant. The Indians have a wailing they call singing and the West Indiands have their own way too. All I am saying is that singers adapt to the circumstances. We will not ask you to sing in a torn cardigan or sing through your nose into your jumper. But you are the only one of us who can sing. Let us stop and consider the matter"

"My vocals may be lacking" admitted Shane

"Me too" said Aengus

"I can do Gregorian chant" said Fr Barry "but that is only shouting out in a funny manner"

"So you men want me to be the singer?" said Hannah "That is sex discrimination. Yes it is. Just like the men. Really"

"let us hear the alternatives. A few bars of "Mary "again Shane if you please"

They all begged for mercy. Dear God let there be peace. Fr Barry said nothing but he thought they had made their point. Best to let things settle. He knew the bond between them was strong enough and a solution would be arrived at. No hurry.

Next week Hannah got in first

"I have listened carefully to what has been said and I have been thinking"

They were waiting. That she had been thinking

Jesus get on with it thought Shane. One could die thinking too much

"Well I will give it a try" she said

She got three great hugs

"Now listen to me" she said. "I will act a singing role. I will have a lot to learn. I will imitate Dolores Keane or whoever and I will sing in Character"

It was a victory for them all.

And they set to work. They would form a cabaret act. They experimented and fought and argued and compromised and fought again and tried to get it together. No Margaret Barry or Dolly McMahon but their own style. Maybe there was some lampooning of some of the old singers but there was true music in what they achieved.

They now had a compact cabaret show. Irish traditional music singing in the sean nos or very nearly sean nos, some bits of poetry and a few stories. But it was not enough to come on stage and perform. Theyhad to control the mood. The lighting had to very according to the mood. They came off stage between acts and they drew the curtains when they moved to another section of their performance. It was miusic and song and talk in the Gaelic tradition. Hannah mastered the half notes and the sliding notes of the olden Kathleens'. Shane was the man for the diddling or the mouth music and because he did not have a note in his head he brought the house down. Good old Shane. And when he was dressed in his bainin jacket and wide Aran trousers and pampootees he only had to lift an eyebrow to have them laughing

Hannah was happy in that she did not have to sing very often at all. But she was the star of the show. She sang to close the evenings' entertaimnment. Slowly and hauntingly in a West of Ireland brogue. Shane acccompanied her with just a quiet echo. And when the last notes of "Thady O Neill" faded into the night there was not a sound to be heard. Stunned silence

They played at one or two of the sessions in Doherty's and at Omagh and the word was passed round. They got bookings for weddings, GAA functions and church funds' concerts

What would they call themselves? The Garton Minstrels?. No.

The Garton 4?. No.

The Lagan Four? Yes Sir. The Lagan 4. Short and asweet. Lagan Valley was their Valley. Not that place in County Down. Their lagan had only one 'g' no matter what they say

So Lagan 4 it was and Lagan 4 it stayed

But even though they played as a goup at many events Hannah would not go to the sessions in Doherty's. Not a place for ladies she said. Especially a Presbyterian lady at that. Theysaid she would be a great favourite as now she had her own singing technique. A cross between Dolly Parton, Ruby Murray nd Dolores Keane with a dash of Delia Murphy to top it off. Like a touch of Grand Marnier in a coffee

Stage names were needed. Fr Barry was to wear black thick rimmed glasses and he was to have heavy sideburns down to the side of his mouth. His hair parted in the middle amnd he was known as Corney

Shane was to wear his bainin waistcoat and a high necked Aran Gansey and a Donegal Tweed cap and pampootees on his feet and he was known as Beartlai

Aengus was to have a high collar and a dark tie and round steel rimmed Glasses and his hair stuck to his head with Brylctreem ans he was known as Duff

Hannah was the problem. They did not wish to dress her up as someone else. Not as a character. Semicomical would not be appropriate

Why not a beautiful name for a beautiful lady?

There was Maeve or Emer or Cliona.

Emer the wife of Cuchulainn

Maeve, queen of Connaught and of the Tain Bo Cooley. It was Cliona they settled for

Cliona, Queen of the Banshees

49

NEIL WAS READING the newspaper when Shane came down the stairs.

"What's the funny smell?" he asked from behind the paper

"What are you on about?." asked Mary

"Just a funny small that's all" Neil said.

Shane knew well. Smart in his old age he was getting. A sense of humour. Better than the sour old bollicks he usually is. Say nothing he thought

"Well I smell nothing" Mary said and she smiled over at Shane

"You trod an anything?" Neil asked from behind the paper

Keep cool thought Shane. Old smelly socks himself. Smart arse

"Must be off now" said Shane and he went

"There was no need for that" Mary chided. "I think he might have a girlfriend. He has never used aftershave before"

"Smelled all right. A bit spicy" Neil remarked

"It is called Old Spice and he got it last week" she said

"I'm happy for him. A bit of female compamny will doo him good" Neil ventured

"Listen to who's talkin' will ya? Mary asked

It all happened so quickly and Shane was a bit embarrassed.

He was playing in goal. It was a friendly agains McCools and no one cared who won or lost. It really was a social. Every player who wanted got a game or part of a game and there was a bit of a gathering after the match. The older players went to the pub and the younger men went to Brady's coffee shop

Shane spent most of the game leaning against the goalpost as all the play was in the McCools half. It did not seem to bother them either. Just to get a game was enough for them all. The honour of wearing a Garton Gael's jersey was enough for Shane

"Hi Gorgeous. Hi there Gorgeous". It was coming from an embankment behind the goalposts. He ignored it. He would look silly if the taunt was for someone else. Just ignore it

"Hello gorgeous. Hello handsome. Lovely legs"

Ignore them, Ignore them. Just ignore them

"Lovely legs. Lovely knees. What a nice bum"

What was he going to do? Tell them to clear off?

Heha to take a kick out and it was a good one

"Ooo Oooo look at them muscles. Show us yer chest"

He did not look back but the next wide he had a peep as he retrieved the ball

There were four lassies sitting on the wall behind the goalposts. Legs swinging and having a good time. Taking the Michael. Yea. Havin' him on.

"Come on Beartlai. Get your cap and Gansey"

That got him. They knew who he was. He fumbled the next ball and the Master shouted for him to keep his mind on the game. But how could he tell the Master that four lassies were baiting him?.

Half time came and he felt better. He would move to the other side of the field down by the river away from his tormentors

But damn me who was down there before him but one of the lassies?. On her own. She said nothing but clapped when he made a moderate save

"Well done Beartlai. Well done" she said. He had a wee look and she smiled at him

The final whistle amnd he was walking up the pitch when she came up beside him

"Beartlai from Lagan4. Right?" she said

"Naw naw, wrong guy" he said

"Will ya stop coddin. me?. I saw you in The Intercounty last week. On the accordeon. You were not bad under that cap. Just admit it"

"What's your name?" Shane asked

"Terry Flynn"

"My name is Shane. Shane O Neill and I am from Lochbeg in Garton"

"I know" she said

"But I think Terry Flynn is a lovely name. It has rhyme to it. There is a tune called Terry Flynn" Shane answered

"Well" she sais "I know there is a book called Tarry Flynn about a poet in Monaghan. Me dad is from around there and he called me Terry. He could not call me Tarry in real lidfe I suppose. I have enough trouble when people think I am a lad"

Some people must be very blind thought Shane

"I am going to Brady's after I have changed and will you join me there and you can tell me all about yourself" Shane suggested.

"You might tell me all about the Lagan4 and I might get your autograph" she said and she gave a cheeky shrug of her shoulders

That was how the romance started

Terry was studying at the Letterkenny Institute of Technology. LIT she called it. Her father was from Monaghan and he was an accountant in the town. She was studying to be an accountant herself. Eventually. But her dad says that eventually will never happen unless she gets her head into her books

Shane started to tell her about himself but she kept interrupting and saying "I know, I know"

Soon old Mr Brady was tidying up and asking if they had any homes to go to and it was time all good people were in bed

They agreed to meet again and go to he pictures at the Ritz. She said she and her best friemnd Eileen Coughlan came in to the cinema every Friday night. But when she saw the look an Shane's face she said that Eileen did not need to sit with them. Gradually they progressed to the back row of the cinema where they could have the wee kiss and the cuddle. Nothing serious. The Redemptorists at the Mission threatened damnation for any hanky panky

But Shane did not get off that easy. The others in the Lagan 4 heard about his romance

Was it a fan club?. Membership exclusive or could they all join?Did one have to be a good looker? Was it skirts only?. Did they screech and throw their knickers?

"Can't a fella have any privacy?" he wailed

"Privacy? Privacy? Anyone talking about privacy? Whats that. In Garton? Ger off wid ya"

But the novelty soon wore off and they left him alone

But Terry Flynn liked Old Spice and Mary noticed a new toothbrush and a change of underpants regularly. Bless his little heart. Neil was more direct and he asked Shane who his girlfriend was and did her parents have lots of money. Romantic Ireland was with O Leary in the grave for certain as far as Neil was concerned

As luck would have it Eileen Coughlan found herself a boy friend. Great stuff. The girls would come in to town together and Shane would drive Terry home. Eileen and her man did their own thing

Terry said her parents would like to meet Shane. Her father had heard of Neil's fame and his history and her mother wanted to see what Shane looked like

"They wont bite you. They will be as nervous as yourself" Terry assured him

Best collar and tie joband he went for tea, Michael Flynn did not have much to say. Suppose accountants do not talk that much.

Shane managed the knives and forks and the evening passed. He was expecting a quiet word from the father as they do in the movies like" I am trusting you with my daughter" and all that stuff but all he said when Shane was leaving was "Now you look after her"

That was not too bad" she said and she leaned over and kissed his ear
"You have to look after me. Look after me young man. Get it?"
They went to the cinema and to dancing ftrom Donegal Town to Mudff and when they had enough dancing they wenyt back to the car and cuddled in the back seat.They became closer

"Have you read "Lady Chatterleys Lover"?" she asked

"Onlythe dirty bits" he said

"How come?" she asked.

"One of the lads has the book with the pages turned down at all the dirty bits so you dont have to read all the dull parts

You ever done it?" she asked

"You? "He said

No not really" she said "but I nearly did once but they say you should only do it with someone you love. Someone special. You want to try?" she said

Yea we must" he said and they left it for another time.

Shane went to the pharmacy in Strabane and bought a big packet of Durex. If he wa going to be embarrassed every time he might as well get them all in one go. They became lovers and Terry was a bit disappointed that the earth did not move. Shane wrote to Maureen and she sent him a manual "The Joy of Sex" as he had seen advertised in The News Of The World. He waited at the bottom of the lane every day. Tommy Martin had seen it all before and all he said when he handed over the brown paper parcel swas "Enjoy"

Terry and Shane read the book and had a giggle.

"Imagine us like that in the back seat of the car" but after a few weeks when Terry gave a shudder and a moan he knew that he was getting better

What about Confession? Should they tell?Certainly not to Fr. Barry. Anyway there was a bishop down South who was up to no good and he was not excommunicated and there was a Cardinal who had a heart attack and died in a Bordello in France

They agreed they were not hurting anybody and they wreere causing no trounble even if he had to avoid Michael Flynn's eye when they met. Maureen phoned and asked how he was getting on with the book. Neil was in the kitchen at the time and Shane had to let on the call was from Omagh about his playing the accordeon and he told her how the listeners were enjoying his tunes. She got the message

He was sure Hannah sussed what was happening. One evening when they were in Aengus' kitchen waiting on the kettle she lookesd at hinm and said

"Shane I think you are in love"

He could not say anything or they would tease him so he looked at her and smiled. She was a woman of the world and she would know what his smile meant.

Women know about these things. Don't they?.

50

THINGS WERE GOING well back at Lochbeg farm. The corn the potatoes the turnips and the hay. They killed the odd pig, sold a few beasts, reared a dozen or more turkeys and Shane still had his eggs. Shane did the odd day for Ivan Ashe and had pocket money. The Master and Fr. Barry and Hannah bought the odd trailer load of logs. The fishing and the caravans were ticking over nicely. He had two caravans and ten fishing pegs or stages on the loch. It suited the old fashioned English fishermen. They liked the solitude and the Guinness

The loch was now well stocked but the facilities were poor. Shane needed proper toilets and an electric supply. He went to Conlons the architects and they drew a scenario for eight caravans around the loch with a central laundry and washroom and a common kitchen. He called in on the AGS and they would not believe it. Only some years ago he was asking about basic farming. Was he not happy in what he was doing? Doing very well from what they heard. Better than most small farmers in the locality.

Neil thought the same. Why could he not settle for what he had? What was the need for more?. But Shane did not agree. Stay where you are? No way. It was forwards and upwards for him. Neil himself would never admit it but he had a begrudging admiration for his son and wished he was forty years younger to keep up

Shane went to the manager of the local Northern Bank

"A holiday village? In Garton?" he sneered. Shane walked out.

The Credit Union were sorry but this was beyond their remit and their limits. But they took hin into the office and together they made a list of his assets

He owned his own farm. He had a business in the farming and in the lake and he traded in livestock and farm produce. He had his youth and his business acumen. But his main assets was his land. He had two fields by the road and they were worth a lot of money

"How is that?" he asked. Farmers never think of selling land. It comes from centuries back in history. Land is sacred. But the Credit Union wre right. Those fields were worth a lot. Building sites. But building sites for high quality houses. Houses for the well to do

Neil did not agree Sell some of our land?. More land is what we need

But Shane kept on, We do not need more land. What we need is to make better use of the land we have. But that takes money We have assets by the roadside.

Who would wish to build in the country? Think man think . . . . Townies

People who worked in the towns and who wanted the fresh air and their open space at weekends and in the long Summer evenings

Shane thought of one man. Mr Lavin. Joseph Lavin the dentist in Strabane. He had been a great Mayo footballer in his day and he had settled in Strabane with his wife and two sons. He lived above his surgery in the Square in Strabane and he often came to Doherty's to the sessions. Fr Barry knew him as well as he came out to watch the football and to fish on the Finn River. His boys were growing up and Strabane was not the best place for teenage boys. Shane called to see him at his surgery and he remembered Shanes playing in Doherty's. He was very interested and he came out and looked at the site and he thought it might suit him and his family.It might even be suitable for a dental surgery if one of his boys qualified as a dental surhgeon.

But all this he would have to discuss with his wife and two boys. Forever the optimist, Shane considered the sale as good as done. One down and two or three to go. Move over Onassis

They say entrepreneurs are born and that they have an innate feeling and it cannot be taught. Shane had that feeling.

He took Conlons plan to the Wynns and the estate agent had a look at Mr Conlon's plans. He told them he had one customer who would take one of his sites and he was a customer who would build a quality house on the site and that he Shane would not sell to anyone below a certain level. All he needed was more quality buyers. That they could feel safe in that they would be among equa;ls. With Herdman's and Fruit of the Loom deveplopment in the locality Wynn's told him there should be executives coming in. They would be in contact.

Wynn's called him within the week. They had a client who would purchase one of his sites. But the client wished to remain anonymous and any attempt to find out awho it was would mean cancellation of the deal.Tax and indemnities and things like that. Meant nothing to Shane as long as he was paid. A deposit was given.

With his new money Shane went on a business holiday to England. He was interested in holiday villages over there and with Conlon's guidance and he modelled his loch set up on the best he saw. The Electricity Supply Board brought in the power lines to ten individual caravan sites. They were not at th loch side but hidden in the woods. No cars were allowed beyond the car park at the front of the farmhouse and the place was quiet for the wild animal life and the dawn chorus. He built a community centre with showers, washing machines and a play room. There was no need for planning permission as Fianna Fail had no time for trivialities like that. The whole country had gone mad building Spanish Haciendas all over the mountainsides and no one cared. And here in Lochbeg out of sight was out of mind

He now had his caravan business going. But he was still not finished. He had seen Bernard Matthews in England with his intensive chicken farms. He applied fotr a Governmenyt Grant with the idea of starting on those lines. The government officials came. It was a nice day out. No. they could not give him any help. Yet the boyos in Gweedore and in Connemara were getting grants to grow tomatoes and mushrooms. Mushrooms? Jasus did you ever hear the like?. Some of them had never eaten a mushroom in their lives

The IDA had empty premises but they would not let him have one. As if they did not want the locals to succeed. Waiting for the Yanks or the Japs and then have them tax free with a government grant

Neil mad a remark "If you cannot beat them then you join them at their own game"

Then what he meant was clear. The politicians looked after their own. Government ministers looked after their own.

At a Lagan 4 meeting the matter was discussed and it was decided theat a political answer was the only one for Garton.

But they knew nothing about politics.

But they knew a man who did. Neil O Neill was invited to the next Friday.

51

THIS MEETING WAS not for music.

Fr Barry spoke first." Neil we are lost here in Garton. Years ago we ewere East Donegal constituency and we had our own TD. Our own man in the Dail. Independent he was. But now the Fianna Fail crowd have it all to themselves with the Fine Gael lot as a side show in the pantomime. Neil you are the wisest and the most experienced man here and we ask you for your opinion and your advice. Maybe we should organise a petition What do you think?"

"Petition my eye. Let us take them on" Neil almost shouted

"Take them on?"

"Yes take them on. In the ballot box"

Aengus cleared his throat and asked" Do you mean we have a candidate in the next election?" There was silence and everyone looked st the old man

"I could do with a cup of tea or a glass of porter" he said. "It will oil the vocal chords. For I have a good few words to say"

"A bottle of stout?"

"The very job "Neil replied and he then continued

"I have been thinking very carefully so listen to what I have to say. I know how our political system works and I think I know a way of having it work in our favour. At least we then get our fair share and not let them thieves take all

To start with we do not need to win any great battles. The fear of what we might be able to accomplish will do for a start. We must enter the local election and win a seat on the local council. Win that seat and keep it safe and secure"

"Only a Council seat?" asked Fr Barry

"It is enough to be going on with. It is an entry into the political arena. What we might do in that arena is what will cause the others to worry"

"What name will we go under.?. I propose Sinn Fein" said Fr Barry

"No no. not Sinn Fein "said Neil

You were a Sinn Feiner once,father" said Shane

"Now as I said. Just listen to me. Sinn Fein is not for us. Let me tell you that"

"You were active in Sinn Fein were you not?" said Aengus

"Yes I was. That is another story. Let us stay with our problem here in Garton. Some other day I will tell you the Sinn Fein story

"We would love to hear it now" said Fr Barry hopefully

Neil went on "I was active up to the end of the Civil War. I sided with the Free Staters after the War of Independence and the end of the fighting. But then I was a DeValera man. Now I am a DeValera man even though he put me iin Jail once. He is the best politician this country ever had. Not because of what he did but because of what he did not do. He had made a truce agreement with Collins before the mad men took over the Four Courts. He even resigned as an officer in the IRA and rejoined as a private. His whole object was to take the extremism out of Irish politics when the Brits had gone. I doubt if he fired one shot after the 1916 Rising. He was in America for most or the horrific and cruel times. When he did enter politics again in 1926 he was a moderate and in the war years he had internment for IRA men who would not obey the civil law"

But you were still an IRA man" said Fr Barry

"Not really. I joined the Irish Volunteers. They were not anything to do with the IRA. We were formed formed to counter the Ulster Volunteers who opposed the Home Rule bill that was passed in Westminster. Redmond had got us Home Rule but Carson and his lot opposed it"

"So there was no need for 1916 at all?" asked Shane

"We were no better off after The War of Independence and the Civil War than we would have been without any of the fighting" said Neil

"Load of rubbish" said Fr Barry

"Cool down Father" said Neil. "those men of 1916 were great and brave heroes who gave their lives for Ireland. But they were not politicians. Poets, teachers authors philosophers, yes. But politicians they were not. Now DeValera was a politician to his finger tips. He was never a true Republican. He only joined the Gaelic Lweague because he fancied Sinead Flanagan. He was never in the secret IRB, those extreme Republicans who took over the Irish Volunteers and the IRA and he let a free State supporter be the first President when the State of Ireland was formed"

"They set out to form an Irish Republic and Ireland will never be at rest until we are all one. All one nation and as one people" said Fr Barry in his true Patriotic Voice. Neil was kind to him

"Fr Barry" he quietly said" but we are one. We are one nation. I can go in to Strabane without any trouble and I can do as any man in Strabane does. I can do what I want. Here in this room one of our group is of plantation descent. She is one of us. A dearly beloved one of us

I am not going to give a history lecture. Too much of what has happened has yet to be told. It is too recent. Leave it lie. So I suggest we stay away from the patriotic or the Republican politics"

'Sinn Fein is out then you think?" asked Aengus

"Yes I do. I think we should go for the voter who is not interested in political ideals. Our neighbour who is more interested in his wage packet or the price of a pint or who wishes they would mend the road up to the bog. Leave the lofty ideals to the intellectuals. Anyone agree with me?"

Hannah spoke "Thank you Neil. Very revealing words. I think we must be independent. Independent for the area"

"Not Fianna Fail?" said Fr Barry" they would appreciate our assistance"

Neil interrupted again

"If ye do not mind let me explain my ideas a bit more. If we side with Fianna Fail they will be delighted. In the election our candidate will get at least their third preference.under the PR system. The big boys in Innishowen and Letterkenny will feel much safer when we take votes from the Fine Gael party. But if we go Independent ane win good support in the Council election the big boys will not know who we will support in the general Election. There will be no need for us to enter the General Election at all. No needed for us to show our hand. Who will follow us and what side we might support?. But we must do well in the Council election. If we get a big vote then they will not know how many of their voters will come to our side in the General election. It could cost any of the main parties a seat. There is not much difference in the main parties agendas. Most voters vote as their fathers did, But our agenda will be about local issues and what is close to them and if we are successful locally we can apply political blackmail

You help us and we help you?. You scratch my back and all that?"

Hannah spoke again

"We must remain independent, We must stay local. Our name will have local connections. Short and succinct"

"Well said" Neil praised her and he went on "That is enough politics for tonight. We will meet again next Friday and each of you must have at least four names for our new political party"

No one bothered toplay a tune

52

THEY MET AGAIN with Neil in the chair. What were they going to name their party?

Fr Barry was for Sinn Fein but they ignored him

"Any names then?" said Neil

The Lagan Locals,Donegal Farmers. The Wee Men, The Bogmen. Home Help. Dirty Hands, Parish People

Neil was not amused. "Thats enough of the funnies. Give me some serious offerings. We need a seperate identity; Away from all the other parties.What do we all share in this part of Donegal?. The land, the river, the Finn, the church, the border?. Come on Come on. What do we all share in this part of Donegal?. Swirl them allaround your minds and let me have an answer"

"Finn Valley" called Shane "Finn Valley"

"But there is a Finn Harps and a Finn Athletic Club" said Fr Barry

"No one has a monopoly on the Finn" said Aengus "and I think it fits well. Short and it locates us"

"What do you think Hannah?" Neil asked

"I think it is a good name. It does not offend any on our side of the fence. Non denominational. Right here amongst us. Finn Harps and the AC will do us no harm"

"Right" said Neil. "Now let us move on. What will we campaign under?. It has got to be local issue like, dredge the Finn, or something along those lines"

"And who will we have as candidate?" Neil asked

"It has gotta be yourself" Aengus said "you have a big reputation from the past"

"No not me please" Neil pleaded "I cannot allow my name to go forward and that is final" he said

"Oh come on Neil." said Aengus "You must lead us You have been a leader in the past. We all know of the wonderful work you did in the Troubles. People will remember you for what you did"

"Naybe I should be remembered for what I did not do" Neil said and his face dropped

Fr Barry wasted no time.

"Neil you must tell us your story. You have promised us you would tell us and we swould love to hear it from you"

Neil looked at the priest and then at his son Shane, and he said

"I will tell you of a burden I have been carrying for many years"

And he began

"Contrary to what people believe I was never a member of the IRA. I joined the Irish Volunteers. Redmond and Asquith had Home Rule passed in 1912 but the Lords intervened and then the First World War started. James Larkin had founded the Irish Citizen Army But in 1913 McNeill founded The Irish Volunteers. They were to oppose the threat from The Ulster Volunteers and Carson and Bonar Law who opposed Home Rule for the whole island of Ireland. The Irish Volunteers were to help Redmond's cause. But the Irish Republican Brotherhood, the IRB, infiltrated the Irish Volunteers. They were the main onsurgents in 1916. We in the Volunteers did not know if the 1916 Rising was on or off. But when the 1916 men were murdered we became the IRA and we did as we were told. I had done a shift in Kilmainham jail before the Rising. Then came The War of Independence against the British and we had our own flying column in Drumkeen. The Truce was eventually signed and then there was the Civil War. The details of that I will not talk about but I was on the Treaty side. I agreed that signing The Treaty at the time was the best thing for Ireland. We had achieved what Redmond and Dillon and Parnell wanted and there was no need for any more killing

But some of the boys down South wre not happy with the Treaty and we started fighting among ourselves. I understood that they felt the North should have been included in the new Irish Free State. But I felt we had won the right to govern ourselves and if the North did not want to join in with us we did not have the right to make them. In any case we did not have the guns or the ammunition to make them to join us

A few gangs of anti treaty men travelled the country trying to raise some support but they finally gave up. Our Column came across a few of them over the mountain beyond and we had no trouble taking them prisoners, We locked them up in Drumboe. They were prisoners of the Civil War. Kerry men. Daly, Larkin, Enright and O Sullivan. I got to know them well and I used to drop in with the fags and a drop of poteen and we played the cards

But the Treaty Government shot those men. In cold blood. Fellow Irishmen. Patriots who were prepared to die for Ireland. They shot them. Shot them like dogs. Our own brothers in war.

I never went back. Never had anything to do with them again. I never asked for a medal or a pension. I have sleepless nights. I find it hard to live with. Shot in cold blood like dogs. They never got a trial. The Treaty Government tried to say they were shot in retaliation for crimes done by the anti treaty forces elsewhere. What crimes?. We will never know the truth because some of the men responsible for those murders are still alive and some are still in authority. I still have a hatred of patriotic politicians and I do not trust them

Now that is all I am going to tell you. But you must promise that what I have said here will never be repeated outside of this room. I want your solemn oath on that"

They sat and looked. Fr Barry had to go to the toilet and Hannah was wiping her eyes

Shane stood up and said "They are afraid of the truth

"I can see now why all out history books end at 1921"

Fr Barry came over and handed Neil a glass of whiskey

"Get that down you. I am sure you have a lot more to tell" he said

Neil shook his head "No more stories. The history lesson is over"

He rose to leave "Come on son. Time to go home. Tomorrow is anotherday and there is work tobe done"

He opened the door and walked out he was seated in the car when Shane arrived. They did not speak. There was a vow of secrecy and Shane never mentione that night again. To anybody.

But the quiet and crotchety old man who was his father was now somethingcompletely different

He was now a silent hero

Not many fathers are heroes to their sons

Neil O Neill was the exception.

53

BUT FR BARRY culd not leave it alone. When ever he was bored or lonely he would drop in on the farm. They almost had an arrangement. Ftr Barry was interested in the Politics and Neil was interested in The Hereafter

Fr Barry wasted no time. He wanted to know.

"You said the 1916 Rising was not necessary and that we would have been as well off if it had neverhappened?. Did all those patriots die in vain?" he opened the debate

Neil replied in a less agresive tone

"The Home Rule had been passed in May 1912.We would have had Home Rule eventually" he said "But the Ulster Volunteers were armed. There would have been a bloody war" countered the priest

"Not really. The North would have been given their own government as a satellite sstate within the Commonwealth. We could all exist within the Commonwealth" said Neil. "Our man Butt had the right idea" said Neil

"But those men gave their lives" Fr Barry countered

"I know" said Neil "and I respect them. They were dreamers and idealistic patriots. But the truth is that the man in the street was not interested in a Republic. All he wanted was a fair government. The original Wolfe Tone rising was not for a Republic. It was for fairer trade laws. The Finianism and the Republicanism was an American pie in the sky dream. We did not fight the Orangemen and the Unionists. We fought among ourselves instead. We killed our brothers"

"So you think it was all amistake?"

"No not a mistake. It was idealistic. All of those IRB men were patriots and men of great integrity. Poets and professors and writers. But they were too far removed from the people. The poor of Dublin jeered and mocked the IRA men as they were marched down the docks on the way to English prisons. You know that" Neil said and he went on

"But I suppoort those men until the day I die. When the Rising got under way I joined the IRA and Ifought with them. What happened had happened and we had to support them but there were other ways"

"So you think Redmond and Dillon might have done better?" Fr Barry asked again

"They might have done. But they handled the Conscription Issue very badly and that lost them some of their credability. But the British Empire was beginning to break up in any case and the world was changing. Look at what happned in Canada, Australia and India. We were in the pipeline if you see what I am getteing at.

But enough of that. Let us get down to important things and my first question" Neil stopped talking and looked at Fr Barry and he asked

"Is there a God?That is the big question" and Neil sat back in his chair.

Fr Barry might have been asked that question before

"What is your definition of a God? The person who created the world in six days and took a breather on Sunday?I do not believe that. The Bible is not meant to be taken literally" said Fr Barry

But Neil was not letting him off that easy

"Is there a Supreme Being up there?" he asked

This got the priest. "I do not know" he answered. "That is a strange answer from a Catholic priest. I want to believe in a God and that there is life after death. It is in our nature to believe in a Higher Power.They had the Sun and the Stars in the olden days.We are the same. We need a God. The need to believe is greater than the belief itself"

"I feel the same" said Neil ' I want there to be the Presence of a God around me and when I die that my soul will not be all alone. So we agree that while we cannot prove for certain that there is a God we do belieeve there is one out there somewhere.

"A Jesuit could not have said it better" said Fr Barry

"How many miles to the gallon are you getting out of the Cortina?" Neil suddenly asked. Back to terra firma

But they loved the chat and the little discussions. Neil had spent time in jails with some of the senior officers of Sinn Fein and the IRA. He listened as they debated and argued and he learned from them. There was much he did not understnd but his mind was awakened.

Fr Barry had been through the Seminary and the University and his professors were as confused as he was himself

If there was a God he believed in Him and if there was no God then he was making a big mistake and it was not his fault

Theyagreed on one thing. One was a Fenian who did not believe in a Republic and the other was a clergyman whowas not sure there was a God.

Only in The Republic of Blessed Ireland

54

FINN VALLEY WAS their name and they were Independent and they would offer nothing to any of the other political parties. But they had to select thir own candidate.

"Definitely not me "said Neil

"But you are the best known of us all in the county" he was told "Aye naybe the best known, But by the older generation. And some of them will not look me in the eye. I still hace enemies among the freedom fighters. Too much history I carry. So leave me out"

"You Fr Barry?" they asked" here have been great peoples' priests down the Centuries. Fr Murphy in Wexford. Fr Flanagan in Derry. FrMcDyer over in the Glen"

But Fr Barry said "No not me. I could be transferred to another parish at any time. Could be out of here next week. Depends on the Bishop"

That left Aengus and Shane and Hannah

Aengus got in first" Not me. I am from Gweedore and the Gweedore men are not loved in this part of the county, Too wild. Not suitable in the public estimation;;

"Well it looks like you son" said Neil and he looked at Shane

"Get off" said Shane "What do I know about politics? Forget it"

Then Hannah spoke "Unless we go for an oustsider it must be you Shane"

Shane gave it his last shot "You could do it Hannah. You would look good. They would vote for you"

But Hannah replied "Things have changed since our man was elected. He was a member of the Orange Order but he was a man for all the people and he was very well respected. There is no way a Presbyterian and a woman could have any influence now. Times have changed and so have the new constituency boundaries. So it has to be you Shane if we go ahead"

Shane had no option

How did the new candidate feel?

He liked the quiet way his father was in control. The old Commandant had come out of retirement. The flame was relit and his steadiness was reassuring. He had the ability to banish fear and with his integrity and his command anything was possible.

They launched their electoral campaign

They would put posters everywhere. On telephone poles, walls, fences;everywhere until Finn Valley was known from Barnes Gap to the Foyle. Just the name. People's curiosity would do the rest. No loudspeakers. Just a couple of men outside at every Sunday Mass with a placard and ready to qnswer any questions. The same on Saturday evenings in the town. They were ready to talk to anyone. Creeping under the blanket was what Neil called it. They knew they were winning when a local councillor asked what the fuck did they think they were doing

Great show. Let them worry. No fighting. Kill them with kindness. They may not like us but we do not dislike them. Help us to help ourselves. That was the old Sinn Fein slogan translated into English. Nothing new ever in politics.

The local papers sent a reporter to interview the new Finn Valley candidate. Shane insisted thet his "advisor" be at his side and Neil was happy to oblige.They did not have a wide agenda. Just to help the local people. The small farmer and the poor man to feed his family

Not one of their public meetings was interfered with. Sergeant Thornton sent a plain clothes Garda to hang about the ghurch gate and he reported all was fine

"Naw Sarge.just a few men having a chat. Not a stir"

A Fianna Fail man called on Shane and asked if he could be of any help

"No no not at all" said Shane "we are doing fine" as Neil rubbed his hands gleefully in the next room. This was just the beginning of their journey and already they wre enjoying it so very much. Neil had told his son about the journey being more satisfying than the arrival. The Fianna Fail man was worried about the young man's sanity, All this about journey and arrival. Funny people.

Neil dropped back and came to the Friday nights when he was asked. He would discuss tactics and all he wanted was for them to keep a high ptrofile. Not to bother with the details. Highland Radio interviewed Shane and had Hannah say a few ords as well. Poor old 'Glasses' Quinn the local Democrat reporter was never as busy in his whole career as Finn Valley bombarded him with their bulletins and reports. He was too polite to tell them that there were others in the county who had activities to report as well.

Hannah put a discreet notice in her gallery window

Support Finn Valley
That was a nod to her own crowd that their vote would be appreciated
No great rush. A slow infiltration. Macra na Feirme, The ICA even the GAA.
No arguments, No great public debates
We listen. We hear you. That was their unspoken slogan.

55

GRADUALLY FINN VALLEY grew bigger and wider. At an Intercounty match in McCool Park they placed their placards where the television cameras would pick them out and the daily papers showed a mild interest. A trickle of support followed. A dollar or two and a few pound notes and good wishes galore. It was back to Horace Plunkett one letter suggested. He started the CoOperative movement. Paddy The Cope would mean more to Donegal ears. But the past was gone Neil warned. We are who we are and we stand alone

Do not worry about the opposition. The floating voter is our target. The die hards will never join us. But the floaters are not that interested in the political scene and they might come to us because we are just like them. We are one of them. The poor people. We do not own big ships or restaurants. We know how they feel. Let them know that we are aware of their feelings. There was a steady growth. A Highland Radio man came to Lochbeg and he left a very happy man. Best cuppa he ever tasted and that brack he could die for. Ane he had a slab of it in his briefcase for the kids and the missus.

Election day was near. Tactics needed sharpening Neil told them.

Derry wre playing Donegal in McCool Park. The Ulster Championship. This was a big game. Radio Telefis Eireann and Ulster Television woud have the match live.

Fonsie was their man. His surname might have been Sweeney but he was Fonsie to them all. Fonsie and Scalp his sheepdog won the Ulster Final of One Man and His Dog and they were presented with s beautiful Waterford Glass Trophy. That finished Fonsie and the fancy competitions. You cannot spend a fancy glass vase. In his opinion a few fivers would look better on the mantlepiece

Now Scalp and Fonsie were able to talk to each other and Fonsie had a silent whistle that only Scalp could hear. Neil had a word with Fonsie. He would sneak the dog in to the sideline seats. He would do that after the Minor match when the Ceili dancers were doing their act on a lorry in the centre of the field. But they might stop him at the gate

No bother.Fonsie had been going to McCool Park before they built the big gates and started charging an entry fee.He never paid an entry fee in his life and no way was he going to pay now. He knew how to get in. All was set

Micheal O Muircheadaigh the commentator was in full blast when he stopped mid sentence.Scalp was on the pitch. The referee blew on his whislle and stopped the game. Scalp ran to the halfway line and sat there his tongue lolling

O Muircheadaigh was a doggy man himself and this was too good to miss. Scalp was wearing a jacket" Vote Fiin Valley" and O Muircheadaigh explained what that meant. The referee tried to grab Scalp and Scalp dodged him. The dog looked as if he was really ejoying himself. So too was the commentator. Fonsie had Scalp run roundthe referee and then sit. And again. The crowd were shouting and laughing. Some of the sideline stewards came on the pitch to try and grab Scalp and Fonsie had the dog run to the corner of the field by the river and they both disappeared

The press had a field day. Literally.All over Ireland Finn Valley were in the news. McCool Park committee were not happy. Someone would pay for this. Who owned the dog? Who let him in?. Sure no one knew anything. Stray dogs come and go.But the Garton men knew and Fonsie had free pints for months

Then the cheques started coming again. The odd Donegal man in Belfast or in Dublin who saw what happened and felt the pull of the fields and the lonely country roads and the blue sky up above.

Scalp was famous. There were plywood cut outs of him at every crossroads. No need to write Finn Valley. Everyone knew.

They did well in the election. Topped the poll with 78% of the valid poll. Because of the massive vote for Finn Valley, another Independent sneaked in as well

Neil called a post election meeting in Aengus house

"We won. Stay silent.We have thousands of votes. But we will not contest the general election. There we can only win one seat but by playing our cards right we can have an influence over two seats in Donegal. We will wait and see which of the parties will be the first to recognise this and who will approach us. We have no conscience, We are open to bribery. We can be bought. What can they do for Garton?. Let them come bearing gifts. But not a word. No gloating. No public announcements. Tactics. Tactics and evil cunning. Morality? Me eye. Politics is the art of the possible. It is what you can get away with"

Shane was so proud. He wanted to tell everyone. That this cantankerous and awkward old bogman was such a wonderful leader. A man who carried a heavy personal burden and who felt his people had been let down years ago but who could not force himself to forget. But he was coming out from under that cloud and the sun was on his face again.

56

THE LAGAN 4 were still practising and they were improving. They had regular bookings in the local hotels. After The Finn Valley Dog the press sometimes dropped in. And the new County Councillor was fresh news. Young and elected with the help of a sheepdog. Echoes of Lassie but no Liz Taylor. Just Shane.

But could they find the bloody dog? No one seemed to remember what he looked like. It was that Finn Valley jacket. Surely a Finn Councillor would know they told Shane.

In Italy they call it "Omerta" but in Donegal they just call it "Dunno"

A reporter who stayed overnight heard the Lagan4 perform at the hotel. Radio Eireann had missed a former Donegal group, The Johnstons, and it was not likely that they would miss another rising group.

Fr Barry owned up. He ha a pal in RTE and he passed on the message and they sent down a repotrter. Joe Mulholland from the Donegal Rd., was a big noise up there in Ardmore in Dublin as well and he might have put a good word in.

The result was that RTE would like to do a program about Garton and its music and its Councillor and its Sheepdog. Just pick a date and a venue and the bold Ciaran MacMathuna would come down and record a show.

Would they have the recording in one of the hotels and have Ciaran enjoy all the comforts? No not likely. The music was the people's music and it was to be shared. Shared with their own. Cooney's bar it had to be.

On the night the place was packed. After a few pints the noise level was too high. Too many "yippeees" and "good on yas" and "gwan gwan"

Ciaran asked for more decorum as they had to redo some of the tapes three times and yet it was not right. Ciaran was puzzled. There was a strange drumming in the music.

"Leave it with me" said Francie Cooney and he stood up

"Ladies and Gentlemen I have a request to make. Would Jamesey Burke take off his hobnail boots and beat time to the music in his socks?"

Jamesey did as he was told and that end of the bar soon cleared. There are some fine perfumes that even good Irish music cannot alleviate

It was good night for the craic and Ciaran replayed them on his Sunday morning programmes and that brought invitations to play outside the county

Then came a call from Donegal's most famous adopted son. Sure doesn't he spend most of his time around Dungloe?.Gay Byrne the man himself and his lovely wife Kathleen Watkins. She of the Harp and the Irish Colleen image.

Would they like to appear on his show? Would they?Would they?

Up to Ardmore they went and played for Gaybo

What they did not realise that the Gay Byrne program was sold abroad and shown on other networks

A very excited Sinead was on the phone and she said she had seen the program and had it taped an she plays it regularly to her friends. It was like being back home in the kitchen again

There were a lot of people in Boston who saw the show and a few other enquiries were made.

57

THE LAGAN 4 were still ptactising aned they wre improving. They had regular bookings in the local hotels. Sfter The Finn Valley Dog the press sometimes dripped iAnd the new County Councillorwas fresh news. Young and elected with the help of a sheepdog. Echoes of Lassie but no Liz Taylor this tine. Just Shane but could they find the bloodybdog?No one seemed to renmember what he looked like. It was that Finn Valley jacket,Surely a Finn Councillor would know they tiold Shane

In Italy they call it "Omerta" but in Donegal they just call it "Dunno"

A reporter who stayed overnight heard te Lagan4 perform at the hotel. Radio Eireann had missed a former Donegal group The Johnstons and it was not lokely that they would miss another rising group.

Fr Barry owned up. He ha a pal in RTE and he passed on the message and they sent down a repotrter. Joe Mulholland from Donegal Rd., was abig noise up there in Ardmore in Dublin and he might have put a good woord in.

The result was that rte would like to do a program about Garton and its music and its Councillor and its Sheepdog. Just pick a date and a venue and the bold Ciaran MacMathuna would come down and record a showd have Ciaran enjoy all the comforts? No not likely. The music was the peoples music and it was to be shared. Shared with their own. Cooneys bar it had to be.

On thenight the place wa packedAfter a few pints the noise level was too high. Too many "yippeees" and "good on yas" and "gwan gwan"

Ciaran asked for more decorum as they had to redo some of the tapesthree times and yet it was not right. Ciaran was puzzled. There was a drumming in the music

"Leave it with me" said Francie Cooney and he stood up

"Ladies and Gentlemen I have a request to make. Woulsdd Jamesey Burke take off his hobnails and beat time to the music in his socks?"

Jamesey did ashe was told and that end of the bar soon cleared. There are some things that even good Irish music cannot alleviate it was good night for the craic and Ciaran played them on his Sunday morning programmes and that brought invitations to play outside the county

Then came a call from Donegal's most famous adopted son. Sure doesn't he spend most of his time around Dungloe.Gay Byrne the man himself and his lovely wife Kathleen Watkins. She of the Harp and the Irish Colleen image.

Would they like to appear ipn his show? Would they?Would they?

Up to Ardmore they went and played for Gaybo

What they didnotrealise that the Gay Byrne program was sold abroad and shown on other networks

A very excited Sinead was on the phone and she said she had seen the program and had it taped an she plays it regularly toher friends. It was like being back home in the kitchen again

There were a lot of people in Boston who saw the show and a few enquiries were made.

58

SHANE LOVED DRIVING past the two building sites and seeing the houses taking shape. H e knew Mr Lavin was building an extension to his house for use as a surgery. For his retirement he said and we would work at a leisurly pace and maybe one of his sons might join him. But the other owner. Not a sign. Not a glimmer. One day Shane nearly drove into the ditch. That car!. He knew the owner.

He went in to the building and there she was, Hannah. Hannah Robinson. She did not see him coming in and he was standing there looking at her

When she turned round and saw him she stammered" Sit down Shane. I could not tell you. I just could not tell you. I knew the money would be useful to you but I did not want you to think I was being charitable. I neeeded the site. I needed it more than you wanted to sell. I had been looking for a site and the land agent advised me it was in prime location and at a fair price. I did not know you as well then and I did not wish to upset our little group. Between you and I this site is ideal. I need to have an art gallery for my pictures and here is what will suit me. When I heard that Mr Lavin would be next door that sealed the deal for me. Two professionals side by side. Just right. That is my story"

Shane took his time

"Hannah I am delighted. Remember when you bought my cipini; the firelighting sticks?"

"Shane" she chided "I know what cipini are. Master Byrne nearly had me a Gaelic speaker"

"Great show" he said "I would like a guided tour" She agreed and the main interest was the picture gallery. She would invite local artists to show their work for sale along with what she had acquired in her travels. Not a gallery open to the publicbut to dealers like herself

She asked about the farm. He knew she would have a good idea how things were progressing. But he did not mind. Things had worked out well and they parted on good terms.

In his car he laughed "Cipini;; And a Gaelic speaking Presbyterian. Maybe her forefathers were Gaelic speakers. There was an elderly lady down in Raphoe who spoke a strange dialect. That was best left to the scholars. But Hannah speaking Gaelic?Robinson. What is the Gaelic for Robinson?The son of a robin? Mac a Robin. Maca Spideoig. That would be enough for now

He was happy now that he knew who was taking the two sites. The land agent was very happy. It had set the tone for the other two that still had to be taken. The agent phoned and asked Shane in for a chat. Mr Wynn himself was waiting. He had some news. A major estate agency in Derry had made enquiries about the two remaining sites. He heard nothing until yesterday when they asked if the seller was amenable to selling both sites and the adjoining wood in the one deal. They would not name the interested party,

"I will have to discuss this with my father" Neil said. This no names again was getting a bit on his necrves. Hewas lucky the last time in having Hannah as the buyer. But what would Hannah or Mr Lavin think if there was a butchers shop or a mosque built next door?. It has happened.

Neil himself was puzzled. Why the small wood?. It would need a lot of work to build there. God knows what the stranger had in mind

They went back to Mr Wynn. He had no worries about selling the two remaining sites. When the builders were finished and Lavins and Hannahs houses were to be seen that would increase the demand for the other sites. It was a lovely location and with two good neighbours most people would see it as an ideal place to live.

"Is there any way we can flush this new buyer out?" Shane asked

"I cannot see how" said a resigned Mr Wynn

"I have an idea" said Neil. "let us have different prices. We will have one price for each seperate site. Then we have another price for the two sites together. Then we have another price for the double sites and the wood. But this last price is a special price for the unknown buyer. It is a huge price he will have to pay for having the wood included and he will have to pay for his anonymity.

Mr Wynn gave his advice "No matter what he offers and even if we accept his offer we are not legally bound until we exchange contracts and by then we should know his identity"

On the way home Neil explaines his tactics to Shane

"If this buyer wants it he will pay. He wants two sites and the wood so he wants privacy. He must be well off to afford his privacy. But because he is wealthy he does not wish us to know his identity. We might raise the price. It is probably company money anyhow and we are dealing with an accountant who is trying to save his boss some money and to show how clever he is. But if the buyer really wants the site he will buy it. If he does not we will sell the sites eventually and I might think pretty soon"

The phone cll came. The two sites and the woodland. An offer was made. Close to their price

Mr Wynn advised them to accept it

Neil smiled "we have him hooked. He would be a poor business man or given bad advice if he did not haggle and try to bargain over the price. He probably knows we can use the money. It is a game with him. He has to be a winner. It is in his character to call the price and then it is his price and not ours. But we will sit tight. It is our land This is our price, The money does not mean that much at his level. He can afford it or he cannot. If he cannot afford it then he will break up the sites into smaller ones and we will have let Hannah and Mr Lavin down. But to give him the feeling that he has won and beaten us we will throw in the fishing rights on the Finn. Not the fishing rights but we will include permission to fish on our land. He will check it out and will find that the best salmon pool between Brockagh and Strabane is on our patch. That will be a salve to his self esteem. He has beaten us. Just trust me. I can feel how his mind is working. The dominant ego. The big man."

The next offer was what they asked for and the deal was set in motion. A sold sign was put up after the deposit was paid and the deal was done within a month. Again the O Neills had money to spare. They paid for a new car for Eugene and they upened an account in the Credit Union in Mary's name. The Union had been good to Shane and one never knows. For their own comfort they built an extension to the farmhouse and had a solid fuel burner and radiators fitted around the rooms. Shane bought Maureen a gold wrist watch and diamond ear rings and put a deposit in her name in the Ulster Bank, For Neil he bought a Purdy Double barrell. Them he loaded his father and mother into the car and booked them in to The Great Northern in Bundoran for two weeks.

Maureen did not believe it had all happened. She was now a sister in Cardiff with her own Ward and all that entailed. Intensive care she called it. She breezed in without a worry. No boyfriend this time. And she had not changed. She told them she had applied for a position in Strabane but they would have to wait and see. Nothing definite She said she had the same amadán of a brother who never did as he was told. Especially what she told him. But she was impressed by their business dealings. Shane told her the whole story and she looked at her father. She thought he was still the same old awkward old man but she knew now that he had a brain that she could never equal

She insisted that they all go out for a meal to celebrate. To a special restaurant in Strabane. It had a great reputation and she pulled up outside The Golden Dragon. Neil was in a dither but he went along with her.He enjoyed his meal but the tea bag in the cup was not the right way for him. The Chinese wine went down a treat and Mary had her Tio Pepe. Maureen had to rush off as she was meeting a nurse she had helped train in Sheffield. She put them all in a hackney car and she was gone to meet her old nursing student Rita in Fintona.

They had waited for Eugene at the house and they phoned him but he must have been called out and he did not turn up to join them.

59

THEY PHONED EUGENE and the housekeeper answered every time, He was always out. They thought he might have taken offence at what they had given him from their sites' sales. Maybe he expected a lot more, They rang and rang. He was never in.

Shane went to his father

"I am not happy Dad. There is something here that does not fit.He has not been to see us in weeks. If he has the hump I would like to talk to him about it"

"Wait 'til Maureen goes back. No use bothering her about it as well'

They phoned and the housekeeper answered. Not in again

A woman walked all on her own on to Lochbeg Farm. Mary answered the door

"Can I speak to Neil O Neill?" the woman asked

"Neil a woman to see you"

Coming" he said and he came down the yard brushing straw from his hair

"I am Neil O Neill" he said "What can I di for you?"

"Can we go somewhere private?" she asked

"Come in to the front room, Like a cup of tea?" Neil asked

Sorry to bother you Mr O Neill" she said. "My name is Bridie Glynn. I am the piests' housekeeper and I have been answering your telephone calls. My own father. Paudie McGowan, keeps on talking about you, Commandant O Neill and he swears you are the best man he ever met. When we found that Fr Eugene O Neill was your son we were so delighted and so proud. To have the old warrior's son as his priest was beyond belief to my father and a blessing

But Mr O Neill I have bad news. It is breaking my heart. Things are not well for the Holy Father. No one else knows this and you are the only person I am going to tell. But the young man has a problem. He is too fond of the auld drop.It's the drink. He takes it every night and I have trouble getting him up in the morning. Sometimes midday. No one knows this. The parish priest is never there. Even my husband and My own father I have not told them. I could never betray the Holy Father"

Neil sat there. He was afraid it might be some thing like this. He could not stop the tears welling in his eyes as he looked at this blessed lady Bridie Glynn

"Thank you Bridie Glynn. You are your father's daughter. You will never realise what you have done for me and for my son Fr Eugene. I will take over from here. I will get my other son Shane to drive you home"

"Thank you Mr O Neill but if he could drop me off in town and I could do some shopping and catch the bus home" Mary Glynn asked

Shane did as she requested and then he and Neil sat in the car for an hour. No need to worry Mary. After the tea they told Mary that they had business in town and they set off for the parish of Glenmore deep in the mountains.

No one answered their knocking

"For the best" said Neil "It is better that we are on our own"

They let themselves in and called Eugene's name but no one answered. They went from room to room and there he was. Spread out on the bed with a bottle of Vodka on the chair beside him

Neil went over and placed his hand on Eugene's forehead and said

"It's all right my son. It is your own farther and your brother and we have come to help you"

Eugene rambled drunkenly "disgrace, drunken priest, show up the whole family, no good,"

Now Eugene stop all of that" said Neil. "You have an alcohol problem. An illness. You are lucky in that not many people know. And the less who know the better. Weare not here to judge you. We are here to help you. Just you let us help you"

Eugene sat up in the bed and looked at his father. Then he looked over at Shane and he started weeping. Shane moved as if to hold him but Eugene put out his hand and stopped him. They could see his agony and they remained silent

When he settled a little Neil asked "Do you want help?"

"Yes, yes please I need help. I cannot go on like this. I hate myself and I have let every one down" cried Eugene. Then he quietened down and they chatted for a while, Shane found it difficult to look athis broken brother. A bright scholar beaten by the booze. The apple of his mother's eye and look at him now

Neil laid down the law;Eugene was not to stop drinking. He was to have a double vodka when he got the shakes. The same as a pub double. No more. On no account any poteen. Those were Neil's instructions and Eugene said he would do as he was told

On the way home Shane asked "Have you done this before?"

"Yes I have. I saw it in Mountjoy and when I was on the run. Sometimes the hospitality in safe houses was too much and many of the men in Jail had a problem with the old bottle. I should think that half the GIs in Korea were well oiled mostof the time. The reason I told him not to stop is that he might have a seizure, A fit. Not a word to his mother, do you hear"

Shane could not believe it. This was the father he thought was dead beat. Look at him now. Election leader, Estate dealer, and now looking after the wounded. It was as if the talk about Drumboe and the settlement of the farnm succession had cleared his mind. He was a new man with enthusiasm and a joy to be with.

They tried to contact Mary's brother Liam, in the States. For advice. They left their number at the American Embassy and for Liam to contact them when he could

Shane called over to see Eugene every evening after dark. No need for the world to know but he was sure that many already knew and that they would not wish to admit the obvious

One evening Liam phoned and Mary took the call and they had a chat. When Neil went on the phone he took Liam's phone number and said when he would call him back

Shane and he went over to Strabane and from the post office there they had a long talk with Liam. It meant that the local exchange was not listening. Liam had one word. Rehab. Just Rehab. It is a serious illness and the man needs help.He needs medical and psychological assistance. It has to be. St John O God's in Stillorgan or James' St. out near Islandbridge. Then it would be Alcoholics Anonymous for the rest of his life

"But there are no AA groups locally" said Shane

"Then let him start one" said Liam "sorry for being so hard but that is how it is. Only one word. Rehab".

Shane and Neil stayed up talking that night and they decided it was time Neil paid a visit to his Lordship the bishop

60

NEIL DECIDED THAT it was best if he went on his own to see the bishop. He pulled in the drive to the bishop's residence, His Palace thank you. And very nice too!.

He was met by a young garsoon of a holy father. Probably not yet using a razor

"Good day to you Father" Neil said "I do not have an appointment but I would like to have a word with the bishop. Is he available?"

"Yes he is. And what do you wish to speak to him about?" asked the young priest

"It is a private matter Father. I am sorry but I do not know your name. What will I call you?" said Neil

"I am Fr Jimmy Cullen. I am the bishop's private secretary" said Fr Cullen

"Well nice to meet you Fr Cullen" said Neil amiably "My name is Neil O Neill and my son Fr Eugene O Neill is one of the bishop's curates"

"Won't be a moment" said Fr Cullen and he left the room

Soon the bishop himself came. Neil had only seen him before in his ceremonial robes, mitre and full regalia. Here dressed like any priest, except for the purple borders to his clerical black, he looked a small and ordinary man. He could be a clerk in the post office or a postman if you saw him sitting in the bus.

The bishop spoke first

"My secretary tells me you are Neil O Neill and that Fr Eugene O Neill is your son"

"That is correct" said Neil

"And what brings you here?"

Wow!, What a way to greet a, man? Neil was on edge immediately "What brings you?" "How can I help you?" might be more appropriate. Keep cool keep the head

"Well its about my son. He is not well" said Neil

"I am sorryto hear that. I thought he and Monsignor Kyle were settling in well together in, in, ah yes, in Glenmore. What is wrong with him may I ask?" said the bishop

"He is suffering from Alcoholism" said Neil bluntly

"Oh dear Oh dear" said his Eminence "you mean he drinks too much"

"No, I do not mean that at all" said Neil. No no.He does not drink too much as you put it. He is ill. He has a medical condition. He is suffering from alcoholism. He is ill"

"Well" said the bishop "all he has to do is stop drinking"

"It is not that simple" Neil said. "It is not that easy. It is not easy at all. He is ill. He needs medical attention"

"O my, O my," said the bishop. "Now Mr O Neill take my word for it. Just you tell him to stop"

Neil had enough. No more "your eminence" or "your honour" or is it "your grace"

Neil stood up and came over to stand beside the bishop

'Take your word for it?. Take your word?. I knew Fr O Flaherty and Fr MacGuinness who were alcoholics and who died terrible early deaths. You were their bishop. You probably told them to "just stop drinking". Did your advice work? No it did not. They were abandoned. Left to die. Abandoned by your good and holy self"

"How dare you speak to me like that. I am the bishop of this diocese. Who do you think you are?" said His Eminence

Neil replied" Some people call me Badger O Neill. I was Commandant of the First Donegal Brigade. I knew your brother Joseph. We used to call him 'Ginger'"

The bishop rose from his chair and went to the far window,

Badger O Neill. The very man himself. Joseph, God rest his soul, worshipped the ground this man walked on. He swore he saved his life when he carried him on his shoulders for two miles over the bogland when his leg was shattered by a British bullet. So this was the man.

"Neil O Neill. Well now.I have heard so much about you. My brother was a great admirer of yours. And here you are. After all those tears I thought you hadgone to meet your Maker'" said the bishop in what he thought was a pleasant tone

"No such thing" said Neil sharply. "I have come here with a problem and I need your assistance. And to use terms I understand if I may. My son is under your command. He is in your regiment. You are his commanding officer. He needs medical attention. Is that very clear?" he asked and then he added "Your eminence"

"yes' said the bishop. The 'your eminence' hit him below the belt. "so you think he has an illness?"

"What I think does not matter. It is what I know that counts. And what you intend to do for my son is what is important. Critical. Yes critical. I will not let you hide him and let him die a horrible death" said Neil

Ok Ok" said a rattled bishop "What do you suggest?"

"Rehab, Rehab. Medically assisted rehabilitation. There are Rehab centres in Dublin. One in Stillorgan. There is a Rehab centre there. It can be a long or medium course of treatment" sai Neil

"You know all about this do you?" asked the bishop

Neil felt like giving him a punch in the eye. Doing his superior act again, I am the bishop

"I know more than you" Neil said. "I will not let you hide my son as a chaplain in a Convent or in a monastic retreat where he can die and no one will know. It must be treatment in a proper Rehab centre and there is one in Stillorgan run by a religious order of Brothers

"Who will pay for all this treatment?" said the bishop

You will" said Neil sharply "the diocese will"

"The diocese does not have the money to pay for expensive treatment" said the bishop

"Noe let us stop playing about" said Neil. "You have a chauffeur driven limousine and you are quite capable of driving yourself around in a Ford Cortina like the rest ofus. Your brother Joseph, may he rest in peace, would soon show you how you could afford it"

Again Neil knew that he was not playing like a gentleman. But this was warfare and tha Queensbury rules did not apply and neither did the Geneva Convention apply either.

The bishop was silent. Neil was in no hurry. Then

"Fair comment. What would you wish me to do?" he asked.

Neil had his answer "I would like to take my son to our own GP. The same man who delivered him as a baby and for this doctor to refer him to the Rehab Clinic. There will be complete confidentiality and we will say he has Scarlet Fever or some highly contagious condition. Then it will be Eugene's own responsibilityto accept the treatment and make progress towards his rehabilitation. In all fairness I think that you as their bishop have a responsibilityto look after all the priests in your diocese. In my terminology you look after your own troops"

"You fight a hard battle Commandant and you do not leave any room to manouvre" sais the bishop

"You are correct on both accounts. You agree to finance my son, your priest, and his rehab and recovery programme?"

The bishop did not answer but kept rubbingthe large ring on his finger. As if he were seeking Divine guidance.

He nodded his head to Neil and they sat and looked at each other'

It had been a hard day.

61

EUGENE WAS SENT to Stillorgan and Rhab. He did not protest as he was a broken man. No Hollywood Whiskey priest ever felt as bad. Barry Fitzgerald would never have been able to play Eugene. The world was told that he had a contagious medical condition and he was not allowed visitors. Shane drove to Dublin everyweek to visit and he saw how Eugene was remade. All his old superiority was replaced by a quiet humility and a belief that he was not a bad person but a man with a serious illness. It was an illness. But he himself was responsible for the management of his illness. Other people might take antibiotics or drugs for their illnesses but it as Eugene himself who had his own remedy. There was no cure but the illness was manageable and it was Eugene's responsibility to manage it. His medical officer and his advisor were very satisfied with his progress and after a couple of months he was told he could go home. But Eugene did not feel ready to go. It was lovely and safe here in the clinic and to go back to a bleak and damp house in Glenmore filled him with dread. He doubted if Monsignor Kyle had noticed his absence. He told Shane of his fears and Shane had a word with Neil

So off the Commandant went to see the bishop. He might even say his friend or comrade the bishop. Well at least as two commanding officers on opposing sides. Rommel and Montgomery. Things quiet on the Western Front old boy. Like two old officers ready to sign the treaty and who had enough of the fighting. No ceremonial uniforms bedecked with medals but a handshake and a respect for each other.

Eugene came back from Stillorgan and was put on sick leave. He came home to Lochbeg and to Mary. Chicken broth and generous helpings of the fruit cake. But best of all she loved to have him in the kitchen. They listened to The Kennedys of CastleRosse and enjoyed Gay Byrne and his witterings. Maureen came home and she told him about her hospital and the carry on of the young nurses. He shot a few rabbits and fished the Finn. Fr Barry dropped in from Time to time and they sat in the front room and chatted, The new radiators in there were working fine

At the next Diocesan Review Eugene was appointed Latin Master at the College. He would not be alone any more but he would live among the other priests and be surrounded by the noisy boys. It was busy and active life. But the new Eugene wanted more. He had met men at Rehab who mentioned a fellowship that they praised.It was the A.A. Alcoholics Anonymous. He had not heard if it and there were no branches outside of the city. He went to the bishop and he asked if he could set up a quiet fellowship for his fellow clergymen. No names but they could meet and discuss their common problem with the alcohol. The bishop remembered the lecture Neil gave him on his responsibilities and he agreed. The Catholic Clergy Association was founded. CCA. No need to mention alcohol in the title even if it was for the recovery if alcoholics. Every young priest was made aware of the CCA's existence and that it was their reponsibility to contact the association if they ever thought the association could be of help to themselves or to any priest. It played an important role in the life of the diocese in the years to come

Neil called in on the bishop again and thanked him for what he had done, The bishop thanked the Lord God Himself that there was only one Neil O Neill in the world and that the present one was not a member of the catholic clergy. He did not think his nerves would stand it.

Eugene was asuccess as a Latin master. He studied all the latest teaching techniques and soon his boys were getting Honours in The Leaving Certificate. It also meant he had a salary and long holidays. Most of the teachers in the college had some contact with alcoholism in their own families and if there was a whisper about Eugenes past they admired his ability to recover and manage his life. With his long Summer holidays and his own salary Eugene took off to America and he made contact with priests over there and he attended AA seminars and he qualified as a counsellor and when The first Irish Nartional Convention was held he was invited to address them

It was achange from lying in the bed in Glenmore in a lonely parochial house. Afraid to face the outside world and hating his inner soul. He was not perfect but he was able to accept who and what he was and he was able to live with that.

62

AGAIN SHANE WAS at his old pasttime of driving past the building sites. He was none the wiser. Men with tripods were measuring but they gave nothing away. He called in to see Hannah when he saw her car outside and she had heard it waas an American of Donegal descent who had made millions in the States or it might have been in the oil business. She was not sure and it might only be a rumour. They knew his name was Adamson and he wished to have a quiet retirement in Donegal. That much Shane already knew and she said when she was told it was to ease any wotrries she might have about her new neighbour. He would build his house at the back of the wood and one of the sites would be for the drive only and would not intrude on her privacy. He was going to have an indoor swimming pool and a three car garage. It was going to be an impressive mansion and would add to the value of the adjoining properties. If a millionaire wishes to settle in Garton the pople would wonder. Word crept out. The parish was agog. A millionaire? Was he Irish? Might be a Sultan? With a Turban? And a houseful of wives?. A harlem?. No you clown a harem.

But Shane and his father did not worry. They had been paid and Mr. Wynn had seen to it that everything was in order. Eugene was settled in the College and Neil and his son were getting on very well together. Now it was time for Finn Valley to go ito action

At the first few Council meetings Shane abstained from voting on any issue. That was the group policy. Just to listen and say little. The Chairman Paddy Breslin was a cute old fox and he wanted to know what The Finn Valley boyos were up to. He asked Shane for his opinion and Shane said he agreed with what had been said. This puzzled old Paddy as there had been a disagreement in the Council all night.

One could not agree with them all. Not on both sides at the same time. That Shane was a funny laddo that's for sure.

The Garton Mafia had their own agenda. They wanted improvemants to their football ground. A changing room and a dressing room with showers. Aengus invited Jimmy 'Glasses' Quinn the local reporter over and he took photographs of the broken shed they were expected to change in. That was a start. 'Glasses' wrote a long piece on how the children had to change in the rain and he compared the shed with the facilities in McCool park and to cap it all he had photographs of the luxurious facilities in Croke Park and Thurles. Were our children tobe treated worse than the farm animals? Good old 'Glasses'. Bless his heart

An appeal was made to the GAA Central Council and they agreed to equal any amount the Garton Club could raise. That was their biggest mistake, Those two little words" could raise" The Mafia saw a way. They began their work

The press informed the people that the government refused to help the local people, Massive stadia were built in the big towns and they were empty except for a few big games a year. But the Garton pitch was used every day and no one cared. Was this what the peopleof Donegal wanted? Did the local TDs care about the local people?. It was time for the people to stand up and be counted. A Garton Fund was launched and promises gathered, This was too good an opportunity and the local TD gave his name to it. Promises gathered. No need to pay. It was "could raise". Just promise us. No need for the money. Yet. We can collect when we need the cash. Business men, shopkeepers, companies sent their promises in. All tax deductable of course, But not the cash, Not yet. Cash when th club would ask for it.

On papervthe club had a lot of money and Garton got their new changing rooms. There might be some of the promised money that never made an appearance but it had served its purpose. The local TD opened the new rooms and said how his party was always ready to help his constituents and they would do so at every opportunity in the future. A few pints were lowered all round.

Neil held a Finn Valley meeting. Just the original five. Five founder members. Tight and close

"Now you can see what we can do. We work behind the scenes. Others get the publicity but we get the results. On the surface the local TD has done everything for the football changing rooms. He is a happy man and his opponent is very angry. Now we go to the angry man" Neil told them

"What is out next proposition? He asked

Parish Hall improvements" some one said

"That is the bshop's responsibility" sid Fr Barry

"I might call and see him sometime" said Neil with a smile. What was so funny?

"We need a school bus" said Aengusvery firmly. "There is an education available to our children now the nuns have come to the town. But our children cannot get there. There is secondary education all around us. The Royal in Raphoe. The

Academy in Strabane and the nuns in the Twin Towns but they are all beyond our children. We need a bus to take them to school and not just from Garton but from the outlying townlands as well"

That had them going. Shane and Hannah looked at each other. They both knew a millionaire was coming to live in the parish. But Hannah silenced him with an eyebrow

Theyall knew a bus was needed They had a makeshift one for the footballers and now it was the childrens' turn

A new era awas beginning. No more dead end after primary school and the inevitabel emigration. They would be writing with thir fountain pens at home instead of Paddy's Pencils on the building sites.

Thy all looked over at the old fox. The wily cute old man. Neil himself

He was he man who helped them decide

This time they would ignore the party in power. Be nice to the opposition instead. Invite them to the concerts and the footbll matches. Get them to throw in the ball to start the games and have them make speeches on how they enjoyed coming to Garton. "Glasses "Quinn was a great help again. He bombarded the paper with exclusives and photographs. Nothing politicians liked better than their name and photograph in the paper

The Donegal Association in Dublin had little to do but provide entertainment for themselves and they were happy to adopt a cause. The Garton Bus Society was formed within the group. Something to do. And to embarrass the Department of Education

This was great fun. Neil was delighted. Education fot all those poor children. Someone up there in Ardmore liked them and sent a cameraman and a reporter and the Six O Clock News had coverage of a protest march outside Garton school with a big placard "Give us a bus" surrounded by the schoolchildren

O Donnell ws not one to miss a chance and "Pa" stood up in the Dail

"Are we going to deny there poor children the right to further education? Are we going to have them go overseas or go on the dole?" he asked with a flourish. Good old 'Pa'. Never misses a chance

No one wanted to know. Who had the responsibility?Government TDs in the counties were afraid of 'Charlie'. Mr Haughey to you and I and An Taoiseach. The Prime Minister

But'Pa' wanted the minister reponsible to come forward and face him personally. There are easier things in life than to stand and face 'Pa' O Donnell in the Dail

Shane ansd Aengus took the footballers minibus and drove a load of children to Dublin and the parents loaded their cars and they all arrived at the entrnce to the Department of Education. RTE came good again and sent a camera along. The children surrounded the department Civil Servants and they came and went and the cameras got their pictures. They were on the news and in the papers the next day. But the picture of the week was of the Minister of Education, o Sean O

Tuathail. Jonny O Toole at home in Mayo. Jonnie was photographed pushing little Mary Kavanagh, bless her little heart, angrily away from His August presence. The head lines ran

"Minister pushes her out of his way"

"Was this the way for a minister to behave?" the paper asked

The bus was sanctioned.

Aengus responsibilities at the school were heavier now. Fifth class had to be ready to carry on in the convent. No just hanging on until they could legally not attend. It was a new world and as his own Master Gallagher told him. There is no limit. It was up to themselves

63

TOMMY MARTIN CAME all the way to the school with the letter. He could have dropped it in to the house if he was not so nosey. It was adessed to Aengus Gillespie, Lagan 4, Donegal. Tommy had no trouble with he address. But he was very interested in the letter. An Americen stamp. There had been plenty of letters addressed to the Lagan 4 but this one had Aengus' name. And pushing a letter like that through the letterbox in any door wold be a poor ending. So he went all the way to the school. He knocked on the classroom door and waited

"A special for you today Master. All the way from America" and he did not give Aengus the letter but looked at it and he turned it over in his hand.

"Thank you Tommy" said Aengus and he reached to take the letter

"Looks very important to me" said the bould Tommy himself

"I will have a look at it later" Aengus said

Tommy did not move and Aengus looked and said "Thank you mister postman. See you at the game on Sunday Tommy"

Tommy was disgusted.All this way and he never gave a clue what it was all about. And from America as well. Some people.

It was from Boston and how she had enjoyed seeing him on Television. She could not believe her eyes. There on the box was her old beau Aengus. How time has flown. She still has fond memories of the wonderful Summer they had together in London. She must give him a call the next time her husband had business in Europe. She was Mrs McKinley now but no doubt he would remember her as Fiona Bruce

Remember her? Good job Tommy Martin was on his way. He reddened at the memory and he felt the old stirrings. He would ask Sinead if she knew Mrs

McKinley. But he was too busy just now. Other things to worry about. They had bought a bus for the school run and there was a driver's rota to be organised. Sergeant Thornton was a great help in getting the insurance organised. Extra cover and limitations and all that.

Some of the pupils could not afford the books for St Columba's and he asked the Reverend Mother for any second hand ones that might be available. He asked her if he might buy them for his own pupils as they went through the system and she agreed. They ran a concert and the inevitable raffle and bought the necessary books and they had their own little library in the dressing room in the village hall. They had a heater and a table and chairs there and any pupil could study there and use the books. It needed good behaviour from everyone and so far it was working well

As backup Fr Barry was good at the Latin and Maths and Aengus for the Irish and the History. They had only six students to begin with but they were so successful that a high standard was set for the rest of the following Garton pupils. Garton school was almost a Preparatory school for St Columba's and St Columba's was the gateway to the wide world.

The music sessions carried on as usual, The Garton 4 practised most Friday nights. Hannah made sure she was at home and Shane was never away and Aengus did not go to visit his mother until Saturday morning. But Fr Barry was often missing. And no warning. He just did not turn up. He said he was too busy. No one asked him much about it. Sick calls or visiting his parishioners. None of their business, But he looked so tired. The priesthood was a demanding vocation.

Maureen had taken a post in Strabane and she asked if ehe might come with Shane and she was allowed to attend. But Shane was definite that she keep her mouth shut. He did not want her laying down the law and telling them what thety were doing wrong. She could help with the cooking.

Maureen knew what music she liked and she did not think they wre that wonderful. Not a patch on Val Doonican or Cliff. Who did they think they were anyway?

One night in Doherty's Omagh came and sat by Shane

"It is time you moved on" he said

"What have I done wrong?" asked a worried Shane

"Nothing like that you amadán. We have discussed you in the committee and we think it is time you entered a CCE competition" said Omagh

"Dont be pullin' me leg" said Shane

"Seriously, seriously" said Omagh "it is time to test your talents against the best. We think you can go far. We will travel with you and you will not be alone"

So they travelled and played. Dungannon, Maghera, Dundalk. Shane won his way to the Final in the Mansion House in Dublin

"Now" said Omagh "there is some serious work to be done. The best player does not always win in Dublin.There are so many regional styles and it is often the player who knows that and who comes best prepared who wins. I will find who is on the judges panel and we will take that into our preperations"

He did as he said. Who won in the past? Where were they from?Who was on the judges panel? Where were the judges from?

There are as many styles as there are regions.And the judges are accustomed to their own region's styles. From the mad an frenzied Donegal to the gentle sweetness of Michael Colemans Sligo and to the West Clare with everyone giving it the full blast. The Dublin boyos were the technical players but they lacked soul and finally there was Joe Burke down in Galway with a magic all of his own.

They decided on the sweetness and light. Hannah knew who would help. They went to Herr Kreid. He asked if they had any tapes of other players for him to listen to and they gave him McMahon and Loughnane. Then he had Shane play for him.

"No no it ees too loud. You have the fingers of the stone, we want the fingers of the body, the fingers of the soul, of the mind. you are an artist An artist who paints in music. Do it again. Not good. But getting better, now again. And again.

Shanes brain was like a stone and his eyes like marbles. All this agony. Mozart or Chopin never had to listen to Herr Kreid or they would have packed it in.

But he was getting there he was told. Now he was to go home and practise and practise what he had been told for tthe last three hours

64

WORKMEN HAD STARTED on thr double site. Thry arrived evrry morning in their minibus. From Maghera they came and they did not have contact with the locals, Shane made it his business to pass that way but he could not see much as most of the work was up in the wood. But he did notice a very nice sports car outside Hannah's door. He would ask her about it as it had been there last week as well. Another fine art expert he supposed. The big boss of the site called in on Lochbeg and asked if they could use the other field by the road, The boss was coming by helicopter and if Shane would let him use his field he would be much obliged. Just to make sure there were no animals and it might be wise to clear the field.

The man they were all waiting to see was George Adamson. He liked to be known as George Adamson IV. George the Fourth. His forefathers came from Ulster.Dissenters who went to America ro escape the Roman dissipation of God's Holy Word. They might have been on the Mayflower. They settled on a desert patch of land and all they had to do after that was count the dollars. They were living on an oilfield. On one of his trips to Europe he visited the Folk Museum outside Omagh and he felt that here in Ireland was where he really belonged. He had his agents find a place and here he was now. Ready to start a life in the old country. He knew that The Lagan Valley was a home to Scottish Dissenters or Settlers since the time of Queen Liz and he would be back among his own kind. He did not say so but he was a Mason and he knew he could be friends with the Orange Order and that gang

"Gaaad is good" was his religion and that was all he had to say.

Garton was ready to welcome him. It would do no harm to have a wealthy Presbyterian or Whatever in the parish. They would look after him and he would be of benefit to them. George Adamson did not know that. Yet.

Aengus was rushed off his feet. Getting his pupils into secondary education was his main purpose. He did as his own old master did in Dunmore National School and he gave extra hours teaching in the classroom and his pupils worked hard and his reputation grew. People move to be near the school. Sergeant Thornton, Shane's old friend, moved his family to avail of the better teaching. If there was an open entrance scholarship examination and the Garton School Bus was parked outside the exanination hall the rest of the candidates knew that their chancess were limited. There were complaints to the Department of Educartion but after Feardorcha O Cathain and Sean O Tuathail and 'Pa' in the Dail no one cared to intervene. An official from the INTO came to have a word and Fr Barry gave him short shift. Not another word was heard.

The football team was coming on well and the red of the Garton Gaels was proudly worn. Terry Flynn turned up at all the home games and cheered her boyfriend. Then her father decided that as she had psessed her diploma examination at LIT it was time for her to go and get further experience. He got her an appointment with an Accountancy firm in Belfast and she and Shane had a delightful farewell.

George IV gave notice that he would like to visit the site and would it be in order to use the field. The village at last had a sure date. The helicopter might have been a twitcher's rare bird. Mothers and their prams and crying babies and the local boyos with their drooping fags and hands deep in the drainpipes. A helicopter landing in Garton!. They had seen the army ones passing to Lifford. Aengus might as well have closed the school for that day. Georgie, their own fully fledged millionaire Yank was coming. Bet he looks like John Wayne.

Is that your man? George? The wan over there?. With the big hat? No. Surely not?. Small and fat and thick glasses. More like Arthur Askey or A smaller Eric Morcambe. Not much hair either. Bloody hell they were let down. Not their own Lochinvar at all. He was only a small human being

That was very unfair to George Adamson. He never claimed to be Superman. All he ever did was to be born an Adamson. And being a millionaire in Arizona wa no great shakes. There was one on every corner and he never thought he was anything special. Being a millionaire was the most natural thing in the world. And now here in Garton they did not even have a 'copter pad and not a Cadillac in sight. He had enough of all that. This would suit him better. He knew there was a bit of a row around the Border and there was a rumble about different creeds and beliefs.

. He was not surewhat religion he belonged to. If any. Unitarian sounded nice and he thought he would belong to that. But it could all wait. He looked about him and enjoyed what he saw. The river close by and on one side the Bluestacks and on the other the Sperrin mountains. This Miss Robinson was a charming lady too and a bit of a looker as well. Then Mr. Lavin with his soft brogue and his old Irish manners and charm. A good man for the chat over a pint in Cooneys, That was something he was looking forward to. Thinking back if his forefathers had not been Dissenters and had not emigrated to America he might have finished up a Fenian himself. Wolf Tone was a great Partriot and he was a Presbyterian. Not many realised what both sides had in common

He loved his coming home. That is how he regarded Garton now. Home. He was not able to stay in his own house but he slept overnight in Cooney's and shared the chat and a pint with Mr Lavin.

He called on Hannah. She was aloof at first but when she saw the architecture of his new house she was won over and he asked for her to help him select and buy suitable works of art. He would be the first to admit thet he did not know his Picasso from his Van Dyke

He would enjoy life in Garton she told him. She was born and reared in the village and would never live anywhere else. She was not a Catholic she said but she was as Irish as any person. Her family had been in Ireland for over 300 years and that was long enough to claim Irish Nationality. George was not going to be outdone. He claimed that his family had lived in Ireland centuries ago and although he was born in America he never was anything but Irish. His family were the Irish Nation abroad. He was coming home to a culture that was in his blood vessels. This was why he could never settle, The call of Erin was always there and he did not know what it was. Now he was so relieved, There had always been something in his subconscious that was troubling him. He had lots of money and he only had to ask, but there was aways something missing. And now this beautiful Presbyterian Irish lady had given him the answer. He needed to be among his own, He was part of an Irish Diaspora and he was making his final pilgrimage. He slept well that night.

65

"EVERYONE IN THE county knew Shane had made it to the All Ireland Final." Donegal man heads for Final was the headline. It was all "Glasses" work. Shane did an interview with him and he was on Highland Radio. He said a few words and played a tune ir two. The famous Mansion House. Neil said the First Dail was held there and it was an honour to play in such a historic building

Shane was worried in case thay might think he was getting big headed. Above his stationas his mother would say. Maureen was nursing in Strabane now and she came home on her rest days, Normally she stayed in a flat she shared with some other nurses, She could have stayed in Nurses' quarters but she said she had enough of the hospital after her shift. He did not see her that often as she led a hectic social life. Maybe that was why she lived in the flat. None of his business. Arrangements were made for the Dublin trip. Shane would take their own car and his parents and Aengus could take three more. Maureen did not wait for an invitation. She was in there in a flash, Tommy Martin asked if he could go. What a daft question?. So Tommy was in the back seat. Fr Barry said he would travel in his own car and Hannah said she would fly in from wherever she might be on the day.

They all booked in to The Dergvale in Gardiner Place and that night Aengus took them to all the pubs he knew and down to the Irish Club in Church St. and when they got back there was Omagh waiting at the bar and he had with him his neice Rita. Hope theydid not mind. Saints above! Rita, the same Rita!! Rita the angelic face of years ago. Did they mind? Shane wa s delighted. Maureen was so happy and she explained that Rita and her had met years ago when Rita was a student nurse and now Rita was back nursing in Omagh. Now wasn'. t that agood one?Shane wanted to sit by Rita but the two nurses had so much to say to each other that they went into the lounge to be alone together. What on earth could they have so much to chat about Shane thought

Just before bedtime Eugene arrivedHe onlyhad the one day off and he would have to go back immediately after the competition

Clerys the next morning for the Ladies and Eugene boughta couple of Soutanes. You could wear your pyjamas under them and no one would know he said. Very handy when one had an early class

Neil had them up bright and early

"We need a plan of campaign. We must think about what we do tonight. At all the competitions the contestants go on stage and play their piece. Cold,. But we will be different. We will play when we are ready. When the audience is ready. We have experience from the Lagan 4. Some will object to our P.A. But by then it will be too late. Shane will have finished his playing. To set up our P.A. we need a special approach. We will be officious and efficient and no one will question us" said Neil taking command.

"Fr Barry I want you to be the Commanding Officer so have your biggest Roman Collar and the most Priestly clothes" he said

"Fine" said Fr Barry

Neil carried on "I will stay close to Shane at all times and I would like you, Aengus, to carry the P.A. system and I want Fr. Eugene to stay close to Shane and myself. So I want Fr Barry to give firm orders to Fr Eugene and Aengus. They will set up the P.A. System and they wil pay no attention to anyone else and they will look as if they have official authority. If anyone questions them or interferes Fr Barry is to intervene and give orders as if the staff do not matter. Do not look anyone in the eye and do not answer questions. Act so very busy and if there is any hold up Fr Barry comes and orders his men to do what they originally intended to do

Shane will come on stage and he will wait and I will stand by him. He will play one note and that will give me a chance to check with Omagh who is down among the audience. He will give me tha nod when the acoustics are right. Now let us go over that again. Fr Barry will . . . ."

The accordeons were on at 7.30, They decided to arrive at 7.00 and go straight backstage. Fr. Barry led them past the booking clerk at a furious pace by waving his arms and announcing to all "The O Neills from Donegal" without as much as a glance at the poor lady behind the glass

When the tme came Fr Barry strode on stage and beckoned to his attendants, Aengus placed the mike on the chair where Shane would sit and Eugene put the speakers behind the chair. There were no speakers down in the auditorium as Shane wanted his subtle variations to emanate from the stage and to float down over the listeners.

"Mr Shane O Neill from Donegal" the compere announced

Shane was slow to move on stage as he was testing the sound with Omagh and when he looked there he saw Hannah as well. They gave him the thumbs up and he walked slowly on stage to mild applause.

He started with a slow air. A gentle stream of notes and chords seeming to be without beginning or end; never descending to a low note but balancing and teetering on the edge of a grief; threatening to die but rising and settling like a soft Summer rainfall. Herr Kreid had taught him well. A hush fell over the audience. No applause but then he did not wish them to awaken. Then he played the compulsory march. No place for a march on a concert plarform. He played an easy reel to get them in the mood and then he set to work. He offered them what hey never before had.Before their memory was awakened. Flights of their imagination among the Celtic Gods and back down the ancient sorrows of the Gael. Feelings they did not know existed. Exhilarated and despondent.Angry and forgiving. They did not understand what they were thinking. Some of their ethnic memories stirred. It was as if they were waking from a dream and they did not remember what the dream was. But they had witnessed something wonderful and they did not know what it was.

He finished and walked off. There was a stunned silence and then a chorus of "More, More"

A very angry compere told them that this was acompetition and not a concert but there would be a concert the following night

Neil and his attendants cleared the stage. Everyone to leave. No need for anyone to remember anything but the music' Neil and Shane were happy with the way things went. Omagh was at the back of the hall and they joined him and listened to the other contestants. And there was Hannah. She said she had flown in frim London and she would have to return that evening; But she would be home next week and they would have a party. She was certain Shane was the winner

The contest was over and the judges were at their table with their notebooks. There was some discussion

Omagh saw his old adversary Sheamus O Grianna there and he went over. "Any trouble Sheamus?" he asked

"Aye there is. One ofthe judges says that Donegal had an unfair advantage. The Pa system"

What PA system?" asked Omagh

"Thim wee boxes on the stage"

"They were a help to him" said another judge. A wizened Kerrymen they later found out

Omagh stood by the table" Gentlemen, he said "do you mind if I say a word?"

"Sure" he was told

"Well "Omagh went on "there is no ban on P.A.s in the entry forms. If you want to ban Public Address systems then put it on the entry forms. Then there are accordeons and accordeons. Chromatic acordeons have an inbuilt amplifying system, Then there are bisonic and unisonic accordeons. And one is much easier to play. Yet they were all allowed. So cancel the competition and start all over again. But we did not come here to moan. We came to play and let the best music on the night be the winner, We do not care what he played. Let the music decide

Omagh had said his piece and he shut up, There ws shuffling and coughing at the judges table. The audience was getting restless and they had to declare a winner

Finally they passed a slip of paper to the compere who announced

Thw winner and the All Ireland Champion Accordeon Player is Shane O Neill from Garton in County Donegal"

"Well done a mhac, well done my son" was all Neil had to say but Shane could see he was moved. He too was puzzled by what he felt and what had entered his soul as he played. But the O Neills were banished from their lands and their castles and had to retreat to the mountais and the bogs. Those people were his forebears and their blood ran through his veins. The Wild Geese may have flown but there were nestlings left at home. It was their music Shane played and it was their ethos he carried in his playing. None of them understood what had happened but they knew it had come from a distant past

They all went back to the Dergvale. Hannah had reserved the Banqueting Room and they had a party All the supporters came and so did Omagh and his gang. Hannah opened a few bottled of Champagne and it went well with the Guinness. Tommy Martin had never tasted Champagne but he agreed it was "your man for the job" There was even bottle of Tio Pepe. For those who suffered from the rheumatism, you know. Whe Neil nodded off at the table it was time for bed

For years and years they would remember it as one of the best nights of their lives

Shane, All Ireland Champion?. It was hard to believe

Back home to Garton and his fame had gone ahead and the Raphoe Pipe and Drum band was there to meet them. Fr Barry had been on the phone and there was a reception in the hall and "Glasses" was there and got them all in the Democrat

Life was soon back to normal. Cows to be milked, children to be taken to school and the Garton 4 started to meet again

Maureen got an interest in the Irish Music. Shane thought this a bit strange as she used to deafen him with Radio Luxemburg. Ceolta Tire and Ciaran was the last thing she would have on.

God but he was slow!. Thick in the head. Irish music me eye?. It was Aengus she was after and as far as Shane could see poor Aengus' goose was cooked. He had no chance. Not that he seemed to mind that much. Maureen was now sharing a flat with her nursing pal Rita Coyle, Omagh's neice and Aengus was spending a lot of his time visiting there

Shane now looked at Aengus in a different light. He might become a brother in law. Let him suffer. The man who told him to lift his feet at school. His old teacher a relation?. Secretly, and he would never admit it, he liked the idea.

But Aengus was getting on Shane's nerves. He kept on that Rita was "asking for him" Likely story. Bet she has lots of fellas in Omagh or Fintona her home town.

But then she started coming to the Friday nights. Very interested in Irish music. Oh Yes?Aengus was at it again. He whispered in Shane's ear "For the love of Jasus will you take that lassie out. Her heart will break or my mind will go mad watching her agony"

'AwJeeze, will ya stop pullin me leg" pleaded Shane. "I am a Garton thickie from the back of beyond and she has been all over and she is highly qualified with letters after her name. What could she see in me?"

"See in you?" Aengus smiled "difficult question. I will have to see whatI canmake up" Then he leaned over

"She is crazy about you. My ears are bent with her questions about you. I tell her you are a thickie and not that great on the accordeon either. Blind she is. Definitely blind. But they say that's what love does. For jeeze sake ask her out. Give us all a break will ya"

But Aengus kept on. "Maureen and I and I are going to the Fiesta next week you ask Rita is she would like to come"'

Next Fridayat the music session Aengus kept nodding and grimacing at Shane and finally he had to do the asking himself

"Rita" he said "Maureen and I are going to the Fiesta next week and would you like to come with us" She said she "would love to go" and then Aengus continued "Shane it is time you had a dance as well so you might as well join us"

And so another romantic liaison in Garton had begun

66

GEORGE ADAMSON THE Fourth was settling in very well. Hannah wa a regular caller and she helped with his house décor and furnishings. He certainly had some lovely works of art around his rooms. He called over to Hannah's house whenever he was bored. She thought she might take him to one of the sessions but when he said he a was a Dolly Parton fan she changed her mind

But she took him to the Kirk and he was made most welcome. Settlers. Dissenters. Scottish Presbyterians were all of a kind. The Kirk would welcome any believer but a millionaire was an extra. As far as they were concerned he could believe what he liked.

Georgie was a lonely man. His wife Melissa was fond of the Californian sun and when she came to Europe she did not venture far fom the Ritz in London or The Carlton in Cannes. Garton was too dreary for her. She would never appreiaate the purple haze over the mountain or the sun trying to break through the morning mist. But George liked the sound of the rain on the window panes and the early cheep of the blackbird calling the world that another day had arrived

But there was something worrying George. Hannah could feel it. He showed her the cause.

It was a big dirty brown envelope. It was torn where the rock inside it had broken out and it had been trown through Georgie's window. Inside was a note

"£100 a week will keep you safe. P O Neill"

He thought the O Neills were after him. The very people who sold him the land.

Hannah assured him that the signature was anome de plume used by one of the Republican organisations

"May I keep the note and the envelope?" she asked

"If you like"

Then she said "You must never mention this to anyone. Never never" she stressed

"I promise" he said but he did not sound convincing

She knew there ws only one man. Only one man who would be able to deal with this so she arranged to meet Neil. No talking on the phone. She would call on him at Lochbeg. She showed him the dirty envelope and the rock and the piece of paper

"Aye, yes indeed,just so now" was all he said. And he looked at her and their eyes met. She was frightened out of her life. Never before had she seen such a human being. This was a different man to the Neil she knew. His eyes were dead in his head and his face had gone a greyish blue. Gone was his easy manner.

"Leave this with me" he said and she could have sworn his lips never moved

"Do not, not, tell anyone else, You are not to worry about this any more. You and George will never hear another word about this. You can tell George that the matter is being delt with and that he is safe. Nothing will happen to him and he need not worry any more"

H thanked her for coming to him and their meeting was over

Neil began his work. He spoke on the telephone often and he stopped if anyone approached. He spent time in the spare room and Mary saw that his old trunk case had been moved. She knew to mind her own business and that it might be something about the olden days

Neil was working out in his own mind what was happening. Who made the threat to Adamson?. Garton had come this far through the surrounding troubles and the peace in the parish was important. He did not think it was the IRA. They did not bully this side of the border in the South. Not their own people. Not individuals in any case. In reality the IRA had become a civil rights movement. If Martin Luther King were given control of the IRA he might not need to change their philosophy or modus operandi. This was the action of a rogue. A breakaway chancer.

But he wa sure of one thing. The time had come for him to intervene and he awas ready

After his tea he said he had to do a message in town and he would be home before bedtime and he would take the van

He drove towards the town but he pulled in to a gateway. He changed his clothing in the back of the van. Then he carried on and drove into town and up a side street and down an unlit alley and he turned his headlights off. There was a semi derelict cottage ahead with a light in one window and he could see the flickering of a Televiion.

He gave a few taps on the window pane and he waited at the door.

After a moment the door was opened and a young girl looked out

"What de ya want?" No "hello or good evening". She must be accustomed to answering the door.

"Is this Sheedys?" he asked

"Aye"

"is your father in?" he asked

"Daddy" she shouted "a man wants to see you."

"Tell him to come in" a voice answered

And there he was. The television was on at full blast and there was no other lighting. There was an oil heater in the corner and the air was thick with the oil fumes and cigarette smoke"

"What de ya want" asked the big fat man sprawled on the settee

"You Emonn Sheedy?" asked Neil

"Who wants to know?"

I am Neil O Neill and I have business with Eamonn Sheedy"

"I'm your man. Now what do you want?"

"I want a wee talk" said Neil and he wentover and switched off the television

"What the fuck you do that for? Sheedy asked

"So you could hear me very clearly Mr Sheedy" said Neil" Very clearly what I am going to tell you. Now Mr Sheedy this is my problem" and he took the dirty envelope and the money demand and showed it to him

"Mr Sheedy I do not wish you to say anything when I am speaking. I want you to listen to what I have to say,. Then I will listen to what you have to say. This note was thrown through the window of one of my neighbours. He is an American of Irish descent and he has settled in Garton. He causes no trouble and all he wants is a quiet life

"What the fuck has this to do with me?" Sheedy asked

"Now listen Mr Sheedy. This is a protection demand. It is not Provo tactics. Not on this side of the border"

"Nothing to do with me chief" said Sheedy' Neil carried on "I know there is a cell or two in the town. I will not name names. You may be a member of a cell. Then again you may not. But take it from me I know this area better than you. You are new here"

"Fuck off O Neill. Whatthe hell do you know? An old bollicks like you coming in here and talking to me like that, Get outta here before I throw you out, you old shite"

"It is very warm in here" said Neil "I must take my coat off" and he took the coat off to reveal his full Commandant's uniform. Shining buttons, Sam Browne and Cross belt. Rifle green uniform and leather kneelength leggings and highly polished oxblood boots. And his revolver on his left hip.

Again Neil spoke" This is what I want. I want Mr. Adanmson to be left alone. There is a rogue Provo in the area and if he gets any more threats I will hold you responsible"

"Ha ha ha. Hold me responsible? You think I am afraid of an old fart like you? What can you do to make me shake in my boots?

"Well" said Neil "there are many things that might happen to you" and he took the revolver from itd holster nd stated examining it closely"

"Where did you get the toy. A Christmas Cracker? "sneered Sheedy

"Would you like me to test it?" said Neil and he put a bullet in the chamber and blew a hole in the wall over Sheedy's head and covered him in plaster. Then he emptied the spent bullet and put another in and spun the chamber and placed the revolcer against his head and pulled the trigger. There was a loud click but no shot.

"Oh dear" said Neil and he replaced the bullet. Then he fired another shot and again the plaster sprayed all over the settee

"Your turn now Eamonn" he said "but I cannot let you have the revolver so I will fire it for you" Again he spun the chamber and aimed the gun at Sheedy who was now very much awake and was almost hiding behind the settee, There was aclick and Neil said "Just your luck. No shot My turn again" and he clicked against his own head. He spun the chamber again

"your turn again Eamon my friend. You might beat me to it this time" and he aimed the revolver

"Say when"

Sheedy was berserk "No more. No more. Leave me out of it. No more shooting" he cried

Neil waited and Sheedy came from begind the sofa and sat down

"Ok ok O Neill" he stammered "You are a fucking head case with a gun and for all I know you are a Mickey Mouse Republican. But I am not afraid of you. What can you do? Shoot me? Kill me?".

"Again I want you to listen and I will tell you. If we kill you we will have the police after us. In their eyes it will have been a murder. Now we do not want a murder,do we?. But if you disappear and your body is never found there is no case for murder. You could be under a few thousand tons of motorway concrete and you would be officially alive. We could have you seen in Glasgow or in London. Gone off with your fancy woman. A midnight flit with your bit of stuff. Never even a mention in An Poblacht.

No killed in action. No hero's praise. Even your children will hate you for leaving them"

"What a load of guff" said Sheedy. "You do not frighten me. Piss off and stop making an ass of yourself"

Neil spoke again "Before I go I will tell you that I do not make threats or promises that I do not keep. My name is Commandant Neil O Neill. I was Commanding Officer ot the East Donegal Brigade from 1914 to1923. I live in Garton. Believe me. Ask your superior officers if you have any. But you may not wish to do that if you are a scavenging loner. There is nothing personal in this. You go your way and I go mine and I hope for your sake that our paths do not cross. Just one other thing. Adamson is never to be touched or even spoken about again. I will let myself out"

He went over and switched the television on again and said good night to the young girl who was waiting in the hallway. On his way home he stopped and changed his clothes.

Then he did a very essential task. He took the bullet from the revolver and he kissed it again and again.

"You hve served me well my old friend" he said Then he put the dummy bullet back in the old uniform pocket.

He had a cup of tea with Mary before he went to bed

67

IT WAS LUNCHTIME and Aengus was eating his sandwich and reading the paper

Mary McGinty rushed in. Eyes like saucers and out of breath

"Master master. A big car pulled up and a posh lady in it"

"What now?" he said and he looked out the window. A large car was parked outside but he saw no lady. There was a rap on the door and when he opened it there she was. As glamorous as ever. Fiona Bruce

"Well Aengus I have found you at last" she beamed and she waited for him to come to her

What should he do? Shake her hand or give her a kiss?. The children will be peeping

"What a lovely surprise" he said "how lovelyto see you" and he gave her a big brotherly hug

"Is that all I get after all those years?" she asked

Straight to the point this lady

"You are a respectable married woman now" he said

"Dont remind me" she replied ".Mrs MacKinley. But enough of that. It took me some time to find you and it was only when I mentioned the Lagan4 that people were able to give me directions"

"We are fairly well known around here "Aengus said modestly "and what brings you to this end of the world?"

"You" she said "My husband has some business in Dublin and I was bored hanging about so I set off on my own and here I am. How are you keeping? Have you been back to Islington at all?"

God she does not waste any time

"No" he said "not since you and I. I am full time here and Ispend my holidays mostly in the parish. There is much to do"

"You the headmaster here?

"Well not exactly the headmaster. There are three teachers in the school and I am what is known as the Principal Teacher. Nothing heroic. But we work with the local clergy to improve the life of the children in the parish"

"Right little Socialist" she said. He looked to see if she was mocking him but she was in earnest and she continued "Good for you.Putting your wonderful talents for the people"

And she moved back and looked him up and down

"As handsome as ever" and she took a deep breath and sighed "and here am I getting old and wrinkled. But I should be grateful for good health. And now I have met you again"

She looked around and saw windows of eyes looking in. Like a goldfish in a bowl she was she told him later

"We cannot stop here all day chatting. You have a school to run. I am staying at the Cromwell. Will you join me for dinner this evening?"

What could he do? It would be churlish to refuse but he was entering dangerous waters. But he remembered their good old times and he was honest with her.

"Yes Fiona I would like that. What time?"

"Eight" "Could we make it seven?" he asked. That would mean an earlier finish. Less temptation.

"See you a seven then" and she went to her car and the children leaned over the school wall to see her drive off.

Aengus was absent minded for the rest of the school day.He could not have refused her invitation. Dinner. Nothing else implied. There had been only one letter between them over the years.But she had sought him out. Just to say hello? Or was he himself the person with the other ideas? Word would spread about the fancy car and he was sure to met someone in Cromwells?. And what would Maureen make of it all?Maybe heshould ask her to join them?. But she was not invited. He would phone her and say a friend of Sinead's was touring Donegal and she had called in to see him for advice on what was worth seeing in the County. He was having a meal with her Mrs McKinley at Cromewells and he would call in later and give her all the gossip

Fiona was waiting when he arrived at the hotel. As glamorous as ever. Maureen would ask what she was wearing but that was where he was wanting. Womens fashion and womens clothes?.

"A dry martini?" she suggested

"Thank you but I will will enjoy a glass of wine with the food instead, Strict on the drinking and driving the gardai are here"

It was delicious meal. She suggested they have the coffee in the lounge and she linked his arm as they went through. They sat in the big soft easy chairs and looked at each other and remained silent

"Mrs McKinley you are now and it suits you" said Aengus

"Yes married for some time now I am. And yourself?" she replied

"Still single. But I have a steady girlfriend. Local lassie and I am very fond of her" Aengus said

"I am delighted for you. My husband is adorable but he is away on business a lot" she said

"You must be a very wealthy woman" Aengus said

"Yes indeed. Wealthy. But a wealthy person can still be lonely" Careful here my son,. Getting personal Aengus thought

"I know I know" he said "but the wealthy can afford a divorce an start all over again"

"No divorce in Ireland?" she was amazed

"There is a legal divorce but not many can afford the seperation and the Church will not recognise or accept divorce." Aengus was happy that they had moved away from the personal

"It is lovely meeting you again" and she reached out and held his hand

"I think so too" said Aengus. "It is lovely to see you again. And you are as beautiful as ever. I wish we were back in Islington again. I have wonderful memories of our times together. I will always remember you. But Fiona my dear, we have moved on in our lives and we have obligations to other people now. What is past is past and I will remember it for ever. But I must leave you now. I really cannot trust myself to behave"

He looked round the lounge and saw no one was watching and he leaned across and kissed her gently on the lips. Then he hugged her and left

As he went through Reception the girls there were smiling and he went over

"Fantastic meal.My first cousin from America. That side got all the good looks. Look after her now.". That would keep them quiet

Fiona was sad. It was adream. And it had not happened. But she was at ease. He had treated her with kindness. It was a foolish dream. Tomorrow she would be back in Dublin and soon she would be in Boston

The dream was over and in the end she felt it had not been a bad one.

But Aengus felt a strange disquiet. He called in to see Maureen on the way home and when she asked what Mrs McKinley was wearing he did not know. He just shrugged

And there was more. He could have spent the night with Fiona. It might not be like the old times but they would have enjoyed each other. He knew that. But there was something annoying him. Why did he not go with Fiona? Maureen kept coming into the frame. Was it Maureen that stopped him in The Cromwell?. He did not know. Was this love? He did not know. He told Fiona he had a lassie. A lassie?

There was more. He could not betray her. He knew she liked him. She was fond of him he knew. But there was more to this than fondness. There was a sharing. A responsibility. Gradually it dawned on him. He would like to share his life with Maureen. To marry her and set up a home together. But what did she think?If he told her would she laugh?. Would he be able to tell her?. Maybe he should get kind and affectionate to her and he might win her over. But the others in the Lagan 4 would see what he was up to and they would laugh at him. He would have to wait and see how his romance developed

At school he spent a lot of time looking out the window. Mary McCarthy asked togo to the toilet and she went to the front gate and looked up the road to see if ther was anything to be seen. At the Friday session he seemed in another world but Maureen was on duty and they did not meet

. He went to Lochbeg farm. The old man was there alone. Aengus followed him about like the sheepdog. He had nothing to say and he would not go away and Neil was getting ratty and said

"I have a job to do in the top field" thinking that he might be left alone

"Might as well go with you" said Aengus

Neil looked out from under his eyebrows

"For the chat" said Aengus

"Whatever" said Neil

Thy got to the field and moved a few whin bushes to close a gap. Neil got his pipe out and sat down against the hedge. What was he going to do with this man?

"The years are catching up on me. Need the break to get me wind. How about yourself?" asked Neil

Aengus was out of breath and had difficulty speaking

"I want ta" and he did not recognise his own voice

"I wanted ta, I wanted to ask you a question" he croaked

"No more questions" said Neil "That Fr Barry has me head worn out with questions. All questions and questions. No more. No more"

"It was something else" squeaked Aengus

"Spit it out then"

"I want your permission to ask Maureen to marry me"

"Jesus Christ" said Nil and he dropped his box of matches. He made a big deal of collecting the fallen matches and then he looked way over into to the mountains.

He turned to Aengus and said nothing. The bastard is having me on thought Aengus. But then he saw the smile on the old mans face

"That would be nice" he said and he offered his hand and they shook. It was a deal done.

"I havn't asked her yet" said Aengus. "Could we keep this between the two of us?"

"No problem" said Neil. "I have been keeping secrets for the past 40years"

Aengus then said "But as soon a anything happens I will tell you first thing. You will be the first to know"

Aengus was able to breathe normally again and Neil was quietly pleased. Ever since she came home with Geriant he never knew what Maureen would land with. Aengus was a Gweedore man but he was one of the best of them. At least they had him house trained. Your friend from faraway and your wife from next door was the old Gaelic advice even if it was more down to earth in its idiom. Then their litle game began. Every time they met Neil would raise a questioning eyebrow and Shane would give a movement of the head. Negative so far

Aengus was back to normal in the classroom. If he asked her would she think he was rushing her and if he did not ask then maybe one of he doctors in the hospital might get in there before him. Then again he did not know what to do or say. In the movies the stars were always saying how much they loved each other but if he said something like that she might ask if he was sickening for some thing and was he feeling all right.

So it had to be one question and one answer

68

MAUREEN AND RITA used to drop in on the Friday night sessions, They were not that impressed by the music and often sat in another room watching TV or cooking in the kitchen. When he had a glass of wine Aengus felt brave enough but Rita was always in the way. He was not afraid of Maureen. He was afraid that she might not agree to marry him. He had not even tried a bit of hanky panky when things got hectic. Certainly he wanted her and in his dreams many times they made passionate love. But his lust in real life was chastened by a love that wanted to share his life, his home, his children with her.Anyhow if she agreed to marry him there would be a lifetime of delight.

. Poor old Fr Barry had hurt himself again. A black eye this time. Rough crowd in Buncrana he complained, Getting their own back on the clergy for too severe penances imposed by the Parish Priest. Less Rosaries and Stations of the Cross and more plain Hail Marys. But Shane and Aengus were worried. What if he were hurt when the Lagan 4 had an important booking, and they were getting busy again?. After all they had The All Ireland Champion but basically theywere an all round family show. Back at Lochbeg Shane was doing well. He was not short of money and he could relax. He tried rearing pigs for the mart but he was not able to feed them with his own produce and the plan failed.

He was passing Hannahs and he saw the lovely car there again. He stopped and knocked but there was no answer. But he had a good look at the car, A Jaguar Etype it was and he had never seen one before. He meant to ask her about it. It was in her drive the next day as well and he called in but there was no one at home so he did not bother, Must be one of the Dublin art dealers.He would ask her about it later.

Neil was acontented man. Ther was no pressure on him now and he was able to attend to his beloved sheep. He was at ease that Shane had settled into farming and he wished that Aengus would pop the question. He did not tell Mary what was between himself and Aengus but he saw her looking at them with their nodding and shaking

Then came the big bombshell

The Shamrock Club had invited the Lagan 4 over to Brightons in Mass.in the Boston surburbs and to play in other clubs in the area. The invitation had come through Fr Barry's father in Buncrana

Aengus was not that keen, He had been there and done that. All that fuss, But the others were delighted and he was outvoted. Hannah was also very keen. But she told them she might have to arrange her own travel and schedule but she certainly would love to go. Shane mentioned the lovely Jaguar he saw outside her house and she agreed that it was a visiting art consultant from Dublin and she was too busy at the time to tell him any more. Tell you later.

Mary and Neil said they did not want to travel. They said they could have Neil as their manager but he awas adamant that he was staying at home

But Maureen and then Rita wre very keen. They would be wardrobe mistresses, Or general factotems. Anything you liked to call them as long as they were in the party. A date was set and the preperations were made. Hannah asked that she fly out in her own time and that was agreed. Apart from that, all was arranged and paid for by the Shamrock Club. A minibus collected them and took them to Shannon and they stayed overnight in the Brian Boru Hotel

Next morning the minibus took themto the airport and directly out on the runway to a waiting airplane. It was not a big fancy number, Maureen thought it looked a bit battered, But she never liked flying. A nervous passenger.

A man in a peaked and braided cap came towards them

"I am your pilot. Brian Monks is my name. I pilot this plane for Mr Maguire. We travel all over the world in this baby. He is an international dealer. Currencies and jewellery. Call me Brian. My father was from Cavan, Great man for the Gaelic football he was, God rest his soul. He would have made John Joe Reilly a saint"

Fr Barry introduce the gang to Brian who said

"Just take your hand luggage on board" said Brian "customs have been cleared" he said with a wink

12seats. "My God this is small" said Maureen and Aengus could sense her tension. Brian must have heard and he said "Plenty of space for all and I have a copilot up front with me"

Maureen thought it looked like the old CDR railway carriage with two aisles of six seats like she used going to the Convent

"America here we come" sang the bold Brian. "I will keep the partition between us closed but I will talk to you all over this little system we have and if you wish to speak to me just press the button on your armrest and talk to me. I will hear what you say'

Afew seconds later he was back on again

"We have been given clearance for take off so here we go. It will take us 7 hours to Boston so try and settle down and sleep"

Maurenn opened her handbag and had a fistful of tablets. "Barbiturates" was all she said "Anyone want some?" but no one answered.

They watched the Aran Islands beneath them and then they went into the clouds and the sun. Brian spoke "I hope you are all settled. All is well. Make sure your seat belts are fastened. There is some turbulence ahead. Nothing we cannot manage. I could fly around it but it will mean another hours flying time. Nothing to worry about but I just thought I would keep you informed No need to worry"

"What what? "Maurenn was wide awake "Turbulence? Turbulence in this little plane. Oh my God" and she began to sob

Aengus gathered he close and triedto comfort her

"Its just a cloud that causes the plane to shake a bit. Just like the pothole in the road outside Noonan's that does the same to the cars at home"

The plane was rising and falling and Brian Monks was on again

"I go through this almostevery flight. Matilda, my best pal this plane, and myself are used to this. Matilda is a good dancer. She can wattz through any turbulence and Mr Maguire swears it is good for the digestion"

Maureen was still shaking. "Will we ever get to Boston?"

"Of course we will love" said Aengus said

"I am so frightened" she said

"No need to be" said Aengus "It is only a bit of a cloud we are passing through. We have a long life to live together yet"

What had he just said? Long life together?

He put his lips close to her ear "Did you hear what I just said?" he asked

"What?"

"I will say it again, Slowly this time. Will you marry me?"

She looked up and kissed him "Yes please. Yes please Aengus" and she lay back and closed her eyes and did not say another word.

Brian came on and wakened them all

"Landing soon, Seatbelts fastened"

They landed and whirred into a large hangar where there was minibus waiting

"Just take your hand luggage. I will have the rest taken to your Hotel.You are booked in the Ferrybank. Mr Maguire owns it. Very superior. You lucky people"

Aengus put his hand to Maureen's face "You have not changed your mind now we are on dry land?" he asked

"No way. Never never." and she hugged him

"Will we tell the others?" she asked

"Not yet. Let us keep our little secret"

They were taken to the Ferrybank Hotel. Very posh, Very posh indeed.

"I must leave you for a moment" said Aengus

"What for?" Maureen asked and kissed him again. Shane looked at the ceiling in disgust and Rita blew him a kiss

"Back in a second" and Aengus was gone and he went to Reception

At Reception he was given a form to fill

Address; Neil O Neill. Lochbeg Farm. Garton. Co. Donegal Ireland

Message; "Yes"

The receptionist read the completed form and she smiled. These Irish have their own ways God Bless them. Sure her own mother would not go any further if she met a black cat. Funny people, Must be the fairies or maybe the poteen

Tommy Martin on the other side of the world felt much the same. He knew the Irish people. And the mountainy men in particular. The poteen was a devil

Tommy had a sneaky read of the telegram. "Yes" What did 'yes' mean?

He handed the telegram to Neil and looked at the mountian and waited. No point in making it obvious that he was dying to know what it meant.

But he could not believe it. The man Neil was doing a dance before his very eyes. The bloody poteen Tommy thought

"Great news Tommy. Great news" That made it worse. Share the great news. One word it was on the telegram. Share it. Tommy could keep a secret. Nothing coming.

"Must be off" Tommy said

"Thank you Tommy" and Neil went back in to the kitchen. He decided he would not tell Mary. That was a woman to woman pleasurable task and they could have a happy time with the tears and the joys all together That would be at home in Garton.

Over in Boston Aengus rejoined the group. They were approached by a man who introduced himself as Sheamus who told them that his job was to look after them. He was their minder for their stay in Boston. Just leave everything to him.

He gave them their room numbers. The two girls were together and Aengus and Shane were sharing and Fr Barry had his own room.

Sheamus told them to have a light meal and an early night. The head waiter came with the menu and Shane asked for a boiled egg. Maureen called him a hick and the waiter did not understand. A boiled egg? Just one? Mon Dieu. Je ne pense pas

They had coffee in the lounge and a waitress came over and asked

"Are you the Lagan 4?" and she handed Fr Barry a telegram

"Welcome to the land of The United States of America. I hope you are all in one piece. I am not far away and I will meet you all tomorrow. Love from Hannah"

Not faraway? Where is she?

"I thought she was in Italy looking at some paintings" said Aengus

"Sounds like she is in America" said Rita

They made their way to their rooms. Maureen waylaid Aengus in the corridor

"We could visit each other?" she suggested

"None of that you hear. We have Fr Barry in our group. And the no good brother of yours would blackmail me. No way. I can hear him already "Ill tell me dad" Off with you before I cahnge my mind"

He was going to have trouble with that young lady and it was a lovely thought

69

"MY GOD BUT I am shattered" said Rita when they reacjed their room

"Same here" said Maureen

"It was one nightmare of a flight" continued Rita "I thought you would pass out"

"It was the best airline flight of my life" said Maueen

"You gone crazy?. You were almost berserk at one stage"

"I sure was. But I got much better whan Aengus asked me to marry him"

Hugs and kisses and dancing round the room. What a wonderful flight?. What a wonderful day?. What a wonderful Aengus?. They both agreed it was going to be a wonderful trip. But in the back of her mind Maureen had another idea making its presence felt. Roll on the next week in Boston

They were woken by the hotel porter, There was a Mr James in reception for them. It was the bold Sheamus himself

"I was sent to get you organised as Mr Maguire will drop in later to meet you all for a chat, So have your breakfat and do not leave the hotel until he has been" They were eating their breakfast when Shane spluttered

"Holy mother of God. I can't believe this". Aengus looked round and said

"Jesus Christ, sorry Father,but this is not real"

"I thought we might join you all for breakfast" said Hannah Robinson herself and standing beside her was Des Shanley

"We thought you were in Italy" Maureen said

"No no. We have serious business to attend to here in Boston. I want you all to keep tomorrow free, all day.Des and I are getting married at 11a.m. in the Registry Office here and we want you all to be there. We have arranged a reception at this hotel and you gang had better be here"

Then there was the kissing and the hugging

Aengus spoke' "It must be the Americen air. I have asked Maureen to marry me and she said yes. Shane looked at Aengus and said "some brother in law you" but he liked Aengus from the day he told him to learn how to spell

Sheamus looked on. Bewildered. Two betrothals at the same table. Irish betrothals and they were all under sixty years of age. Things were changing in The Emerald Isle. Tying the knot before their dotage. There were some questions to be answered'

"So this explains some of the happenings in Garton" said Fr Barry

"Yea" said Shane "I saw the Dublin registration car but it never crossed my mind"

Aengus said "I had an idea this might happen ever since Des called over to see me when Na Fianna were playing in Donegal Town. Fantastic. Congratulations all round" How long have you known?" asked Maureen

"We knew we would marry some time ago but this trip to Boston was too good to miss. Ideal for a Civil Marriage and we can have a great reception when we get home. The Papists and the Presbyterians can get together and no one will be offended" Hannah replied.

Then Mr Maguire arrived.He was a short round man with a fancy waistcoat and a cravat and a shiny head fron his hairoil that was keeping his hair back from his forehead

"My name is Colm Maguire. I waas born in Creeslough and I have been in Boston for forty years. I am active in the Ancient Order of Hibernians and I am Chairman of The Shamrock Club. My God after a few seconds with fellow Donegal men I am back with my Creeslough accent again. As if I had never left. My business is dealing in jewellery and precious metals. It is lovely to meet you all. Any chance of a cup of tea?"

He sat with them and said how they in Boston and the Shamrock Club were so proud of what Fr Barry and Aengus were doing for Garton but Fr Barry interrupted "Not at all. It is you and the Shamrock Club who should take the credit. Without your help we would not have been successful"

Sheamus intervened

"Mr Maguire Sir, I must tell you something. This is a most unusual group of people. Hannah and Des are getting married tomorrow and Aengus has just proposed to Maureen and she ha accepted. In Matilda your plane and over the Atlantic Ocean"

That appealed to Colm Maguire. He could tell that story for many years to come

"Well I do believe?" he said "my old boneshaker as a marriage bureaux. Might get it blessed and give that villain Brian Monks the licence to marry his passengers. But folks. You must all come over to my place and meet my good lady"

Thank you sir and it is very kind of you" said Des Shanley. "But we ave booked our wedding reception in this hotel and we would like you and your friends to join us here. Please invite your friends from the Shmrock Clib to come and celebrate with us. We will be delighted to meet them"

"Great idea "said Colm Maguire. I will invite my friends and my secretary will make the necessary arrangemeents with the hotel. Now I must leave you all but my man Sheamus will look after you"

After breakfast Sheamus asked "What would you like to do today?"

"If we could rest after that enormous breakfast?"

"Then I will come back later and we can decide"

Hannah explained that she and Des had all arrangements made but they needed a best man and a bridesmaid. Witnesses over here. Maureen and Aengus volunteered. Then they settled in the easy chairs and went back over the years of Na Fianna and the R&R and The Loft In Rathmines and the games against Vincents. Des admitted that he crept in to the Mansion House to hear Shane's great victory and that he all their tapes

"He knows the songs better than I do" said Hannah

Shane and Rita and Maureen sat and listened

"Dublin is a bit more exciting than Garton" Des was told

He did not agree "I am delighted to be leaving the city and coming to Garton. The quiet life will suit me. In Dublin I have my little flat and I do not know anyone in the block. Even though I was born in the city. I might see them in the local pub. With Na Fianna I did not know the players as they went their way and I went mine. When I was Captain I only knew the older players but the younger men stayed apart. It was the same at the Golf Club"

Well" said Shane "You will not have the same trouble at Garton Golf Club""

"Oh Yea?" and Des shrugged at the feeble joke

Fr Barry said" Des you will have plenty to keep you occupied in Garton. The GAA, the school, the village hall, the school bus, the students' reading room. No time to get bored. We can easily use any spare time you may have."

"Thank you Fr Barry. Much appreciated. I am into rare books and manuscripts now since I gave up teaching, First editions and that sort of thing. I do a lot of travelling"

It did not matter. It was a pleasant feeling. Garton was getting a new family. With Mr Adamson and his new mansion and Mt Lavin with his dental surgery and now the Shanleys with their picture gallery Garton was becoming a centre of excellence. No longer a backward parish not far from Lifford.

Maureen and Rita were in their room whan Sheamus called for them all.

"What a maevellous day for you Donegal people" he said

Maureen whispered to Rita "It was on the cards. It was the timing that was unusual. I knew in my heart that Aengus wanted to get married but he was so shy I thought I would have to pop the question myself"

"Its a big change from you and Geriant" said Rita

"Yes Geriant. He was a very nice chap. We were really close friends. Two lonely people. But all he ever wanted was to get his fellowship and go home to the Valleys. I never want to hear of Barry John or of Gareth Edwards again in my life. And as for Male Welsh Voice Choirs I feel ill when I hear one now. So there"

But Maureen had other things on her mind

"Thats enough about me. You have some history too. Some tales to tell All those interns after you"

"Yes I had a few passing romances" said Rita. "Undergraduate drinking and snogging"

"But now?" said Maureen

"Now?"

"Yes now" said Maueen again

"Well"

"Well what?" pressed Maureen

"I have it bad this time" admitted Rita

"Is it love?" asked Maureen again

"Yes it is" said Rita and they were silent

Then Maureen was off again "Let me tell you one thing. Shane adores you. He worships you. But you are a more mature person. You have been out in the wide world and you have further education and you have the experience of dealing with people. He has been in Garton all his life. I might have to rely on you to make the decision."

Sheamus herded them together and Hannah suggested they go and have a look at the Registry Office so they would not get lost the following morning and Sheamus said they might go on from there to the Shamrock Club

The Registry Office was a dull and dingy building. It could have been the Council Offices in Lifford. Steps up to swinging doors where a group was having a photograph taken. As they watched people come and go there was very little wedding celebrations. Might as well have been paying theit car tax or the Council rates "Better go in" said Des. A big fat man in a uniform met them

"We are getting married here tomotrrow" said Des "and we thought we might see where to go"

"Over here is the waiting room. In there is you make your marriage declaration and there is a bench for you to sign the documents. Nothing very romantic I am afraid" the doorman apologised

"We mght liven it up a bit tomorrow" said Des

Y'all from Ireland?" the doorman asked "Tell you one thing. You Irish know how to party. Brighten up this goddamn dump when they come. See y'all tomorrow and he gave them a smile that showed every tooth in his head. Then on to the Shamrock Club. It was the Mansion House all over with the steps up to a portico and swinging glass doors and latticed windows. Sheamus went to reception and said the it had been arranged with Mr Maguire that he James Murphy could show this party around the club. He explained that they were the Lagan 4 and that they would be performing in the club sometime during the week

Shamrock Club?. There was not a shamrock in sight. Not a tricolour or even a harp. It could have been the Conservative Club in Strabane. But all that changed when they entered the dining room. White linen tables and Waterford Glass and beautiful chandeliers sparkling overhead. On a raised platform at the far end was the President's Table and that was where Mr Maguire entertained his guests

Then they went to the members' clubroom upstairs. It was a subdued room and it took time for their eyes to see it all. It was Ireland with a capital letter

A beautiful handwoven Killybegs carpet of a Celtic design covered the central floor. There were tables in recesses all about the floor and on the main wall facing everyone there was a light focussed on a large framed copy of the 1916 Proclamation of Independence and on either side photogrphs of DeValera and Gerry Adams. It might have been Jesus and John The Baptist. As they looked around the walls there were photos of Loam Mellowes, Dan Breen, Paraic Pearse. MacGuinness and O Hanlon.

To balance things they had photos of Frank Aitken and Gerry Boland and over an the far corner was Conor Cruise O Brien

"This is an IRA stronghold" said Aengus

"Looks like it" said Fr Barry "Big Republicans here. Whatever they are they helped us in Garton when we needed it"

"More Irish than the Irish at home" said Shane.

Then Aengus said "It is almost as if they feel they have abandoned the old country and they wish to compensate for it. Like a father who abandons his children and tries to compensate for it later in their lives"

"Good an explanation as any" said Fr Barry. It was lunch time and they went to the dining room. Sheamus had said that some members might call in as word of their arrival was out. Mr Maguire arrived and he looked very pleased

"I have had a good day on the markets an what is happening here? He asked

"We have had a wonderful day with Sheamus and we thought we might go back to the hotel and relax" said Aengus

"Will you do an old man a great favour?" asked Colm Maguire. "Will you go to the Ferrybank and freshen up and then come and have dinner with me here in the Shamrock.My wife would love to meet you and I promise I will have you back in the Ferrybank before eleven o clock.

When they arrived back at the Shamrock there was Sinead and Hudi waiting to greet them

"Hannah has kept us up to date with all that is happening and we could not miss out on today with the marriage proposal and the wedding tomorrow" Sinead said

Colm Maguire arrived and he had a great welcome for Sinead. "So Mrs Yehudin is your sister Aengus?. Well it's a small world. This lady has been keeping me out of jail fot the last many years. Some and join us Sinead and Yehudi. Lovely lovely. Well I never"

They were all introduced to Kathleen, Colm's wife. "My little Colleen I call her. A Colleen from Kerry. I lost my heart at the first glance. She wa a student nurse in the Holy Mother Hospital. A healing angel from Heaven above. Broke my ankle and lost my heart on the same day"

Jeeze thought Aengus this is worse than anything Holywood could spew out any time.

But Colleen spoke up and told her Colm that he was being a nuisance and that he might listen for a few moments to give the others a chance "And Aengus proposed to Maureen in Colm's plane" she said "Now aint that wunnerful?" and she looked at Fr Barry and smiled. They all had a lovely evening.

"What did you thinkof Darby O Gill?" asked Rita

"Darby who?"

"Yer man Colm Maguire" she said

"I do not think we should laugh at him" said Shane. "He came over here with nothing and now he is a millionaire. I admire him"

"But he does go over the top" Rita said

"He might overdo the Irish bit" Shane said "but we do not know what he has been through and where he comes from. It may be an act to cover his shyness"

"You may be right there" she said

"I always thought my fatherwas a cold and dry old sod until he told us his story and I saw how he manages things quietly behind the scenes. We never really know who or what any person is" he said

Well that puts me in my place she thought and she leanded over and kissed him on the cheek and said" love you"

Shane thought. A millionaire and his own airplane,. Some Darby O Gill !!

70

RITA WAS HAVING a moan "I haven't a thing to wear. Not a thing"

'Only three suitcases full" said Maureen "and anyway you are not a bridesmaid. I am the one awho has to dress. But it is a Registry Office and there will be no great showing of the trousseau"

They had to mix and match. Sheamus collected them all and drove them to the Registry Office and there to meet them was Colm Maguire and his darling Kathleen. Sinead and Hudi had turned up as well and quite a number of the Shamrock Club. An Irish wedding was not to be missed

Satchmo the doorman apologised fot the dreary waiting room. Dreary it soon was not. Sheamus' wife had a large handbag with a bottle of Irish Whiskey and plastic cups and soon they were a happy wedding group

The wedding ceremony was short and direct. Passports shown; affirmatives given and sign the book.

"All back to Ferrybank" Sheamus commanded and they piled into any available car. The staff applauded the newly weds and they had the red carpet in the entrance. But in the banqueting room they had done their magic. Green and gold tablecloths and shamrocks and harps hanging from the ceiling and a Leprechaun sitting by the wedding cake. It could have been Garton on a Patrick's Day Ceili. Sheamus got everyone seated after the champagne

Aengus knew it.Holy Jesus he knew. Des came over and asked "Aengus will you do the announcements, Will you be fear a tighe.?" Suppose it was a best man's duty in any case

He stood up and thanked them all for coming and that it was his great honour to say a few words. He wished that Hannah's parents were here to see their beautiful and radiant daughter and her fine new husband. He had known Hannah and Desmond for many years and never was there a couple more suited He knew they would lead a happy life together and best of all they were going to Settle in Garton where he and Maureen would be their neighbours"

Hannah was crying an Des stood up "My lovely wife is crying. She is crying wth pure happiness and she wished you all to carry on and have a great day and she will regain her composure"

The wedding feast progressed and Shane went off from his table. Then they heard it. One of the Lagan 4 tapes and when Hannah's singing of "Thady O Neill" came on they all stopped eating and talking and then they clapped. She stood up and bowed to the wedding guests. She was back to her old self. The meal was never ending.No performing or dancing but people changing seats and chatting. A photographer moved among them but there was no group photograph.

Colm Maguire came over to Aengus

"Where is Maureen?"

They found her and Colm said he wanted a quiet word

"You popped the question yesterday on my plane. Kathleen thinks it is the most romantic thing she has ever heard. Now let me ask you a question. Did you put the ring on her finger?"

"Well no. It waas not a planned job" said Aengus

"Then I have a suggestion" said Colm. "I do a bit in that line. Jewellery. Nothing big. Just a sideline of mine. I have a small private office down by the docks and I might have a ring that might suit. Would you be interested?"

"Yes Yes" Maureen almost shouted

"Fine just fine. I must go, but Sheamus will look after it all and Kathleen is having a great time and she is staying on. Sheamus will take care of her"

It was late afternoon when the festivities were nearing an end. Sinead and Hudi stayed on and chatted and Maureen got to know about her intended. They spoke of his childhood and of Ownie Rua's death. Of how Peggy managed on of thir own. The Boston and Gweedore weddings and how wll Peggy was managing even in her old age. Shane and Rita were listening and they understood the words that were not said. But this was a joyous holiday and all those worries could be addressed at another place and time.

They were at ease in each other's company. In spite of what had happened Ireland had been kind to them and Maureen intended that it would include Rita. The Irishness had spread over and covered them. The Donegal connection was intangible but it was there and they knew that whatever life had in store they could manage and an inner quietness permeated their souls

Sheamus drove them down the quays to Colms office and Maureen insisted that Rita and Shane come as well

She took Shane to one side. He would never meet another girl like Rita. She came from a background similar to his own. It was her uncle, Omagh, who set

Shane on his way to being All Ireland Champion. She herself had known Rita for many years and there was no finer woman. Would he take her out of her misery and marry her.She was in love with him. Now was the time and Colm might sell them a nice ring as well. So he had to get that little brain of his working and get engeged to Rita. They could get married at any time later

Maybe she was right.He knew he loved Rita and that she loved him. He could not think of marrying anyone else.

Sheamus pulled up outside a steel door and there were steel bars on the windows. This was Colm Maguire's office. His little store. His little beauty. His little dream. They pressed the bell and there was a buzzing and a question

"Who is it?"

"The Lagan 4 to see Mr Maguire"

More buzzing and a "Come on in"

Colm was waiting and he introduced them to Monica

"I could not have this wee pasttime of mine were it not for Monica. I know about the metal trade but Monica looks after the jewellery. My little jewel she is herself. What have we got in engagement rings Monica me dear?"

"Not too bad at all "Monica said "You picked up some nice ones the last trip to South Africa"

"South Africa was it?. I get confused with all the names in that part of the world" Colm said

Doing his Barry Fitzgerald act again thought Aengus

Monica went to a safe and took a tray of rings and put it before them

"Any tea in the pot Monica?" Colm asked and he said they would leave them to decide

Maureen was in Heaven.She tried on various rings an then she stopped

"There are no price tags"

"I will go and ask" said Aengus and he went to Mr Maguire. He sounded very surprised

"Monica Monica. What is this? No prices?. Tell Maureen to make her pick and then we can check the price"

Monica did not mind his little game. He had phoned ahead and told her to remove all price tags

Maureen settled on her choice. Then she took Shane by the elbow "you told me you had something to tell Rita. Off you go and tell her in private" and she ushered him into the next room

"Come here Rita" she commanded and closed the door' There was asqueal of delight and Rita came rushing back. "Shane has asked me to marry him" she cried and they all cheered. Colm Maguire came rushing out to know what all the noise was about and Rita grabbed and hugged him

"Shane has asked me to marry him" she said

"Holy be Jasus. Me plane and now me shop. No need for the Pakistanis to go home for a wife or a husband any more. Just sit in my plane or in my shop. Kathleen will never believe it. Never"

He was beside himself with excitement. Imagine?. Two Irish weddings and he was the cause of both. His plane and his office.

"This calls for another ring. You choose a ring Rita or my Kathleen will never speak to me again. Another cupof tea then Monica" and he left them to choosse

Rita did not take long and Colm was called back.

"I dont believe it, You have both picked rings I bought in the same deal in Africa. In a mining shop outside Johannesburgh. You have both struck lucky. I got them for a song" and then he named a price that had Monica hold her breath. What he was asking was not even a verse never mind a song. He was giving them away. Somebody down the line would later have to pay extra

"No need to pay me now" he said "When you get home put a cheque in the Northern Bank and the deal is done. Now let us hit the town and celebrate"

"Colm our friend" said Aengus "There is nothing we would rather do than celebrate with you. But we have come to play at the Shamrock and we need some rehearsal. To check the sound system and the acoustics" and he gave Mr Maguire a bear hug. The girls kissed and hugged him and Maureen said "You and Kathleen will please, please come to our wedding. Promise" and Rita chimed in "And to ours as well" The Garton crowd left and Colm stayed with Momica

"I think we deserve a little celebration ourselves "he said. "Close the office and we will have a meal and a drink at Flanagans"

"You real old softie" she said "you real old Irish softie. That was a wonderful thing you did" and she got her coat.

71

FRANCOISE THE WAITER was puzzled and bewildered. Those mad Irish. First there was the one who wanted the boiled egg. And now they were all getting married and he did not know who was marrying whom or what. There might be two or three weddings. Those Irish. Good at the music and the stories. But for organisation?, il est intuile. Aengus called for order at the breakfast table and said

"Now last evening we could not get in to practise in th club because of a function there so we will go today"

They called in at the club and went to the manager's office to collecr their equipment and they were told they would have to wait an hour or so

"Why?" they asked

"Have a look on stage. The mayor of Boston Stephen McKinley heard about the Lagan 4 s coming and the local TV is doing a slot on you. It will be live for most of your playing. Nothing to do with me. All the big brass are in on this and I do as I am told" said the harassed manager

The concert hall was buzzing with technicians on stepladders and lighting men calling and shouting. Fr Barry went to the senior technician and asked if they could have a try out using their own equipment and was told "No problem. It is our job to enhance on what you do tonight. Go off and have a cup of tea and we will see how things work out. If you wish to incorporate your system in ours then that can be done."

They played on the stage and the technicians adjusted everything to the Lagan4s requirements

"McKinley is a stickler and he is the big man here in Boston. No doubt he will have a speech to make on TV after the show. He likes the limelight and the glory. Big Irish vote here in Boston" the foreman said

I was like a Civic Night in the Shamrock. All the ladies' finery and the tuxedos and champagne and the cigar smoke

The Mayor welcomed them all "to this great city of ours that was looking forward to a fabulous night of Irish Music and culture from the Klagan 4 after their great succsss in Europe"

"Were we in Europe?" asked Shane

"Ireland is in Europe you dope "said Maureen

They performed well. But they felt there was someything missing. They got a standing ovation at the end and all stood for the Soldiers Song

Some of the important guests were introduced to the Lagan 4

There again was Fiona Bruce and she smiled at him as they shook hands

"Colm tells me you have just got engaged. Congratulations from us all in Boston" and she moved on

Thank you Fiona Bruce and long may ou live prayed a relieved Aengus. The Boston papers gave them a good review and the TV news praised their evening's work. What then was missing?

Sheamus had the answer

"The Shamrock lot are different. All great Republican heroes in their own hearts. Taking on and beating the Brits. Blood and Glory is what they need. Let it pass. Have a rest. Here is my number if you need anything"

So there was the answer. Not enough death and heroism. Too much culture

"But we are a cabaret act" said Shane

"Not over here we are" said Fr Barry. "You could sing "Sean South" completely out of tune and they would raise the rafters. Music is not that important. But give them 'My Name is O Hanlon" and they will go home happy"

Sheamus was right. What they played had no mention of those who died fighting on the Border or on hunger strike

"We do not do that stuff" said Shane "we are a general cabaret act. We have played to Orangeman in the past and they did not take offence and they did not walk out"

Fr Barry said "We have one more session to do at the Shamrock. Three more bookings at other hotels. Let us play our act for the other venues and we will see what we can do for the Shamrock

They were well received away from the Shamrock Club.

But on the last night in the Shamrock they told the audience that they had requests to play different ballads and songs. But they needed time to practise and to rehearse those songs and ballads if they were to keep up their standards. They asked the audience to accept their regrets

A mumur passed down the auditorium. It was not a mad Irish night. It could have been in any city in the world with a cosmopolitan audience. The Lagan 4 felt the difference and they responded. Gradually they won their listeners over. This was their culture. This was from the land their forefathers had to abandon. The music crept into their consciousness. By the end of the evening they were calling for more. Noy the "Paddy MacGinty's Goat" type of song but the music of thousands of years of Celtic heritage

Sheamus drove them to the Airport, courtesy of the Shamrock Club and then it was home to Garton.

72

PEGGY WAS IN O Neills when they arrived home. Neil who had the secret had driven over and collected her. Neil had kept his side of the bargain with Aengus and he had said nothing about proposals or anything of that kind.

Aengus was the first to give the good news "Maureen has agreed to marry me. I am the happiest man in the world. As well as that wonderful news I can tell you that Hannah and Des Shanley got married in Boston last week. That's all" and he sat down

Hugs and kisses all round. Aengus looked over at Neil who lifted an eyebrow and laughed. Maureen saw what was going on]

"Were you in on this?. Did you know?" she asked

"I had an idea. He asked my permission some time ago" Neil admitted

"God I might have gussed when you called him Aengus instead of 'that Gweedore man'. God sometimes you can be really sneaky" she said

Mary cut in "Thanks be to God. It will give me ears a rest. On and on about him all and every day she was"

Again there was a lull and Aengus looked over at Shane "Your turn"

Rita nodded and Shane said "Rita and I got engaged in Boston as well. Got the ring in the same shop as Maureen and Aengus too"

"Get the Whiskey out" said Neil

"And the Tio Pepe" said Mary

What a night. Comparing and admiring the rings and looking into the future. They were a happy O Neill family and Peggy Gillespie was a happy mother as well

Neil had a few naggins and he went out and sat on the wall with his pipe and the stars above. He had a feeling of sweet quietness. A calmness so deep that his soul was infused with such strength and serenity that would have him face the whole world. He has felt it before when they returned from a dangerous mission and none of his men was killed or severely wounded. It was a sweet peace, A calm that would sustain him against the whole world. One of those moments when the soul experiences its own God. Not a vision but a moment when God speaks by means of the truth to those who can hear Him and a light opens in the darkness. A moment when one's God is near and it is possible to know he is there

He looked up at the brightest star and said

"I must be going in now"

Things had quietened down. The alcohol was making them sleepy. Fr Barry was the first to leave.

Aengus was told he was not yet a member of the family and did he not have a home to go to. Peggy enjoyed this joshing. One had to fight one's corner here. Neil surprised them all when he gave Aengus a hug and "see ya tomorrow son" was all he could say

Maureen hauled Rita off to bed and Shane was left with his father and mother

"This is the happiest day of our lives. Don't you agree Neil?" Mary said

"Aye lass" was all he said and he blew into his handkerchief.

Mary was weeping and Neil held her

"Shush a leanbh, Shush a stoirin" and he looked at Shane

"See you in the morning" and they alll went to bed.

The only thing that Maureen could think of was her wedding. The sooner the better. Why not hop over to Birmingham and get it over in in a day?. To hell with the church. A few words and a sprinkling of Holy Water. That's all it was. It was the Certificate and the Registration that was important. She wanted to be wed. She needed to be wed. She carried on nursing but she could not ignore what her whole body was telling her. Was it love?. If Adam and Eve felt like this what chance did the Angel of God have?. They were not impure thoughts. They were of her nature. God would understand.

They had to give Colm and Kathleen Maguire time to make their travel arrangements and Sinead and Hudi would need time to arrange things as well. The reception would be in Cooney's and Fr Barry and Fr Eugene would conduct the wedding ceremony. Poor Fr Barry had fractured hus right wrist but not to worry he said. He could do a lovely Blessing with his left hand.

Shane was the best man and Rita the bridesmaid

Cooney's did them proud and Aengus and Maureen booked a room there for the wedding day. It was better not to have the old couple worrying about them getting ready on time. They would have enough bother with Shane. Shane as the best man had to make a speech

"I have known Aengus since the firstday he came to Garton school. The very first words he said to me were "lift your feet" and then "learn how to spell". He then spoiled a most superior essay with a red pencil and wrote on it "must improve". Since than we have got on well and we play together in the Lagan 4. No big deal. But then he started being nice to me. I could not understand it. Then I realised Maureen was back in Strabane. I was his bestest bestest pal then. Bestest pal. I warned Maureen but she never listens to me anyway and now I have a new brother. Welcome Aengus"

Other speakers said someting on the same lines. Neil got a round of applause for his words. H esaid he never thought he would meet a Gweedore man he could like. But Mary was a great believer in Blessed Martin De Porres and here was a miracle that could be attributed to the Holy Man and he definitely should be canonised. Pass the word on, Fr Barry.

Then Maureen spoke

"I know it is not usual for the blushing bride to say something but Iwould like to say a special welcome to Colm and Kathleen Maguire and I would like to thank them for thieitr lovely wedding present. It is a painting of Lough Finn by local artist Celine McGlynn. Thank you Colm and Kathleen"

The reception was over and it was time for the young couple to lesve. They went to their room to change

Maureen slipped out of her dress and grabbed him

"Jeeze not now" he whispered

"Yes now Now Just now" and she pulled him down on the bed' That was something, he thought later. And I will have to put up with that for th rest of my days.

Maureen was happy too. Where did he learn that?. Who taught him?. But she did not care. He was hers now.

They both came doewn the stairs and straight into the car that Shane had parked by the door

"Oh My God" she said

'What?" he asked

"No problem. Lucky I am wearing the trouser suit. I can feel somrthing trickling down my inner thigh"

He drove off before she could embarrass him more in front of the watching family

Maureen wanted to see all the old places in Aengus past life and they booked in to a hotel in Ranelagh.Aengus knew the bus routes and they covered the city. UCD and Earlsford Terrece and Alexandra College, Botanic Gardens. The Zoo, and before they came home they spent a night in Moloney's Bar and Lounge.

All the old gang were there and yer man himself Paddy Gorman. God how he missed The Master. Best fu--- best Master they ever had and that was why his Lorcan was going to do his Leaving Cert next year and dere was nuttin' surer than Lorcan would be a Perfesser up dere in the fu---,up there in The Terrace. Mark moy words.

Thay called in at Na Fianna clubhouse and everyone was asking for Hannah. She often dropped in there with Des for a drink and a chat

And they did not know in Donegal?.Well, would you ever believe it?

73

Mrs Collins had reached retirement age and they would have to appoint a new teacher. Fr Barry was doing the selection and he asked Aengus to sit in on the interviews. Their main dilemma was the sex of the new teacher. A lady migt have more empathy with the younger children but she would not be of much help on the football field and the after school activities.

Maureen and Rita saw no reason why a lady could not drive the team bus or referee a match or take the team training. She would be an asset to the ICA and she could organise the choir and play the harmonium in the church.

Garton National School had a very good reputation and they had numerous applicants. Brother Kevin came to the rescue. He sent them a young man from Monaghan. He was not exceptional in any way but he was a good all rounder and James Beirne was appointer assistant teacher at Garton National School.

Maureen moved all her things over to Aengus' house. After dark in the back of the pickup. No point in having nosey neighbours see one's things. They decided that Peggy should come and live with them. She would be handy when the new baby arrived. A son. Maureen was certain.

Shane had given up on rearing the pigs. There was too much labour involved and when he could not grow enough grain and potatoes to feed them it was not profitable. Neil huffed aand puffed but the physical labour was too much and he took his baking soda for his ulcer

Maureen was a week late and she gave birth to a daughter. That did not worry her. There would be sons later. Peggy came in handy and Maureen went back nursing. But after a couple of weeks she resigned to be with her daughter. Maeve. Again was there a saint Maeve? But Fr Barry avoided that one.

Rita asked to be married soon. All the baby talk and the female hormones in the air affected her. The wedding was in a village church outside of Omagh. There was no local priest but a curate from Omagh looked in at weekends and said Mass on Sundays. It was a Protestant and an Orange community and as Rita grew up among them they came to her wedding. Shane and the Lagan4 entertained them all and what they played would not heve satisfied the Shamrock Club

Within a year Rita had a son. Were he born in Americe he would be Neil the Second but in Garton he was Neil O Neill like his grandfather. Neill Og was his name. Young Neil. Fr Barry called in from time to time and had his cuppa and the chat. Neil and himself had reached a truce. One was a political Sinn Feiner who had seen it all and the other was a Socialist Sinn Feiner who was going to change the world

The Lagan 4 sessions were less frequent. They were busy people and musical tastes were changing. Geldorf and that type were in fashion. Hannah spent much time travelling and Fr Barry went home to come back covered in bruises from the rough crowd in Buncrana.

They first heard it on the Nine O clock news. Body found on Roadside Hit and Run

Then the story was told. Two men arrived at the Accident and Emergency and placed a body on a trolley and said they found the body on the roadside. Then they drove off

One of the staff took the car number. It had been stolen the night before from the car park in Buncrana Town Hall

Mr Flynn the consultant pronounced the body as dead and it was removed to the Morgue where the police cme and examined it.

It was the body of Father Barry Morris

Aengus and Shane and all or them were devastated. They knew he was overdoing the fitness and now look at what happened. He awas always getting knocked about. Never ready to admit that he was getting on in years. Must have fallen off his bicycle due to tiredness. Fr Barry's father Liam Morris came and identified the body of his son and he had it removed to a private room. The police had all the details and he would like to take his son 's body home

It was headlines in the newspapers

"Priest Killed by Hit and Run"

"Holy Father dies on roadside"

The people of Garton were disconsolate. Their own Fr Barry. All alone on his bicycle. On the roadside. What a sad way to die.

The reporters came but the parents did not meet or speak to them

Leave them in their private grief

The bishop spoke from the pulpit to say how diminished the diocese was by the death of this young priest. He made a request for privacy for the Morris family in their great loss, Shane and Aengus tried to contact Liam Morris but he would not come to the phone and the funeral was a private affair. The police said the case would not be closed in the hope of further evidence. The whole affair wsas allowed to quietly pass by

Then came another shock. Rita came home fronm town and she was almost unable to tell them the news. She had met a former solleague. They had nursed together and now this friend was a nurse in the hospital where Fr Barry's body was taken. He had theree bullets in his chest. He died from bullet wounds. There had been an attack on an army convoy that weekend and if the army had suffered any casualties it was not reported. But the attackers suffered a casualty. It was Fr Barry

I was all clear now. The accidents at weekends. Dislocations, fractures, black eyes. From training exercises or from actual assaults. The Shamrock in Boston. A Provo associated club no doubt. The cheques sent from Boston. Colm Maguire and all his pals at the Club. The people they met at the functions and the questions they were asked. The pictures on the walls of the club

Neil understood the visionary patriotism of the gallant priest but he knew of the chimera of the irrevocable epilogue

The next edition of An Poblavcht had an obituary notice for "Baire O Muirris who gave his life for Ireland" Mary O Neill at the end of the Rosary said an extra deacade for Fr Barry and that his gentle should rest in peace.

74

AENGUS WAS AWARE of the little girl. She was weeping since she arrived at the school. It was distressing to see and he did not wish to draw attention to the child. He asked Mary MacCarthy to sit with her. Mary was thhe class surrogate mother. She looked after all in Aengus' room. Any cuts or bruises or stings and Mary was there giving comfort and a helping hand

Mary soon had the whole story. The child was Nuala Thornton the daughter of Sergeant Thornton. Shane's old friend. Thornton liked the quiet life and he moved out from town to Garton. The Garton school's reputation had spread and that suited his family. The sergeant himself would accasionallt drop in to give one of his talks and the children loved his Western brogue. They spoke with a Mayo accent for days after his visits.

Mary had the whole story

"Nuala's father is being transferred to somewhere in Kerry. Ballyferriter or something. They are not sure where it is and her mother says she is not going down to that Godforsaken part of the world" Mary told him

"Thank you Mary for looking after Nuala"

Mary's day was made and Nuala's head was soon on her desk and she was asleep

The episode passed and Aengus paid it no more attention

But that was not the end of the matter

A stranger came to the classroom door

"Can you direct me to Sergeant Thornton's private house?" the man asked

"Yes I can. His daughter is a pupil in my class. But you can find him at the Garda Stataion in town" said Aengus

"Yes I know that but I had better introduce myself" the stranger said "My name is Kelly and I am the Garda Sergeants' representative. We have a representative Board and I am the full time secretary. I do not wish to go to the Garda Station"

Aengus could see the man was tense and he aslked

"His daughter is here and she has been distressed. What is happening?"

"It is a disgrace. A thundering disgrace. And we cannot let them get away with it. Bloody criminal it is. Ballyferriter effin hell" said Kelly

"Can you tell me or is it confidential?" asked Aengus

"Confidential?. The more who know the better. I am going to tell the nation. Tell the world. Too much political interference for my liking and the rest of the Garda Force feel the same"

"Come in for a chat" said Aengus and "Mary. Two cups of tea"

Mr Kelly, Sergeant Kelly fom the Representative Board told the story

"A certain person was found in his overturned car in the ditch with his headlights on. Drunk. Someone phoned the Garda Barracks and the squad car went and found him and charged him with being drunk in charge. He was so drunk there was no need to call the doctor so a hackney car was called and he was sent home. He could sober up at home. He is well known to the Garda. He is Secretary to the Fianna Fail party for this area and for the wider county. A summons was issued and the proceedings for prosecution were commenced

Two days layer an irate Superintendent phoned the Sergeant "What's all this I hear about prosecuting Willie McFadden just because his car skidded into the ditch? Have you got a grudge against this man?What has he ever done to you?. There was no need to provides a summons. I think you behaved in an unprofessional way. Leave this to me and I will handle it from now on"

The Sergeant said that the other gardai saw what happened and that he went strictly according to the book

"Bring the other garda into this?" said the Superintendent "I am not having it. You did this yourself. Have you got something personal agaionst this man?" the Super ranted on and said that Sergeant Thornton would be a sorry man and then he hung up

Then came the transfer to Ballyferriter and the Sergeant has three children of school and of college age. This area suits his family and years ago he refused promotion as it would mean leaving Garton" said Sergeant Kelly

"This Super sounds a bad egg" said Aengus

"Rotten to the core. He is from the West of Ireland and his wife is the sister of a Minister of Government. He got rapid promotion from being a sergeant in Dublin and they are still celebtrating his departure. It has all gone to his head and he is a nuisance and a disgrace. Never should have been promoted. Political interference."

Sergean Kelly finished his tea and thanked Mary and he left

Aengus was upset. Sergeant Thornton was a valued member of the parish. Was it any of Aengus business? Yes. He came to Garton to live with the people and to help the people, He could help little Nuala Thornton in her worries.

Maureen sensed his discomfort

"What is worrying you?"

"Nothin', nothing"

"Come on. Out with the whole story. Stop fooling me" And Maureen knew where to go for help in this case. The old man himself. The old fox

"But we will have to tell all the gang. Shane and Rita and Hannah and Des. We can be the Six Garton Muskateers and we will change Neil's name to Athos"

They held a meeting with Athos in the chair. All his old leadersghip and cunning came to the surface

"Now this is a delicate one. We must cover our backs at all times. We are dealing with a crowd who play dirty and who have power above our heads. We cannot meet them face to face. Our enemy here is the party. One of the party pets is not playing the game. We cannot take on the whole party But if we can find a sore spot we can keep at that spot until it becomes really annoying. Or if we can find a weakness. A weak member. Get our claws on a party member ansd squeeze him"

"But that is not fair" said Aengus

"Very correct my son. Who said anything about playing fair?. Are they playing fair?. So that questuon will never be asked again."

"But we might take a man down who has nothing to do with this case" Aengus tried again

"We do not want to take anyone down. All we want is fair play for our own man. All agreed? "Neil, or Athos, asked

They nodded in agreement

"It must be local. Close and tight and local. We know the runs on our own patch and we can catch our quarry on our patch. The sergeant will not be involved. We will not have him mentioned. We will do what is necessary to have the Super change his mind. So we have the Super and MacFadden as our two main characters in this drama. What have we got on any of them?"

Shane spoke "I know MacFadden from the Council. He is a ladies' man and he has a child by a girl from Convoy. A bit on the side. Everyone knows that"

"If it is common knowledge then it is no good good to us" Athos, Neil said

Hannah spoke up "I think I might have something we can use. We cannot really use it but we can threaten as Neil said. Do you remember Josie Ryan?"

"She worked for you' "Yes she did.Cathal Ryan the senator. His daughter. Thats the girl" said Hannah

"She resigned and went to England. She was home in the Summer with her husband and baby daughter" said Maureen.

"Now never a word of this to anyone" said Hannah. "She did not resign. I sacked her. The accountant found that she had taken three hundred pounds from the till. She denied it at first and we called in her father and he agreed to refund the money if we did not call in the police. He paid us and the matter was resolved. But the paperwork is still in my files"

"We cannot involve Josie" said Maureen. "She is married and has a baby now"

"We will not harm her but we can use her without her knowledge to save the Sergeant" said Neil

"How dad?" asked Shane

Neil looked at his son. "let us play about with our ideas. Throw in whatever crosses your mind. We cannot go and face Cathal Ryan. He might brazen it out. We cannot sacrifice his daughter. But we can use what we have got as blackmail. He will know we have definite evidence and that might frighten him"

"Will that be enough?" Maureen asked

"It might not be" said Neil "so let us invent some thing extra" Shane came in again "The AIB contracts were given to Alan Owens and he is a Fianna Fail man. That was government monies and I am sure that Alan greased a few palms. He surely gave a few bachhanders. But we can never prove it"

"No need to prove anything" said Neil. "He will know we have definite proof on one thing and he will not be sure about the other. We can tell him we are ready to go public and blow the whole story. That might frighten him"

"How/" asked Hannah

Neil took a pencil and wrote

Dear Cathal Ryan,

We have evidence that your daughter stole from her employer and that you covered over the crime. We have evidence you refunded the money your dughter stole. We also have evidence that you accepted money as a bribe to obtain the IDA contract for Alan Owens

We are aware that Sergeant Thornton is being transferred over a summons he issued to the secretary of your party. We would ask you to intercede in this matter as the Sergeant was only doing his duty. We hope you will see that what we ask is reasonable. Needless to tell you that any leakage or breaking of secrecy will mean that we will go public. Sergeant Thornton does not know we are interested in his case. We will contact you again later

Yours Sincerely, Colleagues of the Sergeant and Friends of Justice.

"What do ye think?" he asked

"Great. Just right. Like the colleagues and the Friends of Justice bit. Implies that we have depth and it will stop him going to the police as it suggests some of them might be involved" was their reply

"Good" said Neil

"Shane chipped in "We must wear rubber gloves and use a new writung pad and not lick the stamps like in Columbo"

"Never mind Columbo" said Neil "there is much more to do. We must phone Cathal Ryan and say we are from the press and would it be worth our while sending a reporter as we heard a whisper there was a scandal ready to break in the area. Then we make another call saying we are from North West Radio asking the same question. That should get him thinking. All from a public phone box. You see I watch Columbo as well. And as a last kick we phone him saying we are from the Inland Revenue and we need the name of his accountant. I hope it never gets that far"

The letter was posted and a few days later Cathal Ryan teceived a telephone call
"Is that Senator Ryan's house?
"Yes it is"
"News Office of The Democrat here. Are you free to talk?"
"No bother, no bother. Fire away" said Cathal
"Cathal there is a whisper that there is a political scandal about to break in Donegal. We got the word from our man in Dublin.Should we send a reporter over to find what it is all about?What do you think?
Hello hello you still there Mr Ryan?"
"Yea yea, still here. Just thinking. I have heard nothing. Not a thing. Tell yer man in Dublin that someone is having him on. I will give you a bell if I hear anything. Not much happens around here that I do not know about"
What the hell is this all abouthe thought and he was barely able to put the phone back.
"Who was that?" his wife called from the kitchen
"The Democrat looking for news. Nothing special" he replied
But his wife sensed something
"You all right?" she asked
"Yea my dear" he said. No need to bother her as well as she would keep going on and on. The less who knew the better
Next day he took another call. This call from North West Radio
"Senator Ryan?"
"Yes speaking"
This is Sheila from North West Radio. Can you speak in private?" she asked
"Yes I can "the senator replied "I am here in my office at home"
"Good" said Sheila. "Senator this is in strict confidence. There is a scandal ready to break in your constituency"
"Who told you that?" asked a ruffled Cathal
"We cannot divulge our source but they have always been reliable in the past" Sheila said
"Never heard anything so daft in all my life" said the senator
Sheila went on "It could be a resignation job. Do you think we should send a few chaps over to have a chat with the locals and have a mosey around?. RTE have promised us a camera crew if we find anything"

Neil was delighted with his team. Real actors they were. Word perfect and they had only two days practice

"Let him wait a day or two. Let him sweat a bit and soften up" he said

Then they wrote Mr Ryan another letter

Dear Cathal Ryan,

Time is running out. You had better get some results as the madia are waiting. Like hungry wolves. Just get the job done and we promise you all will be over.

But there was one more call to make

"Is that Senator Cathal Ryans office?

"Yes it is. This is really his private residence and his office as well and I am his wife. I take his messages when he is out."

"This is The Regional Tax office. My name is Mary O Sullivan and I am the Regional Tax Inspector's private secretary. Would you get the Senator to phone this number next week. We would also like his accountant's name and telephone number The inspector will be here then and they can make arrangements to meet. This is the number to ring. Just give us a call next week and we can arrange a meeting"

Senator Ryan was now a worried man when he heard this. He got his coat and told his wife that he had buisiness to attend to and that he would be back as soon as he could

Then he went to the local TD's house and the wife was quite cross

"He is in Dublin. The Dail is in session. You should know that" and she almost closed the door in his face.

It was late afternoon when Senator Ryan arrived in Dublin. He showed the two letters he received and he told of the Income Tax Inspecrtor's office phone call. The TD was not surprised. That was politics. No morality in politics. It is the art of the possible. What you can get away with. But there were the anonymous letters. What they knew was correct. William Ryan was distraught and he wailed

"Everything they said is true"

But would they tell?. Would they try again?. Wh at else did they know?. Even the TD himself had some transactions he prefereed to keep hidden

"Give us a break. One more chance" pleaded William. The TD could do Cathal a favour. There is honour among thieves. Yes there is. Until they are found out. The TD had a duty to the Party. It was time to help this man

Especially in this carry on of the Garda Superintendent and the local Sergeant

The case of the Garda Superintendent was not unique. It was the same in the army and in many governmental departments. Look after your own. In the high courts the judges were political appointees. But sometimes serious errors were apparent to the public. What might become public knowledge had to be corrected. For the sake of the Party.

They went to see the Minister for Justice. He listened to their story. Cathal's background in the party and the letters and the phone calls he received. But it was the Superintendent and the Sergeant that the Minister was most interested in . . .

"That effin bollicks of a brother in law. Big headed shite. Never knew what Angela saw in him. The self important fart. Sure the Sergeant might have been in the right and stood up for himself but it is part of an officer's job to manage situations like that"

The Minister walked around the room and then banged his fist on the table

"Yes, leave it with me. I will sort this one out. Never forget that I have saved Senator Ryan's bacon and much more. If the truth got out no one would ever trust the Party again.I never want to see you lot again and a safe journey home"

Then he got on the phone and he swore

"I don't care where you put him. Get him out of my hair. You must have a back office somewhere"

God but Cathal Ryan was a relieved man. He was assured there would be no further bother and that all would be looked after. And the poor old Superintendent had a sudden heart attack. The Garda doctor was called to the Superintendent's house and he ordered that the super be urgently transferred to the Garda Hospital in Dublin. A temporary Garda Inspector took his place. Sergeant Thornton's transfer was cancelled and no one could find the summons the sergeant issued to MacFadden. Maybe the Super took it with him to Dublin. The sergeant knew that things like that happen. He was happy that all had ended well. No one was killed or injured

The Sergeants' representativecalled and had a chat with Aengus. He also went and thanked Mary MacCarthy for the lovely cup of tea she made him. That was why he and come back he said. He was not sure he had thanked her the last time he called. Nothing better than Donegal tea he said as he left the room

Senator Cathal Ryan got a letter thanking him for his assistance and wishing him well with the hope that he had many years service left to enjoy and the Superintendent was made Senior Schools Attendance Officer for Dublin City. A desk job. It would suit him and his weak heart the minister said.

75

IT TOOK THEM a long time before they could even mention his name again. But gradually the pain subsided and they started playing without Fr Barry on Friday evenings. A new curate was appointed to Garton and he was called Fr Eamonn. Not many one knew what his surname was as Fr Barry had set the precedent on names. Fr Eamonn awas only a newly ordained garsoon and he spent most of his spare time visiting his mother the far side of Letterkenny.

But they decided that they needed to have the Garton parish group reorganised. They had Shane and Rita, Aengus and Maureen, Hannah and even though he was a newcomer there was Des. The new priest Fr Eamonn was there as well and of course Neil was availablewhen ever they needed him

To start there was the parish type Council who looked after the Village hall and the school. Aengus proposed that Hannah be coopted to that Council. She objected that she was not a Catholic and was politely told that no one cared a damn what religion she belonged to. So be quiet and get in there and get on with the job. Rita and Maureen were always available and Aengus knew thar Des knew about the football. He said that he was often away on business but he was told that Master Beirne would cover for him then.

Neil was always in the background to keep a fatherly eye on things and Fr Eamonn could be found in the parochial house in an emergency.

Shane said he would like them to share in his greatest idea.

He would like to ask George Adamson. George the Fourth to come aboard the committee

The Yank?. The old man himself?. Silence. They thought. And then they all agreed

George was delighted. He was at home now among his own and they welcomed him. What more could he wish for?. All his life he had just been a nonentity among his own employees and now he could be a fish in his own pond. He would help in every way and he thanked them for the honour they gave him in asking him to join them

Shane looked at Aengus and over at Des as well. They were expressionless. God forbid that they would think that he Shane would have asked the old man because he was a millionaire. It had never crossed anyone's mind. They opened a bottle of Black Bush as George was partial to a wee drop. God bless the Settlers and their descendants

And so life at Garton settled again. Lochbeg and Aengus' house were as one family. Maureen gave birth to a son and Rita had a daughter. With the two grannies to look after the children Maureen and Rita were thinking of going back to the nursing

Then Eugene phoned. He would be home that evening and could they all be there as he wanted a word with them all. He would see them later. Bye.

That morning the bishop had called to Eugene's classroom. He and the class were half way over the Alps with Hannibal but Eungene dismissed the class and sat with His Reverence

"We had better go over to my private quarters" the bishop said

This was really private. Not where the bishop met his official visitors but at the back. On a sofa in the lounge was an elderly priest. Eugene recognised the man as Monsignor Francis Given.

The bishop spoke to Eugene "We have a sick man here"

The Monsignor looked at them and slurred

"You haaave a drunnken preeesth here"

"It is all right Monsignor. You are in a safe place. Just sit easy and listen tio me. I am Fr Eugene O Neill and I can help you. Do you think you need help?"

He looked at Eugene "I know. Know. about you. Fr Eugene. you been doing these last years. The meetings. Magic. Can you help me Fr Eugene?. I need help"

Eugene looked at the bishop "The Monsignor is asking for help?"

"What can I do?" asked the bishop

"Can you keep him here for one day. Keep him here tonight. I will see what I can arrange. Get me a bottle of Whiskey and some Valium tablets. Your own doctor will let you have the tablets. I will be back here later tonight and I will need a bunk in the same room as the Monsignor"

The bishop went over to the Monsignor Given and said

"Thank God Francie me old pal that you have come here. We will help you and soon you will be as big a nuisance as you ever were. So have a sleep now and I will sit with you"

Eugene went to Lochbeg to meet his family.

They all sat around the fire and he told them his story

"The bishop came in to my class and he asked me to go with him over to his house. He has a drunken Monsignor there and he does not know what to do with him

"Send him to the hospital" they said

"No" said Eugene "that is not on. They are old pals and the exposure would be humiliation for the old priest"

"How about one of the convents?"

"That would be worse. How would he spend all day?. He needs to be looked after in a quiet and private place. Now stop me here if you like. We have two highly qualified nurses here and an empty chalet and complete privacy where a priest could recuperate"

"Do you mean a Rehab Centre here in Lochbeg?" Maureen asked

"Something like that. You have both looked after drunks in Casualty and Alcoholics in Psychiatry and I think you should be able to look after this man. See how you get on"

The two women looked at each other. He could see the excitement in their eyes. What a challenge?. And they could still be at home with their childeren

"I am willing togive it a go" said Maureen

"Me too" said Rita

Eugene carried on "I have arrangeed for some Valium to be at the bishop's house and we could have the patient here tomorrow afternoon. That will give you time to get the chalet ready"

Aengus drove back to the bishop

"Your Grace I have fond a way that may help the Monsignor. My sister and my sister in law are two highly qualified nurses and they have experience in treating people who have had trouble with mood altering substances"

He did not like using the word alcoholic as the bishop might feel the hurt for his old and sick friend

"My brother has some chalets on his farm. He lets them to holiday makers and to fishermen. There is one chalet very close to the farmhouse which has all modern amenities and they are prepared to take the Monsignor and nurse him back to health. As you know I have experience in that field and I will be there to oversee things and to offer advice when needed

"Thank you Eugene"

Eugene was very aware that the bishop had used his Christian name. He felt good

The bishop went on "I will pay for the Monsignor's treatment. There are two professionals looking after my old friend and they will be paid. I will set up a direct debit with my bank. The less who know the better"

"That is fine. Thank you very much" said Eugene. "And before I go my father sends you his regards" he added cheekily

The bishop raised his eyes to Heaven

"Down to buiness then. Where is the Monsignor?" asked Eugene

"Still on the sofa"

"have you given him a drink as I advised?"

"yes a wee sup every hour or so"

"Great" said Eugene "then let us put him to bed. Do youhave a plastic sheet ot an oilcloth"

What for?" asked the bishop

"In case we have an accident and wet the bed"

Eugene put the Monsignor to bed. He was a bit stroppy until the bishop came in

"Now Francie. I want none of this carry on. No no. Not a word. Just do as this father tells you.Do as he says or you will have me to deal with and if I lose my temper you will be a sorry man" and he gave Eugene a wink and he left them

Eugene sat at the bedside all night. He kept the old man in the recovery position and took him to the toilet and gave him the odd sup to avoid the shakes. Eugene's classes were to be taken by another Master and he could return when he was good and ready

Maureen and Rita came to collect them and Maureen sat in the back with the Monsignor. Rita drove them to the Monsignor's house and collected his necessary belongings

"Will that be enough?" his housekeeper fretted. She would not look Rita in the eye. She knew.

"Rita tried to put her at ease "Just think that the Monsignor is going on a few weeks' holidays and pack what you think he will wear. We can always phone you and come and collect anything special he may need"

Thw Monsignor settled in very well and slept a three dayValium induced sleep. He was watched over by the two nurses in a constant vigil and Shane and Neil and Aegus took their turns by the bedside. Gradually he made a recovery. Not a cure as Eugene kept reminding them. There is no cure.

Soon he was walking around the lake and talking to the children Neil Og was boasting that he beat the Monsignor at Snakes and Ladders

The bishop was a very relieved man. He had other priests who needed help and succour and he had found the very place. No more rushing up to Dublin and all that hullabalooo.

Here in his own diocese was a place where his men could find recovery and he himself could drop in and have a friendly chat and a quiet word.

So the very first patient had arrived and was being treated and was recovering at Lochbeg Farm. Lochbeg Tranquility Centre

It was the beginning of a whole new era.

76

THE BISHOP CALLED in often to see his old pal Francie Given, He was Monsignor when there was anyone else present but as Francie he was an old and dearly loved adversary. They had opposed each other on the football field as young men; in debates at Maynooth; they argued at diocesan conferences and had they not taken Holy Orders there is no doubt that they would have been suitors for the same woman. His old pal was getting better and the bishop bought a television set and the following week a coffee maker and he had the phone installed in the chalet. Eugene kept a close eye on how things were developing and he collected the Monsignor and took him to outside A.A. meetings and sometimes he had the meetings in the Monsignor's chalet

Before long there were two and then three patients in the Chalet. Maureen and Rita said their limit was six patients and a schedule was arrived at. Breakfast in the chalets at 9am delivered on a trolley. Lunch was at 1.00pm again on a trolley and all the breakfast crockery was collected. Washed and dried thamk you. Evening meal was usually sandwiches at 6.30 but anyone who wished could use the menu card and no one was left hungry. And so the house of tranquility progressed. They did not encourage visitors and anyone calling had to phone and make a prior appointment and only one visitor per patient was allowed.

At one of the monthly parish meetings Mr Adamson approached Maureen

"A quiet word?" and they withdrew to a corner

"I hear you have a rest home in Lochbeg" he said

"Yes" she replied and waited

"Do you specialise in anything in particular?" he asked

"At the moment our limit is six residents" she said by passing his intrusive question

"Well as you know I am the titular head of a large multinational company" he said "I do not have much say in the company policy. That is for the professionals. But I take a keen interest in the human side. I look after the welfare of the families when they need help. I see people break down under the continuous pressure. I do not put the blame on anyone but I help thosee in need. Your house of rest is what I am looking for to aid my disabled. My men. My patients. Aw hell, you know what I mean"

Maureen replied "I am only one of the family. I do not know. We may not be able to accommodate your requirements. It will need to be discussed at a family conference"

"If I can put it simpler" he said "All my men need is a quiet time to regain their strengths. Peace and quiet. MayI have an appointment to meet the family?"

Maureen reported back and there was a serious argument. Their first intention was to help the clergy and that was going well. But already they had reached capacity and other dioceses were refeerring patients to them. Eugene was managing but he was not a qualified psychiatrist or psychologist. They were familiar with alcohol dependency but nervous breakdowns were beyond their scope. But they agreed to meet Mr Adamson

Neil was in the chair. He did not take a very active part in the running of the centre but he knew how to manage a meeting

"Now welcome to you all here and thank you for coming" Neil began. "There is one rule here. It is the most important rule we have at Lochbeg. Every word that is spoken here is confidential. It must never be repeated. Not even among yourselves. If you have something to say or something to ask you must wait and say it at this gathering. We will not discuss our affairs with any other person. Not to wives or to family. Nobody. Repeat nobody. Understand?"

He had each person agree individually to his demands

Then they began their business. They explained to Mr Adamson that they ran a rest house for sick Catholic Clergymen. That was their primary purpose. No matter who else came there was a reserved section for those clergymen. They have two trained and highly qualified nurses who had worked in Psychiatric Wards but they had worked under supervision. They could manage substance abuse as that is what most of the patients suffered from, Some are addicted to prescription drugs, some to non prescription drugs and some to alcohol. All mood altering substances.

"What did you have in mind Mr Adamson?"

Mr Adamson cleared his throat. "This is beyond belief. Here in a small village is a centre that can rival The Betty Ford Clinic. I have employees who will not go to The Ford Clinic because once it goes on their CV veryone knows. Some resign rather than go there and then they go away and die from their illness. But to come here for what we will say as an Irish Holiday is another thing. I would love to avail of your facilities. Might I have a look around?"

He was taken round the lake and chalets

"Just the job" said George Adamson. "I am prepared to rent a lakeside chalet all the year round. Kept in readiness for my company. I will pay the yearly rent and when one of my employees is in residence I will pay for his nursing and his keep. Just let me have your contract terms and I will sign'

The Yanks came and went in dribs and drabs and they were no great bother. Mostly they stayed in their own chalet and they were friendly towards the priests in residence

Different machines and telephones and shredders and a clamour of attachments were installed in their chalet and Shane had security lamps and bells and wires installed

Word was passed discreetly around that there was a respite centre in Garton and there were enquiries from wthe well to do. From all over.When sons or daughters went skiing in the Alps or mountain walking in Tibet the parents rested in Lochbeg. The staff was increased. Shane stopped rearing his pigs and concentrated on helping in the chalets. He bought moresheep and let them graze on the land. They hired young maids to do the laundry and prepare the vegetables. They worked from 9 to5 and had no contact with the chalets

It did not take long until they were fully booked. They could have filled the chalets many times over during the Summer months so they started a waiting system. Any vacancy was offered to those on the waiting list. Then there were the regulars who booked the same chalet for the same weeks every year. Sometimes it was easier to get a Manchester United season ticket than a chalet in Lochbeg

But they kept the chalet fot George Adamson's Americen company. It was known as George's Academy. Good old George.

77

EUGENE WAS TOLD to spend all his time at Lochbeg farm and another teacher would take his Latin classes at the college. At Lochbeg he needed more space as there wre casualties coming in from all over the country. Gradually the other chalets were taken over by the clergy. That left the priests to themselves. Their privacy was important and visitors calling to the Centre were told to use the local Catholic church as their place of worship

The families were growing. Shane and Rita had a baby girl and Hannah and Des a boy. All the children played at the Lochbeg centre and Neil was one of theit guardians. It was a joy to watch him. He taught Neil Og to play draughts. Noughts and crosses were everywhere. He told them of Finn MacCool, Na Fianna. Setanta, Manaan Mac Lir, Queen Maeve and the Cattle Raid of Cooley. They were all going" to rise now and go to Innisfree, and a small cabin build there"

Shane had seen a statue of Sean Paraic O Conaire in Eyre Square in Galway and it could have been his father

Neil was enjoyin his life as The Old Man Of Lochbeg. Nothing he liked better than to go up the hill and walk among his sheep. He did not have a sheepdog. He did not need a sheepdog. His sheep knew him and they moved around him like pets

"Joe Dowling wants the ram for a week or so" Neil told Shane. "I owe him for two days in the bog"

"Ok" said Shane

They got the tractor and the trailer box and headed for the top field. They backed the trailer against a half open gate and went to shoo the ram into the box But the ram avoided the box every time

"God blast the silly old fool. Sure we are only trying to give him a good time"'
Then Neil sat by the tractor wheel "I feel dizzy and out of puff"
"Sit as you are and it will pass" said Shane
"I have a tightness in me chest" the old man said
Shane sat down beside his father
"It's me heart. It's me heart" the old man said
"It could be the old indigestion again" said Shane "have you got any of the baking soda?"
"No it's not the stomach. It's the heart. It is creeping up me side of me shoulder and on to me face"
"Will ya sit and be quiet" said Shane
"No I will not. Listen to me. I know the end is near. I have seen men die and I know it is my time now. But I am not afraid" Neil said
"Will I run for the doctor?
"No time, no good" Neil said
"What about the priest?" asked Shane
"No need. I am ready to meet my God. I can look Him in the eye. But I have one request my son. Will you look after my Mary?. My darling Mary. My my, Mary Mary"
Those were the last words spoken by Neil O Neill

Shane held his father as the life ebbed away. He held him with his head resting on his shoulder. He sat there as he owed the man's soul some peace and time to leave the worn and tired body. No need for the priest or the doctor. There was no hurry, He sat and rested.

Then he carried the body and laid it on the straw in the box trailer. Where the ram should have been. He drove home and he carried his father into the house. He called his mother and he told her what had happened. He held her as she sobbed and then she went in to see her husband. She straightened his hair and kissed his forehead and thanked him for the wonderful husband and father he had been. Then they rang for the priest and phoned the rest of the extended family

They rearranged the small room at the top of the stairs, Mary thought of laying Neil out in the front room but that room would be needed for those who came to wake him, She would not let anyone see him until Susan Slevin had laid him out properly. Susan did a good job and in death Neil looked reposed and at ease. Shane told his mother that was how he looked as he died

Then there was the wake and the funeral to be arranged. Neil had often said that he wanted no fuss. But the local press did features on Commandant O Neill." Last of the Old IRA". "End Of An Era. Old Patriot". "Quiet Man Of The Troubles"

The wake was a crowded affair. Most never made it to the front room or upstairs to kneel by the corpse and the tea and cakes and the whiskey was taken in the front yard. Telegrams from all over the world. There was one from The Shamrock Club and one from Colm and Kathleen Maguire offering their sympathy and that they were coming over to the funeral. Local politicians dropped in but did not stay long.

An Army car with a tricilour on its bonnet and a multi ribboned officer came to the yard

"The President of Ireland woud like to be represented at Commandant O Neill's funeral. With your permissiom he would like his aide-de-camp to attend on his behalf"

Well who could refuse such an honour?. Neil may have been reticent about his abilities but his family always had the feeling that he was never given credit for what he had done. And now they would not deprive him of his few moments of glory

The Bishop came out to the house and asked if he might attend the funeral of his most beloved and most persistent sparring partner

Shane crept into the room late that night to say goodbye. He looked at the motionless face and he closed his eyes and he cried. He wept for some time as he thought back over the years. Of the times they fought and did not speak to each other and how they came together when Shane inherited the farm

But he was not prepared for the sensation of numb helplessness at the immobility and silence surrounding that beloved face and the cold unresponsive hardness of his fathers face when he kissed it.

A Garda car escorted the hearse to the church. The Presidents aide-de-camp and The Bishop shared a pew at the side of the altar inside the railings

Eugene said the Requim Mass and the chapel was full. An army trumpeter played The Last Post over the tricolour draped coffin as it was lowered into the grave

Shane invited some of the mourners back to the house. Hannah and Des and George Adamson. Colm and Kathleem Maguire arrived in time for the Mass and they all gathered in the front room and had a few hours together. Colm Maguire andd George Adamson seemed to get on very well and George invited Colm and Kathleen to stay with him for a few days' rest;Everything passed very smoothly and there was no outside interference

This was The Old Republicans Day and they honoured him

78

THE LAGAN 4 stopped taking bookings. Shane played at home just to keep Neil Og interested and in the hope that he might keep on playing the Irish Music. But they missed the Friday nights. They would sometimes bump into each other in Cooney's bar. But they met regularly every month at their parish council meetings. George Adamson asked that they come to his house and hold the Friday sessions there. They went over but it was inconvenient. Staying at Aengus house was easier and eventually they went there again and started playing together

"My Gaawd" said Mr Adamson or Georgie as he preferred "I love this place and I am full of admiration for your Centre. My company is deeply indebted to you all. The way you saved Michael Dixon when he went down was pure magic. He is a cousin of my wife you know"

Conversation stopped mid sentence. There was a silence and Maureen was given the nod

"Now George we look on you as one of our best and most trusted friends. But we can never discuss any person who attends the Centre. We can never break their trust. You may not be fully aware how sacred that trust is. George I am not telling you off, but what happens at the Centre must never be discussed. It must never be mentioned. Again George thank you for your help and what you have done for the Centre and with that I will say no more"

George was very embarrassed "Oh my God. Folks I am so sorry. So very sorry. I apologise. I apologise and I swear I will never again mention the Centre to anyone"

"Well said Geotrge" Aengus replied

And Rita moved them on with

"Vanilla or Rum and Raisin folks?"

Eugene got a letter asking if he would make himself available for a meeting with executives from Adamsons Corporate and from Maguire Enterprise. It was addressed to him as Director of the Lochbeg Centre' He wrote back that he was the Spiritual Director and that the management was a family and a team affair.

A meeting was arranged and in the hotel was George Adamson and Colm Maguire. The Centre team was Shane, Rita, Aengus and Maureen and Fr Eugene

Colm Maguire greeted them

"I was so looking forward to meeting you all again. You were all so busy at Neil's fiuneral and I stayed out of your way. George looked after Kathleen and I and as you know we stayed in his beautiful mansion. George and I found we had so much in common and we thought we might be able to help you all at the Centre. When we go in to the this meeting there will be high powered executives from Adamsons Corporate and there will be only me from Maguire Enterprise. We have only one member and the same member is the executive officer. Me.There will be much talk about trustees and endowments and all that legal bull but it is simple. Georgie and I wish to make a contribution to Lochbeg Centre. We decided that at Neils funeral. You want to add to that George?"

Mr Adamson said "mmm yes mmm. You all know me and who I am and how happy I am to live in Garton with you people. Colm and I can arrange for some money to be channelled into the Lochbeg Centre. The tax laws or something like that make it practical. That's all I know so let's go in and fix it up"

They all met in the Conference room

There were three Adamsons Corporate men who were very serious and authoritative but as soon as they got high and mighty Colm asked

"Please explain that to me in two simple sentences?"

God how those highly educated men hated this rough Paddy.

The outcome was that both companies agreed to give the Lochbeg Centre half a million dollars fot building developments. Straight away. They would like to see the architects' drawings of course. But then they would give the Centre one hundred thousand dollars every year for educational purpose.To educate medical staff and to help in postgraduate research

"That was not too bad" said George "how about a nice repast?" and he ushered tham towards the dining room

Aengus waited back and he spoke to Colm Maguire

"Mr Maguire, could we have a quiet word?" "Delighted" said Mr Maguire "what can I do for you?"

"You know all those lovely rings you let us have in Boston years ago?" said Aengus

"Only a couple of engagement rings, that was all" said Colm

Aengus continued "I have been paying cheques into the Ulster Bank since then to pay you and they heve not been cashed"

"Listen to me Aengus" and Mr Maguire put his arm round Aengus shoulder "I have all those cheques in my office drawer and I will never cash them. They give me so much pleasure. I often take them out and look at them and and I recall the wonderful day you all came to my little place. Now that I know that Maureen is the daughter of Badger O Neill and that Shane is his son there is nothing that could compensate me for the beauty of those cheques. Just you leave me my little pleasures"

There is no need to say that gifted the money came in useful to The Centre. They built some new chalets and added to the older ones and they held Summer Schools and World Seminars in the Centre. Eugene went to America and qualified as a Psygchologist and hc came home as one of the leading authorities on Alcohol abuse. Maureen and Rita in turn took their diplomas in psychiatric nursing and they had visiting Registrars come and go as they did their Fellowships and their Doctorates. Garton Tranquility centre was becoming world famous

Then they decided to change the centre's name. Tranquility Centre was open to questions. What was it? Why go there? Why Tranquility?

They changed the name to a simple Lochbeg Farm. And you might go there to savour the country and the fresh air and the farming lifestyle

And the Adamson Chalet was renamed Adamson's Barn.

79

COLM MAGUIRE AND George Adamson had formed a great friendship. They enjoyed each others company. Colm and Kathleen came to stay in Garton at George's mansion and he got to know the Garton gang quite well. George went to stay in Boston at the Shamrock Club as Colms guest. So there it was. The Americn descendant of a settler and Dissenter and a staunch Irish Republican did not seem to have much in common. But both their heritages were of Celtic origin.

They dropped in to Lochbeg Farm and were proud of what was being done there. The young O Neills and Gillespies were coming through and the Lochbeg Farm would be in safe hands. There was no doubt in their minds

One day they came aand sasked for a meeting with the Lochbeg Farm committee. They had something to discuss

When they all had settled Colm Maguire rose and he opened the discussion

"I ask that what we talk about here is kept among ourselves. I know that you have the ability to keep confidences in yout running of Lochbeg Farm. I do not suppose it is a secret to anyone here that I am a staunch Republican. You all now know that Fr Barry was one as well. God rest his soul. You all may have gathered that the Shamrock Club is a Republican Club and that we did support the IRA in their efforts to unite the country of Ireland. Well things are changing. The IRA have achieved much in the governing and in the police management of the Six Counties. You may not be aware of this but there have been meetings bertween the Provos and the British Government representsatives. In Tulla in Co Clare and outside of Letterkenny in Donegal and in other places. The IRA have almost done what they can do. There is a process of continuous negotiation at the present time. The general feeling is that everyone is tired of guerrilla warfare and that they would like to give peace a chance. George and I have been made aware ot these secret talks and dealings.

We have been approached and we have been asked if the Adamson Barn might be made available for those discussions

"You got anything to add to that George?"

George Adamson rose" My dear Garton friends. I do hope you do not think we are imposing on your friendship. As one of old Dissenter Stock here I am trying to play a part in the unification of the Irish peoples. I know very little in depth of Irish politics but I do know that the time for a peace settlement has come. And I am so proud that we here in Garton have been asked to play a part. I might add that Colm and I are only the message carriers and that we do not wish to influence you in any way"

It was the longest speech he had ever made in his career he thought and he felt quite pleased with himself.

The Lochbeg Farm committee missed Neils experience and his wisdom. They would have to make a decision on their own. It was a difficult one

Shane asked the first question

"How much will we and our families be exposed to any danger?"

Colm answered "I think I can answer that. I know that the Provos have decided that the ballot box may be the best answer for them. The day of the Armalite is over. The UDA do not have the backing of their people anuymore There is Direct Rule from Westminster and that is a big achievement. Everyone has had enough. Violence has had its day"

"But how can we help if everything is going so well?" asked Rita

"As I said "Colm continued" things are coming on very well. But there are details to sort out. Who will be on this commottee or on that committee and what powers will that committee have and all that kind of detail.

Now you might ask why all the secrecy. It is because of that everpresent feature of Irish Politics and of of Irish History. The Split,. The Split. If the powers that be can agree and present their agreements as complete then there is less chance of subdivisions among the active parties. So there is where Garton can help At Adamsons Barn the agreements can be refinedwithout too much outside interference. The technology is there and the secrecy as well"

That seemed to make sense and George spoke

"At the Adamson Barn we have al the modern communications technology and that will be very useful. We at Adamsones are quite prepard to offer our Barn to the peace movement"

Again Shane asked a question

"if we find it intrusive or disagreeable do we have the right to withdraw the offer?" Colm looked at George and they both said "Yes you do"

It was agreed that the peace movement could avail themselves of Adamsons Barn but no one knew what would happen next. Colm and George said they would see and find out

A week or so later a Post Office delivery man pulled in to Lochbeg Farm and he asked to see Mr Shane O Neill. A registered letter

Rita was very excited and she shouted for Shane." Registered letter. Shane Shane"

The Post Office delivery man asked that Shane sign tfor the parcel and he asked that they go indoors out of the rain

In the front room the man produced his identity card. He was Lieutenant Colonel Marcus Oldfield and he was head of Special Branch

"There is no need for you to worry about anything. And I cannot tell you any more about my assignation here. I will keep these premises under observation at all times and no one will be any the wiser' If there are any doubts about any person you may meet then you ask" You looking for Kathleen?" and they will answer "the dark lady". Anyone else than phone this number. That is all I can tell you about my brief and my job" Then a few days later a builders lorry pulled in and a man said

"you have any idea where I might find Kathleen?" and Shane directed him to Adamsons Barn

They set up some scaffolding around the barn and the lorry came and went sonmetimes as often as three times a week. Shane had an idea that it might be delivering and collecting more than building materials.

Nothing unusual apart from the builders coming and going. Later on Shane was to find little depressions in ditches around the farm. Just enough to take a body. They must have been formed by the Special Branch people. But it had nothing to do with him

Weeks later there was abig meeting between the Taoiseach and the Prime Minister and they announced a settlement had been arranged over the Northern Ireland Question. Celebrations all round. Peace at last.

George invited them all over to his mansion and they had a psarty. Hannah and Des and all the children were there and everyone was so happy

Pity the old man Neil was not here. Fr Barry too.

80

THE O NEILL and the Gillespie children are growing up and into their University education. Medicine and Psychiatry and Psychology is what they are studying. Eugene has gone grey and frail and he does not take an active part in the Lochbeg Farm. Shane and Aengus are old and tired but they enjoy going to the football matches. Peggy has gone to Heaven and so has Mary. Rita and Maureen spend their time sitting in the verandah and sleeping and chatting and George Adamson is driven down from time to time for a chat. His old pal Colm Maguire died years ago but Kathleen calls when she comes home to Kerry.

Apart from the Gated Entrance Lochbeg Farm in not in any way noticeable. Sometimes a big car will come and go and when there is a Conference the place is busy but once they are all behind the gates then the countryside is quiet again.

But it has been part of the Irish Story. Not many know.

So you have been so privileged to have been told that story.

Printed in Great Britain
by Amazon.co.uk, Ltd.,
Marston Gate.